ALEX&ZEE

ALEX&ZEE

Cordelia Strube

Coach House Press
Toronto

Coach House Press
50 Prince Arthur Avenue, Suite 107
Toronto, Canada M5R 1B5

© Cordelia Strube 1994

FIRST EDITION
1 3 5 7 9 10 8 6 4 2

Printed in Canada

Published with the assistance of the Canada Council, the Ontario Arts
Council, the Department of Canadian Heritage and the
Ontario Publishing Centre.

Editors for the Press: Frank Davey and Jason Sherman

Canadian Cataloguing in Publication Data
Strube, Cordelia, 1960–
Alex & Zee
ISBN 0-88910-504-9
I. Title.
PS8587.T78A73 1994   C813'.54   C94–931748–9
PR9199.3.S77A73 1994

For Dorkhead

DECEMBER

ONE

Zee doesn't want to go home. Sitting very straight on the park bench he feels like that statue of Lincoln: solid, all-seeing, immovable.

He doesn't want to go home because Alex will be there and she'll want to know what he did today. She'll want to know when he is going to do something with his life. She'll want to know why a forty-three-year-old man sits around a park all day watching pigeons shit; she'll want to know how much longer he plans to sit around with his "thumb up his ass contemplating the meaning of life".

Abruptly, a wino, reeking of alcohol, flops down on the bench beside Zee and stares at him, bleary-eyed. "Can you spare a buck?" he asks. Zee feels around in his pocket for change and hands some to the wino, who examines it before shoving it in his pocket. "It's cold as a witch's tit," he says. Zee nods in agreement. The wino leans towards him, squinting. "Colder than a witch's aassss." He stares at Zee to see if his words are having any effect. "Colder than a witch's pussseee," he adds, then chuckles and picks his nose. Zee has a feeling that the wino isn't concerned with the meaning of life. He has a feeling the wino understands that if he dies it won't make any difference, and this doesn't bother him. The wino doesn't feel he has to leave a "mark on the world". Alex wants to leave a mark on the world. A big bruise.

A man with a navy wool tuque pulled low over his forehead walks by, slapping himself on the head repeatedly. "I'm going to get you," he says. "No fucking way, man." He slaps himself. "I am. I'm going to sneak into your bedroom, and I'm going to … No fucking way, man." He slaps himself again. "You think I'm kidding. I'm going to kill you." The wino looks at the man, then at Zee, and circles his index finger at his temple. Zee nods in agreement, although lately he has felt the inclination to slap himself on the head but has resisted, aware that this would mean that he is losing his mind. Bird-poop splatters on the bench between them. The wino points at it and snorts. Zee stands up, stretches and starts across the park. "Ciao, amigo," the wino calls after him. Without looking back, Zee waves.

Above the floor of Dini's bar is a neon-tubed, large-breasted woman holding her arms out wide in welcome. How appropriate, Zee thinks, just like a woman, alcohol will lure him inside, promising good times, only to make his life a living hell later. But alcohol, unlike a woman, is predictable. He knows exactly how many drinks it will take to kill the pain and how long it will take to recover. With Alex, he never recovers but lives with the constant memory of the pain, dreading its recurrence. Pushing open the door to Dini's bar, he remembers when he lived alone. He was happier then. He smoked when he wanted to, drank when he wanted to, slept when he wanted to, watched TV when he wanted to.

Now it's a cold war.

He sits at the bar and orders a beer. The beeping and buzzing from the computer games against the wall remind him of the killer bees. What's happened to the killer bees, he wonders. They must have crossed the Mexican border by now.

Alex wants a baby so that it can be swarmed by killer bees.
Watching teenagers in torn, pre-faded jeans bounce around the computers, he wonders why it is that people don't have the patience to fade their own jeans anymore. Used to be faded jeans contained lives. He tries to picture the teenagers older, sitting in suits behind desks. He wonders how they can bear the weight of the knowledge that soon they're going to have to figure out how to be adults. He feels he should warn them that it's not something you figure out once. You have to maintain it, the facade, forever. He feels exhausted just thinking about it. Today, he decides, he will stop trying to be anything. He's always tried to be something, always felt that if he could only figure out how to be something he'd be a happy man. He used to sit on the toilet, studying the "Career Without College / Training at Home" matchbooks, wondering if he'd he happy if he learned how to fix air-conditioners and refrigerators. Today he understands that the key is to X the *if*. Don't try to be anything, people will look at you strangely for a while but eventually they'll ignore you, as if you had no legs or a hump. Maybe he should tell the teenagers about X-ing the *if*. They probably wouldn't believe him.

A little, round man in a worn satin baseball jacket, sitting at the opposite end of the bar, waves at Zee. Zee waves back. The little man shakes his head several times. "Hockey isn't what it used to be," he says. Zee nods and stares at the rows of liquor bottles behind the bar. "Now they hit each other with sticks," the little man adds. "They have to wear so much padding it's a miracle they can skate at all." He shakes his head again. "No, it's not like it used to be. I don't watch much anymore, can't. It's too bad they're always hitting each other with sticks." Zee nods, thinking that there are more crazy people around than there used to be. The little man wipes his nose with the back of his hand. "I guess that's what the public wants." He shrugs. "It's not like it used to be. Too bad." Zee nods, running his fingers over the bar. The wood grain of the counter reminds him of the relief patterns on the maps in grade-eight geography. Things were better in grade eight, he thinks. He knew everything. He could feel his classmates straining their necks and eyeballs to glimpse his answers on multiple-choice tests. He'd fill in the wrong answers then change them at the last minute. *Why? Why bother?*

A man in a turquoise shirt with sweat stains around the armpits pulls up a stool beside Zee. "Anybody like riddles around here?" he asks. "I've got a riddle." He wipes sweat off his forehead with his hand and looks at it, as if he can't believe he's actually sweating. "What politician has a face like a shoe?" Zee stares at him, having difficulty absorbing the question. "Come on. Guess," the man insists. Zee shrugs. The man leans into him. "Our great leader," he declares. "Get it? Heel, as in swine."

Lately Alex has been telling Zee that he's the best person she's ever known and that he mustn't give up but must learn to take pleasure from the little things because life sucks, that's the way it is, he can't expect it to be easy. Alex understands that living is hard work, that planning and constant surveillance are required. Sometimes he wants to put a pillow over her face. Not to suffocate her but to stop her working it out, summing it up. Stop! Just stop! Can't you stop?

Maybe he should go home and have a bath. Baths are good, he feels suspended, weightless. In his next life he wants to be a dolphin. Except they're all dying in tuna nets. The sweaty man leans into him. "Do you believe in reincarnation?"

"I haven't really thought about it," Zee lies. He doesn't want to encourage discussion because he has a feeling the sweaty man is about to tell him he was a Roman Emperor in a past life.

"You know how you tell if someone's been reincarnated?" the sweaty man asks, tilting his head back and looking at Zee down his nose. Zee shakes his head.

"If they're smart." The sweaty man wipes his forehead. "Stupid people are on their first life, that's why they're stupid. Smart people have done it all before so they know better. Every time something shitty happens to you in this life you have to go, 'okay, what am I supposed to learn from this?'" The sweaty man karate chops the bar for emphasis. "Everything's a lesson, and your soul chooses lives depending on what it needs to learn. For example, I could be really depressed right now, but instead I'm going, 'okay what can I learn from this?'"

"What have you learned?"

"I haven't figured it out yet. That's part of the process. You have to go through the process."

Zee nods and looks over the sweaty man's shoulder at the little man in the satin baseball jacket. The little man grins and waves. Zee waves back and orders another beer. The bartender, without taking his eyes from the TV above the bar, pulls a beer from the fridge and opens it. "This one's on me," the sweaty man interjects. "Have a scotch, would you like a scotch?"

"Thanks."

The bartender pours two scotches, notes it on the tab, and stares back at the TV screen where a woman is being submerged in water. Her hair spreads out in tendrils around her, her eyes bulge, her lips pucker as she blows bubbles. "When's your birthday?" the sweaty man asks.

"June 12th."

"Gemini, oh boy." He clucks his tongue. "I had a lover who was Gemini. Dangerous waters. Don't misunderstand me. I don't regret any of it." Only now does Zee realize that the sweaty man reminds him of a hedgehog, the kind in English storybooks. "I'm Sagittarian," the sweaty man continues. "You and I actually complement each other."

Feeling the scotch, Zee is thinking about the single hair growing from the tiny mole on Alex's chin. Once he caught her clipping it with nail scissors. Embarrassed, she tried to look as if she were tidying the medicine cabinet. He couldn't understand why she'd be embarrassed about clipping a hair on her face. He clips his nose hairs all the time.

He tries to remember when he stopped looking forward to seeing her. He always used to look forward to seeing her. They'd share the day's experiences, hug, cook dinner. Now they circle around each other saying excuse me and please and thank you. Now it's a gamble. Should I try to talk to her, make her laugh? Will she flinch if I touch her? He used to know her, like he knew himself, what she wanted, what she needed. Now he watches her sleeping, tidying, baking, updating her files, and he has no idea. She might look up and ask him to make coffee, or she might want to know what he's staring at.

He looks back at the sweaty man who smiles at him. Only now does it occur to Zee that the sweaty man is homosexual. This does not alarm Zee, only saddens him. He almost wishes he could swing both ways just so the man won't be disappointed. He hates disappointing people. He hates disappointing Alex. That's why he stays out of her way most of the time. His toes turn to prunes while he sits in the bath, staying out of her way. He has become a roommate she has to put up with, clean up after in the bathroom. Was she always such a fanatic about cleanliness? He doesn't think so. He never used to notice her chasing after him with a sponge. So why does it bother him now? Why can't he accept her obsession with cleanliness as part of her? Because, he thinks, it's his dirt she hates, his dirt she guns down with her bottle of environmentally friendly cleaner. It used to be their dirt, mutual dirt. Now he has a feeling she thinks it's all his dirt.

When the sweaty man excuses himself to relieve his bladder, insisting that he'll be right back, Zee sneaks out of the bar.

That's another thing Alex says about him. He's a coward.

TWO

At the makeup counter Alex is trying on different shades of lipstick. Each time she tests a new one the salesgirl says, "That's a good colour for you." Alex doesn't like wearing lipstick because it comes off on cups, clothes, men's faces. It bugs her that women on TV have perfectly applied lips after eating, showering, fornicating. She applies a bruise-coloured lipstick just to see if the girl will say that it's a good colour for her. "It's a good colour for you," the girl repeats, leaning languidly against the counter. A woman in a sheepskin coat places her gloved hand on the glass and glances at the girl. "Have you got any of that Shuko Anti-Aging gel?" A three-year-old boy tugs on the woman's coat. "In a minute, pumpkin," she tells him. Alex watches the boy as he turns and hops over to a perfume display. He stares at the exotically shaped bottles and, with his mittens dangling from the sleeves of his snowsuit, tentatively reaches towards them. His mother sees him, rushes over, grabs his wrist and pulls him back to the makeup counter. She glances vacantly at Alex who smiles at her. The woman averts her eyes and ruffles the boy's hair.

Lately Alex has been staring at children, fascinated by their wonder as they make discoveries about the world. Yesterday she stood in the park for twenty minutes watching a little girl explore a wooden jungle-gym. The girl climbed ladders, walked over ramps, swung on tires, pulled on knobs, turned wheels. She behaved as though it was her mission to explore every aspect of the wooden structure. Finally her mother appeared, wrapped a protective arm around the girl's shoulders and stared fiercely at Alex as though she were a pedophile.

Alex finds the Ladies' room, sits on the toilet and rests her head in her hands. She doesn't even really like children. "I only want one," she says over and over to Zee, hoping that somehow "just one," will be acceptable to him, as if "just one" might be less of a problem, something she can slip past him, something small that he can do for her as a favour. "Other people have babies," she points out. "People poorer than we are, I see them all the time, they can handle it." It frustrates her that she has to wait for his consent before she can go ahead with what, primarily, will be her concern; her body, her baby, her pain. It enrages her that she has to beg a man to co-operate before she can act on her decision and subsequently wait for the right time of the month before luring him into bed, trapping him, titillating him so that he will get hard, stay hard and ejaculate. And even then she can't be sure. She read in the paper that women over thirty have only a twelve-to-thirteen percent chance of conceiving each month.

She pictures Zee, slumped on the couch, sipping his scotch and sucking on his pipe even though she has informed him repeatedly that smoking affects sperm production, even though he knows that secondhand smoke is hazardous to her health.

All her life she has tried to believe that you make choices, that you control what happens to you. Now she feels out of control.

She's considered spending time in bars, trying to pick up

men who appear capable of producing quality sperm, but how could she be sure that it would be AIDS-free?

Of course there is always Michael. Why he finds her desirable, when he's only seen her in baggy jeans and sweaters, she has no idea. There was a time when she dressed like a woman, when she still believed in the ultimate relationship.

Now she feels trapped in a skirt and high-heels, unable to run, unable to kick in a rapist's face. Now she has no expectations or delusions. She wants to get on with her life.

Already she knows what sex with Michael would be like. He'd try too hard and ask her if she had come. Not wanting his penis to go flaccid, she'd say yes and try to coax him into ejaculating, her sole object being the acquisition of his sperm.

She pushes open the toilet-stall door, leans over a sink and splashes cold water on her face. In the mirror, she tries not to stare at a woman in a miniskirt lining her lips with pencil. The woman applies lipstick with a brush then steps back to appraise her work. Apparently satisfied, she deftly resurrects the lines under her eyes with a pencil then pulls out her compact to freshen the powder on her nose. Alex dries her face and leaves. She's always felt like a lump around women who line their lips. A lump that should be removed.

She doesn't want to go home because she's afraid that Zee will be there, and she'll start a fight. She can't help it. She can't stand his passivity, can't stand how nothing gets to him the way it gets to her. She prods at him just to get a reaction. When she succeeds he flails his arms and shouts, "So leave me! I can't be what you want me to be, so leave me!" Then he slumps into a corner of the couch and sulks, cleaning and refilling his pipe. Or he hides in the bathroom, soaking in the tub, humming old Randy Newman songs, leaving a disgusting ring she'll have to clean because, if she asks him to do it, he'll say she's "needling at him". She doesn't want to go home because if he is in the tub, she might push his head under water and hold it there.

In the hat department, she tries on a bright red felt hat that makes her look like her mother. Lately, Alex has felt her mother's expression gripping her face like a clay mask. She can feel gravity tugging downward at the the corners of her mouth, forming jowls. People have always remarked on her resemblance to her mother. Alex didn't believe them. Now, wearing the red hat, she sees it too and quickly drops the hat back on the table. An arm darts past her, swooping it up. A narrow, grey-haired woman, her spine bent forward, jams the red hat on her head and stares into the mirror, clutching her handbag with both hands. Alex turns away. She wishes she could rid herself of this trapped feeling.

In the mall, she sits at the donut-shop counter and orders an apple fritter and coffee. Lately she's been eating sugar, hoping it will make her feel better, but it only makes her feel fat. She stares down at her thighs, spreading on the stool. Zee insists she's neurotic about being fat, that she's thinner than she's ever been. But Alex knows she's getting fatter. Why eat donuts then? *What kind of sick person eats donuts when she knows she's fat?* She licks the sugar from her fingers and places her palm over her coffee cup, absorbing its warmth. A frizzy-haired mother in a yellow, down coat, at the counter with her fat-cheeked ten-year-old son, orders a muffin for herself and an eclair donut for him. "You said something very true before," the mother says. The boy stares hungrily at the donut the waitress sets in front of him. "About bad teachers," the mother continues. "There will always be bad teachers but you have to remember that they're unhappy people, and that's why they yell at you." The boy licks the cream oozing from his eclair. "And when you get older," the mother warns, "in real life, there will be lots of people yelling at you, and you'll just have to remember that they're yelling because they're unhappy."

Once Zee yelled at her, called her a bitch, grabbed her shoulders and shook her until she pointed out that he looked ridiculous resorting to physical violence. She tried to appear calm, but she was frightened because he seemed to hate her, seemed to blame her for his despair. So why does he stay in the relationship? It doesn't make any sense. All day at the Centre, she tells young girls to get out of relationships that make them unhappy. You stay in a relationship because it makes you happier than you would be out of it. That's what she tells them.

Sometimes, seeing him sitting on the couch staring at the wall, she feels as though it makes no difference to him whether she's there or not. Sometimes she has to say his name twice or wave her hand in front of his face to get his attention. She worries that he stays with her because he's too lazy to get a job; that he stays with her because she doesn't have the guts to make him go. Often now, in the evenings, he doesn't even talk to her but watches stupid sitcoms on TV—and actually laughs—or goes to some bar and charms people into buying him beers. Alex wipes the ring under her coffee cup with her napkin and decides that they can't go on like this. She can't waste any more time waiting for him to get his life together. *She has no more time.*

THREE

Cutting through the park, inhaling the bittersweet
smell of crushed and sodden leaves, Zee thinks how
wonderful rain is really; how it cleanses, rejuvenates.
He almost feels ready to start all over again. Even with Alex.
Who knows, maybe tonight's the night. Maybe they'll go to
Dini's for a beer, stare at the rain sliding down the window-
pane and just feel lucky, incredibly lucky to be together. They
used to feel that, or anyway he did. He'd watch her sip her beer
and wipe her mouth with her hand and feel so lucky to know
her. But they don't go for beers anymore. He doesn't know
why or when they stopped. It just doesn't happen.

A squat man in a trenchcoat, under an umbrella, hurries
past him, trailed by a tiny terrier on a leash. The terrier hangs
back, pulling on the leash, stopping to pee on a trash can. The
man averts his eyes, respecting the dog's privacy. Zee considers
telling the man that it has stopped raining and that he can
close his umbrella. Then it occurs to him that maybe the man
likes holding his umbrella, feels safe under it, yearns for rainy
days just so he can hold it over his head. The dog finishes his
pee, circles the trash can, hikes his little furry leg up and starts
another one. The man cops a quick glance at him. "Otis, we
haven't got all night." Suddenly Zee wishes he had a dog like

Otis who'd love him as long as he fed him regularly. He reaches down to pet him. "Please don't pet my dog," the man says abruptly. Zee's hand freezes in mid-air. He looks at the man, expecting some explanation as to why he is not allowed to pet Otis. Does he look like a dog kidnapper, a dog molester? But the man tugs on the leash. "I warned you not to waste my time," he tells Otis who pricks up his ears and wags his stumpy tail. Zee wants to say, "Fuck you, too." Instead he says, "Nice night out." Ignoring him, the man hurries off, pulling Otis behind him.

What is the world coming to when you can't even pet a person's dog?

It is, in fact, a nice night out. He can even see stars. What he hates most about living in the city is not being able to see stars, just little tiny specks of sparkle, nothing dazzling or uplifting. But tonight he can actually make out the Big Dipper; ever-present, unshakeable. Humans must be a joke to look down upon, running around frantically like ants, trying to build empires, holes in the sand. What's the point?

"Haven't you got a home to go to?" a voice calls from behind him as a hand clamps onto his shoulder. "Zee buddy, how ya doin'?"

"Oh hi Dave, how are you?"

"Can't complain," Dave says, tapping his fist into his palm.

"Were you jogging?" Zee asks, noting Dave's fluorescent orange windbreaker, grey spandex running tights and bright-green and purple running shoes.

"I'm done." Dave pulls on his nose with his thumb and forefinger. "Listen do you want to stop by for a beer?"

Zee hesitates. When Dave used to go out with his sister, Jenny, he would phone Zee periodically to chat and confide. Once he told Zee that he knew he had poor communication skills and worried that he pushed himself on people.

"I want you to meet someone," Dave says, leading Zee down the street. "I've met an amazing woman." He looks around as though afraid someone might overhear and contradict him. "I'm marrying her."

"Congratulations."

"Thanks. I'm having a stag. I wanted to invite you, but I didn't know how you'd feel about it, you know, being Jenny's brother."

"I feel fine about it. I'm very happy for you."

"Thanks." Dave slides the zipper on his windbreaker up and down. "It sounds corny I know but I swear, when I met this girl, I knew she was 'the one'." He stares at the pavement, shaking his head in disbelief. "I never thought I'd hear those words coming out of my mouth. I feel lucky, really lucky."

Up in Dave's high-rise apartment, a full-bodied, young woman, wearing nylon running shorts, lies on her back on the floor with ankle weights strapped around her calves, pulling her legs together then lowering them again.

"Honey?" Dave says. "Remember I told you about the nicest, decentest guy I ever met? This is him."

The young woman glances at Zee and sits up. "Hi," she says, pulling her feet towards her groin to unfasten the weights. Zee, noticing her pubic hair poking out from under her shorts, looks away, out the sliding glass doors to the balcony. "You've got quite the view up here."

"We like it," Dave says and hands Zee a can of Coor's Light. "Zee this is Glenda, Glenda this is Zee." Both Zee and Glenda nod and smile politely. "Nice to meet you," she says, pulling herself up off the floor to sit cross-legged on the sofa.

"Glenda's an R.N.," Dave tells Zee.

"A what?"

"Registered Nurse," Glenda explains, almost apologetically.

"Oh good for you, that's a tough profession. I admire nurses for putting up with ... what they have to put up with." She stares at him. "I mean doctors, and low pay and all that."

"It's not that bad," she says, and Zee worries that he has offended her.

"Anyway, good for you," Zee repeats, staring down at Glenda's weights, nervously tapping his sneaker on the parquet floor.

Dave looks closely at Zee. "You look a little wasted. Everything okay with you?"

Zee shrugs, nods and sips his beer, trying to avoid glancing at Glenda's crotch. It's not that he wants to look at it, it's just that it's right there in front of him.

"How's Alex?" Dave asks.

"She's fine."

Dave looks at Glenda. "Zee's girlfriend is a social worker, works with teenaged mothers. What a pair. Good people, the two of them. Soul mates." He grins. "When are you two going to face up and get married?"

Zee tries to smile mysteriously, but he's thinking that Glenda's thighs are very round and smooth. Pink enamel glints off her toe-nails. He wonders what it would be like to touch her, if his fingers would sink into her flesh or if she would feel firm underneath all that roundness.

"Anyway I think you two have a good thing going," Dave says. "Mutual respect. That's important." He looks at Glenda. She nods in agreement.

Zee pictures Alex's solid, angular frame. He can't remember what a soft woman feels like and wonders if he will ever feel a soft woman ever again. "I should be going," he says.

"So come to the stag," Dave reminds him. "Here on the twelfth. Eight o'clock." Zee has never been to a stag and pictures men sitting around with antlers on their heads. "And I'd love it if both you guys could come to the wedding. Maybe Glenda can send you an invitation." Dave glances at Glenda who nods in agreement.

"That would be nice," Zee says, knowing they won't go. Alex boycotts weddings, doesn't see the point of them, or of marriage for that matter. She believes that the commitment is in your head. Besides, she says, I don't see how two people can live together for more than ten years without eating each other's livers. Zee thinks it's interesting that she should choose a large gland that secretes bile to symbolize ten years of marriage. Why the liver? Why not the heart?

FOUR

Staring at the girl in the panty-hose ad, Alex wonders how anyone can have legs that thin. How are women supposed to feel good about themselves when advertisers keep telling them they should look like emaciated fifteen-year-olds? The man sitting beside her, smelling of mothballs and Clorets, stands, preparing to get off the train.

If Zee's home she'll just bake the muffins and go to bed. She won't "needle at" him. She knows it accomplishes nothing, only makes her feel as if there's a gash in her stomach. Always, after the fight, she cries and wraps her arms around him, aware that nothing has changed between them, but at least she hasn't lost him, chased him away. At least she can continue to hope, to delude herself that one day they will have a house in the country and a baby. Right at the start he established the house-in-the-country fantasy. And it has hung there, like a mirage, for seven years. On the days when they came home frayed from work, he would hold her and murmur, "We have to get a house in the country." She always agreed but asked how they would afford it. And always he said, "We'll get there." But of course they're not getting there. They're getting nowhere fast and her eggs are rotting.

What does it say about her if he's a loser? It must mean

that she's a loser. Why would someone who isn't a loser spend seven years with a loser? She must be a loser otherwise she would have snared a more dependable man. A doctor, a carpenter, a plumber; someone who understands and can cope with the adult world. Someone prepared to make the necessary compromises to build a life.

A mother and child step into the subway car. The child, walking awkwardly on artificial legs, has no arms, only withered flaps of hands stemming from her shoulders. The mother places her hands around the child's rib-cage and hoists her onto a seat. The child stares past her mother's shoulder at Alex with curious, hopeful eyes. *How can you hope? How can you be curious? How can you believe in anything?*

Alex has seen cocaine babies at the Centre. And babies with AIDS. Most of these infants die, yet the mothers continue to take drugs, go back on the street and get pregnant again. Alex has a feeling that if she continues to be a social worker she will go mad. She no longer feels that she is helping these teen-mothers, these victims of sexual abuse, these drug addicts. She knows that they don't listen to her, that they want her pity not her help. They come to the Centre for food, shelter, baby-sitting and to use the phone. They avoid her eyes and stare at the walls. Some of them tell her about being raped, beaten, burnt, locked up, tied up. They sit lifeless, waiting for her to feel sorry for them. They want to be victims, choose to be victims. Alex tries to make them understand that they are, in part, responsible for their own lives. She tries to make them believe that they can do something to improve their situations, but they resist her. They want to blame their problems on the world; they feel justified in blaming the world because the world, the one they see on TV, owes them fast cars, microwave ovens and swell houses filled with beautiful people drinking beer. The way they see

27

it, the world hasn't kept its part of the bargain.

Alex used to agree that society was to blame. But now, when she stares over her desk at young women who continue to take drugs and fornicate without contraception, she no longer feels compassion for them, no longer feels that they have been wronged. Now she feels that they are stupid. "Why didn't you use contraception?" she asks.

"Didn't have any."

"You know that condoms are always available here."

They shrug, pick at their pimples and play with their hair.

"Why didn't you ask him to use a condom?"

"He says it don't feel right."

Alex feels like reaching over and shaking them. But no, she leans back in her chair and wonders what she's being paid for. To listen to these people? To tell them that everything will be okay? To assist them in getting an abortion so that they can run off and get pregnant again?

"I just want to be with my kids," they say.

"You can't just be with your kids. Nobody can just be with their kids. You have to support your kids."

She's acquiring a reputation for being "hard on the girls". Some of her co-workers are saying that she's starting to burn out. Sometimes she imagines herself walking into McDonald's with a machine gun and blowing people away. She knows that this is not a healthy attitude for a social worker, which is why she has started to bake muffins. Zee thinks she's crazy to get up at five in the morning to deliver them. He doesn't believe it's worth the money. Apparently there are no jobs that Zee considers worth the money. He seems to believe that he should be paid to do nothing, to hang out in bars, to sit around the park with his thumb up his ass contemplating the meaning of life.

Often now, walking down the street, she searches the

crowds for a man like Zee, with a similarly humorous face and twinkling eyes. Someone like Zee but who works for a living and wants a baby.

The woman sitting across from Alex in the plaid coat with frayed cuffs and collar is wearing a white fake-fur hat shaped like a marshmallow. Balanced on the hat is a pair of sunglasses. She notices Alex staring at her. "You have to be careful," the woman cautions. "They give you cancer." She tugs on her bare hands as though taking off gloves. "Certain times you're more likely to get sick from them because your body's vulnerable. It happened to me." She presses her hand against her hat. "Don't listen to what the doctors say." A man with acne, wearing a nylon parka, leaning back in his seat, opens his eyes for an instant, looks impassively at the woman in the marshmallow hat, then closes his eyes again.

"Don't listen to what the doctors say," she repeats. "I spent two years in hospital. Lost all my hair. It never grew back the same. It used to be jet black." Alex stands, offers the woman what she hopes reads as a sympathetic smile and steps off the train. On the platform wall, directly in front of her is an ad for men's briefs. A headless man stands flexing his muscles, his pectorals bulge, his stomach ripples, his penis and testicles push impressively against the briefs.

It maddens her that there has never been anyone in her life she has liked as much as Zee. Never been anyone who could make her laugh when she felt ready to put her fist through the wall. Never been anyone she's felt could withstand all forces of her personality, both negative and positive.

Pushing through the turnstile, she thinks he'd probably be better off without her. He could smoke himself to death, drink himself to death, sit in the bath and never clean the ring; he could think about whatever he thinks about for hours. He wouldn't have her to remind him that the day is over, that it's meal time, bed time. He could just stay the same twenty-four hours a day, an amoeba; a simple microscopic organism. A blob.

FIVE

Zee's glad Alex isn't home yet; glad he doesn't have to justify himself; glad her battleship-grey eyes aren't bearing down on him, boring a hole into his brain. But it's awfully quiet without her, almost spooky. He looks at his watch: ten forty-eight. It occurs to him that maybe she's having an affair. Except he doesn't think she'd screw somebody unless they were going to "build a life" together. She's holding out on sex until she can do it with a purpose. She used to like it. They weren't your regular-without-fail-three-times-a-week couple, but he thinks she used to enjoy it. He used to call her his little sex machine in an Inspector Clouseau accent, and she used to laugh.

Suddenly he misses her so much his gut throbs. Suddenly he's convinced she's been raped and killed, lying broken in an alley. No not Alex, no one would dare rape Alex. She took classes in self-defense, knows how to maim, knows how to bust balls and noses. She carries her keys in her hand, ready to rip an assailant's face apart.

He looks in the fridge for the fourth time. Lettuce, shrivelled brown around the edges, and sprouting carrots lie in a pile on the middle shelf. In a plastic bag, bean sprouts have grown roots that look to Zee like white worms. Alex insists bean sprouts are important for their potassium. Zee dislikes them because they crunch like insects in his mouth. He reaches down to the bottom shelf and discovers some mouldy cheese in a paper bag. He pushes it to the back of the fridge and closes the door then sniffs his hand and washes it in the sink. He opens a cupboard and stares grimly at rows of jars filled with whole grains, flours, oat bran, wheat bran, dried beans.

He wants some potato chips.

He looks out the window at the rain splattering down on the street, and wonders if it's worth a dash to the corner store. A man in a suit rushes past holding a newspaper over his head. Zee looks back at the cupboard, pulls out a jar of unsalted peanuts, leans against the counter and eats several handfuls. In his head he hears Alex saying, "Those are pure fat."

If only he could live on a farm somewhere. Grow things. Maybe then he wouldn't want to sleep all day. Maybe then he'd rise with the sun, eat a bowl of porridge and stride purposefully into the fields, welcoming another day.

He has tried to grow things on the balcony—basil, parsley, cherry tomatoes—but everything dies. He waters them, drips plant food into the soil, but still they die. He even tied a sheet of canvas against the balcony railing to protect them from the wind, and still their leaves turned brown, shrivelled and dropped off. He felt hopeless, inept, unable to protect a single tiny plant from the outside world.

How could he protect a child?

Inside, his aloe plants are spreading through the apartment. As each plant grows too large for one of his sawed-off plastic milk jugs, he transplants clumps of it into another. When Alex complains that there are too many of them in the apartment, he reminds her that the aloe is a healing plant. When he cuts himself shaving, he triumphantly demonstrates to her how rubbing aloe on the wound stops the bleeding.

One night he woke up to see Alex sitting very straight in bed, terrified, asking him what the spiked heads were doing there. He looked to see what she was staring at. "Aloe plants," he whispered. "It's just the aloe plants."

She continued to squint into the darkness. "I thought they were warriors' helmets."

Warriors' helmets?

Still half-asleep, she'd shoved her head back into her pillow and pulled the covers up around her ears, her short hair standing away from her head in tufts. Always, in sleep, she reminds him of a burrowing, furry animal. Always, he wants to protect the furry animal from her waking-self, her warrior-self.

When he plays back their conversations in his head, he tries to see himself from her point of view, because from his point of view, his arguments make perfect sense. From his point of view there is no point in arguing. He has facts to substantiate his arguments, hard facts, while she has only the biological clock to shake in his face.

He wonders if she's at Mel's. Mel with the pear-shaped bum, always in search of a man. Mel who hasn't yet figured out that they can see her coming and take off before she can eat them alive. He considers phoning her as he's done before when Alex has taken refuge in Mel's coral-pink apartment. He decides against it, looks down at his belly, the belly that's betraying him, pushing up against his jeans, forcing him to loosen his belt a notch. Alex tells him to stop eating "fats"— peanut butter, cheese, Hungarian salami—things he thought were supposed to be healthy. She tells him to stop drinking. Her nagging doesn't make him stop eating and drinking, it just makes it less fun, because wherever he is, he hears the little voice saying, "You've got to take responsibility for your body." This responsibility thing's a hoax. It is possible to live irresponsibly and relatively contentedly. Look at his wino amigo. You just have to find a way to short-circuit your brain.

When he hears her key in the lock, he considers making a run for the bed and pretending to be asleep. Except that he wants to see her: her serious little face; her long, solid body. And who knows, maybe she'll be in a good mood, maybe she'll want to go for beers.

She looks up at him as she closes the door then quickly averts her eyes, and immediately he understands that he is in dangerous waters. He pulls a hand out of his pocket and offers a tentative wave.

"Hi," she says, recognizing that he is drunk. She drops her shoulder bag on the sofa and hangs up her down jacket. She feels him watching her, waiting, like a blob waiting to be poked. She runs her fingers through her hair, shaking out the rain. "So what did you do today?"

"Not much." He slides his hands in his pockets and hangs on tightly to some change.

"Did you call that firm?"

"No."

She sighs, walks past him to the kitchen, fills the kettle and slams it on the stove. He follows her and leans against the fridge. "They want lawyers with clientele," he says. "They don't want some old fart who's been working in government."

"You have a lot of experience."

"Not the kind they want."

She rinses and empties the teapot. "I just can't believe there's nothing you can do."

"I'm open to suggestions."

"Legal aid."

"Prosecuting bums and junkies, I've done it, I hate it."

She drops tea bags into the pot. "Well some of us have to do things we hate."

"Can we not have this conversation?"

"How many more months do you plan on doing nothing?"

"I don't know."

She pulls two cups off the shelf, sets them on the counter and stares at them. He knows he must change the subject, otherwise they will spend the evening in gloom. He wonders if he should tell her about his wino amigo or the hockey fan in the satin baseball jacket or the hedgehog man. But then she'll know he went to a bar, spent money in a bar. "How was your day?" he asks.

She pours boiling water into the teapot. "I saw a little girl with no arms on the subway."

"Really?"

"She had no legs either." She looks at him, surprised to see him actually disturbed by this information. But of course he doesn't see how the little girl's plight relates to their situation; how the odds of their having a baby without arms or legs are getting greater every day. "Her mother was older, forty or something. She just looked ... I don't know, beaten." Zee nods and moves a ladybug magnet to a new position on the refrigerator door. Alex smears peanut butter on a piece of Ryvita. "A forty-year-old friend of Mel's had a baby with no fingers. Another one had a Down's syndrome child."

"Really?" He lifts the ladybug a quarter inch off the fridge then lets the magnetic pull suck it back on.

"Before the baby was born," Alex continues, "she'd organized this party for all the women in her pre-natal class. She couldn't cancel it, so they all came with their healthy newborns and lined them up on her couch so they could take pictures. She didn't tell anyone that hers was retarded. Can you imagine seeing all these healthy babies, knowing that yours is retarded? That would be devastating." Zee nods and leans against the fridge. Alex bites into her cracker. "Another baby was born dead."

"These were all friends of Mel?"

"No, these are stories I've heard through other people. If you have a normal child after thirty-five, it's a miracle. Can you imagine having your baby born dead? Apparently she knew it was dead when she was still in labour. Can you imagine pushing out a dead baby? "

He winces, envisioning a woman's spread thighs, the bloodied gloves of doctors, a tiny skull tearing a vagina. A baby born dead. What do they do with it? Show it to the mother? Drop it in a bin? Wrap it in plastic and freeze it for its organs? He pictures Alex, her feet in stirrups, screaming. He has seen actresses simulating childbirth in movies. He can't understand why any woman in her right mind would want to put herself through that. He can't understand why any woman in her right mind would want to put a baby through that when there's nothing out in the world for it, nothing left, all has been consumed and transformed into waste. Even the sky has been used up.

Alex has been watching him leaning against the fridge, playing with the magnet, shifting his weight from one foot to the other. A blob. "It just amazes me that none of this has any effect on you," she says.

"It has an effect on me."

"What?"

"It's sad, very sad."

"Right." She screws the lid back on the peanut butter, shoves it into the cabinet and wipes the crumbs off the breadboard. "You don't care that if I'm lucky enough to conceive at all there's a good chance the baby will be deformed?"

"You're not even thirty-five," he says. "Lots of women have babies at forty."

"My eggs are going bad. That's what happens when you get old. Your eggs go rotten." She stares at him and plants one

36

hand on her hip. "And your sperm's getting sparser all the time. Soon you may not even have enough motile sperm to fertilize my egg."

They'd watched a show on the human reproductive system and he'd been appalled at how easily the tiny-tailed sperms lost their sense of direction. They'd flitted about, bumping into one another, spinning in circles. He'd always imagined sperm as a well-organized team, determined to do whatever it takes to score.

"There is the problem of my brain," he says.

"What are you talking about?"

"What good would a brain-dead father be to a child?"

"What do you mean, brain dead?"

He taps his temple. "There's nothing going on up here. Nada."

"So do something about it. Read."

"I try to. It's meaningless. My life has no meaning."

"How can you say that?"

He shrugs. "Nothing in my life has meaning."

"What about our relationship?"

"It has no meaning if my life has no meaning."

"How is that supposed to make me feel?"

"Women always do this, bring the conversation back to themselves."

"Oh please."

It's true, he thinks. Always, when they fight, it comes down to, "Doesn't this relationship mean anything to you? Don't I mean anything to you? Why are you staying in this relationship? What does it say about me if you're brain dead?"

Many times he has asked her, sometimes told her, to go away, insisting he just wants to sit quietly, smoke his pipe and drink scotch. "I don't feel fulfilled," he says, "I can't find fulfillment in a relationship. Bringing a baby into it isn't going to help, it'll just keep us busy, and we'll have to work at stupid jobs to buy it what it wants and pay the baby-sitter."

"Nobody is fulfilled," she argues. "Nobody gets to do exactly what they want to do, get paid for it and feel fulfilled by it. That just doesn't happen. It goes against human nature. We always feel dissatisfied. That's what keeps us going."

"Well I'm going nowhere and I'm dissatisfied, so I guess I'm a freak. Maybe I'm not human. Maybe I'm an alien." He grips his ears and stretches them away from his head.

She rolls her eyes, crosses her arms and sighs.

He has always admired her ability to get things done, once she has decided to do them. She has a focus, a concentration, that he has always envied. When he quit work, and she began baking muffins to make extra money, he'd watched in awe as she worked eight-hour days then came home and baked. Progressively she has baked more and worked less. The word seems to be out on her low-fat muffins because she can't meet the demand. He imagines that soon, if she wishes, she will have a low-fat muffin empire.

Sometimes he feels that spending seven years with some-one so focussed has been his downfall. He allowed himself to be drawn into her current because he was too lazy to venture out on his own. He doesn't like this about himself; doesn't like the feeling he has, more frequently now, that he is a lazy fart who has blown it. People who used to smile at him, defer to him, now pretend not to see him on the street. His eyes meet theirs for an instant before they look away, suddenly engrossed in a store window. He wishes this didn't bother him; he reminds himself that these are people he didn't respect when they did speak to him so why should it bother him when they look past him now? Why should he care? He regrets that he hasn't done something drastic to deserve their cool treatment, wishes he had shaken the system. But no, he only irritated a few bureaucrats more firmly entrenched in the system than he. Bureaucrats who labelled him "treacherous" when he suggested that the system wasn't working. Bureaucrats with sizeable pension plans, waiting for retirement so they can spend their days watching TV and their evenings on the curling rink.

With his finger, he draws a stick-man in the condensation on the window. She considers booting him in the ass but knows that this will only weaken her position, knows she must remain rational, work this out. "What makes you so special that you deserve to be 'fulfilled' while the rest of us have to work for a living?"

"I don't think wanting to be fulfilled is asking too much. Lots of people are fulfilled."

"Like who?"

"People who love their work."

"Who?"

He draws a smile on the stick-man. "Certain artists, filmmakers, architects, people who are their own bosses."

"I'm sure if you asked them, they'd have something to complain about."

"Yes, but at least they're working at what they want to do. They believe in it." He draws very large ears on the stick-man.

"So what do you want to do?"

"I've told you. I wanted to effect changes in government, but they wouldn't let me."

"You're blaming the world again." She opens the fridge, pulls out a bottle of mineral water and unscrews the cap. "It amazes me that you think the world owes you a living."

"Can we not have this conversation?"

"Seriously, what makes you so special that you're above the politics and all the other bullshit the rest of us have to put up with?"

He rests his forehead on the cool of the window-pane,

knowing that there is no point in having this conversation because they have had it many times before. It only leads to frustration and a desire to throw things.

She leans her hip against the counter and stares at a wet tea-bag in the sink. She can't believe, *can't believe* that he is conceited enough to think that he should be allowed to do exactly what he wants in life. "You're not dealing with reality," she says.

"Your reality."

"There's another reality where you don't have to work for a living?"

He throws up his hands. "Find yourself a banker. I can't be what you want me to be so leave me."

"I just want you to help out."

"You want me to get some stupid job I hate so that you can have a baby. Great, that's just great. I'll hate my life but at least you'll have experienced motherhood."

"I don't want you to get some stupid job you hate."

"Sure you do. How are you going to afford daycare, computers? All children must have computers. All children must have nice toys and clothes otherwise their lives are made a living hell by other children who have nice toys and clothes."

She picks the tea-bag out of the sink and pushes it past the flap in the trash can. "There must be a happy medium somewhere."

"Yeah, marry a banker."

"That's good, take the easy way out."

"I don't know what to tell you. You want answers. You want everything to add up in that tight little brain of yours. I can't do that for you. I have no answers. Marry a banker. I no longer want to have this conversation." He walks out of the kitchen into the bedroom and closes the door.

For a moment she imagines her arm growing long and

furry, as in a horror movie, her hand busting through the door and grabbing his throat. She sees his eyes bulging in terror, his mouth gaping. She takes a slug of mineral water, puts the bottle back in the fridge then reaches into the cabinets and pulls out oat bran, flour, baking powder, brown sugar. She reaches into the freezer for frozen blueberries and cranberries. She must bake six dozen muffins for tomorrow morning. She must push the Zee problem out of her mind and deal with the matter at hand.

•

He dreams that he is a Hollywood director filming in a luxurious hotel lobby. The crew mills around him, dragging cables, setting up lights, arranging furniture, making the actors up. Zee waits nervously for someone to ask him for direction. He worries that he won't know what to say and that they'll find out that he isn't really a Hollywood director. He holds his hand against his chin and squints, hoping to appear deep in thought. He knows that at some point he will be expected to call out "action" and hopes that when the time is right, it will be obvious. All will become quiet and still; the actors will stand poised, ready to deliver lines; the cameraman will have his eye pressed to the camera; the soundman will hold his microphone over the actors. Zee waits. No one asks him anything. No one seems to notice him. Finally the hotel lobby becomes quiet, the actors stand poised, the cameraman squints into the camera, and the soundman holds up his microphone. Zee can feel his heart pounding and sweat forming on his forehead. Suddenly the actors begin to say their lines, and the camera starts to whirr. He looks around at the crew, wondering if anyone has noticed that he hasn't said "action". They all stare attentively at the scene in progress. He feels both relieved and distressed that no one has noticed his lack of leadership; that no one seems to care.

He wakes up to see Alex on all fours beside the bed. "Zee wake up."

"What is it?"

"I think I'm having a heart attack." She gasps.

"You're what?"

"I think I'm having a heart attack. I can't breathe."

He kneels down on the floor beside her. "I don't think so, sweetie. I think if you were having a heart attack you wouldn't be able to move at all."

"I can't move!"

"I don't think you'd be able to talk."

She rolls onto her side. "Zee, I think I'm dying. I'm serious. Call an ambulance."

He feels around on the floor for his pants. "I'll get the car."

"There's something wrong with it."

"I thought you had it fixed."

"There's something else wrong with it."

"It still runs though doesn't it?"

•

In the car she sits hunched over, resting her forehead against the dash. "Why didn't you call an ambulance?" she asks.

"I thought this would be easier."

"You're not taking this seriously." She gasps. "You think I'm making this up. Why would I make this up? You think I'm enjoying this?"

"Just try to breathe, sweetie."

She loses patience with the admitting nurse who happens to be Asian and can hardly speak English. Zee fills out the necessary forms while Alex leans against the wall, clutching her chest. Other patients slump in chairs around her. A leather-jacketed teenager holds a wad of toilet paper up to his bleeding head. A gaunt man, with a sparse beard, sits staring at his feet, his entire body shaking. A fat woman holds a coughing, spewing child in her arms. Alex turns to face the wall, wondering if she really is dying and if she is, why it should disturb her. What has she got to live for anyway? She doesn't live. She survives. She feels Zee's arm around her waist. "How're you doing?" he asks.

She shrugs. He nods and stares at the coughing, spewing child then looks up at a television set bolted to the wall high above the waiting area. On the screen a man crouches behind a car, holding a gun. From a window, another man fires shots at the man behind the car who ducks then fires back.

"I can't believe you're watching TV," Alex says.

He looks at her. "What do you want me to do?"

She turns her face back to the wall and shakes her head, thinking that as usual he continues to float undisturbed while she is drowning.

He looks back at the TV, thinking that he hates it when she does that, shuts him out as though he were worthless scum. She does it on purpose, he knows, to make him feel small. Amazing that even while in pain she can still find the strength to make his life a living hell.

Without looking up from the dirty-beige linoleum, she knows he's watching the TV. What if she dies? Will it devastate him? Will he weep on his knees by her grave? Will the sight of her belongings send shudders of despair through him or will he have a yard sale then sit in the park, drinking from a bag?

On TV the man lunges from behind the car and runs towards the building, dodging shots from the man firing from the window. Zee slides quarters into an automat and pulls out

43

a can of Five-Alive. It is only when he offers it to Alex that he notices the tears. "Don't cry, sweetie," he says. He opens the can for her and again holds it out to her. She shakes her head. "Sweetie," he whispers, "I think if it was a heart attack you would be dead by now, you know. I think maybe it was something you ate. What did you eat yesterday?"

She bangs her forehead into the wall. "Quit patronizing me."

"Sweetie, don't get excited."

"You don't take me seriously," she says loudly, attracting the attention of the fat woman with the baby. "Whenever I'm upset about something you act like I'm over-reacting."

"Well, sometimes you are." He waves at the fat woman who looks away.

"Like when?"

He swirls the juice around in the can. "The money thing," he mutters. "You always freak out about money."

"With good reason."

"It's never as bad as you think it's going to be."

"That's because I take care of the problem before the shit hits the fan," she whispers hoarsely. "You sit around waiting for the shit to hit the fan."

"Why freak out about the shit hitting the fan before it hits the fan?"

She stamps her foot. "So that it doesn't hit the fan! You take preventive measures. You protect yourself."

"You always assume the worst is about to happen, and it doesn't. I've seen you predict disaster a hundred times and it doesn't happen."

"That's because I don't let it happen!" She gasps and grabs her chest again.

"Sweetie, don't get excited."

"You know I'll take care of everything, that's the problem, you know I'll clean up after you. It's pathetic."

"Sweetie, stop talking. Drink some juice."

She shakes her head. He sips the juice and watches nervously as she rests her forehead against the wall. "It hurts," she says. "You don't believe it hurts."

"I do, love." He rubs his hand between her shoulder blades. "Just try to breathe normally." On the TV, the man who was behind the car chases the other man up some stairs then jumps on top of him and pushes his gun into the man's throat.

Alex slides down the wall and crouches against it. "I'm scared," she mumbles. She pulls her knees into her chest and closes her eyes tight, wincing. He squats beside her, brushes his open hand against her forehead and feels her sweat in his palm. Only now does he realize that she may be really sick, only now has he become sufficiently disarmed to appreciate her pain. If he could, he would kick himself. He hurries over to the Asian admitting nurse who doesn't look up from her desk. "I think she's really sick," he says, "I mean I think she's getting worse."

"Car accident just happen. Emergency."

"Yeah, but you see, there's something wrong in her chest. She can hardly breathe."

"Car accident just happen."

He crouches back down beside Alex, very pale now, slumped against the wall. "It won't be long now, sweetie."

"If I'm really sick," she says weakly, "none of what we argue about would matter would it? I mean, it wouldn't matter because I would be dying. We wouldn't give a shit about whether our lives have any meaning, we'd just … we'd just live for the moment. We'd be glad for the moment. Wouldn't we?"

Zee nods, shocked at how fragile she has become. Suddenly he wants to throw his body over her, protect her.

After she has been led away, he sits and waits for what feels like hours, telling himself that there can't be anything seriously wrong. Alex eats whole grains and soya margarine. Alex takes brisk walks to stimulate circulation.

On TV a man and woman are dancing close. The man starts to unzip the woman's dress, the woman starts to undo the man's tie.

Zee opens and closes his fingers, wishing he'd brought his pipe then notices the no-smoking sign. Close by, a young woman in a miniskirt, a rabbit-fur jacket and stiletto heels sits staring at the TV, chewing her fingernails. One of her ankles is viciously swollen. Pimples poke out from beneath her heavily applied makeup.

Life without Alex. This is not possible.

On TV the man slides the woman's dress off her shoulders, pushes her onto the bed, climbs on top of her, plants his lips on hers and slides his hand down her body. He begins to kiss her neck, then moves down towards her breasts. The woman tilts her head back as though in ecstasy.

What if it is a heart attack and she's paralyzed? He'll have to look after her. She will depend on him, will hate depending on him. She has always prided herself on not depending on anyone. What if her speech is impaired? He will have to learn to interpret the guttural sounds she emits. She will probably drool; will probably urinate into a bag that he will have to empty. How do paralyzed people shit?

He does not know if he can handle this situation, doubts that he is that good a person. As she has said, he is a coward.

When he sees her walking towards him, he feels as though he must be dreaming. He stands, stunned, then hurries over to her and wraps his arms around her, inhaling her smell. "How are you sweetie?"

"It's alright."

"Is it?"

She nods meekly. "I'm really tired. They gave me some

46

drugs to help me sleep."

"Okay, well, we'll go home."

She nods again and starts to walk. He puts his arm around her shoulders. "What did the doctor say?"

"They took a cardiogram and everything."

"And?"

"Everything's fine."

"So what was it?"

"He says it's stress-related. He says I should take stock of what I'm doing with my life."

"Take stock?" He pictures her jotting numbers down on a clipboard.

She nods. "That's what he said."

"What is that supposed to mean exactly?"

"It means my life isn't working. It means that if I don't remedy what's wrong in my life I could get really sick."

He studies the side of her face, since she won't look at him, then kisses her temple. "You wait here. I'll get the car."

SIX

I never meet men." Mel spoons some froth from her café-au-lait into her mouth and sets her spoon down on the edge of her saucer. "I'm not interested in going to bars and so on. I don't believe you meet men in bars. When couples say they met in a bar it usually means they met through friends in a bar. Strangers don't meet in bars."

Alex flicks a crumb off the marble-topped table. "I met Zee in a bar."

"Did you really?"

"We were playing darts." For a moment Alex pictures Zee against the barn-board walls of the Catcher's Mitt, leaning back on his heels, closing one eye, taking aim.

"I've never played darts. I'm always afraid I'll jab someone's eye out." Mel runs a finger under her eye-lashes, checking for smeared makeup. "In fact I don't play games. Maybe I should. Join a bowling club or something." She looks at the mascara on her finger.

"I can't see you bowling."

"No, you have to rent the shoes, don't you? I hate the idea of wearing other peoples' shoes."

"And people stare at your bum."

"Well I don't mind people looking at my ass," Mel says.

"God knows I work out enough that I shouldn't be ashamed of it. Of course I'd still like to lose a few inches but what can you do?" She sighs heavily then squints at something over Alex's shoulder. "I think I've slept with that guy."

"Which guy?"

"In the green." Alex turns in her seat to look at a portly man in a green lamb's-wool sweater. "He wasn't bald when I knew him," Mel adds. "He's a criminal lawyer."

"He doesn't seem to recognize you."

"No. Well, I was a brunette then."

"Why did you sleep with him?"

"Oh, I don't know," Mel says. "I was articling with his firm. I thought maybe I could learn something from him."

"By sleeping with him?"

"Pathetic, isn't it? He had a wife, a drinking problem. They all do, you know. They can't take the stress, working twenty-hour days to pay for their boats and so on. They sleep with their secretaries or whoever else will put up with them. It's sad. Law's a sordid business. To be honest with you, I can't blame Zee for wanting out of it." She leans her chin on her hand and continues to squint over Alex's shoulder. Alex studies Mel's new nose. When she pictures Mel in her mind, it's with her old majestic nose. The new one is shorter and turned up at the end.

"How is Zee?" Mel asks. "Any change?" Alex shakes her head. Mel sighs. "What a waste of an education. Didn't he want to be a lawyer?"

Alex notices a robust young man and woman in matching Norwegian sweaters hold hands across a table. The young woman lifts his hand to her lips, kisses it and smiles at him. "He wanted to be a lounge singer," Alex says.

"A what?"

"A lounge singer."

"Seriously?"

Alex shrugs. Mel drains her coffee cup. "Can he sing?"

"I think so. I mean he sings at home and it sounds alright. You know, folk songs from the Sixties. And old Randy Newman songs."

"Lounge singers don't sing folk songs."

"No, well he sings pop songs, too. You know, those golden oldies that you see advertised on TV, only available by mail order."

Mel shakes her head. "He's definitely losing it."

"When he was a teenager, he used to practise singing like the guys on Ed Sullivan, you know, Frank Sinatra and Wayne Newton, Tony Bennett."

"That's sad."

"He used to pretend to be holding a microphone so he could practice his mike technique. He thinks Julio Iglesias has poor mike technique because he lets the microphone down after each phrase."

"So?"

"Apparently you're supposed to keep it up," Alex explains. "Zee says it looks better."

"He's actually told you this?"

"We always tell each other stuff like that. Or anyway we used to."

Mel leans back in her chair and crosses her legs. Behind her a man whose neck is the same width as his head smokes a cigarette. She tries to wave the smoke away with her hand. Alex stares out the window. A little blond boy, wearing very thick glasses and holding a white cane stands alone on the sidewalk. After a moment his father steps back from the newsstand and takes the little boy's hand. Why, she wonders, does she keep seeing disabled children? She contemplates the grounds in her coffee cup. "You know what's weird is I can't remember if I ever wanted to be something when I grew up, did you?"

Mel tightens her lower lip, thinking. "I think I wanted to be a brain surgeon. Then I got repulsed dissecting frogs."

"I can't remember wanting to be anything. I must have wanted to be something."

"Most girls wanted to be fashion models."

On the street a man and a woman argue, gesticulating wildly. The man turns his back on the woman and starts to walk away. She runs after him and grabs his coat. He looks at passers-by and, obviously embarrassed by the situation, grips her arm and pulls her down the street.

"We had to go to the hospital last night. I thought I was having a heart attack."

"Seriously?"

"I had this pain in my chest."

"An anxiety attack," Mel says. "I know someone who has those. She works in advertising."

Alex has, of course, thought about Zee all day; has tried to sort out what is left of their relationship; has tried to weigh the pros and cons of staying together. She pictures him meandering around the apartment as though nothing out of the ordinary had happened. He has probably opened the fridge fourteen times, has probably had a bath and is probably watching TV. Lately, when she comes home at night, he tells her about the "real" people he's seen on "The Oprah Winfrey Show". He insists that they have valid concerns, and he finds it interesting that they want to tell the world about their personal problems. He wonders why they expose themselves on national television. Do they feel validated? Is it cathartic? Does confessing on "Oprah" actually help anybody? Alex doesn't comment, doesn't know, doesn't care. She half expects him to appear on the show. He could tell Oprah about the cruel woman he lives with, the hard bitch who needles at him.

"Zee's a nice guy, but he's lazy," Mel says. "I've never seen such a laid-back individual. Initially I thought he was on Ativan or something. I've never said this before because I don't believe in judging other people's relationships, but maybe you should get on with your life. Maybe it's time to move on."

To what though? To where?

"Maybe it's time to cut your losses."

But she's so used to him being there, counts on him being there. Who would she talk to? Who would listen to her? Who would understand what she's talking about?

There is a hollow between his neck and shoulder where she can rest her forehead and feel completely safe.

Mel pulls out her wallet and puts three dollars on the table. "People change, and there's nothing we can do about it. Anyway I've got to get going. I want to put on a skirt."

"I thought you were going to a movie with Doreen."

"I am."

"So why are you wearing a skirt?"

"Because there might be men there, and men like skirts. I know this for a fact. My brother told me. The first thing men notice are legs and bums. Apparently breasts aren't such a big issue anymore."

•

In rush-hour traffic, the Mazda sputters then stalls at a red light. Alex revs the engine, but it continues to cut out. She panics as drivers behind her honk and shake their heads. When she finally makes it to her service station, she steps into the office with what she hopes is a winsome smile for Larry. Experience has taught her that harassing the mechanic only prolongs her wait for service. He glances at her as she comes in then finishes filling out an invoice. While she waits Alex stares at the shelves of bottles of oil and antifreeze and at a poster on the wall of a large-breasted girl in a hot-pink bikini.

"What's the problem?" Larry asks finally.

"It's still stalling."

"Let's have a look."

She follows him out to the car, noticing, not for the first time, that underneath his coveralls, he has nice legs. He opens the hood. "Start her up." She does, the car idles briefly then stalls. "It's the carburetor," he says.

"What will that cost?"

He reaches up and massages the back of his neck. "Around two hundred, depending on the price of the kit."

"I see." She pushes open the car door, gets out and leans against the roof. He slams the hood shut, rests his hands on his hips and stares at her.

"Maybe you can explain something to me," she says.

"Un-hunh?"

"You just put in a new distributor, a new alternator and a new battery …" Larry tips his head to one side and narrows his eyes, waiting patiently for her to come to the point. Feeling patronized, she stiffens. "What I mean is, how can we be sure that doing those things to the car worked when it isn't working. Is it possible we did the wrong things to the car?"

He squints out at the traffic, reminding her of Clint Eastwood staring across the plain. "The things that weren't working before are working now, right?"

Suddenly, for no particular reason, she has a feeling that this man would like to see her naked. It has been a long time since she has felt that a man she didn't know would like to see her naked. Michael would like to see her naked, but he admires her personality. This man knows nothing about her. This man just likes her body. Flustered, she steps backwards, into a puddle.

"Whoops," he says.

"All I'm saying is it's hard to tell if the car's working when it keeps stalling."

"The symptoms were different."

Alex marvels at his self-confidence. Where cars are concerned, Larry has no doubts. She wonders if he stands as grounded in his personal life. She doubts it. He hides behind long hair and a beard.

"This is a different problem," he says.

"I've just never had so many things go wrong with a car in such a short time."

"It's expensive."

"Yeah."

Larry nods, apparently pondering the car. "It's an old car."

"It's only five ... six years old."

He shrugs and nods, still staring at the car. She wonders what he would look like naked. It has been a long time since she has wondered what a man looked like naked. The reawakening of this curiosity does not please her. She had thought it dead in her, gone and buried. She'd thought herself free of it. She wants to get on with her life. "Well I guess I'll leave it," she says.

"Sure."

Sitting on the subway, she tries to recall if he wore a wedding ring.

SEVEN

Zee holds up a strip of cooked pasta and lays it carefully over the sauce. He spoons some ricotta cheese from a carton and smears it over the layer of pasta then sprinkles it with grated mozzarella. It occurs to him that he should have put the cheese over the sauce before he covered the sauce with the pasta. He spreads more sauce over the cheese then begins another layer of pasta. He hears Alex come through the front door and stops to listen while she takes off her boots and jacket. When she doesn't come into the kitchen but goes into the bedroom, he considers calling out some form of greeting but decides against it, preferring silence. On "Oprah" today, there were deaf and dumb people. He liked how they didn't sign at the same time but waited patiently for one to finish before another began. It seemed to him that they thought before they signed. He has decided to think more before he speaks. All day he has been thinking about what to say to Alex, knowing that she will expect him to say something. Finally, he has decided to say nothing as, certainly, she will say something. He sprinkles more mozzarella over the sauce then lifts up another strip of pasta. When he hears Alex's socked-feet approaching, tension creeps into his neck. She leans against the doorway.

"Hi," she says.

"How do."

"You were talking to yourself again."

"When?"

"Just now, when I came in."

"You're kidding."

"I can't believe you don't realize you're doing it."

"I don't."

She opens the fridge and drinks from a bottle of mineral water.

"What are you doing?"

"Making lasagne." He lays the strip down carefully.

"I can see that." She wonders if this is some kind of peace offering. Does he think that, by making lasagne, he will cure her of anxiety attacks? "Since when do you make lasagne just for us?"

"It's not just for us. We have guests."

"Guests?"

"Lucas and Abby."

"Lucas and Abby?"

He nods and picks up another strip. She puts the bottle back in the fridge. "When did you invite Lucas and Abby? I thought they were in New York."

"They were. They're back. He has cancer." He does not look at her when he says this but suspects that her mouth is gaping slightly.

"What do you mean he has cancer?"

"He has this big malignant tumour on his spine and he's going to die, Abby says. He's in town for chemotherapy. Apparently there's a clinic here that specializes in his kind of cancer." Alex sits heavily on a chair at the kitchen table. "I tried to call you at the Centre but you weren't there."

"When did this happen?"

"He was diagnosed five months ago. It's spreading fast."

Alex pictures Lucas as she remembers him, youthful, athletic, dark-eyed, always smiling with a hint of mischief. "He's only thirty-three."

"I didn't think you'd mind them coming, I mean you really like Lucas. You two had a bit of a thing going as I remember."

"What do you mean 'thing'?"

"You got drunk and necked in the kitchen, as I remember. I didn't mind except that I was stuck talking to Abby. Or should I say, stuck with Abby talking to me."

Alex had been attracted to Lucas but wouldn't have necked with him if she'd felt that Zee would mind. She'd wanted him to mind, had hoped that by necking with Lucas she would force Zee to admit that he did mind. But of course, he didn't. He said he thought it was very funny that they were necking out of sight like two teenagers. "He used to run eight miles a day."

"He had a tumour on his leg as well. They removed it but it's grown back."

Alex drops her head into her hands and stares between her feet at flakes of oat bran on the floor. She really liked Lucas and had wondered if, under different circumstances, they might have ventured into a relationship. He'd had Zee's ability to slide through the world unscathed. Zee's ability to appreciate the humour of a situation. Of course, this was before she had become disenchanted with Zee's inability to take anything seriously. She looks up at him sprinkling mozzarella. "When are they coming?"

"Abby said 'sevenish'. She warned me that he can't eat much because of the chemotherapy. And she asked us not to comment on his appearance. Apparently he's lost some weight."

"Oh god."

Abby steps through the door first, wearing a bright orange fake-fur coat and a pink pill-box hat. She smiles tightly. "Hi guys." Zee waves at her. Lucas follows, hobbling like an old man. On such a gaunt and sickly face, his smile of greeting looks grotesque, reminding Alex of heavily made-up actors on TV pretending to be dying. She tries not to gasp or stare or look away but to appear glad to see him. She hugs him, shocked at how he has shrunk, then remembers the tumour on his spine. "I'm sorry, am I hurting you?"

"No, no."

"He's been taking mega doses of morphine," Abby says, helping him off with his coat. "He's stoned."

"I wish I could enjoy it," he adds, still smiling.

"It's still not killing the pain," Abby says.

Zee offers Lucas his hand. "Good to see you."

"Same here," Lucas responds. Alex wishes he would stop smiling. It looks spooky on his sunken face, a death mask. She takes their coats. "Is there anything we can get you ... tea, wine, I have herbal tea, juice?"

"Nothing for me thanks," Lucas says.

Abby burrows in her bag. "I brought some wine. It's a Chardonnay, really nice."

"Great," Zee says and takes the bottle into the kitchen.

Lucas looks towards the kitchen. "Smells good. Italian."

Alex gestures towards the couch. "Sit down."

"Actually I prefer to stand," Lucas says. "Sitting's real uncomfortable for me at the moment."

"His back," Abby interprets.

"Of course."

Zee brings out glasses of wine. Lucas waves his away, but Abby and Alex each take one. "Cheers," Alex says, immediately realizing how stupid this sounds. Zee squats down into his beanbag chair.

"I've thought about this apartment often," Lucas says. "I have fond memories of it."

Zee looks at Alex and winks. She ignores him and sits on the arm of the couch, trying to determine the best way to behave. She suspects that pretending everything is normal is not a good idea. "So what do you know about this treatment?" she asks.

"It's supposed to be the best," Abby says. "It better be, for the price."

Lucas smiles. "Fortunately I'm starting to understand that after a certain point, hospitals stop expecting you to pay. They sort of write you off after a certain point, depending on your condition I guess. It's the one good thing about being really sick. You can stop worrying about debt."

"You still worry about it," Abby mumbles.

Lucas lowers himself onto the couch and slowly crosses one leg over the other. Alex notices the bandage wrapped around his ankle and foot. "It's a surgical stocking," he explains. "They removed a tumour from my ankle. The foot hasn't quite got itself together to function properly so every morning I have to force it into a surgical stocking. Quite a feat, actually. It's pretty funny. I feel like an old lady."

"It's not funny," Abby says. "I don't know why you keep referring to these gruesome details as funny."

"I think it's pretty funny," Lucas says, "a thirty-three-year-old man jamming his foot into a surgical stocking."

Abby shakes her head irritably then starts to chew on her cuticles. They all sit for a moment. "So you just started this treatment?" Alex asks.

"I'm on my fifth day."

"Is it helping at all?"

"They say it'll be a couple of weeks before I feel any improvement. I do a week at a time, then go off for a few weeks then try again." He smiles. "I'm kind of looking forward to going bald. I have a feeling I've got the right shaped head for it."

"Oh stop," Abby pleads.

"I thought maybe I'd start wearing an earring."

"Would you quit making a joke of everything?" Abby looks at Alex. "He's been driving me nuts. We had a fight this afternoon over some stupid woman in this group for people with cancer and their loved ones. This bitch was being really rude, kept interrupting everyone, so I told her to shut up. She got really angry."

"Red as a beetroot," Lucas says.

"I thought she was going to have a heart attack or hit me, so I backed off because I didn't want to cause a scene. So, later in the car I'm telling Lucas how angry I am with this woman, and he says, 'Why can't you let it go?' I said, 'I can't let it go. I have to express my anger. You can't go around with all this pent up emotion inside you.' That's always been Lucas' problem. He doesn't express his feelings. He's too busy being laid back." Alex looks at Lucas who shrugs, smiles then excuses himself and heads for the bathroom. They can hear him throw up. "He was sick twice in the car. It's the chemo. Makes him nauseous. Also the liquid morphine is really hard on the stomach."

•

During dinner, Lucas pokes at his lasagne with his fork then goes to the bathroom to vomit. Suddenly Alex realizes that Lucas really is going to die. For a moment she feels as if she has been gagged. Abby stares at her then reaches across the table and grabs her wrist. "Don't let him see you cry," she whispers. Alex goes to the kitchen, runs the tap and throws cold water on her face. Zee considers following and wrapping his arms around her but decides against it, afraid she might push him away.

"I wanted to freeze some of his sperm, before he went in for chemo."

Zee looks up at her, then at Alex standing in the doorway, drying her hands on a towel. "Did you?" she asks. They hear Lucas flush the toilet and run the tap. He opens the bathroom door. "Never got around to it," he says.

Abby watches him. "And now it's too late."

Lucas avoids her eyes and settles on the couch. "It just didn't seem right, Ab. I'm sorry, I don't know why."

"He's never believed in babies," Abby explains.

Lucas shrugs. "I've never grown up."

Silence. The electric clock on the wall hums. Outside the apartment door, they can hear their neighbour take out his keys and unlock his door. "That was some earthquake in California last week," Zee says. The neighbour's door closes.

Abby shakes her head. "I can't imagine why anyone would want to live in California, knowing that, at any minute, the earth could crack open."

"It takes a certain type of person," Lucas says.

Abby nods. "A stupid person."

Lucas arranges a cushion behind his back. "I don't know that they're stupid."

Abby wipes her mouth with her napkin. "You'd have to be." Lucas looks over at Alex and smiles as if to say no point in arguing with her. Alex tries to return the smile but feels uncomfortable under his stare, wondering if he still considers himself capable of sexual relations. If not, does he want to be considered capable? She feels certain that he doesn't want to be treated as an invalid, but she can't imagine that he expects her to respond to him as she did a year ago. He must, when he looks in the mirror, notice his grey pallor, the dark circles under his eyes, death. Or maybe, because he has lived with the illness for five months, and the decay has been gradual, he doesn't notice any great change. Just as one doesn't notice the aging process from day to day. Suddenly we're just old.

"First of all," Abby continues, "why would you want to live in L.A.? You can't breathe the air; you can't drink the water. Everything is plastic. Everybody's smiling, but nobody's sincere."

"Nobody smiles here, and nobody's sincere," Lucas says, placing his hands on his knees, preparing to stand up. Lifting his bum off the couch, he falters slightly and presses a hand against the armrest for support.

"Okay," Abby concedes, "but at least people here don't pretend to be happy all the time. I can't stand that."

Lucas straightens up then puts his hands on the small of his back and stretches. "Maybe by pretending they're happy they feel happier."

"You mean they delude themselves," Abby says. "That's healthy."

While Lucas hobbles to the kitchen, Zee looks at Alex and shrugs helplessly. Lucas starts to run water in the sink. "No, don't do those," Alex says.

"It's alright. I like to have something to do."

"Let him do them," Abby says. "He's stubborn."

Lucas glances over his shoulder. "Just don't whisper about me, alright? I hate that."

"We aren't whispering." Abby picks at some grapes in a bowl on the table. "He always thinks people are whispering about him. I can't get him to stop spending money. The medical bills are astronomical, and he's buying all this fancy food he can't stomach. The man will drive me insane."

"I like to cook," Lucas says simply.

"Yes darling, but who's supposed to eat it?"

"You eat it."

Abby leans towards Alex and whispers, "He had a bad night last night, was kneeling on the bathroom floor crying and planning his funeral. It was rough, really rough."

"You're whispering," Lucas says.

"Don't you want her to know what's going on?" Abby asks. "She's your friend."

"Nothing's going on. I'm getting treatment."

"Fine, okay, I'll shut up." Abby picks off another grape.

Lucas shakes water from his hands and turns to them, leaning against the door jam. "It was pretty funny today. After they hooked me up to the IV, I went to the coffee shop to get a paper and had to drag the IV contraption along with me."

"It's on wheels?" Zee asks.

"Yeah. Anyway, I'm standing by the magazine rack, and this woman says to me, 'Excuse me, do you work here?'"

"I don't think that's funny." Abby chews on her cuticles.

"I'm hooked up to the machine, and this woman is asking if I work there. I think that's funny."

"It is funny," Zee offers.

"Come on, Ab. Where's your sense of humour."

"I don't happen to think that's funny," Abby says. "It's tragic. The whole thing's tragic. You keep trying to make light of it. It's just another form of denial."

"What am I denying?"

"Never mind."

"You don't like it when I plan my funeral, you don't like it when I try to see the humour in the situation. What do you want me to do?"

"Just forget it, alright. I'm sorry. I'm just really stressed out. This is hard on me too."

Silence. Zee squats into his beanbag chair, which emits a crunching sound. Abby looks at him. Lucas shuffles back into the living-room. "I feel like some ice cream. Does anyone else want some ice cream?"

Alex looks around for her bag. "Sure, I'll go get some."

"I'll come with you," Lucas says. "I could use some air."

She looks at him, trying to imagine how he will be able to walk down the stairs, up the block and back. "Does anyone else want to come?" she asks.

"No. You two go ahead," Zee says. "We'll make some coffee."

Alex wonders why he's doing this? Is he enjoying forcing her into an awkward situation, or does he genuinely feel that she and Lucas should spend some time alone together?

•

Outside light snow has begun to fall. "Snow, great!" Lucas says, offering his arm. She takes it, slowing her pace to match his. Normally she's a fast walker and can't imagine what it would be like to be sick and unable to stride. When she has been ill, she has always known that she would recover. She tries to imagine what it would feel like to know that she was never going to recover; that she would continue to slow down until, eventually, she died.

"I had this realization the other day," Lucas begins.

"What?"

"I realized that I've always had relationships with women who finish my sentences for me. I wonder why that is." Alex squints into the falling snow, trying to think of an appropriate response. "It's hard on her," he says. "She's a very energetic person, you know. I ... I wish I could calm her down. I wish ... I don't know. I worry about her worrying. It doesn't help."

"Do you talk about it?"

"She becomes very defensive, thinks I'm implying that she's not a good wife. She's a very good wife. This just isn't what she bargained for." He stops still for a moment and looks up at the sky. "It's funny, you know, I've heard that fatal illness brings couples closer together but I don't think it does. Not us, anyway. I don't want her to see what I'm going through. It's killing her." He tries to smile. "And it's killing me to kill her." Alex puts her arm around him. He reaches up and cups his hand over her hand on his shoulder. "I don't see why, just because we're married, she has to watch me suffer. I know this sounds terrible, but really, I'd rather be alone. The problem is, it looks like soon I won't be able to look after myself."

"What about your parents?"

"I'm thinking about it. A couple of months ago, I would have said no way, but we've been talking lately. They're doing okay. They want to be there for me."

"Abby would freak out, though."

"She would." They walk on, both staring down at snowflakes melting into the sidewalk. "Sometimes I have this feeling that it's all a dream, and I'm going to wake up, and everything will be okay. It feels like that sometimes." With his good leg, he kicks an empty Coke can and watches it roll into the street. "This city's dirty now. It used to be clean. What happened?"

"Too many people."

"Watch your step," he says, pointing to a dog turd. Alex steps around it. He slides his hand over his hairline and scratches his head. "I have to believe it's attitude. If I let it get to me, like last night, I'm finished." He tries to laugh. "I used to have a pretty bleak view of things, you know, and now … jesus I'm just glad to wake up in the morning."

"I wish we could learn that lesson without getting sick."

"Oh, I think you can."

On the way back he leans against a traffic light to catch his breath. "I hope you're not sorry about what happened between us."

"Not at all," Alex says.

"I enjoyed it."

"So did I."

He smiles, reaches for her hand and squeezes it. "Isn't life funny."

·

Back at the apartment, Zee has Johnny Mathis on the stereo. Abby stares at them. "You two were gone a long time."

"There's coffee," Zee says.

"Excuse me," Lucas mutters and goes into the bathroom. When he throws up, Abby covers her face with her hands. They hear the toilet flush and watch him as he steps out, steadying himself against the wall. "I think we'd better go, Ab. I'm not feeling so good."

Abby helps him on with his coat, picks up his bag of painkillers and guides him carefully to the door. He turns to Alex and Zee and smiles, "Thanks for the dinner. It was great. We should all get together again some time, maybe go to a movie."

"Sure, give us a call," Alex says, knowing in her bones that she will never see him again.

·

Sitting on the bed, Alex sucks the ice cream from her spoon. "Why do you think he married her?"

Zee shrugs. "Who knows what makes a marriage work."

"She's looking after him. That's something." She jabs her

spoon into the ice-cream carton. "Maybe it's the mother thing."

He sits on the edge of the bed. "Maybe she's a different woman in the sack."

"I can't imagine it." She watches him pull off his socks. "Can you imagine it?"

"No." He tosses a sock into the laundry basket.

"And anyway you know that sex can't be the basis of a lasting relationship."

"I don't know anything."

Alex stares at her bug-eyed reflection in the stainless steel spoon. "I really want to like her."

He tosses the second sock. "She's greedy. Me me me."

"Poor Lucas."

Zee turns on the television. Alex stares at his back. "You're not going to watch TV now, are you?"

He stares at a pizza on the screen. "You don't want to?"

"Well, no. I mean, we've just experienced something pretty devastating. I think we should talk about it."

Resigned, Zee shuts the TV off, flops back into the bed, grabs his foot and stares at his toes.

"What are you doing?"

"I'm wondering if this is a wart." He holds his foot up for her to examine. "Do you think that's a wart?"

"You are unbelievable."

"What do you want to talk about?"

"Doesn't seeing Lucas have any effect on you at all?"

"Sure. I feel sorry for him, very sorry."

"But doesn't seeing what he's going through affect your view of things?"

Zee folds his hands over his stomach. "You mean that I should be glad to be alive and all that?"

"Yes."

"No." He picks up a section of the newspaper lying on the

bedside table and glances at it.

"I can't believe you're reading."

"I'm listening. What do you want me to do, look at you?"

"That would be nice."

"Alright." He puts the paper down, folds his hands over his stomach and stares at her.

"You're an asshole," she says.

He throws up his hands. "What do you want me to do, tell me what you want me to do?"

She waves her spoon. "This is such a bullshit relationship. This is a non-relationship."

"Then end it, for fuck's sake, end it. I'm tired." He sits up abruptly, swinging his legs over the side of the bed and rests his elbows on his knees, gripping his head in his hands. Stalled by the anger in his voice, she stares at the knobs of his vertebrae pushing through his shirt. "You're ready to give up," she asks, "just like that?"

He doesn't move. "I can't please you. You're unhappy. I don't know what the fuck I'm doing. I don't need you needling at me."

"I'm not needling at you."

He holds his hands over his ears. "Stop talking, please, can you just ... stop talking!"

"There you go getting irritable again. You hate your life so you take it out on me."

"I get irritable when you harass me."

"I see. So I'm supposed to sit around with my mouth shut while you jerk off."

He snatches a pillow. "I'm going to sleep in the living-room."

"That's good. Run away from it."

"If you don't stop talking, I'm going to hit you."

"Oh good, be the big man. You really scare me."

He leaves, slamming the door. "You're a fucking coward!"

she screams. "Other people fight to get by, but you sit around with your thumb up your ass, feeling sorry for yourself. You're a loser. A whiner and a loser." She jams the lid on the carton of ice cream, opens the door, marches to the kitchen and stuffs the carton into the freezer. When she closes the fridge door she sees him standing, staring at her as though she has only just appeared to him.

"If you really believe that," he says quietly, "what are you doing with me?"

"I don't know. Pretending that everything is okay." She pushes her hands into her pockets and stares at the hole her big toe is wearing in her sock. "It feels empty to me now. Like there's no point to it. We used to have fun. We never have fun anymore."

"It goes through cycles."

"We've been going through the same cycle for two years."

He nods and stares down at his palms. "I'll leave tomorrow."

She braces herself against the fridge, feeling as though she has been whacked by a powerful wind. She hadn't expected him to give up so easily. She's always pushed him to the edge because she was certain he wouldn't jump off. "Are you sure?"

"This makes no sense, does it?" He looks up at her, hoping for an answer, something low-cost but effective.

"Unless we try to work it out," she says.

"We can't work it out. You want me to be someone I'm not."

"I just want you to take responsibility for your life."

He holds his hands over his ears. "Don't start, please, don't start." He goes to the couch and slumps into it, then rolls onto his side, pulls his coat over his shoulders and pushes his face into the pillow. She stands in the doorway watching him, knowing that if she were to curl up beside him and press her face into his shoulder, tell him that she loves him, that she's sorry, that she didn't mean it, he would stay. And tomorrow would be just another day. All of a sudden she desperately wants tomorrow to be just another day.

With his eyes closed, feeling her standing there, he craves and yet dreads a truce; craves and yet dreads being free of her. She is, he thinks, the last of his chattels.

She looks out the kitchen window at the snow drifting down. "It's really snowing now. It's staying on the ground." She watches him lying motionless, an impenetrable lump. She goes into the bedroom and closes the door. On her side of the bed, she pulls the covers up over her shoulders and stares at an aloe plant. After a moment she shifts her weight to the centre of the bed.

EIGHT

Zee rings the bell because he knows that when he uses his key, it startles Daisy. He sets his suitcase down and leans against the railing, watching his breath puff into the cold. As a child, in weather like this, he sucked on pieces of rolled-up note-paper and puffed into the cold, pretending they were cigarettes. He thinks it's a shame that, as an adult, he never pretends things. He used to pretend to be Spiderman, a nightclub singer or the illegitimate son of a Hell's Angel.

He hears Daisy's heavy tread behind the door and sees the peephole darken as she peers out at him. He waves. She opens the door and holds it ajar, watching him warily.

"Hi, Mum." He knocks his feet together, warming them.

She draws her cardigan closed over her stomach. "Did something happen?"

"No, can I come in?"

She steps back into the house, patting her pin-curls. Zee follows her into the living-room, takes off his coat and drops it on the couch. Daisy picks it up, shakes it and hangs it in the closet. "I keep thinking I should have you two over. Then I can't decide what to cook for Alex." Zee blows on his hands to warm them.

"I cut out a recipe for rice casserole, but you have to soak the beans overnight, and I never remember. Do you want some tea?"

"I'll make it."

"No, no."

As she plods towards the kitchen he notices that her ankles are more swollen than he has ever seen them. "Your arthritis bad?"

"You get used to it." She fills the kettle from the tap.

"Didn't the doctor say you should try to lose some weight?"

"You try to lose some weight. It's not easy being alone with nothing to do." On the table is an open box of Sugar Crisp.

"It's the cereal, Mum. That's pure sugar."

She slides the kettle onto the stove and turns on the burner. "I don't like cooking for myself. You try cooking for yourself."

"Well, at least you could eat Shredded Wheat or something. Something without sugar added."

Ignoring him, she holds the teapot over the sink and shakes out the used tea bags. He notices that the flesh under her arms jiggles. "You should invite a friend over. You could cook together, make it sort of a potluck. You could make potato salad. You make great potato salad."

"Mayonnaise is fattening." She pulls out a bag of chocolate chip cookies from the cupboard, arranges several of them on a plate and places it on the table. Her belly bulges over the counter as she reaches above the sink for cups and saucers. Studying her, Zee tries to remember how she looked when she wasn't fat; tries to remember the shape of her face, her jawline, what she looked like with a waist. She was attractive once, he thinks. He remembers construction workers whistling at her while she held his hand at traffic lights. He'd ask her why they were whistling, and she'd tell him that construction workers always whistled while they worked. Then she'd sing, 'Whistle while you work'.

He sits at the table and drums his fingers on the plastic tablecloth. "You should get out more. See friends. Is Mona around?"

"Mona is no longer with us."

"You're kidding?"

"Why would I kid about something like that?"

"Why didn't you tell me?"

"Haven't seen you. And anyway why would I bother you with something like that? You're young, you have other things to think about."

Zee plays with a teaspoon on the table, repeatedly pressing his finger into the bowl, tipping up the handle. "Poor Mona."

"Yes, well, it wasn't easy for her. They kept her lying around for weeks before they operated. They had to strap her down because every time she moved she had an attack. All I can say is that when I go, I hope I go fast." Ever since he can remember, Daisy has said that she doesn't mind going so long as she goes fast. He used to have nightmares about his mother being hit by a bus or pushed in front of a subway car. Rushing over to try and save her, held back by throngs of curious onlookers, he'd see Daisy smile up at him and call out that he shouldn't worry, at least she was going fast.

"What about bridge?" he asks. "Are you playing bridge at all?"

"Once a week. And to tell you the truth I'm thinking of giving it up. Erma is such a poor loser, she spoils everything. It's reached the point I'd rather not win so what's the use in playing?" She holds the teapot over the cups and pours. Zee realizes he has absolutely no idea about the state of his mother's physical or mental health. For years he has not returned her calls, has avoided coming home for Christmas, has had flowers delivered on her birthday. Now, staring at her red face, her girth, her swollen legs and hands, he is reminded that she will not live forever. "So what do you do all day?"

"Why all these questions all of a sudden?"

"I'm just concerned."

"Have a cookie."

He takes two, bites one, stretches his legs out and stares at her fake-wood cabinets. "Has Durham or Jenny been by?"

"He says it upsets him to see me fat, and she's started singing in a band so she's always busy."

"A band?" Zee asks. "What kind of band?"

"A band. They play guitars and drums, and she sings."

"I didn't know she could sing."

"There's a lot about your sister you don't know." She picks up a cookie and nibbles at it delicately. "I don't see why you can't be nicer to her, she loves you very much."

"She gets up my nose."

"She's just like you, that's why."

"No she's not."

Daisy shrugs and reaches for the teapot. "Why are you wearing sneakers in this weather? Why don't you wear the rubber boots I gave you?"

"They make my feet sweat."

"You'll catch cold."

"Mum, can we not argue? I really don't want to argue." He kicks his running shoes off, picks them up, goes into the hall and drops them on the boot tray.

"Something's up with you, I have a feeling," Daisy calls from the kitchen.

"Alex and I are separating." He looks at a black and white photo of himself and Jenny at ages eight and six. Jenny, grinning toothlessly, brandishes a candy apple while he stares at a model airplane he holds in his lap. In his mind he hears Daisy urging him, "Zee, smile for the camera!"

Her chair scrapes as she stands up and plods to the middle of the kitchen so that she can see him in the hall. "Are you separating for good then?"

"I don't know."

She nods, picks up a sponge from the sink and absentmindedly wipes around the faucet and taps. "Do you want to stay here then?"

He has spent the day racking his brains, trying to think of someone he could impose on other than his mother. Someone who wouldn't ask questions but would nod sympathetically and give him shelter for a few days. No one came to mind. He has realized that he doesn't have any friends. Alex was his friend. "If that's alright with you," he says.

"I don't mind, just don't make a mess. Pick up after yourself. Clean the bathtub after you use it."

"Thanks, Mum." He moves towards her, considering hugging her, but she turns to the table and adds another bag of Sweet n' Low to her tea. "I'm sorry," she says. "I always said you made a nice couple."

"You always say Alex makes you nervous. You think she's finicky."

"Yes, but you wouldn't be happy with a slob. You can't have two people the same." She pushes the plate of cookies towards him. He sits back down, takes two more, bites one and brushes crumbs off his sweater. Daisy watches them fall to the floor but says nothing. He knows that she is making a mental note to clean them up later.

She pulls her cardigan closed over her stomach. "She's keeping the apartment then?"

"It's her apartment."

Daisy nods and scrapes at something on the side of her

cup with her thumbnail. "Have you been looking for a place?"

"I have to find a job before I can look for a place."

"You still haven't got a job?"

He shakes his head, stares at the apple-shaped clock on the wall and watches the minute hand move three times. Daisy sips her tea, takes another cookie from the plate and nibbles it. "There's no sheets on the bed."

"I'll put some on."

"I don't want to start doing laundry again. You do your own laundry."

"For sure."

She wipes the plastic tablecloth with the flat of her hand. He watches the minute hand move twice. The tap drips. "Do you want to watch TV with me?" she asks.

"I think maybe I'll just sit quietly for a bit."

"Okay. I'm going to watch TV."

"You do that."

She leans on the table to stand up, picks up the cups and saucers and puts them in the sink. "Eat anything you want."

"I will. Thanks, Mum."

•

After Alex left for work this morning, he lay on the couch staring at all her shoes crammed into the bottom of the closet. He has never understood why she needs so many shoes and repeatedly cursed her when he stumbled over them. This morning, staring at the pile, he had a revelation. They all have the same shape. Regardless of style, Alex's feet have forced the shoes into the same shape. All have a bump on the inside from her bunion and a bump on the front from her hammer toe. All the outside edges of the heels were worn down in exactly the same way. It seemed to him that, like everything in Alex's life, her shoes bent to her will. His shoes have always opposed him, forced him to wear band-aids and extra socks. Only the occasional running shoe has been a true ally. This morning he told himself he was like one of Alex's shoes. He told himself he was fortunate to be given the chance to escape before she forced her shape into him. Now he isn't so sure.

He wonders if she'll notice that her Reeboks are missing. She has two pair: one black; one red. He fetches his suitcase from Daisy's hall and takes out the red pair. He sits back down at the kitchen table and slides his hands inside them. The leather is chafed, the rubber soles are coming unglued from the foam. He hopes that holding the shoes will release something in him; a feeling, a revelation, an understanding.

Nada.

He wonders if she is sitting in the apartment with her hands in his shoes. He doubts it.

"Zee, come and watch this," Daisy calls from the living-room. "Come watch the elephants. He's got them on their hind-legs."

He gets up, puts the Reeboks back in his suitcase and joins Daisy on the couch. She points at some elephants on the television, parading around a circus ring with their trunks hooked through each other's tails. "You used to worry about if they were happy, remember that?" she asks. "I said if they minded they'd roll over and squash the tamer, remember that?" He nods. She picks up a dish of hard candies from the coffee table and holds it out to him. He shakes his head. "It's the French poodles I worry about," she adds, "having to dress like people."

He leans back, adjusts a cushion behind his head, rests his feet on the poof and feels as though nothing has happened in thirty years. He's still sitting on Daisy's couch watching elephants walk in circles. No progress has been made, nothing has been accomplished as Alex would say. What was it all for, the angst, the pain? Why didn't he just stay on Daisy's couch?

"Maybe I will have a candy," he says.

Daisy offers him the bowl. "I bought butterscotch, your favourite."

He sucks on the candy and stares at the TV, letting his brain go dead.

NINE

Michael drops some change while paying the cashier for the coffees. Both he and Alex bend down to pick it up. "I'll get it," he insists. "That's okay," Alex says, handing him the quarter she's already retrieved. He straightens up, puts the quarter in his pocket and hands her one of the styrofoam cups.

"She wants to rent a chalet for the winter," Michael explains. They look for a vacant table. "She has this idea about a white Christmas. She wants the kids to be able to toboggan then come back to the chalet and drink Ovaltine." They push aside a tray of styrofoam cups and plates and sit. "What are you doing for Christmas?" he asks.

"Not much. Keeping quiet." Through the window of the cafeteria, Alex watches a Santa in the mall ring his bell and adjust his beard. A little boy stops to stare at him. The Santa looks down at the boy, pats his padded belly and chants, "Ho, ho, ho." Frightened, the boy turns abruptly and runs back to where his mother is examining humidifiers in the hardware store.

Alex has decided to ignore Christmas, now that Zee won't be around, although she had already bought him a pure virgin-wool sweater.

"Her doctor called me," Michael says. "It seems she's anorexic."

"Really?" Alex tries to appear as though she hadn't already figured this out.

"She's still losing weight. I never see her eat. She'll go out and buy bags of groceries but I never see her eat. Or cook for that matter. She tells me she's eating big lunches, that she prefers to get her 'carbo-loading' over with by three o'clock."

"Is she still running?"

"Of course. Miles and miles." He looks down at his cup. "I don't think she's feeding the kids properly, and I don't know what to do about it. She denies there's a problem, refuses to seek help. Frankly, I'm scared." He looks hopefully at Alex, as though expecting her to offer a solution.

"I don't know, Michael. It's a dangerous illness."

"Do you know anybody who can help?"

"I can give you some names, but she has to want to go."

He nods, leans back in his chair and stares into the mall at the Santa's sled filled with bags of boxes wrapped in shiny paper. "I hate Christmas," he mutters.

"Me too."

"What are you doing for Christmas?"

"You already asked me that. Nothing."

"I'm sorry. God." He plays with his Rolex. "She was a beautiful woman. Not in the classic sense, of course, but she had ... I don't know, sensuality. Now it's like making love to a skeleton. The irony is that I encouraged her to get fit. I thought it would make her feel better about herself." He rubs his eyes with his fingers. "She used to say all she wanted in life was to be loved. Well, I've certainly done that." He takes his hand away from his eyes and stares fiercely at the sled. "God I hate Jane Fonda. Laura uses her videos, you know. I used to tell her over and over again that she wasn't fat. She'd ask me if

I liked Jane Fonda's body. I'd say yes, and she'd argue that she wasn't as thin as Jane Fonda. It seems that no matter what I say, she can turn it around."

"All women think they're fat," Alex says.

"You don't."

"Sure I do."

"You can't be serious?" Alex shrugs and wraps her hands around her cup. "You've always struck me as being comfortable with your body," he says. "God. I love your body. I mean, what I've seen of it." Embarrassed, he reaches abruptly for his coffee, spilling some on the table. "Damn" he says.

"Here." Alex pulls a Kleenex from her pocket and mops it up.

She called Michael today because she is trying to decide whether or not to try to capture some of his sperm. For the past half hour, she has been studying his features, trying to picture the baby they would make. Always, when she has imagined "the baby", it has had a combination of her own and Zee's features: a bouncing, dark-eyed, dark-haired bundle. Now, while surreptitiously assessing Michael's hair and eye colour, skin tone and teeth, she tries to picture a blondish baby. At least, she thinks, it wouldn't be pigeon-toed. Both she and Zee are pigeon-toed. But Michael is shorter than Zee, in fact shorter than Alex. This would be alright if the baby turned out to be female, but she would hate a boy to be short. Also, Michael is losing his hair. She can only hope that, by the time the baby grows up, science will have found a cure for premature baldness.

"I should get back to work," Michael says.

"Do you have any pictures of your kids?"

"What?"

"I've never seen any photos of your kids."

"Oh." Looking puzzled, he reaches into his jacket pocket

and pulls out his wallet. "I don't have a recent one." He flips open the wallet and pulls out a shot of a small boy and girl standing in front of a pile of leaves. Both sandy-haired, the boy appears to have an overbite, but the girl looks fairly attractive.

"Does William take after Laura?" she asks.

"Yes, as a matter of fact. Only the teeth look cuter on her. We're going to have to straighten those out for him, spend more money I don't have." He grimaces good-naturedly and slides the photo back into his wallet. "Well, it was good to see you. For some reason you always have a calming effect on me. I ahh ... I really appreciate your continuing to see me knowing how I feel about you."

Alex lays her hands flat on the table and stares at them. "Michael?"

"Yes?"

"Zee and I have split up."

"You can't be serious? When?"

"Yesterday."

"That surprises me, you seemed to love him so much."

"Yeah well ..." She lifts her hands from the table and holds them in her lap. "Anyway I'll probably be pretty lonely now so if you want to visit, don't hesitate. I need all the friends I can get."

"Of course. God. I'm glad you called. Listen, if you want to have lunch or anything, just give me a call. Days are better for me."

"I understand."

He stands and slides his arms into his cashmere coat while Alex zips up her down jacket. "Which way are you going?" he asks. She points across the mall. "Okay. Well, I'll leave you here then," he says, kissing her on the cheek then tapping his index finger on the side of his nose. "Take care of yourself." She offers what she hopes reads as a brave smile then watches him walk through the revolving doors.

Last night, in a frenzy, she cleaned the bathroom, removing every one of Zee's head, pubic and nose hairs; every nail clipping; every used disposable razor. Items left behind but still usable she dropped into a plastic bag and stored under the sink. When she had finished spraying, scrubbing and wiping, she sat on the edge of the tub and studied the transformation. Once again the bathroom belonged to her alone. No longer would he pee while she was in the bath. No longer would he brush his teeth alongside her, spitting in the sink just as she was about to rinse her mouth. No longer would she have to wash his bristles from the sink or smell his farts. She snatched the towels off the rack and his bathrobe from the door then went into the bedroom, yanked the sheets off the bed and stuffed everything into a Glad garbage bag. She put on her jacket, threw the bag over her shoulder and trudged to the laundromat.

The night before, in a dream, she had been running from a bald man who was trying to stab her with a knife. She managed to keep ahead of him until, suddenly, the pavement dropped off into a raging torrent. She jumped into the water, as did the bald man who grabbed her shoulder, wielding his knife at her. She pulled her legs into her chest and rammed her feet into his solar plexus. He gasped and flailed. She pushed his bald head under water and held it there. Struggling to stay afloat, he struck out blindly with the knife. At that moment Alex understood that she was a stronger swimmer than he and that, if she chose, she could drown him. Treading water, watching air bubbles erupt above his fleshy pate, she had to decide whether to risk letting him go—knowing for certain that he would continue to pursue her—or to continue to hold his head under water until his body grew limp. She didn't want to kill him, though she felt angry with him for forcing her into this situation. If he hadn't tried to stab her, he would-n't be drowning now. It was his own fault. Still, she didn't want to live the rest of her life knowing that she had killed a man. So she tried to grab the knife, but he slashed her thumb, caus-ing her blood to blossom against the green water.

She woke up before killing him.

In the laundromat, during the rinse cycle, she had tried to figure out why, if the man was supposed to represent Zee, he was bald. Lucas had talked about going bald. Maybe the man was both Lucas and Zee, both victims; Zee of her, Lucas of cancer and of Abby. Add to this list Michael of the receding hairline. All three men complain about their women, yet they stay in the relationships, allowing themselves to be victimized. It occurs to her that having the nagging wife validates them, enables them to experience male-bonding and to make deri-sive comments about their demanding mates. Meanwhile the wives suffer guilt because the men insist that women are mak-ing their lives a living hell; because they want children; because they worry about money; or because they feel unable to offer enough variety in the bedroom. Michael's wife must be starving herself out of guilt.

As she concluded that the bald man must have represented men in general, a young man wearing jeans, fashionably ripped at the knees, leaned over her, holding a laundry basket. "You work at the Centre, right?" he asked. She nodded. "Marika," he mumbles, "my girlfriend, knows you."

"That's right."

He dropped the basket at his feet. "How's she doing?"

"Ah ... well the baby is teething so she's not getting much sleep."

"Her mom's helping out though, right?"

"I think you know as well as I do that she and her mom don't get along."

He bobbed his head sheepishly, sat on one of the plastic chairs beside her and pulled the laundry basket towards him. "Does she talk about me?"

"A little."

He began pairing socks. "I don't know what she wants from me." He dropped the socks into a garbage bag.

"She wants you to be there for her."

"Oh, right, like what's that supposed to mean? Like as if I wasn't. I mean I'm not saying I'm perfect, but I was doing way more than she was. I was going out on the line for her, I mean I was working till late then doing the laundry. I cleaned the place." Alex watched him fold his T-shirts and jeans.

"She says that you go out with your friends and come home drunk."

"At least I come home," he said. "She goes out with her girlfriend and doesn't come home at all and her girlfriend's the biggest slut in the world. I don't ask what they do together."

"She says she sleeps over there sometimes."

"Yeah right," he said dubiously. "Anyways I wouldn't go out if she didn't hassle me. Like last week, a friend phones me just to shoot the shit you know. I get off the phone and right away she says, 'So you're going out?' I says no, he just called to say hi. She doesn't say anything, like she doesn't believe me. So I go out, because I can't stand it when she does that."

"What?"

"Treats me like dirt. She gets mad about everything. Whenever anybody calls me she gets jealous. If an ex-girlfriend calls me I hear about if for three days." He collected his jockey shorts into a pile and stuffed them into the bag. "Anyways," he said, "I've got to get going. Don't tell her you saw me, okay? I just wanted to make sure she's alright."

How can she be alright? She's eighteen with a baby. She can't find a job that will cover rent, food, diapers and a babysitter. Are you acquitted because she makes you feel like dirt when you go out and spend money on beer?

But she didn't see the point in saying any of this because she has said it many times before, and nothing changes. She placates, encourages, sympathizes, tactfully reprimands, but nothing changes. Now, walking through the mall, seeing Christmas decorations she recognizes from last year and from the year before that, she wants to scream because nothing changes. She has tried to believe that life is a process, that things are always moving, evolving; that she must appreciate the small things, the small changes because they all make up the whole. But now she's just bored with it, all of it; her messy, sloppy, useless life. Even though she reminds herself that she could be dying like Lucas. Even though she knows that Lucas is glad to just wake up in the morning.

What astonishes her is how, no matter what, she will go on. Nothing stops her. Right now she will go to the grocery store and buy food, even though she can't stand her life. She will even eat the food. Ordinary people stop eating when they despair, or drink alcohol, or take drugs, or commit suicide. But she just continues on with her messy, sloppy, useless life. Zee has stopped. Just stopped. As much as she wants to kill him, she envies his ability to stop. She is a slave to the system, clings to the system, earning her daily bread so that she can put it in her mouth, go to sleep, wake up, shit it out, and start all over again.

•

At the service station, Larry is tinkering under a car on the lift. "Hi," Alex says. He glances at her. "Is my car ready?"

"Yeah."

"Great."

He wipes his hands on a rag and walks into the office. She follows him, wondering how anyone can stand to work in an environment that stinks of oil and other toxic chemicals. He thumbs through a pile of invoices on the counter, pulls one out and peruses it. "So I overhauled the carburetor."

"Great."

He pushes the invoice across the counter so that she can see it. "One fifty?" she asks. "I thought you said it would be two hundred?"

"You want to pay two hundred?"

"No, no, I'm just surprised. I mean it's usually more than I expect it to be."

"Well not today." He avoids her eyes, shuffling the invoices around on the counter. She pulls out her wallet, takes out her credit card and hands it to him. While he processes it and fills out the form she notices that he is not wearing a wedding ring. He slides the form along the counter for her to sign, which she does.

"Thanks," he says.

"Thank you." She wonders why he seems so distant, maybe she has offended him in some way. All of a sudden she feels ugly. She reaches into her bag for her sunglasses, appalled that she could be so deluded as to imagine that this man would want to see her naked. This is a young, attractive man who must have a young attractive girlfriend. She adjusts the glasses on her nose. He reaches up and massages the back of his neck. "The clutch'll go next," he says. "It's high."

"What does that mean?"

"It means it's going to go."

"Yeah but I mean how will I know?"

"You'll know. You'll feel it sliding."

"Right. And how much will that cost?"

"You don't want to know." He hands her the keys.

"Good luck."

Pulling the seatbelt across her chest, she has a sinking feeling that she will never experience anything she hasn't experienced before. Every experience will be reminiscent of a previous one, consequently she will be able to predict its outcome. Zee says that she is a pessimist. She argues that she is a realist who yearns for her predictions to prove false, but they don't. Her expectations are met, over and over again.

Outside her building, Mrs. Merchant and her middle-aged daughter slowly climb the steps to their front door. Alex makes a vain attempt to step around them. "Hello," Mrs. Merchant says.

"How are you, Mrs. Merchant?" Alex asks, raising her voice so that she won't have to repeat herself.

Mrs. Merchant grips the banister with both hands and peers at her. "Do I look different to you?"

"Different?"

"You haven't seen me since the stroke."

"Oh, I didn't realize you had a stroke. I'm sorry to hear that. Are you alright now?"

"She's fine," her daughter mumbles.

Mrs. Merchant pats the banister. "That's why I have trouble getting around."

The daughter sighs. "You're just the same as you were before, Ma."

"Miserable as ever," Mrs. Merchant says and grins, crinkling her thickly powdered face.

"Come on, Ma," her daughter says, "I'm freezing."

Alex suspects that she, herself, will live to be a very old lady, survive a stroke and say that her life is as miserable as ever.

As soon as she steps into the apartment she notices that it still smells of Zee. She had left the windows open a crack but his wooly, tobacco smell still clings to the walls and furniture. It's not that she finds it unpleasant, she just doesn't want to be reminded. She hangs her jacket in the closet and takes the groceries into the kitchen to unpack them. Usually, at this time, he has the radio on, forcing her to listen to reports on traffic accidents and to ads for lottery tickets and trips to the Bahamas. She knows that he doesn't actually listen to the radio because she has commented on items just read on the news, and he hasn't known what she has been talking about. "They just said it on the news," she'd say.

"They did?"

"Weren't you listening?"

"I missed it."

"You've got the radio on, and you're not even listening to it."

"Sure I am." He knows that she hates it. She thinks he keeps it on to irritate her.

Without the radio on it's very quiet. Of course the tap is dripping. She asked him a million times to replace the washer even though she suspected he doesn't know how.

It is not until after she has eaten four strawberry Pop Tarts that the desolation sets in. She picks up the box of Pop Tarts and reads the ingredients, which include dextrose, sucrose, glucose and sorbitol. She would never have bought them if he were here. Whenever he hovered around the Pop Tarts in the cookie aisle she told him "Forget it, pal." Now she is taking her revenge by buying the food she wouldn't let him eat. She stares at an aloe plant on the kitchen window-sill, picks it up, holds it over the garbage pail, pushes open the flap and stares into the black hole. After a moment, she sets the plant back on the window-sill.

TEN

When Daisy leaves to do her volunteer work at the hospital, Zee pulls down the blinds and unplugs the phone. Sitting in her pink bathtub, he thinks it's wonderful that he can unplug the phone and not answer the door; that he can disconnect. He couldn't disconnect with Alex around. Now he doesn't have to do anything; doesn't have to go to the park or a bar because he doesn't have to keep out of her way. He can eat what he likes, although somehow he's lost his appetite, now that she's not around to tell him not to eat. Leaning his head back against the rim, he tries to decide what to do with his day. He could go for a walk, or maybe a movie. He could do his laundry or go for a donut. He sets his feet on either side of the faucet, thinking that it's quite peaceful really. Without her. Maybe it's better this way. Why put himself through it?

Taking her Reeboks was a mistake. Even though they're hidden under the bed he feels them through the mattress. He can't help it, he misses her feet. She's always hated her toes but he thinks they're wonderful, dextrous; he's always said she should take up toe-painting.

He wishes he could bring himself to dispose of the shoes, hand them over to the garbagemen to be mashed by the hydraulic compressor. He grabs his foot and examines the wart. Warts spread don't they? Soon his body will be covered in warts. What is a wart exactly? What causes it? A bad attitude? Is it like Pinocchio's nose, growing with every dishonest remark?

When the doorbell rings, he ignores it and dunks his head under water. When he surfaces and squeezes shampoo into his palm, it rings again. While he massages his scalp, he hears pounding on the front door. Suddenly it occurs to him that it could be the police, maybe something has happened to Alex. Or maybe Daisy has had a heart attack. He steps hurriedly out of the bath and slips on the tiles, then realizes that his bathrobe is at home. The pounding continues while he scrambles to the bedroom, shoves his dripping legs into jeans and rushes downstairs to the front door, flinging it open.

"Mom told me you were here," his sister says, smiling cheerily. "How are you? She told me things aren't so good with you." Zee, stunned, doesn't invite her in but feels the cold prickling against his naked chest. "What are you doing here?"

"Damian and I had a fight. He threw me out." She pulls a package from her handwoven shoulder bag. "Look, I brought some Swiss Miss hot chocolate, remember how we used to drink that?" Zee nods and backs into the house. Jenny follows him, hopping up and down and flapping her arms. "Holy moses it's cold out."

He notices that she has on steel-toed cowboy boots. "Nice boots."

"Thanks, aren't they great? They make me look taller on stage. All the guys are around six feet. I was looking like a dwarf, but I didn't want to wear heels because I can't walk in them, so I bought these. They're wild, don't you think?"

"Wild." Zee heads back upstairs.

"Your hair's wet."

"Yup." He closes the bathroom door, sits on the toilet and stares at his dirty bath-water, trying to ascertain why he can't stand his sister. When they were small, she followed him around. He tried to discourage her by screaming at her and gripping his hands around her throat, but she adored him blindly. As a teenager she looked to him for advice about school, boys, algebra. Always he would respond to her questions in monosyllables hoping that she would figure out that he didn't know what she should do with her life and didn't care. But instead of becoming discouraged by his indifference, she began to refer to him affectionately as her strong, silent brother. It seemed that the more remote he became, the more convinced she was that he harboured great spiritual strength. He pulls the plug on the tub, telling himself that she has no grasp on reality. She's always going to be an actress, or a writer, or a painter or a rock-'n'-roll singer, but she never gets off her ass to do anything about it. She's lazy. And fucking cheerful, all the time. The world could end, and she'd still be drawing smiley faces beside her signature on Christmas cards. Last Christmas she sent them wool slippers. Alex said it was nice of her, actually wore the slippers and sent Jenny a thank-you note. Zee passed his on to Mrs. Merchant down the hall.

Jenny knocks on the door. "Come out of there, bro. I even found some marshmallows. They're getting all gooey, just the way you like them."

He rests his elbows on his knees and grips his forehead with his hands. Daisy and Jenny in the same house with him. This is not possible.

•

She sits at the table with one leg crossed over the other, swinging her cowboy boot. She hands him a cup of Swiss Miss. "I made it with milk instead of water." He nods grimly and sips. She gestures towards a chair. "Sit down, stay awhile." He does. She points at him. "You've got marshmallow on your upper lip." He grunts and wipes his mouth with the back of his hand. "It's so neat that you're here," she says. "I wasn't sure I could handle Mom by myself. She seems real spaced out these days and fat, jesus, what is she eating."

"Everything."

Jenny laughs. "I guess. Maybe we should take her in hand, feed her oat bran or something. A friend of mine made an omelette with skim-milk mozzarella and egg whites, and it was really good. I was surprised. Only two hundred calories or something. It's the yolks that are fattening ... and high in cholesterol. She didn't use butter, sprayed the pan with Pam. It was good." Zee feels his grip tightening on the coffee mug. He stares at the apple-shaped clock. "I'm sorry to hear about you and Alex. I had a lot of respect for her. I thought she was good for you. A stabilizer. You and me need stabilizers. I think it comes from growing up without a dad. I think we're always looking for someone to guide us. I mean look at me and Damian. You know what I figured out today? I don't really love him. I've been following him around because he got me into the music business and I thought he was a genius. It turns out he wants a slave. Well, I'm not slave material. He can just forget it. You know he actually expects me to pick up his dry-cleaning?" She pulls two marshmallows out of the bag, drops one into her mug and the other into Zee's. "Anyway, the point is, I don't need him anymore." She pokes the marshmallow with her finger. "I'd love it if you'd come and see the show. I know you hate hard rock, but we're not your average band. We're high-concept. We don't just get up and play. I mean, I'm even writing songs. It's wild, I experience things differently now. Like I'll be walking down the street, and I'll see something, and a song will just pop into my head. Well, not a whole song, but an idea, you know?" She tries to sink her marshmallow with her spoon. "All these years I've been searching for something to do creatively, and I think I've found it. It feels really good." She looks at him, waiting for a response.

"Good."

"So what happened with you and Alex? I'll understand if you don't want to talk about it."

"I don't."

"Okay. I just want you to know I'm here for you. It's hard I know. Especially if you really love somebody. It took me a long time to get over Dave, even though I was the one who called it quits."

"He's getting married," he says, immediately wondering why he is telling her this, why he wants to hurt her. He watches the life seep out of her, her mouth collapse. "I'm sorry. I shouldn't have told you that."

She drags the bag of marshmallows towards her and ties it closed with a twist-tie. "No, that's okay. I mean, I would've found out. I'd rather hear it from you than anybody." She gets up and stands on tiptoe to put the marshmallows in the kitchen cupboard. He'd forgotten how tiny she is. From behind she could pass for a teenager.

"He was really broken up over you. He used to call me to talk about you."

She rubs her hands on her jeans. "Yeah, well, you're lucky if you have one great love in your life, right?"

"Right."

She holds out her hand to him, palm upwards. "Put it here, bro."

Reluctantly he slaps his hand over her palm. Then she holds her hand palm downwards, ready to slap his. He complies with this comradely behaviour only because he feels like a mean-pig-brother.

She hooks her hair behind her ears. "Anyway it's nice we'll both be here for Christmas. Maybe Durham will come by. Is he still living with what's-his-name?"

"I think so."

"Man, is he ugly, that guy, have you ever seen him? Pockmarked as hell. I don't know what Durham sees in him. I bet they're into S & M." She glances at Zee's cup. "Are you finished? Do you want me to make you another one?"

"No. Thanks. I think I'll go for a walk."

"You want company?"

"Actually I just want to be by myself for a bit."

"I understand." She smiles, and he notices the front tooth he chipped when he pushed her face into a drinking fountain.

On the street, he becomes acutely aware of the sound of his running shoes padding on the frozen pavement. Around him, colourful Christmas decorations flicker. Amazing how, regardless of what's going on inside, lit houses always look cosy at night. Wives might be battered, children abused, but from the outside, everything looks dandy. Daisy's house looks cosy from the outside. "Peachy," he says out loud.

Who the fuck was his father anyway? What kind of man deserts a wife and three children? What kind of man takes a seven-year-old boy to the zoo to see the rhinoceroses then vanishes the next day, poof, just like that? Zee can hardly remember him, just the smell of his pipe and the feeling of supreme safety he had while sitting on his shoulders. But he can barely remember the face. After he left, Daisy removed every trace of him and went to work for the phone company. When ordinary people complain about rate increases, Daisy says the phone company has been very good to her.

What kind of man has no curiosity about his own children?

Daisy said he went to New Zealand, became a sheep

farmer, remarried and had children. Zee took this to mean that he liked his new children better. As a teenager, Zee entertained thoughts of tracking down the son of a bitch and whacking him in the head with a boomerang, but he decided against it. His father didn't deserve to know that he'd been missed.

What kind of man walks away from the past he has created, what kind of coward?

A man like me, Zee wonders, *like me?*

ELEVEN

At the Centre's Christmas party, Alex and Mirv help a few teenaged mothers decorate the artificial tree. Marika, in tight jeans and a cropped sweat-shirt, circles them scornfully, jiggling her crying baby in her arms. "I hate fake trees," she mumbles to Alex.

Alex feels the baby's forehead with her palm. "Marika, I think he has fever."

"He's always like that. He gets hot when he cries."

"Maybe you should put him on the couch anyway."

Marika shifts the baby to her other shoulder. "He's teething, alright? I know how to look after him." A glass ball crashes to the floor. They all look at Suzy who stares down at it, horrified, holding her hands over her mouth.

Marika snorts. "Had a little too much to drink, Suze?"

"Leave her alone," Alex says.

"She's pissed."

Mirv puts an arm around Suzy's shoulders and guides her to the kitchen. "It's alright, Suzy, but we better sweep it up before somebody steps on it."

Marika stares after them. "She makes me sick. She'll suck off any dumb john for a couple of bucks. She's so dense I swear half the time she doesn't even get paid."

Alex picks up a bag of pink popcorn. "That's her choice." With her glass of egg nog, she settles on the couch and begins to string popcorn. Mirv and Suzy come out of the kitchen, Mirv carrying Suzy's baby and Suzy holding a dustpan and broom. She crouches over the shattered glass and carefully sweeps it up. When she's finished she straightens up and stares at the tree. "It's so pretty," she says. Marika snorts.

"You know what we could do …?" Suzy asks. "We could go out carolling."

"Give me a break," Marika says and drops down on the couch beside Alex. Her baby, surprised by the sudden motion, becomes silent for an instant then resumes his wailing.

"Maybe the neighbourhood would appreciate it," Suzy says. "Maybe they'd stop thinking we're rejects."

"We are rejects," Marika says. "Who gives a fuck?"

Suzy takes her own baby from Mirv and cups the infant's head protectively with her hand. "You know why you talk like that, Marika?"

Marika widens her eyes feigning wonderment. "Why, Suzy?"

"Because you're scared you'll be rejected so you won't even try."

"Gosh, Suze, you're really deep."

Mirv claps her hands. "Okay, guys, lay off it. Where's your Christmas spirit?" She picks up a carton of eggnog. "Anyone for refills?"

"Put some bourbon in it, and I might consider it," Marika grumbles. She lays the baby on his stomach and rubs his back.

Alex sticks her needle through another popcorn kernel. "I saw your boyfriend the other night."

"Oh yeah, where?"

"He was doing laundry." Marika snorts and plays with her baby's hair. Alex watches her. "He told me he used to do laundry for you. And clean the apartment."

"Maybe once in a million years. He won't change a diaper, it's like he's scared the shit'll jump out at him."

Alex nibbles thoughtfully on a piece of popcorn. "It's funny, you know, because I didn't get the feeling the baby was the problem for him. He seemed more concerned about his relationship with you."

"Oh, really?" Marika snorts again and pulls out a cigarette from a pack in her diaper bag. She lights the cigarette, inhales heavily, then turning her face away from the baby, exhales in a slow stream. "What did he say about 'our relationship'?"

"He seems to feel that you don't trust him."

Marika folds one arm over her stomach and props her other elbow on it, holding up the cigarette. "He said that?"

"No, I just had that feeling. I think he wants to be with you, he just doesn't want to feel that he can't go out on his own with his friends."

"His friends are dickheads."

"Whatever they are," Alex says, "they're his friends, and if you love him, you should respect his judgement and let him go out with them."

"Every night?"

"I didn't get the impression he was going out with them every night. Was he?"

Marika shrugs, balances her cigarette on an ashtray, slides her hands under the baby's armpits and lifts him to her chest. Again, surprised by the movement, he becomes silent for a moment, rests his pudgy cheek against his mother's shoulder and stares at Alex. She smiles at him. He stares back.

"It's funny," Alex says. "The more you tell somebody not to do something, the more they want to do it. We just don't like being pushed around."

Marika pats the baby's back. "I wasn't pushing him

around. I just want him to act like a decent human being."

"Your idea of a decent human being. Maybe your idea doesn't exist. Maybe you're going to have to compromise a bit and settle for someone who loves you, helps out with the laundry and housecleaning but likes to go out with his buddies."

"Would you?"

"I don't know. Nobody's made me the offer."

Marika tips the baby sideways, sniffs his diaper and wrinkles her nose. "Jesus." She takes a last drag on her cigarette, stubs it out and grabs the diaper bag. "I've got to change him."

Alex slides another kernel along the thread, wondering what Zee is doing at this very moment. He has no money, no friends. He must be at Daisy's. Doing what, though? Probably nothing. Probably building a jungle of aloe plants. She looks around at the crowd of babies, some smiling, some irritable, some asleep, and feels that yearning again, to have one of her own—to love, to hold, to watch grow, to buy cute little shoes for. She feels that without one, something inside her will shrivel and die. Without one, her life will be hollow, incomplete. Her hair will grey, her skin will sag. She'll spend her days lingering over cups of tea, mourning the child she never had. The life she never had.

•

For a moment, Mel stares at Alex past the safety chain before unhooking it and opening the door. "You want a brandy?" she asks. "I don't have any food. I ate an almond croissant which contains more calories than I'm supposed to consume in a day." She takes a bottle of Remy Martin from the cherrywood cabinet, pours cognac into two large brandy snifters and hands one to Alex who leans back on the couch and sips.

Mel sits cross-legged on the floor. "Tough day?"

"The Christmas thing is getting to me."

"Tell me about it. If I hear 'Frosty the Snowman' one more time I may kill somebody. Norm bought Christmas decorations for the office. The poor secretaries have to work overtime putting up his asinine decorations."

"Do they get paid for it?"

"Of course not. I think he gives them fifty bucks or something as a bonus. Mr. Christmas Spirit. It's reached the point I can barely talk to him without spitting."

"Maybe you should switch firms."

"And start all over again? No thank you."

Alex feels the alcohol slide down her throat, enter her blood stream, heat her up, melt her down. Mel nudges Alex's knee. "So talk to me, you feeling alright? You look troubled."

"I tripped on a curb on my way here."

"Are you hurt?"

"No."

"So what's the problem?"

"This man tried to help me. You know, grabbed my elbow to steady me. Instinctively I shook him off."

Mel stares at her blankly. "So ...?"

"I was ready to fight him. This man had tried to help me and I was about to hook him with my elbow."

"Well that's natural. You're a woman. You have to protect yourself." Mel lies back on the carpet, lifts her legs back over her head and touches her toes to the floor behind her.

"But maybe he was trying to help me."

"You couldn't know that. How are you supposed to know that?"

"I should've given him a chance." Alex drinks from her snifter and stares at Mel's floral wallpaper. "It just seems so sad."

"How do you mean sad?"

"Sad. That women can't ever let down their defenses. We're so used to creeps ogling us, hissing at us and grabbing our asses that when a nice guy tries to help, we treat him like he's a rapist. I hate that. I hate that I have to feel that. He thought I was a bitch. Right now he's probably saying, 'I tried to help this bitch today.'"

"He's probably forgotten all about it."

Alex adjusts a cushion behind her head. "Maybe I am a bitch. Lots of people think I am, you know. People have told me, 'So and so thinks you're a bitch.'"

Mel sits up and pours more cognac. "You're not a bitch."

"I just don't like wasting time talking to people I don't want to talk to. Zee'll talk to anybody. The number of times I've stood around waiting for him to finish a boring conversation with someone he met in a bar once."

Mel nods. "He's a friendly guy."

"He just does it because it distracts him from his own life. He'd much rather sit around talking than actually do anything. Also he wants to be liked. You know, ever since he quit, he's tried to act like it doesn't bother him that all those nerds can't stand him, but it bugs him. I know it bugs him."

Mel laces her fingers and stretches her arms over her head. "I can't imagine anybody not liking Zee."

"They know he thinks they're incompetent."

"That could be a problem."

Alex holds the snifter under her nose, inhaling the fumes. "That man might have been a nice guy, just wanting to help. He might've been a friend. I need a friend. I don't have Zee anymore."

Mel swishes the cognac around in her snifter. "Now, now, don't start getting morose."

"Did you hear about that guy who stole a woman's car, dragged her into the woods, raped her then stabbed her nine times with a screwdriver? I mean can you believe that? Why would he do that? He must hate us. Why does he hate us? What have we ever done to him?"

"I don't know. Maybe his mom molested him or something. Al, maybe we should talk about something else. I don't think this is a healthy topic for you right now."

"It's so sad we don't trust each other anymore. Did we ever trust each other?"

Mel straightens her legs in front of her and grabs her toes. "I don't know. I think women shut up more in the old days. Now we're letting them know what we think, and the boys are panicking."

"Zee would like me to shut up."

"There you go. Maybe he wouldn't have left if you shut up."

"I can't, though. I mean, I try, you know, to keep it in, but it comes out anyway. Sometimes I really want to shut up because I know mouthing off won't do any good. But then I feel like I can't breathe. I mean what are we supposed to do? Shut up so they won't rape us and stab us with a screwdriver?"

"I don't know, Al."

"Another woman was raped in our neighbourhood. In one of the corridors of her high-rise. She was fifty-five years old." Mel shakes her head and lies on her side, fingering the stem of her glass.

"You know why I think men want women to wear high-heels?" Alex asks.

"Why?"

"So we can't escape. They want our feet bound. So they have power over us."

"I think that's a bit extreme. I wear high-heels because I like them."

"How can you like having your feet squished into little pointy shoes?"

"They aren't squished," Mel says. "And I like the way they look."

"But you're not looking at them, you're on top of them."

"I still see them."

"You wear them so men will think you have nice legs."

"That's part of it."

"What kind of sick man thinks a woman's legs look nice when her feet are jammed into little pointy shoes?"

Mel studies her. "You're drunk aren't you?"

"You told me yourself you wear skirts because men like to see legs."

"I've never seen you drunk."

"You're letting them dictate how you dress, how you behave."

"I like wearing skirts."

"When it's cold outside, and you have to wear icky nylons that run all the time? You've told me yourself you love weekends because you can dress the way you want."

"Alright, so I'm a victim. What do you want me to do, wear jeans to the office and give Norm a heart attack?"

"We keep telling ourselves we're making progress, but we're not. We're still dressing up for them, shutting up for them."

"Making less money."

"And they still go and rape us."

"Al, I think you have to be careful using the 'they' word, you know. I mean, they're not all bad."

Alex nods then stands. "I should get going. I've got baking to do."

"You going to be alright? Do you want me to call a cab?"

"I'll be fine."

On the subway platform she waits for some bastard to approach, some drooling creep muttering 'pussy' and 'cunt' and 'suck me off'. She feels coiled, ready to spring at him and ram her knuckles into his Adam's apple. But there's only a pasty-faced young woman reading a romance novel, a Pakistani security guard and a weary construction worker holding a lunch box.

She tells herself she mustn't start hating men just because Zee has let her down. Or because they have sperm, and she doesn't. Or because so many of her teen mothers have to turn tricks for a living. Not all men are cowards or perverts or manipulators. Some men are good. She knows this. Like the man who helped her on the curb. Maybe.

TWELVE

Zee decides to go to Dave's stag because Jenny's band is setting up to practise in the basement. And because he's lonely. He's been able to fill his mornings in the bath and in the Donut King, contemplating the vicissitudes of life over coffee and a Bavarian Cream. In the afternoons, he's walked around downtown, just feeling lucky, really lucky, not to be cooped up in an office. But he's still lonely. He hadn't expected this.

Standing by the drinks table in Dave's apartment, he notices that Dave's buddy, Harvey, shaves between his eyebrows. He tries to imagine how Harvey would look with one solid band of eyebrow.

"My three-year-old son," Harvey says, hitching up his red sweat pants that keep falling down at the back, "wanted to know why his girl cousin didn't have a penis. So my old lady explained to him that girls don't have penises. You know what he said?" He looks expectantly at Zee who shakes his head. "'Poor them.' He said 'poor them' because they don't have penises." Harvey chortles. Zee tries to look amused while he reaches for the scotch bottle and refills his plastic cup. He wants to get drunk, very drunk, wants to short-circuit his brain. "Do you have any photos?" he asks politely.

Harvey smirks and hitches up his pants again. "I don't make a habit of carrying around photos of my son's penis, you'll just have to take my word for it."

"No, I mean of your kids. In your wallet. Do you have any pictures of your kids?"

Dave, wearing a long-sleeved T-shirt with a tuxedo and tie printed on it, clamps a hand on Zee's shoulder. "What's cookin', good-lookin'?"

"Not much."

Dave pokes Harvey's belly. "Harv, you're putting that weight back on. I bet Nancy's not too happy about that."

"She could lose a pound or two herself."

"Listen, man, she had a baby, she's allowed."

Harvey pats his stomach. "Sympathy fat."

Dave grabs the roll of fat around Harvey's middle. He shakes his head and clucks his tongue. Then, beer bottle in hand, he jumps up onto the couch, puts his fingers in his mouth and whistles. "Okay listen up, fellas, I've got a special guest here tonight. Her name's Dawn ..." Everybody whistles. "And she's going to do a little dance for us." Harvey and a red-haired man with pumped-up muscles stamp their feet. "Now the rules are," Dave continues, "you look, but you don't touch." The red-haired man shouts out 'boo'. Some of the others join in. Dave holds up his hands, "Come on guys, give the girl a break. She's a professional entertainer." He jumps off the couch. "Let's have a warm hand for Dawn." Everyone whistles again and claps. Dave pushes a tape into the stereo; drums beat, a saxophone wails as a curvaceous young woman comes out of the bedroom barely clothed in an array of billowing scarves. She undulates and swivels to the music before pulling a scarf loose and winding it around the neck of a man with very large teeth who sniffs the scarf and barks. She twists through the crowd, pulling each scarf free from her body, then slowly draping it around a man's neck, brushing her breasts close to him, causing his face to turn either very red or very pale. When she approaches Zee, he waits to feel aroused, but nothing happens. In his head, he hears Alex saying, "Poor woman. Do you think she enjoys that?"

When Dawn is naked except for two scarves attached to her nipples and a sequined G-string, she kneels on the floor and arches backwards, shaking her shoulders, thrusting her bouncing breasts forward. Then she lies back on the floor, spreading her knees and thrusting her pelvis while sliding her tongue over her lips and running her hands over her breasts and stomach towards her groin. The men say nothing; they stare, transfixed. It occurs to Zee that this position must be difficult to maintain, if not painful. Slowly Dawn eases herself into an upright position and cups her hands under her breasts. Abruptly she yanks the scarves—Zee decides they must be attached by suction cups—away from her breasts. He is surprised at the size and deep brown of her nipples. Alex's are smaller and more pink, delicate. The brown nipples look almost grotesque to him. He pulls the scarf from his neck and turns back to the drinks table for more scotch. The music stops. Dave claps, leaping back onto the couch. "Let's have a hand for Dawn." Everyone applauds, cheers and whistles. Dawn, suddenly graceless and absurd in her nudity, quickly collects her scarves and scurries back to the bedroom.

Harvey waves a pretzel at Zee. "The temperature went up a few degrees in here, wouldn't you say?" He bites his pretzel. "You know, it's funny," he says, "watching that gal, I kept thinking about my wife." He munches thoughtfully. "We've been married ten years. She's a fabulous woman." He holds the pretzel up as if about to make a point. "The funny thing is, we're really very happy." He looks at Zee as though expecting an argument.

"That is funny."

Harvey pops the rest of the pretzel into his mouth and wipes his hand on his sweat pants. "You're being sarcastic. Listen, I understand where you're coming from."

Where am I coming from?

"I used to feel the same way." Harvey reaches for another pretzel. "It hasn't happened to you yet that's all, but when it does, when you find the right girl ..." He shakes his head as though he can't find words to describe what happens when it happens. "When you find the right girl ... everything changes, your whole outlook on life, you know what I'm saying?" Zee narrows his eyes and juts out his chin to suggest that possibly he does. "My old lady," Harvey continues, "she knows me better than I know myself, you know what I'm saying? She knows what's going to happen before it happens, and it's no big deal to her. All she says is ... you know what she says?" Zee shakes his head. "'Just make sure you wear a rubber, Harv.'" Harvey holds his arms out like a stand-up comic who's just delivered a punch-line. "Isn't that something?"

"It is," Zee responds, wondering if Harv's old lady feels defeated and bitter about his philandering or if she just doesn't care anymore, is glad to have Harv out of the house.

"She's fabulous." Harvey puts his beer bottle to his lips.

Zee wonders why he, himself, doesn't need the odd shot in the dark anymore, the odd conquest. When he was single, he'd get nervous if he hadn't used it in awhile, would worry that there was something wrong with him, that maybe he was emitting impotent radar. He'd try it out to make sure, pick up a girl in a bar and go to her place so he could leave in the morning. Only once did he think he was in love. For about a week he clung to a woman who wore a garter belt until he realized that he'd created her and that he didn't even like her in fact. But at least he got hard, stayed hard and ejaculated. He wonders what has caused this change in him, this lack of sexual drive. Doesn't he have anything to prove anymore?

Very drunk now, Dave clambers back onto the couch, pushes up the sleeves of his tuxedo T-shirt and announces that he loves his buddies, they're the best. "A man's gotta have buddies. I don't want you guys to think now that I'm hitched up I don't want my buddies around. It's important in a marriage to have good friends, separate friends." Some of his buddies stick their fingers in their mouths and whistle, some shout "Hear, hear." Dave holds up his hands like a politician at a rally quieting supporters. "I'm still playing football on the weekends, and I'm still hanging out at the Mustang, maybe not as late because ahh … I've got stuff to do at home." He tries to wink but closes both eyes instead. His buddies stamp their feet and clap their hands, the man with very large teeth barks. Dave, melting into smiles, steps off the couch and several of his buddies slap him on the back. The red-headed man pours beer over his head.

Harvey reaches into the cooler and pulls out another beer. "I think he's made the right decision. I have a good feeling about it. Have you met Glenda?"

"Yes." Zee pours more scotch.

"Fine girl." Harvey twists the cap off his beer. "You know, it's funny, a lot of people get married for the wrong reasons; they're horny or they're scared they can't get anybody better, you know what I'm saying? It's a shame." He points a pretzel at Zee. "Your wife's got to be your best buddy, it's like … there's a world out there and we're in here … you know what I'm saying?" He bites the pretzel. "Me and my old lady, we have an understanding." Zee feels a headache growing over his right eye. Harvey holds a hand to his heart. "I don't ask her, she don't ask me, finito, pas de problème." He puts his beer bottle on the table. "Excuse me. I've got to use the facilities."

"No problem," Zee says and watches him hitch up his pants as he crosses the room. Dave, towelling his hair dry, fixes on Zee and barrels through his buddies towards him. Zee considers taking flight but isn't sure he could move fast enough with all the scotch sloshing around inside him. Dave clamps a hand on Zee's shoulder. "Sit down, buddy, you've been standing for two hours." He pushes Zee down into the couch and collapses beside him. "Man, what a night." He turns to stare at Zee with what Zee suspects is intended to be meaningful eye-contact. "I'm really glad you came. I know we don't see each other all that much, but I feel there's a connection between us. And that's important to me. A lot of these guys, they're buddies right? We hang out in the gym, play ball. But we don't really connect. You know me better than any of these guys." He lifts his feet onto the coffee-table and stares into his crowd of buddies. "You know ... sometimes I lie awake at night trying to think of people who love me, I mean really love me. And you know what?" He turns to look Zee in the eye. Zee shakes his head. "I'm not sure who those people are. I mean how can you know for sure somebody loves you? They could just be saying it so you'll love them, kind of like 'scratch my back, I'll scratch yours'. But it's not real love. Sometimes the people I think love me one year are gone the next. There's no consistency. I mean, isn't that what love's all about? Sticking around come hell or high water? Isn't it supposed to be something you can count on?" Zee looks vague. "Sometimes," Dave continues, "I just want to cry, for no particular reason it's just ... I don't know, man. I just keep messing up." He covers his eyes with his hand. "I'm so scared I'm going to blow this."

"You won't."

"It's like I look at you and Alex and I mean ... to me, you're it, man. You two chime together. I mean, remember when me and Jenny came over for dinner? Sometimes when you're around couples they bitch at each other right? Or maybe they're really touchy-feely, and you think maybe they're doing it in front of you so you'll think they have this really copacetic relationship. But you guys …" He shakes his head, remembering. "You guys don't even have to touch, there's a … I don't know, an aura about you. Hey, I know that sounds corny. I'm a little drunk, okay. But I mean it, there's magic there."

Zee can't bring himself to tell Dave the truth, thinks it would be a cruel thing to do on this night. Instead he sits inert, numbed by the alcohol.

"Come to the wedding," Dave pleads. "I'd really appreciate it."

"Alex might be busy, but I'll certainly make it."

"She's busy on a Sunday?"

"Oh, well, you know in her line of work, you never know what might crop up."

Dave looks serious. "I understand." Abruptly, he hugs Zee. Locked in Dave's embrace, Zee feels like an impostor, feels that he should explain to Dave that he is not the man Dave thinks he is. But then it occurs to him that Dave needs to believe in him. He, Zee, is nothing but an icon to Dave. It costs him nothing to keep quiet. Inhaling Dave's pungent cologne, he wishes he believed in something.

•

Huge, soft flakes tumble around him, muffling the city. The silence awes him. The street lamps create welcoming pools of light. The snow engulfs his ankles, creeping over his socks and stinging his skin. If he believed in God he would really believe in him now. He bends down, scoops up a handful and rubs it into his face, enjoying the burn.

All he wants, all he wants in the whole world, is to sleep in his own bed with his own woman. That's all he wants.

Please God?

The lights are off. He decides she must be asleep because she never stays out late. He tells himself to leave her alone. But his feet are numb with cold, as are his hands, as is his brain. He tries to make a snowball to throw at the window hoping that if she sees him perishing in the storm, she will be overcome with feelings of love and invite him in for Red Zinger tea. But the snow is too dry to make a ball. He feels dry, petrified, like a tree, like petrified wood. He saw it in the museum; beautiful, layered with rich earthy colours.

He uses his key in the lock, stumbles in and squats into the beanbag chair. His chair. He bought it in his youth. It's his chair. His youth. He looks up to see her glaring at him, cinching her robe around her. "What are you doing here?"

He tries to speak, but his tongue clogs his mouth.

"Zee, this isn't funny. You're drunk."

"I just wanted to see you."

"Try and see me sober some time."

"I'm sorry."

"Sorry is a waste of time. You're wasting my time."

"I'm sorry."

"God, you really are pathetic."

All he wants, all he wants in the whole world, is to put his arms around her, rest his forehead on her shoulder and inhale her soapy smell.

She picks a magazine off the floor and tosses it on the end-table. "You know I'd be happy to talk to you sober. You're just too chickenshit to face me sober."

What does chicken shit look like, anyway? He isn't sure. Little pellets. Or is it white, like bird doo-doo?

She stares at him. "Do you want some tea? I'll make you some tea." At first, when she'd seen him crumpled in the bean-bag chair, she'd hoped that maybe, just maybe, he had come to repent, or at least to make some attempt at reform. As she fills the kettle and slams it on the burner, she wonders how he can imagine that showing up meek and drunk will accomplish anything.

Leaning back in the beanbag chair, he doesn't think he's really drunk really. He's quite lucid, actually. He puts his hands on his knees and watches her reaching for the tea-bags, knowing exactly, without looking, where they're stored in the cupboard. He arranges himself so that he is more or less sitting up straight. She'll be impressed if he can sit straight. He clings to the vinyl of the chair to remain upright and tries to work out the best way to behave. Should he be witty, make light of the fact that he has woken her up at whatever time it is in the morning? Maybe he should act like everything's normal, maybe he should pretend to fall asleep. He notices a bruise on his wrist; a big purple bruise. How did he get that?

"What are you hoping to accomplish by coming here drunk?"

He traces the outline of the bruise with his index finger. It occurs to him that if he doesn't say something, do something, she'll tell him to leave. He should say something meaningful. Something succinct but meaningful. He wishes there were a dog folded at his feet, a dog they had bought as a wriggling puppy, a dog that would be his ally, that he could pet right now, that would lick his hand and make Alex sad because she would know the dog was missing him.

She places a cup on the floor in front of him. "What do you want from me?"

Unbelievably tired now, he flops forward in the beanbag chair like a man who has been shot.

"Oh, christ, Zee … I want you to go. Please go. I want you to go. You have to go." The force behind her voice surprises her because she feels very weak, as though she can hardly stand. "I'll call a cab for you. I'll even pay for it. Where are you staying, at Daisy's?"

It feels like someone is sticking a knife in his eye.

"I'm not going to feel sorry for you just because you're stupid enough to get pissed out of your mind. Nobody forced you to drink, did they?"

Darkness slides over his eyelids.

"Oh, for god's sake." She grabs his upper arms and drags him to the couch. "This means I'm going to have to change the lock doesn't it? Do you think I want to do that? Our entire stupid life together you've forced me to do things I don't want to do." She grabs his ankles, swings his legs onto the couch and yanks off his running shoes.

He sinks down down down and feels something soft land on top of him. Snow?

•

Lying on her back in the middle of the bed, she wants to scream. Once again she has been made to feel like the villain; the bitch-wife throwing her man out because, poor guy, he drinks a little too much, poor guy, life is tough, poor guy.

"Fuck right off," she says to the air then rolls onto her side, trying to find a comfortable position for her arm. She slides it under the pillow, then stretches it across the bed, then curls it into her chest. Her legs feel cramped. She tries to shake them out, stretch them, relax them but they remain tense. She throws the blankets aside, gets out of bed, opens the door and stares at him. He's lying on his stomach, snoring, with one arm dangling to the floor, his mouth gaping.

If only alcohol had the same effect on her, knocked her out, darkened her windows. But no, it only depresses her, forces her to watch every detail of her messy, stupid, useless life lurching past in slow motion.

She goes to the kitchen, pulls a garbage bag out of a drawer, lifts an aloe plant off the window-sill and drops it into the bag. In the living-room, she picks up the other aloe plants and drops them into the bag. One by one, she hears them thud. She marches back to the bedroom and jettisons five more. With each thud she feels her lungs contract until she can hardly breathe. She drags the bag back into the living-room, twist-ties it closed, slides her bare feet into her boots and her arms into her jacket. She heaves the bag over her shoulder, opens the front door, walks to the rear of the building, out the back door and shoves the bag into the garbage bin.

Standing very still, blinking into the falling snow, she wishes she had the guts to lie down and freeze to death.

THIRTEEN

Sitting at the Woolworth's counter, Daisy seems fatter than Alex remembers. Her rump bulges over the stool. "Hi, Daisy."

Daisy pushes herself away from the counter to look at her. "Oh, there you are. For some reason I expected you to come from the other side."

Alex slides onto the stool beside her. "How are you?"

"Oh, not too bad. Not bad, you know. And you?"

Alex shrugs and tries to get the attention of an emaciated waitress in a pale-blue uniform who is funneling ketchup into bottles. "Could I have a coffee, please?"

"Have some pie," Daisy coaxes. "The pie's good here. Apple. Have it à la mode. My treat."

"No, thanks. I just ate, actually."

The waitress puts down the large ketchup tin, pulls out an order pad and stares at them glassily.

"I'll have a piece anyway," Daisy says. "I hardly ate lunch."

The waitress looks at her. "With chocolate ice cream on it?"

"If it's not too much trouble."

When she first met Zee, Alex was impressed by his concern for his mother's health and by his tenacity in trying to interest her in the diets and exercise programmes he clipped from magazines. Daisy appeared interested in what Zee showed her, but she never seemed to lose weight. Then Zee began to sneak into Daisy's house when she was out. He discovered bags of cookies and sugared cereals. He would confront Daisy with them, but she would deny everything, insisting that they were leftover from "before the diet". Zee would complain to Alex that Daisy had lied to him.

"Not about important things," Alex would say.

"You don't think her health is important?"

"It's her problem. Let her do what she wants about it."

"It's my problem if she has a heart attack."

"Everybody has to go some time."

The waitress sets the pie in front of Daisy who pokes at it with her fork as though she's not exactly sure how to eat it.

"Why did you want to see me, Daisy?"

"Well, to be honest with you, I'm worried about Zee. You know he's staying at my house."

"I thought he might be."

"He's not happy, I have a feeling." Daisy looks for something on the counter. "Don't tell me they're out of Sweet'n Low again. Oh well." She shakes a packet of sugar into her coffee. "He didn't come home last night at all. I almost called the police, but I said no, he's his own person. Still, I can't help worrying. I don't know where he goes. To bars, I have a feeling."

"He was at my place last night."

"At your place?"

Alex nods. Daisy, surprised, stares at her then dabs at some spilt coffee on the counter with her napkin. "Are you two getting back together then?"

"No."

"Oh." Daisy stirs her coffee, taps the spoon against the edge of the cup, then sets it on a napkin on the counter. "Well, he didn't seem too happy this morning, I can tell you. He sat in his room with the blinds down. Jenny even made apple pancakes, but he wouldn't come out." She breaks through the pastry crust with her fork, lifts a piece of pie to her mouth, chews and swallows. "Something happened between you two last night, I have a feeling."

"Nothing happened, that's why he's depressed."

Daisy, looking sceptical, prods the pie with her fork. "He misses you, I have a feeling."

"I miss him." Alex leans on the counter and stares down at her coffee cup.

"He doesn't go out hardly at all," Daisy says. "He sits around the house watching that black woman on TV. Yesterday he was standing on his head."

"That's an exercise to make the blood flow to his brain."

"I see. Well, it gave me a start, I can tell you."

"What do you want me to do about it, Daisy?"

Daisy sips her coffee. "It's none of my business but you two still love each other, I have a feeling."

Alex stares at a mailman hunched over the counter, eating french fries with gravy, slowly lifting them to his mouth, as though he can barely stand the weight of them. His empty mailbag sags on a stool beside him. Daisy finishes her pie and pats her mouth with the napkin. "He's heart-broken, I have a feeling."

Alex has always believed that underneath Daisy's roly-poly exterior lies a woman of iron who keeps a firm reign on her "boys". Alex has been careful never to interfere with Daisy's treatment of her sons even though she suspects that Zee's reluctance to face responsibility comes from knowing that Daisy will always be there for him.

"I never said he should be a lawyer," Daisy says.

"I know."

"Lawyers have to defend criminals."

"He wasn't in criminal law."

Daisy picks up a shopping bag. "Look what I bought him." She pulls out a purple baseball cap with little quilted silver wings sewn to the back.

"It's cute," Alex says.

"There was a super-hero that had wings on his head. Zee used to like him, used to run around the yard pretending to fly. He'd hold his arms out ..." Daisy demonstrates stretching her arms in front of her, "and run around the yard jumping off things."

Alex feels around in her bag for her wallet. "Look, Daisy, I've got to run. I wish I could help you, but really, we've reached an impasse, and I'm as lost as he is."

Daisy fixes her eyes on Alex. "You're much stronger than him."

Alex slides her bag over her shoulder. "I'm not so sure. I think it might be the other way around."

"Do you have another boyfriend?"

"No, no." Alex puts a dollar on the counter.

"No, let me," Daisy says.

Alex puts the dollar back in her wallet. "Thanks. Okay, well, I'll see you later."

Daisy, defeated for the moment, nods and tenderly puts the winged baseball cap back in the shopping bag. "Alright then."

•

Alex sits over coffee in the mall cafeteria, watching a young family eat pizza. The father, sitting closest to the children, explains how pizza is made. With furrowed brows, they look dubiously at the pizza then at him. "How do you know?" the boy asks.

The father wipes tomato sauce off the boy's chin. "I've seen them make it."

The woman, sitting on the other side of the man, leans forward and smiles across him at the children. "Sometimes he thinks he's so smart, doesn't he?" she asks. The children stare at her blankly. The man turns to the woman and presses his lips against hers. Alex thinks they make an attractive couple; thinks they've made attractive children; thinks it's wonderful that the woman is in such good shape after having two children. When it becomes apparent that the man is sliding his tongue inside the woman's mouth, Alex looks at the children, wondering if it disturbs them that their parents are necking. Apparently unconcerned, they chew on their pizza and swing their legs. When the man stops kissing the woman and sticks his tongue in her ear, Alex looks away, thinking it's extraordinary that a couple that have been together long enough to spawn two children should be so passionate. Usually the mother's attention is with her offspring. She wipes the tomato sauce from their chins; she holds their Cokes for them while the father stares off into the distance, thinking about a squash game or a business transaction or another woman. Only when the man slides his hand under the woman's jacket does it occur to Alex that this is the other woman; that this is a shared-custody weekend. Not once have the children referred to the woman as "Mummy"; nor have they tried to break through the barrier of their father to reach her. They sit by his side, on the outskirts of his passion. Alex wonders how their mother would feel if she were watching. Would she run up and grab her children's hands? Slap the man? Slap the woman? Or would she slink away, accepting defeat, understanding that she can no longer spark his lust and consequently must surrender the job to someone new. Or perhaps she would be delighted that he has found new love because she has found new love.

Perhaps she would smile knowingly and dash home to her new love and frolic in her house, temporarily empty of children.

Alex tosses her styrofoam cup in the trash-can. It concerns her that lately she has been loitering instead of getting her life in order. Sometimes, while loitering, she imagines that Zee is loitering in another public place. Sometimes she thinks she sees him. Her heartbeat reverberates in her head, and sweat collects in her palms until she discerns that it is not him. They will, she knows, have to meet again. They can't leave things as they are. *Messy.* They have to sort things out, divide things up. She knows that Zee will put this meeting off for as long as possible; knows that she will have to make the call.

New love. Impossible to imagine. Where would she find the resources? There is nothing left inside her, nothing left to spare. Every time a relationship has failed, she has lost a piece of herself while tearing a chunk from someone else. She looks back at her twenties, shocked at the carnage she left behind.

On TV last night the hero lifted the heroine effortlessly, carried her up some stairs to a bedroom and placed her carefully on the bed where their arms and legs entwined in a heated embrace. Alex longed to be lifted effortlessly, carried up some stairs and placed carefully on a bed. At five foot ten and one hundred and thirty-three pounds, she doubts this will ever happen to her. Zee tried it a couple of times, but she felt herself slipping from his grasp and worried he'd hurt his back. She'd ask him to put her down, but he wouldn't release her until, gasping, he could drop her on the bed.

•

Mel stands in the movie line-up waving at Alex, who joins her. "So what's this movie about?" she asks.

"Corruption in the police force."

"How original."

"I didn't think you'd want to see a love story."

"That's certainly true." The line begins to shuffle forward. Alex notices that the crowd consists of heterosexual couples or single women in pairs.

"I've been thinking about it," Mel says, "and I don't understand why, if you're really fixed on this baby thing, you don't just go to a sperm bank."

"Can't afford it. Also I'd like to at least see the guy in person, see how he moves, hear how he talks."

Mel offers her a stick of gum. "I have never seen a single mother that wasn't a wreck."

"I don't want to be a single mother."

"So you're hoping either Zee will grow up, or some wonderful guy will materialize?"

Alex bunches her gum wrapper into a ball and, not wanting to litter, puts it in her pocket.

"I'm warning you," Mel goes on, "there are no attractive men out there, anyway none over thirty and single." She takes a tube of lipstick from her handbag and dabs at her lips. "Martin Lovitch, an associate with Calder & Roth, called me up and asked me out. His wife died eight months ago. Ovarian cancer. What's really peculiar about it is that I haven't noticed any change in Martin since her death. I mean he's always looked depressed. If anything, he seems less tense. He tells me they were having marital problems, but even so."

"Are you going to go out with him?"

"He's not really my type. I like a full head of hair." In front of them a young woman wearing a pink, furry sweater stands on tiptoe to whisper in her boyfriend's ear. Alex wonders if she's commenting on Mel's assessment of Martin Lovitch. The boyfriend nods and shuffles his feet. Mel forages in her handbag, pulls out a Kleenex and blows her nose. "You know, Alex, babies destroy your body. They rob you of sleep and spare time. They also cost money. I tell you one thing, I have no desire to put myself through that. I'm too old. I need my sleep."

"I know all this."

"I don't think you do. I don't think anybody knows until they do it, otherwise there would be considerably fewer babies in the world." She stuffs the Kleenex in her pocket. "Also they're talking about banning disposable diapers. I mean, have you really thought it through? Why is it so important to you?"

"I don't know. It's a feeling."

"It's a little selfish don't you think? To bring another human being onto this fucked-up planet because you feel like it?"

"It is selfish." Alex stares at the backs of heads and coats. She feels Mel watching her and expecting her to defend herself. But she can't, doesn't know how, doesn't have a strong case. Mel forages in her bag again and pulls out her wallet. "Let me buy the popcorn. Do you feel like popcorn?"

"Sure."

•

The movie is graphically and relentlessly violent. Alex, unaccustomed to such films, watches the men shoot one another, torture one another, karate kick one another; and she feels an urge to do the same. Suddenly she understands why people buy guns and kill people. They feel powerless and believe that killing people will stop the crowd from rushing past them. Murderers must be very lonely.

In the movie, guns are revealed in close-up. Well-oiled, they glimmer and make satisfying metallic sounds as the hero loads and cocks them. At one point the hero holds the gun to his face and stares down the barrel, preparing to kill himself. Alex knows that he won't kill himself because he is the star of the movie. She tries to imagine how it would feel to hold a gun to her face. She can't.

The villain continually evades the hero. At the end, when the hero finally does gun him down, Alex feels great satisfaction. Were she not Alex, she might boogie on down to the gun store and buy herself a piece.

Instead she goes home and bakes muffins.

●

In the morning, the phone rings, waking Alex from a dream in which a car is chasing her down a dark alley, trying to squash her against a brick wall.

"Hello, Darling."

"Hi, Mum." Alex pictures her mother sitting demurely with her cordless phone on the deck of her Florida condo.

"I was wondering if you had any plans for Christmas?"

"I'm keeping a low profile," Alex says.

"Why don't you come here? It's beautiful here. Nick is coming. He's got another new girlfriend. It astonishes me that, at his age, he behaves as he does."

"It astonishes me that he's still alive."

"I beg your pardon?"

"Forget it." Alex pushes her head into the pillow and closes her eyes.

"You know what your problem is?" Elizabeth says. "You're too critical."

"You brought it up."

"I merely commented on his behaviour, I didn't condemn it."

"I didn't either, I just think it's astonishing he's still alive."

"You have such a negative view of things. I don't know

where you get that from."

Alex rubs her eyes. "Mum, please don't yak at me, I just woke up." Silence. Alex thinks she hears her mother sip coffee.

"How's Zee?"

"He's fine."

"Why don't you both come? It's gorgeous here."

"We'll talk about it. Mum, I have to get off the phone. Zee's expecting a call."

"Well, give him my regards."

"I will."

"Let me know what you decide. Arthur would love to see you. You won't believe what he did yesterday. We had the Allbrights for dinner, and I'd made fresh fruit salad, but I'd forgotten the cream, so I asked Art to go and buy some. You know what he came back with? Cool Whip. Never in my entire life have I bought Cool Whip. I'm sure he did it to irritate me because I asked him not to golf."

"Mum, Zee's giving me dirty looks. He needs the phone."

"Well, let me know what you decide."

"I will."

After she puts the phone down she curls into a ball and pulls the covers over her head. She knows she must get up and deliver the muffins; knows she will get up and deliver the muffins. All her life she has been punctual if not early. She has sat in restaurants waiting for acquaintances to rush in and say, "Sorry I'm late, I got held up at a meeting," or "Traffic was bad," or "My cat was throwing up." It puzzles Alex that she never has similar problems or that when she does, she doesn't get "held up" by them. Her precision irritates her. She has tried to be five or ten minutes late to avoid sitting alone in restaurants, stalling the waiter even though she feels he resents her for occupying a table without ordering. But always, in spite of her efforts, she is on time.

•

Sitting in the frozen Mazda, listening to the engine wheeze, she wants to know what it is that makes her go on. What it is that makes her hurry across the street to avoid being crushed by a car. What it is that makes her stand back from the railings of high balconies, from the edges of subway platforms. She must want to live. Then why doesn't she feel as if she wants to live? Why does she feel like a blob? Why do days stretch ahead of her in sombre greys instead of exuberant yellows? If she values her life, why doesn't she get off her ass and enjoy every moment of it? What's stopping her? She feels that if she could only pinpoint what's stopping her, she could confront it, annihilate it, blow it away.

The cars revs into action. Her day begins.

FOURTEEN

Sitting at the Woolworth's lunch counter, Zee forks apple pie into his mouth. He lets the ice-cream melt over his tongue before chewing. It surprises him that they still bake apple pie, he would have expected artificial cream pies or Jello or instant tapioca pudding.

When he was small, apple pie gave him a reason for living. He could never ask Daisy directly to take him out for pie. But he knew that if he behaved with suitable melancholia she would take him for pie to try to discover what was troubling him. Usually it had to do with school, like Irv Crangle tripping him all the time. But he could not discuss such matters with Daisy. He was afraid she might try to do something about it, like phone Irv's mother. So he would invent stories for her, saying he saw a little girl run over by a truck, or a dog caught by the dog catcher or a blind man taunted by teenagers. While scraping the last of his pie from the plate, he would feel her watching him, touched that he could be so affected by the distress of others. "It's all part of being a grown-up," she'd say, brushing hair from his forehead.

A black woman, even fatter than Daisy, hoists herself onto a stool not far from Zee and orders two muffins "heated up, cut open and buttered". The waitress, apparently familiar with this order, barely looks at the woman before she wanders into the kitchen.

Only now does he realize how often he lied as a kid. At the time it didn't feel like lying, more like omitting unattractive details about his life; his father leaving him, for example. When he first met Alex, he wanted to give her the impression that he was a lawyer with promise. As they became better acquainted, and he could no longer keep up the pretence, it amazed him that she liked him in spite of his flagging career. She never seemed surprised when he recounted tales of backstabbing in the civil service, and always, when he took a stand, she stood behind him, even though she believed he would lose. Although he appreciated her support, he hated her for expecting the worst and being right. Sometimes he blamed her for his failure, insisting that her negativity was affecting his view of the world.

But at least she used to believe in him, he thinks, believed he was doing the right thing.

The waitress places the muffins in front of the black woman who stares at them, making certain they meet her requirements. "And tea," she commands. "Bag in." Zee suspects that this woman lives in a rooming-house and that the muffins are the highlight of her day. Why, then, is she hostile to the waitress? What pleasure can she derive from being rude? Her negativity hangs in a cloud around her. She will consume her muffins and trudge back to the rooming-house, disgruntled as ever.

It never ceases to amaze him how people mishandle one another, how war can be declared over a parking space or a left-hand turn. He remembers the night Alex discovered that the Portuguese dry-cleaner had lost her favourite shirt. When she insisted that the cleaner reimburse her, he bellowed at them and lunged against the service counter like a bull against a gate. "I kill you, I kill you!" he screamed repeatedly then reached into a drawer for what Zee thought might be a gun. Sensing that Alex intended to hold her ground, Zee grabbed her arm and dragged her out the door. "That was my favourite shirt," she protested, jerking her arm free.

"You ready to die for it?"

"He wouldn't have done anything. He was trying to scare us."

"It worked on me."

"I hate being bullied." She booted a trash can. "If I were a man, he wouldn't have done that."

"I'm a man, and it didn't seem to faze him."

"Yeah, but he could tell you wouldn't do anything."

"What was I supposed to do, grab his jugular?"

"If I were a man, pigs like that wouldn't push me around. It's because they know they can beat the crap out of me. I hate that. The simple fact of being physically weaker. I hate it."

She is the only woman he has ever met who has admitted to suffering from "penis envy". "Of course I'd love to have a penis. You think I enjoy being up against the boys' club? You think I enjoy PMS and menstrual pain and other "female problems"? One out of nine women gets breast cancer. Of course I'd rather be a man. Men never grow up. I see that as an advantage."

Savouring his pie, Zee concludes that there are two kinds of women: the ones who tell the truth and the ones who don't. In his experience, the ones who don't are better company. They arrange their bodies in attractive poses and laugh at his jokes. They let him drive and don't comment when he brakes suddenly, or makes a wrong turn or rushes a red light.

Why, then, is he with Alex?

He is not with Alex.

He scrapes up the last of his pie with his fork. Someone

behind him pokes him in the ribs. "Zee, can you believe this, the three of us back here again?" Jenny pulls his new, winged baseball-cap down over his nose. "Durham, come over here. It's Zee," she shouts. Durham, the tallest and youngest, slouches towards them. "Hi," he says.

"How are you, Durham? Long time no see."

Durham nods, sticks a finger in his ear, then sits beside Zee and slowly revolves on the stool.

"Durham needs a shower cap," Jenny says. "And I'm looking for those little hair-elastics, remember the kind I used to wear as a kid, with the bobbles on the end? They were really wild. Daisy said she got them here." She notices Zee's plate. "You had pie, didn't you? Remember, Durm, how she used to take us for pie, one at a time, never all of us together, remember that? It was like this special treat to go out for pie with Mom. Nobody else was supposed to know about it. I thought she just took me. It was like this big secret."

Zee pushes his cap back and scratches his forehead. He had thought that Daisy only took him, that it was his special treat. Because he was the oldest. Why did she let him believe that it was his special treat? He feels betrayed. For years— although he'd been bursting to tell Jenny that Daisy loved him the most because she bought him pie—he'd kept the secret.

Daisy is one of those women who never tells the truth. She doesn't lie exactly, just withholds information.

"Do you want pie, Durm?" Jenny asks. "My treat."

Durham shakes his head and pulls out a pack of cigarettes from his shoulder-padded jacket. Because he stoops, the shoulder pads slip back towards his shoulder blades, making him look deformed.

"I'd eat a piece," Jenny says, "but now that I'm a stage persona I have to watch my figure. I've got Mom's genes, I could bloat up in a minute."

"So how are you, Durham?" Zee asks. Durham holds his hand out flat, palm facing downwards and tips it from side to side then reaches into his jacket for a lighter.

"Durham has made a decision," Jenny says. "He has decided to tell Daisy he's gay."

Durham lights his cigarette, takes a drag then tugs at his earlobe. He has the largest ears Zee has ever seen and was constantly teased about them as a kid. Later he became a punk rocker and jabbed safety pins through them. The last Zee heard, via Daisy, was that Durham was considering having his ears "tapered" by a plastic surgeon. Jenny wraps her arms around his shoulders. "I'm so proud of you, Durm. You'll feel better after you tell her, believe me."

"Why should he believe you?" Zee asks, trying not to sound vindictive.

Jenny plops down on the stool beside him. "Because he's living a lie. He never sees Daisy because he feels like he's lying to her. He loves her, but he hardly ever sees her. That's crazy."

Zee swivels on his stool, away from Jenny, and faces Durham. "So what brought you to this decision, Durham?"

Durham studies his cigarette. "I don't know. It just seems like the right thing to do."

"Why?"

Durham flicks his cigarette over an ashtray. "Just about everybody else I know has done it."

"Everybody does it," Jenny echoes.

"Is that a good reason for doing it?" Zee asks.

Jenny pinches Zee's cheek. "You don't have to do your big-brother number. He's thirty-seven years old."

"I'm not doing my big-brother number. I'm just curious as to why, all of a sudden, Durham has decided to tell Daisy."

"I just think she should know," Durham says. "I'm not

ashamed of it."

"Of course not," Jenny says. "He wants to bring Kyle home for Christmas which I think is a great idea. Won't that be fun, all four of us plus Mom?"

At this very instant, if it were possible, Zee would exchange bodies with the black lady. "When do you plan to tell her?" He asks because he plans to be out.

"I guess I'll have to play it by ear."

"It better be soon," Jenny says. "I want to know who to get presents for. What do you want from Santa, Zee?" She pokes him in the ribs again.

"Nothing, please, don't get me anything."

"Oh you're no fun. Is it because you don't have any money and can't buy us presents? You don't have to give me a present. I just like giving. I bet I know what you'd like." She smiles wickedly and watches him from the corner of her eye. "Beatle records. Remember yours got all scratched, and you threw them out finally? I bet they sell a greatest hits CD." Zee pulls his winged cap low over his eyes and rests his elbows on the counter. "You should sing us some Beatle songs tonight," Jenny coaxes. "You always used to sing Beatle songs. Remember Durm? He's got a nice voice."

"You used to sing both parts," Durham adds. "Paul's and John's."

"That's so cute," Jenny says. "Both my brothers are such cutie-pies. Okay I'm going to find my hair elastics." She bounces off the stool and charges into the store. Zee and Durham lean on the counter like two heavy drinkers at a bar.

"How long you planning to stay at Mom's?" Durham asks.

"I don't know."

"It seems like Jenny's moved back for good."

"It does seem like that." Zee shoves his empty coffee-cup back and forth on the counter.

"She wants to be Daisy's friend," Durham says. "She's really into family, says a lot of people don't have families."

"That's certainly true."

Durham stubs out his cigarette. "How does Daisy feel about her being there?"

"Daisy's been out a lot. Doing her hospital work and whatever else she does."

"She didn't used to go out much, did she?"

"I don't think so." Zee wipes melted ice-cream off his plate with his finger then licks it.

"So maybe she's not too happy about Jenny being there."

"It's hard to tell with Daisy."

Durham flattens his hands on the counter and interlaces his fingers. "It's too bad she's so fat. She could die from it."

"She could."

"I heard about a fat lady foodaholic who got diabetes and died." He bends his long torso over the counter and rests his chin on his knuckles, reminding Zee of a great hound resting his muzzle on his paws. He stares at a ketchup bottle. "You don't think I should tell her about Kyle?"

"Sure, if you want to."

Durham reaches for the ketchup bottle and slowly turns it around. "I wonder if it's really Heinz or if they just refill the bottles with some cheap crap."

"It's probably some cheap crap."

"Could they get sued for that?"

"Not unless they say it's Heinz."

Suddenly alert, Durham sits up and signals the waitress. "Excuse me, is this real Heinz?" He holds up the bottle.

The waitress, sipping from a glass of Coke, stares at him. "No."

"Oh." Durham puts the bottle down and slumps back on the counter. "You know what?"

"What?" Zee asks.

"I'm not sure if I want to. I mean, I can't figure out what I want."

Zee reaches back and fondles the wings on his cap. "I know the feeling."

•

When he returns to Daisy's, Alex is sitting with her in the living-room, with a cup of tea balanced in her lap. Zee feels as though he has been naughty at school and come home to find the teacher conspiring with his mother. "Well, hello," he says.

"Hello."

"We just made tea," Daisy offers.

"Ah, no thanks." He stands, waiting for a cue. His arms feel long and heavy, as if his knuckles were grazing Daisy's broadloom.

Alex sets her cup and saucer carefully on the coffee-table. "I was going to call, then I decided this isn't something we should do over the phone."

He starts to unbutton his coat. "What are we doing?"

Alex stands up. "Don't take off your coat, I think we should leave Daisy in peace."

"Oh, don't worry about me," Daisy says. "I can go have a nap."

Zee holds up his hands. "Would someone please tell me what's going on here?"

"I think we should go out," Alex says. "I think we should find neutral territory."

He pictures Switzerland, snow-capped mountains, green pastures, cows.

•

They walk on opposite sides of the pavement, as though a deadly electric current were rushing between them. It occurs to Zee that maybe Alex didn't expect him to leave. Maybe she misses him. Maybe she wants to "work it out". Well, what if he doesn't want to "work it out"? What if he's happy? What makes her think she can just show up and demand his undivided attention? What if he has other plans? It bugs him that she's assumed he didn't have other plans. What does she think he does all day? Suddenly he feels an enormous rush of adrenalin because for once, he thinks, he has the power. He's the one who left, made the decision; he's the one who will decide whether or not to return. He can bust her up, shake her up, break her down. He looks down at the slushy sidewalk, step on a crack, break your lover's back. For the first time in weeks, he feels alive.

Sitting across from her in the Mexican restaurant, listening to her complain about the shortage of vegetarian cuisine on the menu, he wonders how he could have lived with her for so long. When the food finally arrives, and she informs the waiter that it's cold, Zee wants to crawl under the table. Never mind the greenhouse effect; never mind that farmers are going broke, that people are starving. Alex's food is not piping hot. The waiter sulks audibly, then tramps off to zap Alex's food in the microwave. Satisfied that her concerns are being looked after, Alex stares down at her hand wrapped tightly around a glass of water. Zee notes that her eyebrows are pushed together, which means she is going to say something, but he's going to have to wait for it. What if he doesn't want to wait for it? Why should he sit mute, like a convicted felon awaiting his sentence from the judge? Why not wield his new-found power; employ surprise tactics? "I saw a dead man on the street today," he says cheerfully. "Or anyway he looked dead, his body jutted out at weird angles. He'd jumped off a building. Imagine doing that, having the guts to jump off a building. What if you changed your mind in mid-air?"

She stares at him, unfazed. "Why are you telling me this?"

"I just think it's interesting."

"I see." She has noted that he has lost a little weight. Maybe he ate excessively as an attack on her. He hasn't shaved, knows she hates facial hair. He's obviously avoiding the issue. She'd expected this. Even so, she resents having to be the one to table the discussion. As always, the blob waits for her to reveal her perception of the situation so that he can say it's all in her head. She watches her knuckles turn white as she grips her glass and thinks how effective it would be if it shattered. She's always wondered how they do that in the movies, shatter glasses without cutting their hands. The waiter sets her plate in front of her and stands back, waiting for her approval. "It's fine," she says. "You sure you don't want anything Zee? I'm eating now because I won't have time later."

Why, what are you doing later, he would like to ask but doesn't. He must appear not to care. She's probably not doing anything interesting; she's probably baking her muffins. Suddenly, for no justifiable reason, he feels an urge to touch her tit, not a sexual urge, he just wants to confirm that it's there, still intact, still his. He used to stand behind her while she was chopping vegetables and cup his hands over her breasts and say they were his. She used to laugh nervously, as though she wasn't sure she liked it that he thought he owned her tits. Now she'd probably belt him. "Did you know," he says, "that there are men in Nepal who make their living burning corpses? All day long, people bring bodies for disposal. The men flip the bodies, to make sure they burn evenly. The heads take longest. The men poke the heads with sticks like they're poking logs."

She appears not to hear him but slashes at her enchilada

with her fork. Obviously he wants to upset her. He is hurt and wants to hurt back. This is normal. She should have expected this.

Zee is surprised at the pleasure he feels seeing her like this: unsure, restrained. He wonders if this uncertainty on her part can be sustained, if he can get her back but keep her scared. In their first year together, they went to San Juan on a package deal. It was dirty and crowded, and they fought all the time. One night he refused to fight and sat alone in the bar while she fumed over the one-armed bandits. A man who looked pregnant, wearing a T-shirt with "I'm fat but you're ugly" written on it, told him, "The only way to satisfy women is to keep 'em scared."

"I met a guy," Zee says, "who had a body fall on his car when he was driving under a bridge. It smashed his windshield, nearly made him crash. The driver wasn't hurt but he had to crawl out from under the dead body. Can you imagine that? Having to crawl out from under a corpse? He's got a blood-stain on his leather jacket to prove it."

She shoves her plate away. "Are you trying to make me sick? What do you hope to accomplish by making me sick? Are you hoping to piss me off? You don't have to try to piss me off, Zee. You piss me off!" She stands, knocking the table. "I have to use the phone." He watches her stride to the back of the restaurant and say something to the waiter who jumps to attention and points down some stairs. When she disappears from view, Zee stares out the window, wondering who she's phoning. Probably someone at work. Maybe that's what she's doing later, looking after some abused teenager. He wishes he had his pipe or even a cigarette. Maybe he'll ask the waiter, he needs to use the can anyway.

Alex is phoning Michael now because if she doesn't do it now, she never will. She'll never be angry enough. She'll get soppy and sentimental about Zee and won't do it. She reaches Michael immediately because he has given her the number for his private line. "Michael, it's Alex."

"Alex, how great to hear from you. How are you?"

"Are you doing anything later?"

"How much later?"

"I don't know. I just thought maybe we could get together for a drink or something."

"Ummm ..."

"If it's a problem, forget about it."

"No, no I just ahh ... where do you want to meet?"

"Anywhere, wherever you're comfortable."

He hesitates. "Well, I'd prefer to be out of this neighbour-hood."

"Of course."

"Why don't I come down to where you are? I like it down there."

"Sure, how about Dini's. I'm sure no one will recognize you there."

She gives him directions, hangs up and clings to the phone because she feels physically ill suddenly, lost suddenly, cut adrift. She realizes that she never really expected Zee and her to end, never believed it could end.

While urinating, Zee stares at the graffiti. *The best pussy in town call 283-1010.* He wonders what would happen if he called the number and asked for the best pussy in town. Who would answer, a man sounding like Marlon Brando, threatening to kill him? *Suck my cock,* it says on the wall. It occurs to him that people must carry felt pens specifically to mark up washrooms. As Alex would say, what are they hoping to accomplish by marking up washrooms? Do they think someone will read what they write and that it'll change their lives, force them to confront their homosexual tendencies? Outside the washroom he studies a sombrero nailed to the stuccoed wall because he's in no hurry to get back to Alex. He pictures her, legs crossed, staring out the window, flexing and unflexing her foot. He really doesn't know what to do, he really doesn't know what he wants. He wants to want nothing.

Back at the table, Alex has her jacket on and is settling the bill. He doesn't want her to leave. "You don't want a coffee?" he asks, disgusted by his feeble tone.

"No, I should get going. I just want to set up a time for you to come and pick up your things."

"You didn't eat your enchilada."

"When can you pick up your stuff?"

He used to call her buttercup. Hard to believe. "Whenever you want."

"Good, how about tomorrow?" She zips her bag shut.

"Sure."

"I'd prefer not to be there, can you do it during the day?"

"Sure."

Although he isn't sure.

What if you jump off a building and change your mind in mid-air?

Like an earthquake, it is all over in seconds. He stands alone, staring at her mutilated enchilada, waiting for his world to settle.

FIFTEEN

When she first steps into Dini's, she can't see Michael and panics, thinking that she is going to have to wait, alone, in this seedy bar. But when her eyes adjust to the dim lighting, she spots him at a corner table, studying a newspaper. As she approaches, he looks up and smiles warmly.

"I'm so glad you're here," she says.

He stands and helps her off with her jacket. "Why wouldn't I be?"

"I don't know. Usually I have to wait for people."

"Not for me. What'll you have, brandy?"

"That's a nice idea."

"I'll have to get it, there's no table service."

She watches him walk to the bar and admires his clean stride. While giving the order to the bartender, he stands very straight; no slouch here, she thinks, a man in tune with his mind and body, meeting life head-on, in spite of being short and bald. She has tried to make Zee stand straight, but he resists, even though she has warned him that he is developing a hump. Occasionally his back rebels and goes into spasm, forcing him to lie on the floor with pillows under his knees. The warning signs are there, but he doesn't heed them. He will fumble into old age, stooped, smoking his pipe, wearing a ratty cardigan with sagging pockets containing matches, bits of paper and crumpled Kleenex. Where is he now, she wonders, what is he feeling? Is he feeling? He's probably sitting watching TV with Daisy, stuffing his face with chocolate-coated Oreos.

Michael sets the drinks on the table. "Laura's volunteering at the museum so we can take our time. I wouldn't mind getting pissed, to tell you the truth. It's been awhile. And I can't think of better company to get pissed with. Have you eaten?"

She reaches for her drink. "Yeah."

"Good. So you can handle a shot or two?"

"No problem."

He studies her. "You look harried. Is the single life not agreeing with you?"

"Something like that."

He nods grimly. "I've been feeling pretty single myself these days."

"Laura isn't improving?"

He slides his glass around on the table. "No, she might have to be hospitalized." He stops moving the glass and stares at it. "It's gruesome. You don't want to hear about it."

She folds her hands on the table. "I do if you want to talk about it."

"You sound like a social worker."

"I'm serious."

"I don't want to talk about it."

"Okay."

During the second brandy, she asks if he has ever been unfaithful to his wife. He shakes his head. "You're the first person I've ever thought about it with," he says. "I mean, it had never occurred to me before. I just haven't been interested."

"How long have you been married?"

"Eleven years. I still love her, I mean I can't imagine life without her. I just hate what's happening to her, and there's not a damn thing I can do about it. When she sees me, she looks like she's afraid I'm going to hit her." He leans his forearms on the table and hunches his shoulders. "We never have sex anymore. Not that I want to when she's in this condition. But it's hard for me. I know this sounds coarse, but I need it a couple of times a week. I can't help it. I'm just a guy like any other."

It seems to Alex that Michael is the perfect sperm donor. He needs it a couple of times a week; he wants her; he doesn't want to end his marriage, has been monogamous, which means he is unlikely to have AIDS, and has healthy children, which means his sperm is functional.

He leans back in his chair and slides his hands into his pants pockets. "She was unfaithful to me once. Some college friend of hers was staying with us until he got settled. I didn't mind, he seemed nice enough. I didn't realize what was going on until she told me after he left. I wondered why she told me. I would have preferred not to know."

"Did you ask her why she slept with him?"

"Oh sure. She said she felt that I was overbearing, that she was losing her sense of self and that this guy helped her get it back." He rubs his eyes with his fingers. "The worst part about it—the part that really got to me—was they fucked in my sheets. She didn't change them." He shakes his head. "I found that hard to take."

"Understandably," Alex says. "What was the guy like?" She hopes he will say introverted, unlikely to sleep around on a regular basis, very unlikely to be a drug addict, very unlikely to be HIV positive.

"Very ordinary, I thought. Not her type. Although I'm not exactly what she calls her type either."

"What's her type?"

"She says she likes dark men with lots of hair and olive complexions." He crosses an ankle over his knee. "I don't think I'm overbearing. Do you? I would love her to take charge of things, but she vacillates like crazy, and when you have kids, you have to make decisions." He clasps his hands behind his head. "She wanted them. I didn't feel strongly one way or the other. Now it's as though they belong to someone else but happen to live in our house. They spend all their time with their Filipino nanny. My little girl speaks with a Filipino accent." He tries to laugh then drinks his brandy.

Aside from Zee pissing her off, Alex has invited Michael here tonight because, according to her kit, she is ovulating. When she dipped the litmus paper into her urine sample at six this morning, it turned aquamarine, meaning she has twenty-four hours to fertilize an egg. It is now eight-thirty. She has nine and a half hours left. She grips the edge of the table, wondering how she can get him to ejaculate inside her; how she can make him think she desires him when, not long ago, she implied that she didn't.

"You look thoughtful," he says.

"I'm just listening."

"You're good at that. I talk a blue streak then later wonder what was going through your head while I told you my woes." He scratches his nose. "You'd tell me if you thought I was an asshole wouldn't you?"

"I would." Two young men wearing jeans, work-boots and crewcuts pass their table on their way to the john. "Last night," the shorter one says, "I saw this movie where they made this guy sit on a razor blade."

Michael leans his elbows on the table, his chin in his hands, and stares at her. "What's going on in that head of yours?"

"I was just thinking about how much I miss physical contact."

He blinks and sits back in his chair. "Do you mean ... physical or sexual contact?"

"Both."

He swills the brandy around in his glass. "I know what you mean."

"Maybe you and I should try to give each other that."

He looks worried. "What?"

"Physical contact."

"Does that include sexual contact?"

"Why not? I mean, neither of us has any illusions about it. We can just enjoy it for what it is. You can stay married, and I can stay single."

"Interesting idea." He crosses his legs and looks down at his argyle socks. "But I thought you didn't feel that way about me."

"Not while I was with Zee."

Michael rotates his ankle one way then the other.

"I'm still on the pill," she says. "So it would be easy."

He flexes his foot. "You surprise me."

"Why?"

"Well, for one thing I wouldn't have thought you were the type of woman to be on the pill. Secondly, I wouldn't have thought you were the kind of woman who could treat sex lightly."

She sits on her hands. "I'm not treating it lightly. I miss it. It's a human need, and I don't see why, since we both miss it, we shouldn't partake of it with each other."

He grimaces and nods. "Seems logical."

She can tell that she has blown it; that she has become sullied in his eyes. Zee has told her that men enjoy the "chase"; that once the conquest has been made, and the woman is no longer mysterious, the excitement goes out of it. Mel has told her that men don't want women who sleep with them on the first date; that men don't want women who are too aggressive, or too desperate. Alex realizes that she has been all these things with Michael. "It was just an idea," she says. "Forget about it."

"No, don't say that. It's a nice idea, just let me think about it." He reaches for her hand across the table and squeezes it. She feels like a charity case.

She pulls her hand away. "I'm tired. I'm going to head home."

"Have you got your car? Are you okay to drive?"

"Oh, yeah." She stands and feels around in her bag for her wallet.

"I'll get this," he says, then grabs her wrist and looks up at her. "I've upset you."

"No, it was a stupid idea."

He lowers his voice. "I don't think it's a stupid idea. It's just a bit sudden. I'd just like a little time to think it over. It's not something I do every day."

"Why did you want to do it before?"

He glances nervously around the room. "I wanted to, that doesn't mean I would have."

"I see."

"You're mad at me."

"I'm not. I'm not. Michael, please let go of my arm."

"I've offended you."

"Forget it, can you just forget it!" Bloated faces turn from the bar to gaze at her. She jerks her arm from his grasp, grabs her jacket and begins what feels like a moon walk to the door.

"Nice ass," one of the crewcut boys calls after her.

Outside, it's snowing again. "Jesus fucking christ," she mutters, knowing that her tires will spin, her car will swerve, and she will have a head-on collision with a snow plough.

"Fine, that's just fine." With large swooping motions, she brushes snow from her windshield. It is only when she inserts the key in the door that she notices the flat tire. "I can't believe this."

Michael, panting, halts beside her. "Have you got an auto association membership? There must be a pay-phone around here somewhere."

She snatches the key from the lock. "I'll deal with it in the morning."

"Can you leave it here?"

"I don't care." She begins to trudge across the park; Zee's park, Zee's hangout. She wants to kill him for making her go through this; kill him like a kosher cow, hang him upside down and slit his throat, let the blood drain out of him.

Michael grabs her arm. "Alex, wait." She plods on, head bowed against the wind. Michael hooks his foot through her legs and trips her. She falls face down in the snow. He drops down beside her. "Bug off!" she says, jabbing at him with her fist.

He grabs her wrist. "Alex, I want to fuck you," he says hoarsely, "very, very much." He pulls off her mitten, slides her hand inside his coat and holds it against his groin. It feels hard and hot. "Believe me, I want to fuck you."

The question in her mind becomes how to get him to penetrate before she gets frost-bite. "Then let's do it," she says.

"What? Here?"

"Why not? It's pretty. Nobody's around." She begins to rub his genitalia, feels around for his fly.

"You're crazy," he mutters, barely audibly and lies back in the snow. "My ears are freezing," he says. She licks them, nibbles them, blows into them. He unzips her jacket. She pushes his hand down her pants. "You've got jeans on," he says. "How are we supposed to …?"

She unbuttons his coat, spreads it open around him, lies on it and pulls one leg completely free of her jeans, then, kneeling over him, she pulls his penis out of his pants and inserts it inside her. It feels strange, narrower than Zee's, she can't quite get a grip on it. Worried that it will slip out, she tightens the walls of her vagina and slides up and down on his penis in what she hopes is a stimulating manner.

"You're out of your fucking mind," he groans.

She pictures the magnified sperm from the documentary on the human reproductive system.

Please, God, don't let him have lazy sperm.

Abruptly he rolls her onto her back. The snow stings her bum but he doesn't take long to ejaculate. He jolts into her and moans, arching back, then collapses over her. When she feels his penis soften, she gently nudges him. "I'm having trouble breathing here, Mike."

"Oh, sorry."

"That's okay. Also my ass is numb."

"Oh, of course. I'm sorry."

"That's okay."

He sits up and helps pull up her pants. She helps pull up his. They stand, button and zip their coats and stare at the shapes they've made in the snow.

"Not quite an angel, is it?" he says.

SIXTEEN

Standing on his head, Zee wonders how long it would take for his brain to explode. Surely all the blood and fluids would drain into it and bust the skull open like an overripe cantaloupe. Interesting that no one tries to kill themselves by standing on their head. Aside from the brain exploding, you'd think you could easily snap your neck by toppling to one side.

He hears Jenny knocking on his door again. "Zee, I know you're in there." He feels as though his cheeks are about to squash down on his eyeballs. Soon, he imagines, the flab around his waist will slide down his chest onto his face and smother him.

"Mom won't come out of her room," Jenny says. "Durham keeps calling from work, he's really upset."

On "Oprah" today they were discussing lipo-suction. Zee thinks it's unfortunate that some women get gangrene from it, but on the other hand, how wonderful it must be to suck out fat. He hopes that, in future, more vacuum devices will be designed to suck out other unwanted substances from our bodies: kidney stones, cancer, parts of our brains.

Jenny slams the flat of her hand against the door. "Zee, quit acting like the superior older brother." He hears her pacing.

"Okay, maybe we made a mistake. But she had to know some time. She'll get over it."

"Then leave her in her room."

"She's been in there for eight hours. She's not even eating the food I bring her."

"Maybe she escaped through the window."

"Very funny."

He smiles, picturing Daisy trying to squeeze her bulk through the upstairs window. He drops his feet to the floor, kneels and sits back on his heels. Dark red spots dance before his eyes as the blood rushes from his head.

"She won't talk to me," Jenny says. "It's like she blames me because he's gay. I told her I had nothing to do with it. I just thought she should know about it. I mean I think one of our problems as a family is we aren't honest with each other."

Why be honest? He sees absolutely no reason for being honest. It doesn't make you feel good, it makes you feel bad because people hate you.

"Zee, please come out," she pleads, sounding like the little girl on the ad seeking donations for Muscular Dystrophy research. "Please help us," the little girl says while strapped to a wheelchair. He wonders how many times she had to repeat "Please help us" to the camera before they called it a day.

"Zee ...?"

"Okay, I'm coming."

She stands back as he opens the door, shoves her hands in her jeans pockets and stares at him. He leans an elbow against the door-jamb and rests his temple on his hand. "It's none of my business, really," he says, "but it seems to me that none of this is your business really, and that if you'd minded your own business in the first place, Daisy would not be cloistered in her room right now."

She crosses her arms. "Great, so now you're blaming me too."

"Who else? Durham would not have opened his mouth. It is not in his nature. He could have invited his pal for Christmas and said they were boy scouts together, Daisy wouldn't have known the difference." He walks down the hall towards Daisy's room. Jenny scurries after him. "Don't you ever get sick of turning your back on everything?" she says. "Whenever something doesn't work out the way you want it to, you just close off. That may be easy for you, but some of us want to communicate. You'd just as soon we all dropped dead." Ignoring her, he knocks on Daisy's door. Jenny hooks her hair behind her ears. "You just think you're so fucking smart. I bet Alex ditched you because she figured you out, Mr. Walk-away-from-it-all, Mr. Never-give-a-shit-about-anybody-but-himself." He holds his index finger against his lips then knocks again. Jenny prods his shoulder. "You make me puke, to tell you the honest truth."

He raises his eyebrows. "The honest truth?"

"There you go with that superior tone again." She tries to kick him, but he blocks her.

"Jenny, don't get excited."

"Don't have feelings is what you mean. You stink."

Zee presses his ear to Daisy's door. "Ma, we know you can hear this stimulating conversation. Why don't you come out and join us?"

"You were supposed to be our big brother," Jenny says. "But all you did was jerk off in your room. You think I don't know that? You were too scared to actually try it with a girl so you whacked off in your room. I know that. And when I had to have an abortion, you acted like I was dirt, like I was some slut. You were just jealous because you'd never done it with anybody. Nobody would've touched you with a ten-foot pole. You were an ugly, zit-faced dork!"

"Shut up, the two of you!" Daisy shouts from behind

the door.

"Oh, good. Signs of life," Zee says. "Don't you want to come out and play?"

"I'm leaving, Mother," Jenny says, "since you obviously don't want to talk to me."

"I don't want to talk to anybody," Daisy declares.

"Fine, just starve to death for all I care. Here I am trying to pull this family together, and all I get is shit on."

"Bye, Jenny," Zee says.

"Go fuck yourself."

"I think I will. According to you I'm quite good at it."

She stomps down the stairs in her cowboy boots. "You make me sick."

"I'm sorry about that."

"You're not sorry about anything!" Jenny screams. "You're just one big selfish prick!"

"Say goodnight, Jenny."

"Shut up!"

He hears her march to the front door, open and slam it. He scratches on Daisy's door. "She's gone, Mum."

"You're a horrible brother."

"*Gone With the Wind* is playing at the Review. I thought you might like to see it. It's the new one, you know. They polished it up so it looks brand new."

"Why are you so mean to her?"

"She doesn't take responsibility for her actions."

"You're grown up. You shouldn't act like that."

"She's grown up too," he says and stares at the door. "Are you coming out? The movie's at seven. I thought maybe we could grab a bite to eat first."

"I don't know what I did wrong," Daisy moans. "I did something wrong, and I don't know what it is. You've all turned out so strange. I don't know what I did." He hears huffing and puffing and nose blowing and realizes that she's crying. "Maybe if you'd had a father, I don't know."

Zee sighs heavily, slides down the door and leans against it. He looks around at the fading, textured wallpaper that would be impossible to paint over and consequently has been left untouched since he was a boy. He hears movement behind the door. "What do they do together?" Daisy asks. "Two men. Zee ...?"

Zee rubs his face with his hands. "I think pretty much what men and women do together only they utilize different orifices."

Silence. Zee stretches his legs in front of him and crosses his ankles.

"It's a shame," Daisy says.

"I don't think they see it that way. I think for them it feels quite natural. I think for Durham it feels quite natural. He's not a rapist, Ma, or a child molester. He just prefers men to women."

Silence. He pulls off his sock and examines his wart, trying to determine if it's getting any bigger.

"Was he always like that?" Daisy asks.

"Most homosexuals claim that it's genetic."

"Nobody in my family was like that."

"Well, maybe dear old Dad had a few in his family."

Silence. Zee puts his sock back on.

"Are you going to apologize to her?" Daisy asks.

"Who?"

"You know who."

"Why should I?"

"Because she was only trying to help."

"I think she's tactless."

"Even so, you should be nicer to her. You're older and smarter than she is. You take advantage of that. She just wants you to like her a little."

"Well then she shouldn't do stupid things."

"Everybody makes mistakes," Daisy says. "Anyway, to be honest with you, I'm glad I know. I'd hate to spend the rest of my life wondering when he's going to get a girlfriend. So your sister did the right thing. I think you should tell her." Silence. Zee gazes down at the flab around his middle, grabs and squeezes it. "You tell her she did the right thing," Daisy says, "and I'll go to the movies with you."

"Oh, some sacrifice, Ma."

"That's the deal."

"Okay, I'll tell her."

Daisy cries when Rhett tells Scarlett he doesn't give a damn. Afterwards they go to the Donut King. Daisy dips her Cinnamon Twist in her coffee. "I never did like that ending. You know when she talks to herself about Tara. It never seemed real to me." Daintily, she bites into the soaked donut.

"What wasn't real about it?"

"The way she talked to herself."

"I talk to myself." Zee bites his French Twist.

"Yeah, but it was the way she did it. So hopeful and everything. You wouldn't be so hopeful after something like that."

"Like what?" Zee wipes sugar from his mouth.

"The love of your life walking out on you."

"She hopes to get him back."

"You wouldn't hope that right then. You couldn't."

"Why not?"

"Because you feel like nobody wants you." She dips her donut back into the coffee. "There she was with this big grin on her face. I never believed it. It wasn't like that in the book."

"What was it like in the book?"

"I can't remember. But it wasn't like that."

Zee realizes this is the closest his mother has ever come to revealing how she felt after his father's departure.

"Why don't they make men like Clark Gable anymore?" she asks. "They're all dirty now, in the movies. They look like they never wash. And you can't understand what they're saying. Why don't they speak clearly? Except Tom Selleck. I like him."

Daisy pops the rest of her donut in her mouth, bunches up the wax paper and stuffs it in an ashtray. "I don't know how I'm going to look him in the face."

"He's the same Durham. Just look at him like you've always looked at him."

"To be honest with you, it makes me queasy. The whole idea."

Zee turns on his stool to face her. "You've always said all you wanted was for us to be happy, right?" She nods. "Well, I think he's as happy as anybody."

She runs her fingers along the edge of the counter as though checking for dirt. "I guess I'll just have to get used to it." She shakes her head. "I don't know how I'm ever going to have grandchildren with you three." She finds a Kleenex in her purse, blows her nose then wipes it. "Are you going to tell me what happened between you and Alex the other night?"

"Nothing happened. Everything's as it was."

She stares at him, wiping her nose. "She was ready to make up, I had a feeling."

"No she wasn't."

She stares at him.

"Ma, you've got sugar on your chin."

She wipes her chin with the Kleenex. "Jenny's right about you not communicating. How's anybody supposed to know what you're feeling?"

"What does it matter what I'm feeling? How does what I'm feeling affect you? Why do we have to run around telling

155

each other how we feel all the time? It doesn't change anything. It only hurts people if your feelings don't happen to be
the feelings they want you to be feeling." He frowns at the
sugar dispenser.

Daisy bunches up her Kleenex and stuffs it in the ashtray.
"People that love you want to know how you feel."

"You want to know how I feel?" Zee says. "I feel canned.
Like a vegetable that was once alive then got boiled and sealed
in a can. A beet. I feel like a canned beet." Daisy's eyes shift
away from him and wander towards the donuts lined up on
shelves. "Do you feel any better now, Ma, knowing how I feel?
Or are you just worried that I'm losing my mind? Wouldn't
you have preferred not to know that I feel like a canned beet?"

She shakes her head and pulls another Kleenex from her
purse. "The three of you, you break my heart."

"There, you see? What did I tell you? You were happier
when you didn't know my feelings." She stares down at the
rumpled Kleenex in her hand and shakes her head. "Oh come
on, Mum. I was only kidding. I feel fine. Dandy. Really. Let's
head home, alright?" He hops off his stool and holds up her
coat. Slowly, like a child who has been scolded and has no
fight left in her, Daisy stands and slides her arms into the coat.

"Remember, Mum, when I was little, I wanted Elvis'
'Hound Dog' record, but I didn't ask you for it because I knew
you were short of cash? Remember how you went out and
bought it for me?"

She nods. "It had 'Don't Be Cruel' on the other side. That
was your favourite. You played it over and over."

"The point is, I didn't have to ask you for it. Somehow you
knew I desperately wanted that record. That's the best kind of
communication, when you don't have to say anything. You
just know." He ties her scarf around her neck and reaches for
his overcoat.

"What kind of coat is that?" she says. "It looks too big for you."

"That's the style, Ma."

"The wind goes right through it, I have a feeling."

"It's okay."

"You'll catch cold."

For the first time in his adult life, he feels lucky to have a mother. Someone who cares enough to scold him, forgive him, help him up off the floor after the crowd has moved on. He holds the door open for her and watches her wobble into the night.

"Do the buttons up at least," she says.

SEVENTEEN

Larry sends the tow-truck out to retrieve Alex's car then asks her if she wants a coffee. She says yes before realizing that he has to run across the street to get it. Waiting for him to return, she studies the poster of the pouting, large-breasted girl in the hot-pink bikini. It amazes her that men are aroused by photos of naked women. Her brother Nick used to masturbate while looking at porno magazines. She knows this because she caught him at it one evening when she went into his room to look for an eraser. He pulled the covers up to his chin and tried to look like he'd dozed off. She wonders why she doesn't look at photos of naked men when she masturbates. Probably because she knows the naked men would have big cocks and muscles but no brains. The man who satisfies her in her fantasies has a big cock and muscles but no face. She prefers it that way.

This morning Michael phoned her in the middle of a counselling session with a teen mother. The young woman was worried about a cold sore on her lip, believing that it was affecting her brain because she'd seen a news item on TV about a man who had herpes that affected his short-term memory. Alex had asked Michael if she could call him back, but he didn't think she'd be able to reach him. He said he just wanted to know that she was alright.

"I'm alright," she'd said.

"That was strange last night."

"Yeah." Alex watched the girl gingerly touch her cold sore.

"I hope you don't regret it," Michael said.

"Not at all."

"Maybe we can do it again some time, in less harsh conditions."

She'd laughed politely and said that she thought that maybe they could some time.

But, for the moment, she doesn't want to see him again. She wants to see if the sperm swimming around inside her will latch onto her egg. She pictures the egg, dark and bumpy as the egg had looked magnified in the TV documentary. She hadn't liked the look of it, or of the ovaries for that matter. It disturbed her that, when magnified, the organs inside her looked like deep-sea creatures.

Larry pushes open the glass door and hands her a coffee. "I forgot to ask what you take in it so I guessed just cream."

"You were right."

He smiles a little, sits on a stool by the service counter and pries open his styrofoam cup. She does the same and takes a sip. He stares out the window at the gas pumps.

"Slow day today?" she asks.

"Yeah but I'm not complaining." He massages the back of his neck. Uncomfortable in the silence, she pulls out her day-timer and pretends to study it.

"You married?" he asks.

"No. Why?"

"You look married."

"Why?"

He shrugs and pulls on his beard. She hates facial hair because it provides a trap for food particles, because it feels rough and because she feels men hide behind it. If she were his girlfriend she would ask him to shave it off. "Are you married?" she asks.

"No. Not even close." He picks a pen up off the service counter and begins scribbling on a pad. He really does have nice legs, she thinks. Strong thighs. It looks like he might have a little extra weight around his middle, but what man over thirty doesn't?

"Do you think my car's a lemon?" she asks. "I mean with all these things going wrong with it?"

"Hard to say. Usually if it's a real shitbox they start costing you in the second year."

She nods, pondering, trying to think of something else to say. "Do you have a car?"

He points to a hatchback in the lot. "Cost me seventy bucks."

"You're kidding?"

"It needs a new clutch, though." He stares at the car.

"I would have thought you'd have a fancier car."

He looks at her. "Why?"

"I don't know. You're a mechanic, you're into cars."

"So long as they go, I'm happy." He pulls on his beard.

She wonders what he spends his money on. He must have money. Maybe he's a drug addict.

"Here comes the tow," he says and goes outside.

•

Twenty minutes later he returns to the service area. "It was a screw, lodged in the outer wall. It's a tough place to patch but I think it'll be okay."

"So I don't need a new tire?"

"Not for now."

She stands. "Great, what do I owe you?"

"No charge." He stares at the counter and massages his neck.

"You're kidding?"

"I don't charge my customers for fixing their tires."

"Great ... okay, well that's ..." She backs towards the door, adjusting her bag on her shoulder. "Well, I guess I better get going before you change your mind."

"Bon voyage."

"Thanks for the coffee."

"My pleasure."

•

While strapping herself into the Mazda, she thinks it's perverse that she should be attracted to one man's legs while incubating another man's sperm. She wonders if Larry has a good sperm count. He should. She hasn't seen him smoking, and he's a good age for procreating. Maybe if Michael's sperm can't capture her egg, she'll try Larry's. She could invite him out for a beer, fondle him under the table then slap his face and run out into the night. That should get him excited.

In her early twenties, she believed she would meet the right man. They would buy a pretty brick house, rip out the old walls and bang up new ones. They'd sand its hardwood floors and install skylights. They'd have Mexican tiles laid in the bathroom and a deck built out back. In her early twenties, things were going to be good.

Now she's seducing strangers for their sperm.

She doesn't even like babies. Not really. Doesn't like their mushy, soggy, smelly bodies.

If she were a decent human being, she would adopt a little brown child without a future. But no, it has to be her baby, sprung from her loins. This is selfish, she tells herself, why does it have to be her baby? Because she wants to remake herself? Take another shot at it? See if she can make her child into a better person than herself? Why does it have to be hers? What about the starving children? Why create life when those already living lie exposed in the mud, with bloated bellies and flies on their faces?

She doesn't know. She really doesn't know.

•

While completing her muffin invoicing, Alex listens to Mike Wallace report that, in the United States, millions of children suffer from malnutrition. Millions of children eat macaroni twice a day, every day of their lives. Alex glances at the screen showing two frail little boys in an unfurnished living-room, staring up at a commercial on TV that shows, in close-up, slabs of charbroiled beef, steaming baked potatoes dolloped with sour cream, carrots dripping with butter. Alex can't imagine how the little boys must feel watching commercials abundant with food they can't have. They must feel desperate, betrayed, forgotten, hungry. She hears knocking on the door and doesn't move but stares at it, thinking it must be someone trying to sell her something. Nobody drops in on her without calling first. Unless it's Zee coming to apologize for acting like an asshole. The knocking persists. When she opens the door Jenny smiles at her tentatively. "Hi, Alex."

"Hi," Alex says, wondering what this is about. Has Zee sent his little sister to spy for him?

Jenny hops up and down and flaps her arms. "Holy moses, it's cold."

"What can I do for you, Jenny?"

Jenny stops hopping and stuffs her hands into the pockets

of her jean jacket. "Well, actually, I know this is kind of weird because you split up with Zee and everything, but I really wanted to invite you to my show so I thought, what the hell, I'd give you the tickets, and you can do what you want with them."

Alex notices that Jenny's eyes are red. She's either been crying or smoking dope. "That's very nice of you."

Jenny hands her a pair of tickets. "It's not really your style, but you might find it interesting."

"Thanks, I'll try to make it."

Jenny looks down at her salt-stained cowboy boots. "This weather's ruining my boots."

Alex knows that if she doesn't invite Jenny in from the cold, she will feel guilty for the rest of the night. "Would you like to come in?"

"Well, not if you're doing anything."

"That's alright." Alex steps back into the apartment, turns off the TV and goes to the kitchen to put the kettle on. Jenny follows her and stands in the kitchen doorway, bouncing on the balls of her feet. "I hope you don't mind me coming over. It's just that I don't believe because you broke up with my brother, we can't be friends." She hooks her hair behind her ears. "I mean, I've always liked you a lot."

Alex attempts to smile reassuringly then drops tea bags into the pot. "How's your mum?"

"Oh, she's fine. Fat. I swear to god, one of these days she won't be able to get out of bed, she'll be so huge."

"How's Durham?"

"Oh, he's fine." She slides her hands into her back pockets. "Well, to be honest with you, things are a bit weird right now, since he came out."

"I thought he already had come out."

"Yeah, but Mom didn't know. He just told her. She's

really upset. She won't come out of her room."

"Why did he tell her?"

"He just thought it was time." Jenny wanders into the living-room and leans on the bookshelves. "Why? Don't you think he should have told her? I mean, now he can be honest with her. Before he really loved her, but he hardly ever saw her because he felt so uncomfortable about it."

"Do you think he'll feel more comfortable about it now?"

"Well sure, I mean, it might take awhile."

"Do you think she'll ever understand it?"

"I don't know." Jenny stares at the floor and nudges the base of the bookshelves with her cowboy boot. "I still think he did the right thing."

Alex pours boiling water into the teapot. "Where was Zee during all this?"

"Oh he was there. He threw a fit."

"A fit?"

"Well yeah. He didn't think we should've told her."

"We?" Alex stares at her.

"Durham." Jenny hooks her hair behind her ears. "I'm not saying I wasn't behind him on it, but it was his decision."

Alex carries the teapot and cups into the living-room, sets them on the end-table then sits on the couch. Jenny squats on Zee's beanbag chair. "I didn't force him to do it," she says. "Zee's acting like it's all my fault. Whenever I try to bring the family together he gives me a hard time." She watches Alex pour the tea. "All three of them drive me crazy. They never deal with anything. Durham just says I'm over-sensitive, and Mom refuses to talk about anything real." She rests her chin on her knee and pulls at the tassels on the fake Persian carpet. "I just wish I didn't care. I mean I wish I could just forget about them. I had my cards read the other day, and they said that family will always be important to me, and it's true." Alex hands her a cup. Jenny holds it with both hands and sips. "I just wish Zee wouldn't do his superior-older-brother number. I happen to know that it's a power thing. He gets off on pushing me around. I guess I'm stupid to put up with it. It's like with Damian, he started to do the same kind of number on me, you know, where they treat you like shit so you'll feel like shit. They're just scared of women. In fifty years, it will be a matriarchal society. It's inevitable. They just want to keep us down."

"I don't think that's why Zee does it."

"So why then?"

"I think both of you have always had big ideas about what you were going to do in life. He thought you could never pull it off. Now he's thinking that maybe he can't pull it off, and you're singing in a rock band."

"You think he's jealous?"

"Not jealous exactly, just really scared he's not going to be what he wanted to be."

"So he takes it out on me." Jenny wraps her arms around her knees and rests her forehead against them. "He told me Dave's getting married."

"He is married. He asked us to go to his wedding."

"You didn't go?"

Alex shakes her head. "But he called last week and invited us to go to his housewarming so I think maybe I'll put in an appearance there. It seems rude otherwise. I couldn't bear to tell him we've split, so I'll just say Zee couldn't make it."

Jenny looks up at her. "Tell me what his wife is like, okay?"

"Okay."

"I still dream about him, you know. These really erotic dreams where he's doing it to me in all these really weird positions that I know in real life would hurt. But in the dream it's great. Then I wake up and miss him. The sex part. The rest of it was a write-off."

Alex rolls onto her side and rests her temple against her hand. "What about Damian?"

"I came up with the beginning of a song about him, it goes: My passion for you was a bonfire, now it's a flickering candle. If you piss on it, it will go out."

"Interesting metaphor."

Alex had a relationship once that was based on sex. She had no interest in the world outside their bedroom. Her body felt incomplete unless pinned to his. On the good days he craved her as much she did him, but later when he began using phrases like, "I need space," and "We should get out more," and "I hate routines," she pleaded for his attention and, when it was not returned, hungered for it even more. Finally she could stand herself no longer. He didn't try to stop her from leaving although, when they embraced, there were tears in his eyes, and she knew that if he'd asked her to, she would have stayed.

She and Zee didn't make a conscious decision to stop having sex. Just gradually, it became too much of an effort to bypass the block between them. She'd never felt a strong sexual attraction for him anyway but understood that this was not essential to their relationship. On the other hand, like everything in her life, she thought it was something you could work on. You couldn't expect it to be easy, you had to persist. To some extent this was true. They developed a rhythm, a system that satisfied them both, a comfort zone. Zee pointed out that they made "caring" rather than "erotic" love. But eventually he stopped initiating sex, and when she asked him about it, he said he always felt that she was doing it for his benefit, that she didn't seem to enjoy it very much. He began to make sarcastic comments about women and sex; said they didn't like it, used sex as a tool to lure men into the "cave". She suspected that he was making these uncharacteristically chauvinistic comments because he felt undesired. But she couldn't fake desire. When she asked him how he felt about their non-existent sex life he denied that it bothered him; insisted that their relationship was "not about that". "We're best friends," he'd said. "We don't want to jump on each other's bones because there's no mystery between us. Maybe, deep down, we're too much alike. I don't see this as a problem. It's just different. But every time we talk about it, it makes it into a problem, it becomes a head thing. Sex shouldn't be a head thing."

So she stopped talking about it, and they stopped having sex.

She suspects that her declining sexual interest was a result of her declining respect for him. She'd waited for him to pull out of his slump, get on with his life, quit licking his wounds. She hadn't expected him to fight his enemies, just to get up off the floor and walk away from them.

Jenny hooks her hair behind her ears. "You know what really bugs me about men?"

"What?"

"Is how whenever something goes wrong in a relationship, they don't want to fix it. They just want to move on and stick their wickies into somebody new."

Alex scratches her head. "I don't think they're all like that."

"They get bored so easily. It's like if you want to keep one you have to be acting all the time so they don't know what to expect. They hate it when they think they know everything about you." She licks her thumb and rubs dirt off the steel toes of her cowboy boots. "I mean, there's no way you can know everything about a person. They're just too lazy to keep looking. They make me puke, to tell you the honest truth."

After Jenny leaves, Alex lies in the bath wondering if the tiredness she's feeling is due to pregnancy. She tells herself not to think about it, not to expect anything, remembering Mel's story about a woman who couldn't conceive and finally adopted a little black baby then, a year later, did conceive. The baby was born blind and deformed. Now the woman has to insert contact lenses into the baby's eyes so that he can at least see the outlines of things. "Imagine trying to insert contact lenses into a baby's eyes," Mel had said.

Alex took Marika and her baby to the hospital today. He was running a high fever and couldn't bend his neck. The doctors diagnosed viral meningitis and said there was nothing they could do but wait and see if he pulled out of it. They explained that a virus isn't something they can see under a microscope, like bacteria. Bacteria they can fight with antibiotics but a virus has to run its course. Marika slammed her hand into the wall and told them they were fucking useless. Alex wrapped an arm around her and led her to the waiting area. They sat in silence listening to the calls over the hospital PA system. She bought Marika a Coke and a bag of potato chips and told her she had to get back to the Centre. Marika, pale and listless, only nodded and stared at a little girl in a hospital gown shuffling like an old woman down the hall, connected to an IV unit pulled by a nurse trailing her. "I need a smoke," Marika muttered and went outside. Alex followed, trying to think of something encouraging to say. As if reading her thoughts, Marika shrugged. "I just have to wait and see." Alex knows that she, herself, would not have patience like this. She would pester hospital staff, hover over her baby's bed, study his chart, insist that she be allowed to stay by his side night and day. To what end, she wonders. Marika is probably smarter to just wait and see.

Zee often says, "We'll just have to wait and see." This irritates her because it implies that they can do nothing but wait and allow some unexplained force to control their lives. "How can you live like that?" she asks him. "You wait and see long enough, and suddenly your life is over."

When the phone rings, she reluctantly gets out of the bath, wraps herself in her robe and answers it, hoping it isn't Michael. It's Abby. "Lucas died yesterday," she says. Suddenly without breath, Alex tries to think of something appropriate to say. "It was really sudden," Abby continues. "He told me he didn't want to live like that anymore. The doctors say he let himself die. They'd expected him to last another couple of months."

"I'm really sorry, Abby."

"He didn't want any fuss so I'm just calling his friends to let them know."

"I'm glad you did ... I mean ..."

"He's got this Eskimo sculpture he's been wanting to give you. A walrus or something. I'll try and drop it off to you. It would cost a fortune to mail."

"Or I could pick it up."

"No, I'll drop it off at some point. Anyway, I've got a number of other calls to make so I'll let you go."

"Of course."

"Have a good Christmas."

"Thanks. You too," Alex says, before realizing how tactless this sounds. She hangs up, pulls her knees into her chest and wraps her hands around her cold toes.

He has been dead in her mind since she last saw him but now that he really is dead, she can't quite believe it; can't believe that she will never see him again. He is a corpse now, waxy, drained of blood. Now she understands why people want to see the dead in their coffins. They need to see it to believe it.

She still can't understand why he liked her so much; why he wanted to give her an Eskimo sculpture. She wishes she could have reciprocated his feelings in some constructive way or at least phoned him even though she wouldn't have known what to say. She'd told herself that he didn't need her because he had Abby. They must have been very lonely, the two of them, occasionally entertained by do-gooders who, they must have known, would later sigh heavily and say, "Poor Lucas", "He looked terrible" and "It must be hard for her".

Lucas is dead.

Why should it make any difference, really? She barely knew him, rarely saw him. She has lost contact with people before. How is this any different?

Because if she'd fallen off a cliff into rapids, he would have tried to rescue her.

If it's a boy, she'll call it Lucas.

EIGHTEEN

At Dave's housewarming, Harvey, wearing a leather jacket and pressed jeans, points at a plate piled high with balls of deep-fried dough. "Try one of these suckers," he tells Zee. "They got cheese in 'em. The wings are good too," he adds, pulling one apart with his fingers. "You weren't at the wedding."

"Yeah," Zee admits, "I was sorry I missed it."

"It was beautiful. I even cried." Harvey eats another cheese ball. "The most important day of a person's life, I swear. Certainly of mine."

"Is your wife here, Harv?"

Harvey shakes his head and picks up another chicken wing. "One of the kids has scarlet fever."

Dave ambles up to them and slaps Zee on the back. "So how's the old Zeemeister?" he asks. "Where's Alex?"

"She couldn't make it."

"That's weird. She told me you couldn't make it."

"She did?"

Dave nods. "Sounds like you two got your wires crossed." He grabs Zee's arm. "Come over here, I want you to meet my wife."

"I already have," Zee says as Dave pulls him through the

crowd to Glenda who is bent over the stereo, inserting a CD. "Everybody gets one dance with the bride," Dave says. "Glenda, honey? Remember Zee?"

As Glenda straightens up, Zee notices her breasts bouncing under her tight, lamb's-wool sweater. "Of course," she says.

"You want to dance with him?"

"Sure," she says, taking Zee's hand.

Zee clears his throat. "I actually don't dance."

"It's a slow song, just hang on to me." She wraps her arms around his neck and begins to sway slightly. Zee feels his belly pushing against her flat stomach. He places his hands lightly on the small of her back, although he notices the men around him clutching their partners' bums. When she rests her cheek against his shoulder, he can feel her breasts pressing against him. Her hair smells of apricots. He wonders how he smells to her. Her nose is about four inches away from his armpit. He perspired in the crowded subway coming here. She must be inhaling his stench. He tries to keep his arms close to his sides so wafts of body odour won't reach her. He wishes he could forget about his smell and enjoy the soft warmth of her breasts. He imagines sliding a hand under her sweater and cupping one, sucking on her nipple, feeling it harden against his tongue. His penis stiffens. He clears his throat again and pulls away from her slightly, trying to create space between them, trying to will his penis to deflate. He wonders what it would be like to be married to someone like Glenda, with soft, round breasts and a soft, round ass. What would they do in the evenings? Copulate? Do crosswords? Shop? Watch videos?

When Alex arrives and sees Zee rubbing up against the buxom brunette, she wants to puke, scream, bash his head in, but instead she quickly turns away and jabs a celery stick into some dip. An arm reaches across her for a cheese ball. "Pretty crazy weather out there," Harvey says, popping the ball into his mouth. Alex looks at him, realizing that he's talking to her. He wipes his hand on his jeans and holds it out to her. "My name's Harvey."

She shakes his hand. "My name's Alex."

"Short for Alexandra?"

"That's right."

"Wasn't there a Russian queen called Alexandra? Yeah, she did it with horses." He chortles. "No offense intended. It's a beautiful name, really." He drinks from his beer bottle. Alex, keeping her back to Zee, scouts the apartment for Dave.

"How do you know Dave?" Harvey asks. "Or are you Glenda's friend?"

"I'm Dave's friend. Is he around?"

"He went to get more ice." Harvey holds his hand under his chin and squints at her. "You're probably sick of hearing this," he says, "but has anybody ever told you you look like Twiggy with dark hair?"

"No one ever has."

"It's the eyes. You've got that same haunted look. And I don't mean that as a negative thing. You're a good-looking woman, really."

"Thank you."

"Can I get you a drink? You don't have a drink."

"That would be nice. Scotch with ice."

He winks at her. "The hooch is in the kitchen. I'll be right back."

Alex glances in Zee's direction and sees that he has disappeared. The brunette is also missing. They're probably off in a corner, soldering their groins together. Disgusting, Alex thinks, then reminds herself that she shouldn't care. It's over, the whole stupid thing, he can screw whoever he likes. He'll probably do it without a condom and get AIDS. Anyway, she fornicated with someone, didn't she? So why should it upset her when he does the same? What did she expect, that he stay celibate? Why should he stay celibate? She should wish him good luck in the free world, and good riddance. She rams her celery stick back into the dip.

In the kitchen, Zee watches Harvey hack at a clump of ice cubes with a knife. "There is one beautiful woman out there," Harvey says. "A classic beauty." A chunk of ice falls on the floor. He picks it up and puts it in the plastic cup. "She doesn't look available, though. Doesn't have that look about her."

Zee nods vaguely and drains his glass.

"It's all body language, you know what I'm saying? If they want you they shift around a lot, to make sure you see their best angles. This gal stands like a statue." He points the knife in the air. "Statuesque, that's the word I was looking for." Abruptly he turns to Zee as though he has only just noticed him. "How you doing?"

"Alright. You seem to be pleasantly saturated."

"You might say I'm not feeling any pain."

Zee holds his plastic cup under the bottle of scotch Harvey is holding. Harvey pours. "I've been thinking," he says, "about how lucky we are to be married."

"I'm not married."

"You're not?"

Zee shakes his head. Harvey scratches his eyebrow. "Why did I think you were married?"

"I don't know."

Harvey looks at Zee steadily then places a hand on his shoulder. "I hope you don't mind my saying this," he says, "but it seems to me that you're a depressed person. The only reason I'm saying this is that I used to be a depressed person. Seriously. Then I developed a philosophy of life." He puts the bottle down and leans against the sink. "There's something I call the wheel of fortune, and I don't mean the game show."

He holds out his hands as though he's about to say "the fish was this big". "You're on this wheel only you don't know it's a wheel. And it keeps turning, and you keep thinking you're going to go some place different, some place new, you know what I'm saying?" He rotates his hands slowly. "But the thing is, you end up in the same places, not the exact same places because it's a wheel you know what I'm saying? But pretty much the same places. And the thing to remember is, that even though you don't remember this exact spot, all you have to do is wait a couple of seconds because the wheel's going to start turning again, and pretty soon you're going to end up in familiar territory. By the time you're forty, you've covered every spot on the wheel, but you've been at it so long, you've forgotten some of them so it feels like new all over again, you know what I'm saying? The point is, there's no point getting depressed over stuff because you've been depressed over the same stuff before, and it didn't change anything."

This makes sense to Zee, that he can go around and around but always end up in the same place. Harvey prods his shoulder. "It's not a negative thing, you know what I'm saying?"

When Dave comes back with the ice he surprises Alex from behind, wrapping his arms around her middle. "You made it," he says. "Saint Alex is here, how's tricks?"

"Fine. How are you?"

"Adapting to married life, and you know what? I like it. We cook together, go shopping. It's great. It's like everything becomes a party because you've got somebody to do it with."

"That's great Dave. I'm so happy for you."

"Have you met her?"

"Not yet."

He glances around the room, shifting his bag of ice from hand to hand. "It's funny, you know, I used to try to figure out the kind of girl I was going to marry. But you know, there's no way of knowing. It's like marriage finds you, says okay this is it, get on with it." He holds a hand up to his forehead and shakes his head. "Why am I telling you all this? You know all this. But honestly, when I said those vows, it shook me up a little. I mean those are pretty heavy words, till death do you part etcetera." He tosses the bag of ice in the air then catches it. "But I have a good feeling about it, I'm going to make a go of it, give it all I've got."

How do you know when you've given all you've got?

"Zee's here," Dave says. "Did you see him?"

"Yes, I did."

He tucks the bag of ice under his arm. "I'll see if I can find Glenda for you. I want her to meet you."

"Dave, actually, I really should be going. I just wanted to say hi."

"Oh, come on. You just got here. Have some wings, relax. I'll be right back."

When Zee sees Alex at the food table, he ducks back into the kitchen then considers that he's being silly. They're adult; they should be able to talk civilly to one another. He walks over to her and taps her shoulder. She turns to look at him. "Hi," he says.

"Hello." He notices that her mouth is tight, meaning that she is still angry with him. She jabs a carrot stick into some dip.

"Is the dip good?" he asks.

"Alright. Cheesy. You'll like it."

He picks out a piece of cauliflower then dips and eats it. "How long have you been here?"

"Half an hour."

"I didn't see you."

"No."

He wipes his hands on his jeans. "I'm sorry I was so flippant last week, with all that talk about dead bodies. I don't know why I did that."

"To upset me." She crunches on her carrot. "You haven't picked up your stuff."

"No, well, I haven't gotten around to it."

"What have you been doing?"

"Oh, the usual."

"Right." She crosses her arms. "Well, I'd appreciate it if you would move it. Otherwise I'll have to come up with an alternative."

"Of course." He pictures her striking a match to a pile of his belongings. She could do that, would do that. "Maybe next week," he adds, unable to meet her battleship-grey eyes. Instead, he surveys the food table, even though he has no appetite.

"Lucas died," she says.

"Really? I'm sorry to hear that. Recently?"

"Last week."

"My god." He shakes his head and stares at a plate piled with chicken bones.

She watches him, wondering if Lucas' death has had any effect on him. "What are you thinking?"

"What …? Oh I was thinking about the frogs."

"What frogs?"

"All the amphibians are dying because we've contaminated the planet. They reminded me of Lucas. Innocent victims." He adjusts his winged cap.

Harvey lopes clumsily towards them, grinning. "Statuesque was the word I was looking for." He looks at Zee. "Don't you think she's statuesque?"

"She is."

"You forgot my scotch," Alex says. "You went to get me a scotch."

Harvey claps his hand over his mouth. "Oh, that's right. Excuse me, I'll be right back." He hurries back to the kitchen.

Zee leans against the table. "Everything alright with you? The car running alright?"

"Alright. You?"

He nods, watching a man in tight jeans lick something off the chest of a woman in tight jeans.

Alex reminds herself that she has no right to ruin Zee's fun. If he wants to make an ass of himself chasing after bimbos, that's his business. She should leave, let him get on with it. "I've got to get going," she says. "Say goodbye to Dave for me."

"Sure." He follows her to the door and watches her put on her jacket, wishing he could think of something to say, something she would respect or at least find amusing. She opens the door. "Enjoy yourself," she says without looking at him. He doesn't respond but watches her walk steadily down the corridor.

Harvey pants over his shoulder. "Where's she going?"

"She had to go home."

"Is that right?" Harvey looks at the scotch in his hand, unsure of what to do with it, then takes a sip.

Zee pictures Alex standing in the elevator, ducking into her car, fastening her seat belt, turning the key. He pictures her driving home, cursing at drivers, climbing the front steps, opening the door, switching on the lights. He imagines her brushing her teeth, washing her face, dental flossing. He sees her taking off her clothes and climbing into the bed, pulling the covers up over her head. It distresses him that her movements, still so familiar to him, are no longer part of his life. They are no longer any of his business. He wonders how long it will take to forget exactly what she looks like, exactly how she moves, smells. If he could forget he would be free.

"Did Alex leave?" Dave asks.

"She had to go," Harvey says.

"Shit, I wanted her to meet Glenda."

"She said to say goodbye to you," Zee says.

"Is there some crisis going on?"

"No crisis." Zee turns back to the party.

Just like the frogs, he tells himself, his feelings will die out, and he won't even remember they were there.

NINETEEN

On Christmas morning, Alex wakens in her mother's guest room with the headache she's had since booking the flight. She presses her fingers into her temples, trying to squeeze out the pain. No sane person spends Christmas with her family when she's emotionally distraught. She stares at the vase of daisies on the dresser and remembers how Elizabeth likes to spend hours trimming and arranging fresh-cut flowers. Alex's old Teddy with the chewed ears sits beside the vase. Whenever Alex visits her mother, the Teddy appears. She suspects that Elizabeth wants to remind her that she was a child once, a baby once, helpless once. She lies still, not wanting to move. As she'd expected, her flabby, useless body has betrayed her. Her period started three days ago.

She heard her brother Nick and his new girlfriend arrive late last night but stayed in her room pretending to be asleep. She felt she needed a good night's rest before facing Nick's big-man-with-the-money talk. Ever since she can remember, he has been a gloating thief. In his teens, he stole family belongings, sold them and spent the money on himself. Elizabeth allowed it, thought it amusing, a boy's game. Dotingly, she insisted that he would grow up to be a successful entrepreneur. Instead he became a salesman, selling cars first, then escalators, then computer software and finally junk bonds. Four years ago his wife jumped from a moving cab in an attempt at suicide. The night after she was released from the hospital, her handbag was found on a bridge. The police dragged the river for three days before finding her broken body in a tree. At the funeral, Alex asked Nick to introduce her to his in-laws, but he put his arm around her and told her not to bother with them. Last year he admitted that he'd wanted the in-laws to believe that Alex was his new girlfriend. "Why?" Alex asked.

"They hated me."

"So you wanted them to hate you more?"

"I wanted to give them some of their own back."

Elizabeth had argued against the marriage from the start; had insisted that Nick and Greta were incompatible. At one point, Nick agreed with her and asked Alex to tell Greta that the marriage was off, that he was going to South America to visit friends who were making a fortune trading sugar for guns. When Alex refused to give Greta the bad news, Nick sulked but did not break off the engagement. After they married, Greta's modeling career took off. She spent months abroad and became pregnant. Without Nick. When she told him, he asked her to come home, which she did, after having an abortion. She became penitent, claiming that she wasn't worthy of Nick. She developed a rash on her legs that she scratched in her sleep, bloodying the sheets. She picked at tiny blemishes on her face causing them to flare up with infection. Her modeling career came to a halt. Nick took Elizabeth's advice and had Greta admitted to a psychiatric clinic. It was when she was discharged from the clinic that she jumped from the moving cab. Alex has never understood how Nick could remain unchanged after Greta killed herself. She imagined that, in his position, she would be plagued with guilt and remorse. Once he said he missed her.

She hears a knock on her door. "Are you getting up?" Elizabeth asks. "We're all waiting for you."

"I'll be right out."

Alex came to Florida because the crowds of frenzied shoppers, the TV commercials exploiting the "holiday season" and the malls filled with Muzak carols had finally convinced her that she couldn't face Christmas alone. Unless she was pregnant and had the embryo for company. When she started to bleed, she got on a plane. Staring down at clouds, she tried to push from her mind the picture of Zee lying naked, straddled by the buxom brunette.

Elizabeth, her boyfriend Art, Nick and Courtney sit around the artificial tree, waiting for Alex. Art stands and hugs her awkwardly. Nick salutes and introduces Courtney who, Alex knows, sells real estate. While Courtney shakes her hand firmly, professionally, Alex notices that she has tiny ear-lobes and that the orange blush on her cheeks does not match her pale pink lipstick.

Then Elizabeth kisses Alex on the cheek. "You slept for ten hours."

"I guess I needed it," she says, although she didn't sleep well. She dreamt that she was giving birth to a dead baby; that someone was riddling her knees with bullets; that she was screaming at her dead father. She can't remember why, only that after she screamed at him she felt terrible, knowing that he was terminally ill and that she had hurt him needlessly. She woke lying flat on her back, feeling weighted down, as though she were buried in sand.

"Let's get down to business," Nick says. He rubs his hands together and begins to distribute the presents under the tree.

Yesterday she bought everybody one-hundred-percent cotton T-shirts printed with exotic fruits. Art unwraps his, slips it over his polo shirt, then looks down at his chest and runs a hand over the print. "That's a kiwi, isn't it?"

Alex smiles at him. "That's right." When she first met Art she found him dull, ineffectual, without personality. Now she appreciates the buffer he provides when family discussions threaten to turn ugly. "Very nice," he says, smoothing it over his belly.

Nick presents a parcel to his mother. "This is for you, Elizabeth." She unwraps it and displays suitable appreciation for a luxurious and obviously expensive angora sweater.

"For those cool evenings," Nick says.

"Oh, it's beautiful." Elizabeth rubs it against her cheek, reminding Alex of the women holding towels against their faces in commercials for fabric softener.

No one else seems as pleased as Art with Alex's T-shirts, but they thank her politely. Alex receives bath oil from Courtney, an underwater watch from Nick, a vegetarian cookbook from Art and gold-plated, leaf-shaped earrings from her mother.

"Ah, I have an announcement to make," Nick says abruptly, holding up Courtney's hand. "Courtney and I are engaged." Alex glances at Elizabeth who, still fondling the angora sweater in her lap, stares at Nick. Courtney extends her arm, spreading her fingers to display a sizeable diamond and sapphire ring.

"That's some rock," Art says.

Nick puts his arm protectively around Courtney. "We're planning a spring wedding."

"Congratulations," Art says.

"We've found this wonderful old church," Courtney says. "And we've got an eye on this fabulous house. I don't want to make an offer until it's been on the market a few weeks, and the vendors are feeling it. Luckily, I know they're bridging a deal."

Nick sits very straight, puffing out his chest. "Is something wrong, Elizabeth?"

Elizabeth folds the sweater and places it back in its tissue paper. "I'm very happy for you. I'm just a little surprised that's all. We've only just met Courtney."

"Well that's why we're here now, so you can get to know each other."

Courtney smiles at Elizabeth the way beauty pageant runners-up smile at the winner. Elizabeth smiles back like the celebrities on talk shows who don't want to be there but who need the publicity.

"Anyone interested in more coffee?" Art asks.

Alex stands. "I'll help you."

In the kitchen, Art grins at her through the loud, high-pitched whine of the coffee-grinder. "What a racket, hunh? I'd be happy with plain ground but your mum says it tastes stale. When she's out, I drink instant."

Alex rinses the coffee cups. "Is your son coming to visit?"

"He doesn't believe in Christmas, said he might come the day after though." He spoons the coffee into a filter. "I sent him a ticket."

"How is his writing coming?"

"Hard to say. He's working in a bookstore. He likes it, says he meets some interesting characters who give him ideas for poems."

Courtney pokes her head around the door. "Is there anything I can do?"

"We've got it under control," Art says. Courtney hesitates, apparently not eager to return to Nick and Elizabeth dueling in the living-room. Art notices her discomfort and points to a cardboard box. "Maybe you can take out some more of those crescent rolls."

"Sure, I'll get the plate." Courtney hurries out to the living-room. Art pours water from the kettle into the filter, nodding in Courtney's direction. "I feel sorry for her. She's going to have to live with a skeleton in the closet."

"Yeah but at least the closet will be in a 'fabulous house'."

Art lifts an eyebrow at her. "That doesn't sound like you."

Courtney carries in the plate. "Here we are." With a napkin, she lifts the croissants out of the box, carefully arranging them on the plate.

When Alex takes the coffee into the living-room, Elizabeth is sitting by herself, folding wrapping paper. "Where's Nick?" Alex asks.

"He went to the car to get his camera."

"How long has he been gone?"

"Oh, ten minutes."

Alex had thought mother and son had been alone together, working things out. But no, he'd run off to hide. When they were teenagers, and Elizabeth went away on sales conventions, she would phone them each evening with instructions for meals, lawn-mowing, watering, garbage disposal, grocery shopping. Alex would listen and sometimes disagree, but she would listen. Nick would put the phone down and pick his nose or scratch his armpits until he heard Elizabeth shouting. Alex told him he was chickenshit because he never told Elizabeth what he really thought or felt, always circumventing discussion by ignoring her or shouting at her and storming out.

He steps through the French doors with his camera. "I want a shot of everybody standing in front of the tree." He sets the camera on a tripod, dashes to the group, tugging on their arms, lining them up. He rushes back to stare through the camera with one closed eye then steps forward again to nudge them closer together. "I have about six seconds to get into the shot," he explains, "so you'll have to hold your smiles until after the red light goes on." He adjusts the camera one last time, hurries over to them and wraps his arms around Courtney and Elizabeth. When the red light finally flashes, Alex can already see the photograph: Nick and Courtney grinning as though they're having the time of their lives; Elizabeth wearing her photo smile, her lips pulled back, revealing gums. And, of course, Art, whose pale blue eyes turn pink in photographs and make him look possessed. He'll have one hand in his pocket, jangling change, while Alex, standing on the periphery, not actually touching anyone, will look as though someone cut her out of another picture and pasted her onto this family portrait as a joke.

When her father got brain cancer, Alex was eleven and old enough to be a "big girl" about it. Old enough to understand that, because he was sick, he couldn't remember that he'd already had a bowel movement or a meal, a bath or a shave. But later, when he couldn't remember who she was, she lost her understanding, locked herself in her room and read Harlequin romances, wishing that she were a nurse swept up in steamy romances with swarthy, dark-haired men on the Riviera. Her mother would rap on her door and plead with her to come out, insisting that his illness was a burden they all had to share and that it was time for Alex to read him the newspaper. Elizabeth believed that, like a child, her husband needed structure in his day-to-day life, routine. After his nap every day, when she returned from school, Alex read him highlights from the sports and business pages. In the latter half of his illness he would blink at her and interrupt, asking where he was and the time. "You're at home in bed, Dad."

"I'm what?"

"You're at home in bed."

"What's the time?"

"Four-thirty."

"In the morning?"

"In the afternoon."

He'd blink. "Where am I?"

When he finally died, she didn't mourn but felt relieved because now she would be free to go to movies and begin her life. Later she thought it unfair that her father had died an imbecile, without the love or respect he deserved. She tries to remember the man he had been before the illness. The man in the three-piece suit who smelled of cologne and carried a sharp-cornered briefcase. The man who, when she was especially good, took her to his office and let her sit at his desk doodling with all his wonderful pens and pencils.

Nick claims not to remember his sane father at all, never mentions him except to say, "My old man died of cancer". Elizabeth blames Nick's obstinacy and greed on his having grown up fatherless. Alex once asked Elizabeth why there were no pictures of her father in the house. Her mother said because there weren't any; he was camera shy. But when Elizabeth was packing to move to Florida, Alex found two in a box in the basement. Both were taken on a golf course. In one, he is leaning on a golf club with his ankles crossed, his cap low over his eyes. In the other, he is bent over with his head between his legs, thumbing his nose at the camera. Alex pinned this photo above her dresser. He thumbs his nose at her every morning as she combs her hair. She feels that this is the least she can do for him.

•

As she stacks the dishes in the dishwasher, Nick comes in and stands like Mr. Clean with his feet set firmly apart and his arms crossed. "So what's the plan?"

Alex empties a coffee cup into the sink. "Plan?"

"You going down to the beach?"

"I don't know."

"I thought it would be nice if we all went down to the beach, lay around and had some lobster. I'll buy."

She closes the dishwasher. "That sounds like a good idea. Why don't you do that? I'm actually kind of tired. I think I'll stay here." She studies the machine's buttons, trying to determine which to press and in what order. She can feel Nick hesitating, trying to decide whether or not to coerce her into joining his family-together-at-Christmas plan.

"Suit yourself," he says finally. "I just thought you might like to try that waterproof watch out."

She presses a button, the dishwasher rumbles. "It's a bit cold for swimming isn't it?"

"What do you mean? It's gorgeous out."

"It's cloudy."

"What do you expect for December?"

Later, while she's leaning over the washing machine, studying the buttons, Elizabeth comes into the laundry room. "What are you doing?"

"Laundry."

"Why?"

"I need clean clothes."

"Why won't you come to the beach with us?"

"I don't feel like it."

"Nick wants to take us for lobster."

"He told me."

Elizabeth crosses her arms, not unlike Nick. "Why do you always make it so hard for him?"

"What?"

"He's trying to be nice."

"He's trying to buy me off, Mother, he wants to impress me with his cash."

"Is that so terrible? That he wants to impress you?"

"That way, yes."

Elizabeth shakes her head, pulls some towels from the dryer and starts to fold them. "I think it would be good for you to get out. What are you going to do here by yourself, mope?"

"Maybe."

Elizabeth stops folding and stares at her. "Alex, it's Christmas."

"I know."

Elizabeth makes a "tsk" sound and sighs. "I don't blame Zee for getting fed up with you."

"Thank you for your support."

"You know what your problem is? You're too negative. If you wish trouble you get trouble, that's the way it goes."

"I don't wish trouble," Alex says, shaking Tide into the washer. "I just don't want to go to the beach so that you and Nick can avoid screaming at each other."

"What makes you think we're going to scream at each other?"

"Oh, please."

"You see, there you go wishing trouble again. That's exactly what I'm talking about. I don't know where you get that from."

Alex slams the lid down on the washer. "Can we not analyse me? Can you go on your picnic or whatever the fuck it is you're going to do?"

"Don't use that word in my house, young lady."

"I'm sorry." She stares at the washer. "How do I start this thing?"

Her mother leans over and jabs the "start" button.

"That's all?" Alex asks.

"That's all."

•

After they've gone, Alex steps out onto the patio among Elizabeth's potted plants. She tells herself to relax. She settles into a deck chair, pulls Art's brimmed canvas hat low over her forehead and stares at the condominium development across the lot where a middle-aged man and woman in pastel pantsuits circle an unlit barbecue. The woman gesticulates, and the man shakes his head. They both point to the barbecue. The man shakes his head again and trudges up the slope towards the parking lot. The woman clambers after him. They both get inside a Cadillac and slam the doors. Alex wonders where their children are, if they have any. She thinks it's sad if they don't. In the A&P once, Zee pointed out a squat Portuguese woman, dressed in black, and her gangly son. The mother selected tomatoes from a pile, feeling them, sniffing them while the son stood by, slouching, obviously bored, his eyes wandering through the store. "What about them?" Alex asked.

"They look so miserable," Zee said.

"I don't think so. They're just grocery shopping. I'd like a son who could help me out like that."

"You want a son so you can force him to do grocery shopping?"

Alex grabbed a bag of carrots. "Maybe he enjoys it."

"Doesn't look like it."

It made her wonder, not for the first time, how she could imagine that she might raise a child who wouldn't grow away from her; reject and despise her. How many sons really want to help their mothers shop for groceries? How many offspring really want to visit their parents at Christmas? Why should her offspring be any different? Why is she pitying the childless, middle-aged couple in the Cadillac? Maybe they're better off. If she, a "trouble-wishing, negative bitch", is any example of a daughter returned home, what joy can a daughter possibly bring a mother? What satisfaction does Elizabeth feel when Nick announces his engagement to a girl she has only just met? She must feel out of control. What makes Alex think that she would fare any better? She snatches a *House and Garden* magazine from the table and begins to flip through it, determined to steer her thoughts away from procreation.

"Anybody home?" A curly-haired youth in rumpled dress pants, suspenders and high-topped black sneakers, pops up from behind a bush and steps onto the deck. "Is this Elizabeth's place?"

"It is."

"I'm Art's son," he says, dropping his knapsack.

"Hi." She can see the resemblance, the soft, round face, the slightly bulbous nose, the pale blue eyes. "He wasn't expecting you until tomorrow."

He hangs on to his suspenders. "I got lonely."

"Would you like some iced tea or juice or anything?"

"That would be nice."

"Which one?"

"Tea would be nice."

She stands. "Come on in. They're all down at the beach."

"That sounds like fun."

"If you want to join them, I'll give you directions."

"Thank you."

In the kitchen, he leans against the dishwasher, pinching his lower lip between his thumb and index finger. "So you must be Alex?"

"That's right."

"I'm Dwight." He smiles, revealing crooked teeth, as he looks around at the white and salmon-pink kitchen. "I can't imagine my father here."

"What's his house back home like?"

"Things disappear in it. You put something down, and next thing you know, it's gone. Dad says an old lady ghost does it." He takes the glass from her. "Thank you. I have some bananas, would you like one?"

"No, thanks."

"How was Christmas?"

Alex puts the jug back in the fridge. "Alright. Nick has a new girlfriend. Actually, she's his fiancée, so that was interesting."

"Why?"

"He announced the engagement this morning."

"So it was a surprise."

"That's right."

Back on the patio, Alex settles down in her chair again while Dwight sits on the steps. She notices that his shirt cuffs are frayed. "Do you mind if I smoke?" he asks. She shakes her head. "I've tried to quit twice," he says, lighting up, "then I think, Do I really want to live longer?" He inhales on the cigarette, rests his forearms on his knees and stares at the condos across the lot. "I thought Elizabeth lived on the beach. I wanted to buy one of those inflatable things and float around the ocean."

"You can still do that."

"It won't be the same," Dwight says. "I wanted to run from Elizabeth's place with my inflatable thing and plunge into the sea. I wanted it to be spontaneous. Now I'll have to think about it. Plan."

"You don't like to plan?"

He shakes his head and examines a hibiscus blossom, gently caressing its petals with his thumb. "A friend of mine socked money away for years. Then his blood thickened. They cut off one leg, then the other, then he died."

"I'm sorry."

Dwight shrugs. "It was some rare disease. The opposite of

haemophilia. One of those diseases that nobody's supposed to get."

"Why did they cut off his legs?"

"They got bunged up with blood. He couldn't move them." He pulls at his lip again and looks across the lot at a woman with fat thighs shaking out a lawn chair. "Anyway he was a planner," he says. The woman arranges a towel over the chair, sits on it and rolls her shorts up her thighs. "The last time I saw him, he wanted to buy a camera so I smuggled him out of the hospital. He still had one leg so I put him in a wheelchair."

"Why did he want a camera?"

"He wanted to take pictures."

"Why, though?" Alex asks. "I mean if he was dying. Did he know he was dying?"

"I don't know. He said he did, but I don't know if he really believed it. I think he wanted to take pictures for the same reason anyone takes pictures. He wanted a record of things. That's what pictures are all about, aren't they?" Dwight drops his cigarette in the grass. "You look at a picture and think you had a swell time back then, but in fact you were as bummed out then as you are now." He drains the the last of his iced tea then sets the glass on the step beside him. "I'm glad we got him the camera. He'd been wanting one for a long time, but he didn't want to spend the money."

"Did he take any pictures?"

"A few. Of people who came to visit. And his other leg. Before they cut it off. And there's a couple of shots of his shoes."

For a moment he stares over at the woman on the lawn chair as she pulls a towel from her beach bag and drapes it over her face. Then he rolls up the sleeves of his shirt and stretches his arms above his head. "What a wonderfully cloudy day. A soft day. I have to buy some shorts. Some Bermudas, with fish and shells on them. That would be nice. Do you know where I might find some of those?"

TWENTY

Ma, you're bleeding."

Daisy sets down the open tin of cranberry sauce and looks at her finger.

"Here." Zee grabs her wrist, turns on the tap and holds her finger under the faucet, inspecting the cut.

"Do you have any disinfectant?"

"It'll be okay, it's not too deep," Daisy says, still staring at her finger. Zee dries her hand then makes her squeeze the wound together while he pulls a band-aid from a drawer and binds the cut closed. "I wouldn't have done that normally," she grumbles. "It's because he's here."

"I think he's very nice," Zee says.

"He looks like Frankenstein."

"He can't help that." Zee carefully picks up the lid of the cranberry tin and tosses it in the garbage. "He thinks you have a remarkable face."

"He does?"

"That's what he said."

"What would he know," Daisy mumbles, scrutinizing her finger. "Should we put another one on?"

"I don't think so, you want it to be able to breathe."

"When did he say I had a remarkable face?"

"When you went to get more cookies," Zee says, watching her spoon the cranberry sauce from the tin into a fish-shaped dish.

When Durham and Kyle arrived, Daisy said very little but sat stolidly in the armchair by the tree, staring at them, fiddling with the buttons on her cardigan. Jenny questioned Kyle about his work as a hairdresser and asked him if she should cut her hair. Kyle ran his fingers through her hair and suggested she might experiment with under-cutting and streaks. Then she asked Kyle to recommend hair-styles for Zee. "He goes to any old barber," she said. Kyle smiled politely and said, "It shows." He suggested that Zee would do well with more volume on top, which would balance his face and make him look more sophisticated.

"What about Daisy?" Jenny asked. It was then that Daisy scurried to the kitchen for more cookies, and Kyle observed that she had a remarkable face.

Daisy bends over and peers through the greasy oven window. "I don't know about this turkey."

"It looks fine."

"It's pale on top."

"No it's not." Zee wants to get the food onto the table and into their mouths. He wants Christmas to end. Last night he dreamed that he was still with Alex and had forgotten to buy her a gift. She eagerly presented him with a C.D. player and sat on the bed, waiting for him to give her his present. Gradually her expression flattened as she realized that he had no present, that he had forgotten. She did not reproach him but began to remove the C.D. player from the styrofoam casings, enthusiastically pointing out its features. He realized that she was pretending that she hadn't expected a present, as though it didn't matter to her. Zee, awed by her willingness to forgive and forget, couldn't move, wanted to be extinguished, very quickly, like a bug.

"It should be crispy on top," Daisy says.

"You don't want to cook it too long, Ma. It might dry out."

"It's a Butterball."

"Even so."

She chews on her fingers and stares back at the turkey. "I don't know. I don't like cooking turkeys. They're too big. What if it's pink inside? We'll get that disease that makes you yellow."

"Jenny," Zee calls, "can you come in and look at this bird?"

Jenny's boots click on the floor as she approaches. She looks in the oven. "It should be brown on top."

"That's what I said," Daisy says.

Zee groans, looking up at Daisy's calendar. A fluffy white kitten wearing a Santa Claus hat stares back at him.

Jenny hooks her hair behind her ears. "Leave it another twenty minutes." She has on dangling earrings shaped like Christmas trees. "Come on back in the living-room, you guys. We're talking about cheap vacations."

Daisy pulls her cardigan closed over her stomach. "I don't want to go back in there."

"Don't be dumb," Jenny says.

"I don't like it. Any of it. The whole idea."

Jenny sticks her finger in the cranberry sauce and licks it. "What idea?"

"You know," Daisy says.

"Mum," Jenny says, "you can't discriminate against someone because of their sexual preference."

Daisy yanks open the fridge door. "I don't want to talk about it."

"I think you have to talk about it," Jenny says. "Our entire lives you haven't talked about things that upset you. That's why we're all fucked up."

"I beg your pardon," Zee says.

Jenny turns on him. "It's true, you just won't admit it. You're too busy acting like nothing gets to you."

Daisy shakes a bag of frozen peas into boiling water. "That's enough now."

"No it's not enough," Jenny insists. "Whenever we're on the verge of a breakthrough, you shut us down. That's why we're dysfunctional. Why can't we express an honest emotion for once?"

"An honest emotion?" Zee asks. "Is that related to the honest truth?"

Jenny flings her hands in the air. "There you go with that superior tone again."

Daisy shoves some dinner rolls into the oven. "Shut up, the both of you."

Durham enters, carrying dirty tea cups. "Do I hear arguing?" He sets the tea cups in the sink. Zee turns back to the calendar, picks up a pen and draws a Salvador Dali moustache on the fluffy kitten. Durham looks at the three of them. "Why are you arguing?"

"Because," Jenny says, "Mother is freaked out about you and Kyle."

"I know that," Durham says. "And Kyle knows that." He pulls on his earlobe. Zee draws pointy eyebrows on the kitten. Jenny leans against the fridge, crosses her ankles and sighs. Daisy mashes potatoes. Durham watches her. "Do you want us to leave?" he asks.

Jenny looks at Daisy. "Of course she doesn't. I just think it's time we all talked about it."

Kyle appears and sets the teapot on the counter. "Talk about what, Jenny?"

Zee draws horns on the kitten's hat.

Jenny flings her hands in the air again. "Isn't there something either of you would like to say to Mom?" Durham looks at Kyle who shakes his head. "Oh, that's great," Jenny says. "So as usual I'm made to look like I've made a big deal out of nothing."

"We appreciate your concern," Kyle adds. He looks at Durham who nods in agreement.

Jenny stomps into the living-room. "I don't know why I bother."

"We don't either," Zee mutters.

"I heard that, pig-brother!"

•

Jenny sulks through Christmas dinner, which leaves large black holes in the conversation. One good thing about Jenny, Zee realizes, is that she fills uncomfortable silences. Durham eats heartily and welcomes a second helping, but Kyle refuses, insisting that he has to keep an eye on his waist-line. Daisy fusses, complaining that the turkey is dry, the peas overcooked, the potatoes too runny. All of this is true, but Zee and Kyle deny it. During the mince-pie, Durham surprises everyone by expressing his concern about the resurgence of malaria due to global warming. "You should see a malaria victim," he says. "I saw one on the news." They wait for him to elaborate, but he doesn't.

After dinner, Durham suggests they play Dictionary, but no one seems interested. Jenny retreats to her bedroom, saying she has a headache, and her body feels tingly. Kyle suggests that he and Durham do the dishes then call it a night because, believe it or not, he has to work in the morning; clients want to look nice for their holiday parties.

When they are standing in the hall, putting on their coats, Daisy approaches and thanks them for coming.

"Thank you for the lovely meal," Kyle says.

Daisy stares at the floor and pulls her cardigan over her stomach. "When you get old like me, you hate to spend Christmas alone."

"No one should spend Christmas alone," Kyle says.

Why not? Zee wonders.

When the door closes behind them, Daisy asks Zee if he wants to watch TV with her. "There's a Christmas ice show on," she says.

"A what?"

"Ice skaters. A Christmas show with skaters."

Zee shrugs. "Sure."

They sit on the couch. She offers him a chocolate boot covered in tin foil. "There's liqueur inside," she says.

He unwraps it, pops it in his mouth and lets it melt over his tongue. On the screen a Christmas tree skates around the rink, forlorn because it has no decorations. Suddenly Santa's helpers appear, skating around the tree, draping it with tinsel and glittering glass balls. The tree begins to hop up and down, delighted with its decorations, until it realizes that it has no star. It squats in the middle of the rink, curls a branch under its chin and begins to sob. An angel appears from above, hovers over the rink and asks the tree what it cherishes most about Christmas. The tree answers, "Giving," and sadly declares that it has no presents to give. The angel assures the tree that all those who truly possess the Christmas spirit will always be blessed with the joy of giving. She crowns it with a star. Suddenly coloured dots of light flood the skating rink as Santa's helpers pile presents around the tree.

"It gets better," Daisy says. "They've got world-champion skaters on."

"How do you know?"

"I watched it last year."

Zee pictures Daisy last Christmas, sitting alone, eating chocolate boots, watching the skating Christmas tree. He and Alex had been alone in their apartment eating free-range chicken, trying to pretend it didn't bother them that their Christmas wasn't like the rosy Christmases in commercials: Grandpa bouncing giggling tots on his knees; Mom holding up her new gloves; Dad carving the turkey. In the commercials, everyone is filled with good cheer, no one gets drunk, and everyone delights in their presents. Zee rarely delights in his presents because they're usually something that he doesn't need, something that will clutter up his life, like scarves or tuques with pom-poms.

Last Christmas, he convinced himself that Daisy was experiencing good cheer with friends, or at least with Jenny or Durham. Why didn't he ask her what she was doing? He could have invited her over. Why didn't he? What the hell was the matter with him that he couldn't invite his mother over for Christmas dinner? In his head he hears Jenny saying, "Mr. Walk-away-from-it-all, Mr. Never-give-a-shit-about-anybody-but-himself." Suddenly he wants to put his arm around Daisy, hug her, make up for lost time, but he's afraid to, afraid he'll feel foolish, afraid she'll recoil from him because she's unaccustomed to displays of affection. Instead he reaches for another chocolate boot. Daisy points at the TV to a man and woman in sequined skating costumes circling each other. "He's going to lift her over his head in a minute, you watch" she says. "I'm always scared he'll drop her."

•

After Daisy goes to bed, Zee lies on the couch and stares at the tree. The lights flicker, the tinsel sparkles, the glass balls shimmer. He has placed the phone on the floor beside him. Twice he has rolled onto his side, started to dial Alex's number, then slid the receiver back into its cradle. He lies on his stomach, resting his cheek against the sofa cushion. He tugs at Daisy's shag rug.

Why does he want to call Alex? As she would say, what does he hope to accomplish by calling her? What if she has someone there, some man, some goof who tells her she's beautiful over and over again? Zee used to tell her she was beautiful, even called her a handsome woman, but she never seemed to believe him, so he stopped.

Or what if she's alone and depressed and wants him to come over? She'll use her helpless female voice to lure him back into the cave. She'll be sweet for the night. They'll drink wine, maybe even make love, but in the morning, grey light will filter into the apartment, and everything will look the same.

He flips over on the couch and stares at Daisy's stuccoed ceiling. He hears feet padding down the stairs then Jenny appears in her bathrobe. "Oh, hi," she says. "I didn't realize you were still up. I just wanted to get some milk."

"Go ahead." He listens while she opens and closes the fridge, takes a glass out of the cupboard, pours, then pads back down the hall towards him. When her footsteps stop at the foot of the stairs, he closes his eyes and pretends to be asleep. He feels her looking in at him. He tries to breathe evenly and attempts a snore. "I know you're awake," she says. He does not open his eyes but senses that she is sitting on the stairs. "I've always felt like the reject in this family," she says. "I guess that's what you wanted. I guess you wanted all Mom's love for yourself. I can understand that. I mean it's hard to share one parent. And you were the first-born so you got all Mom's attention, then I came along and took it away from you. It makes sense that you would resent me. I can understand it."

He hears her sip from her glass. "We're all the products of our childhoods. It's dumb to deny it. I was just hoping that, with both of us being back here, maybe we could reach some kind of an understanding. But I can see that that's not going to happen. Maybe we're not ready for it yet. I just want you to know that, whatever happens, I still love you, and I happen to know," she pauses, "that you love me."

He listens while she climbs the stairs, then rolls back onto his side and stares at the phone, whistling through his teeth. Finally he reaches down, picks up the receiver and dials Alex's number because he needs to talk to someone sane. Alex, he knows, is sane, maybe the only other sane person on the planet. If he can relate the day's events to her, he'll be able step back and see them humorously. She will laugh and suddenly it will seem unimportant, just more of life flashing before his eyes. Listening to the ringing through the line, he realizes that he misses telling her about his days; misses feeling secure in her presence, confident that she will understand his point of view.

Not long ago, on one of their bad days, she'd said, "So if we don't have sex, and we don't have the same attitude about how to function in life, why are we together?"

"Because it's the only safe place to be. Why would we be anywhere else?"

He listens for sixteen rings before he hangs up.

Maybe she went out with Mel; maybe there's some event at the Centre; maybe she went to Florida.

Maybe not.

He begins to sing quietly to himself. "Chestnuts roasting on an open fire, Jack Frost nipping at your nose, Yuletide carols sung by a choir, and kids dressed up like Eskimo-o-s ..."

If she has found someone else, he doesn't want to know about it. He doesn't want to know.

TWENTY-ONE

At the beach, Alex watches Dwight scoop sand into a mound with his hands. "Do you ever get the feeling," he says, "that the world is going to explode? Not from nuclear shit but just because there's too much stuff on it? Maybe it'll cave in." He pats the mound. "I'd like to see that. I mean if it has to happen."

"Maybe it'll implode," Alex says, watching two darkly tanned men rub suntan lotion over each other's shoulders. "We'll plug up all its breathing holes, and it'll burst open."

Dwight nods gravely. "It's really hard to eat now, you know. I mean they do horrible things to the cows and the chickens. And the fish are swallowing the crap in the sea." He pushes his index finger into the mound. "Whenever I eat a tuna-fish sandwich, I feel like I'm killing a dolphin."

"Me too." One of the tanned men slides his hand over the other one's buttocks.

"And all the fruit is covered with carcinogenic pesticides," Dwight says. "I can't get into peeling fruit. Elizabeth says you should peel the fruit before you eat it."

Alex looks up at sea-gulls soaring and swooping above her. "I think the bad stuff penetrates the skin. I eat it anyway."

"Me too." He bulldozes his mound with his arms and

starts again. Alex notices that his brand-new, yellow Bermuda shorts, decorated with pink starfish, are already crumpled and soiled. He glances at her then back at his mound. "Nick says you're testy because you just broke up with someone."

"I'm testy because he's an asshole."

"Nick or the guy you broke up with?"

"Both."

"Did you break up for any particular reason? I'm a writer, I'm just curious."

"No particular reason."

One of the tanned men rubs suntan lotion on the other one's thighs. Dwight stretches his skinny white legs on either side of the mound. "It's hard staying together," he says. "You start becoming another person around this person, and if you don't like the person you're becoming, you get bummed out." He slides his hands under the mound and lifts his arms up, letting the sand run over them. Alex stares at a pudgy, pale young woman applying blue sunblock to her nose. The woman passes the tube to an equally pale but thin young man with hairy legs and forearms. He squeezes sunblock from the tube onto his index finger and draws a thick line of it down the bridge of his nose. They both sit, with blue noses, staring somberly at the cloud cover.

"Her reflector sunglasses," Dwight recites, "revealed who he had become, a pinhead, bug-eyed; all nostrils gasping for air, drowning, in black swill." He looks at her. "That's one of my poems."

"I like it."

"Thanks." He smooths his hands over the sand. "The worst thing is when you don't think the same things are funny, you know, you're busting a gut over something, and your lover's looking at you like you're insane." He uses both hands to dig a hole, places his feet in the hole then and covers them with sand. "Do you think Nick and Courtney are for real?"

"I don't know. I'm not the person to ask."

"They look like they're trying to be a commercial for California wine. She's always sitting on his lap, you noticed that?" Alex nods. Dwight's toes break through the sand as he wiggles them. "The only girl I ever thought maybe I really loved thought I was weird. She said that all the time, 'You're so weird.' She also didn't like sex."

"Maybe she didn't like sex with you."

"That's possible." He stares at his toes. "Anyway that was the closest I've come to having a relationship like in the movies. You know, where you're obsessed with the person. Except in the movies, things work out."

"What happened to you?"

"I'm not exactly sure. I guess maybe we got tired of trying to understand each other." He pulls his feet out of the sand and lies back on his towel, folding his hands behind his head. "We used to have completely different ideas about things. I'd be so affected by something, I don't know what, some old guy eating garbage, or a pigeon with a busted wing, but she wouldn't even notice it. She didn't see the things I saw, even though she was right there with me." He sits up again, pulls a cigarette from his pack and lights it. "I started to think maybe I was crazy. I tried to be more like her because she seemed so sure that the way she saw things was the way they were. I loved that about her. Nothing threw her. With me, all it takes is one bad vibe from a person, and I'm bummed out. But nothing could shake up Shauna. I admired her for that." He inhales on his cigarette. "But then the little things that I thought were really wonderful, like some crazy guy on a street corner having a good time pretending to soft-shoe, or some person smiling because I held a door open for them, or a little kid getting off on ice cream. Those kinds of small things that keep me going, she didn't even notice them. They didn't matter to her."

Alex scoops up a handful of sand and sifts it through her fingers. "How did it end?"

"Oh, she met a guy who sold water filters." He flicks ash into the sand. "It hurt for awhile. I had to keep reminding myself that she made me feel like a freak."

Alex brushes an ant off her foot. "Memory edits out the bad things."

He nods. "I remember looking at our reflection in store windows and thinking, this can't work. I knew all along but I wouldn't admit it." He shakes his head. "The tricks the mind can play." He pushes his cigarette into the sand, buries it then rubs his hands on his shorts. "I'm hungry, are you hungry? Is there a weenie stand around here?"

•

In the supermarket, Elizabeth pulls a box of crackers from the shelf and studies the ingredients. "I can't find a whole-wheat cracker that isn't saturated with chemicals." She shoves the box back onto the shelf and looks at Alex. "What do you think of her?"

Alex puts a package of Wheat Thins back on the shelf. "What do you think of her?"

"I'm asking you," Elizabeth says. Alex shrugs as she stares at a box of Champagne Crackers. Elizabeth drops a packet of Ryvita in the shopping cart. "I don't trust her."

"Why not?"

"I have never met an honest real-estate agent." She pushes the cart down the aisle.

"That's in business," Alex says, following her. "Nobody's honest in business."

Elizabeth holds her hand under her chin, squinting at the

pasta shelf. "Quite frankly, I think she regards this marriage as business. Nick says he's going to make two million this year."

"I know. He told me."

"Why can't they just live together? Nick says he wants children, what's he going to do with children? He's never expressed an interest in starting a family before. The whole thing sounds calculated to me." She tosses a package of spaghetti into the cart. "He should insist on a pre-nuptial agreement."

"Mum?"

"What is it?"

"Why are you telling me this?"

"What do you mean?"

"I can't help you. I have nothing to do with either of them. Talk to Nick."

"He won't listen to me." Elizabeth glances at her shopping list. "Green beans."

"Well, I don't want to hear about it."

"I would have thought you would be concerned."

"I'm not."

Elizabeth stares at her, tightening her lips as though she were about to spit. Then she pushes the cart down the aisle and around the corner. Alex knows that she is expected to follow, but instead she lingers in the tea and coffee section. She notices a man nearby glaring at a woman who is taking hold of a shopping cart. "What do you think you're doing? That's mine," the man says, gripping the cart.

"It is not," the woman says, grabbing the cart with both hands, letting her handbag dangle from her wrist.

"What are you talking about? I left it right here." The man yanks at the cart, but she keeps a firm hold as the wheels lift off the floor.

"You most certainly did not," the woman insists. "I collected it from the front of the store."

"Alex," Elizabeth calls from the opposite end of the aisle. "Are you going to help me?"

Alex joins her. "Those two people are fighting over a cart."

Elizabeth stares down at her list. "People will fight over anything."

"Why though? Why fight over a cart?"

Elizabeth shrugs. "Why fight over anything?" She taps the list against her chin. "I was going to ask Art to barbecue, but then you don't eat meat at all now, do you?"

"I'll eat salad and cheese."

"You're looking very thin."

Alex takes the list from her and studies it. "So what's left?"

•

In the car Elizabeth pats her knee. "I'm worried about you."

"Don't be."

"You're very unhappy, aren't you?"

Alex gazes out the window at gas stations and car dealerships. "Who's happy? Are you happy?"

"Of course."

"No, you're not."

Elizabeth reaches towards the dash and turns down the air-conditioning. "How would you know whether or not I'm happy?"

Alex watches a little girl turn cartwheels outside a Baskin Robbins. "How would you know whether or not I'm happy?"

"Why do you do that?" Elizabeth asks.

"What?"

"Mimic me."

"Mimic you?"

"There you're doing it again."

"I'm sorry," Alex says. "Can I open the window, or is that going to screw up the air-conditioning?"

"You haven't answered my question."

"What question?"

"Why you mimic me."

"Oh." Alex opens the window a crack. "I didn't realize I was doing it. I'm sorry."

Elizabeth stops at an intersection, gripping the steering wheel with both hands. "All I want is for you to be happy. That's all I've ever wanted for both of you."

"The light's green."

"What?"

"The light has changed."

"Oh." Elizabeth steps on the gas, the car lurches forward. "Has Zee got another girlfriend?"

"No."

Elizabeth's rear tire hits the curb as she makes a right-hand turn. "I must say," she says, "I've always felt there was something not quite right about him."

"Not quite right?"

"Something strange. I can't quite describe it. He never seemed all there, somehow. He was polite and charming of course, but I was never sure if he was actually absorbing what I was saying. You know how when you're talking to someone who doesn't speak fluent English, you keep talking even though you're not sure if you're being understood? You don't want to keep asking them if they understand because they might infer that you think they're stupid. That's how I felt with Zee."

In private, Zee used to call Elizabeth "Dear Old Fish Face".

"Maybe it's good that you've ended it," Elizabeth continues. "That's really the only way to look at these things. Onward and upward." She smiles at Alex, revealing gums, and pats her knee again.

In her teens, when Elizabeth said "Onward and upward" to her, Alex understood that she had failed and that her failure wasn't worth discussing. She tried to appear to be moving "onward and upward" so that Elizabeth wouldn't say she was moping. But each failure clung to her, warning her that it could happen again, probably would happen again. She envied Elizabeth's ability to erase mistakes, although she hated her for erasing their father from her mind. Years after he died, Elizabeth told her that if Alex's father hadn't had cancer, she probably would have divorced him; that she considered him "a weak cup of tea". Alex knows that Elizabeth put on the "onward and upward" front to protect them, not realizing that it weakened them, filled them with doubt because they couldn't find it in themselves to be as strong as their mother.

•

Alex dreams that she is comforting Sylvester Stallone who's depressed because nobody likes his latest movie. He stands on jagged rock, bare-chested, glistening with sweat, with his feet set firmly apart. His arms hang at his sides; his hands curl into fists. Balancing precariously on the rock below him, Alex reaches up to pat his sweaty forehead with paper towel. She tells him that she liked the first Rocky and that he should be proud to have made one good movie in his life. Besides, if he likes his movie, what does it matter what other people think? "Onward and upward," she tells him. Sylvester juts out his lower lip and stares morosely over her shoulder. She wonders if she should dry the sweat off his bulging pectorals or if he would think this forward of her. She doesn't want him to think she wants his body or his money—although she wouldn't mind his money—and she wonders how someone with so many millions can be so depressed. She decides to take a chance and pat his pectorals with the paper towel; they feel hard, like a car fender. Something cold and wet touches her leg, startling her, causing her to lose her balance on the rock.

"You mean you were really asleep?" Nick asks, standing over her deck chair, holding a glass against her leg. "You weren't faking it?" He offers her the glass. "Tanqueray and tonic."

"No thanks."

"You mean you don't drink either?"

"I drink," Alex says. "I just don't want to drink now."

"Why not?"

"Because I don't feel like it."

"I think you don't want to drink now because I offered you one. I think if I hadn't offered you one, you probably would have gone to get one."

Dwight appears and takes the glass. "I'll have it."

Nick stares down at Alex. "I think that whatever I suggest you do, you'll do the opposite. Maybe I should start suggesting things I don't want you to do."

Elizabeth steps through the French doors carrying a plate of crackers and cheese. "Is anyone interested in anchovy paste? I've put some on a few crackers. It's delicious."

"Sure," Dwight says, taking one, sticking it in his mouth then wiping his hand on his Bermudas. Elizabeth watches him, waiting for him to comment. Uncomfortable under her stare, he gobbles the cracker quickly. "Very nice," he says.

Elizabeth holds out the plate to Nick. "Was it a successful phone call?"

Nick takes a cracker. "It was."

Elizabeth offers the plate to Alex. "Nick has bought a gold mine."

"A gold mine?" Alex asks, looking at Nick, waiting for

him to explain.

He brushes cracker crumbs from his slacks. "I'm going prospecting next week."

"How can you buy a gold mine?" Alex says. "You mean you bought shares in a gold mine."

Elizabeth sets the tray down. "He bought a gold mine."

Alex looks at him. "Is there any gold in it?"

Nick finishes his cracker. "We haven't started digging yet."

"You bought a gold mine, and you don't even know if there's any gold in it?"

"There's active mines all around it."

"Where is it?" Dwight asks.

"Northern British Columbia."

"I can't believe," Alex says, "you bought a gold mine without knowing if there's any gold in it."

"You don't make money without taking risks."

Courtney steps through the doors and sits on Nick's lap. "Are you talking about the gold mine?" Nick nods. "Isn't it exciting?" she says, kissing his forehead.

"It's cold in gold mines," Dwight warns. "Wear something warm."

Alex sstares at Nick. "Do you think you'll ever make enough money?"

"Is that a trick question?" Nick asks, squeezing Courtney. "Oh Alex, don't get your knickers in a knot. It's just a game. A numbers game. I happen to like having higher numbers than the other guy."

"Forget about the homeless," Alex says, "just make sure your numbers are higher than the other guy's."

"Oh, spare me your socialist crap."

Art appears carrying a plate. "Liz made me wrap these water chestnuts in bacon. They're tasty, try one." Dwight leans forward and lifts one from the plate.

"I don't know how you can live with yourself," Alex says.

Art looks around. "What ...?"

"Do I ever comment on your life?" Nick demands. "No, and you know why? Because it's none of my business. If you want to live like a hippie when you're fifty, that's fine by me. I happen," he looks at Courtney, "we happen, to enjoy living in comfort. I happen to enjoy making money. You happen to enjoy catering to junkies. I think you're wasting your time, but do you hear me saying anything about it?"

Elizabeth places her hand gently over Alex's on the arm of her chair. "He's right, you know. He doesn't criticize you."

"That's because he's disappeared up his own asshole. He's blinded by his own shit."

Nick holds up his hands and smiles. "What can I say? I like it up here."

"I know it's really none of my business," Courtney offers, "but I sense a lot of hostility between you two, and I think you might benefit from outside help. I went through dream therapy myself, because I was harbouring a lot of anger and resentment towards my mother, and it helped, really. You have to forgive. Each other, but also yourselves." The sound of someone plunging into a neighbouring pool drifts over the fence. A yelp, and someone else jumps in. They splash and laugh. Courtney fondles her sapphire and diamond engagement ring. "It's just a suggestion."

Alex stands. "I don't know why I brought it up. I'm sorry. Forget about it. It was stupid of me." She steps off the deck onto the grass.

"Where are you going?" Elizabeth asks worriedly.

"For a walk. I'll be back soon."

"Oh, Alex," Elizabeth says, "we were just about to have dinner."

"Mum, I'm not great company. That's obvious."

•

Walking along the residential street, listening to the lawn-mowers and barking dogs, she wonders what she hoped to accomplish by arguing with Nick. Did she really think she could change him? People don't change, she knows this. Outward appearances change, behaviour changes, but the core remains intact. She has no right to impose her views on Nick. His life is none of her business. But then, what is her business, really? She used to believe she could change things, that it was worth the effort. Now, just like Nick, she's disappearing up her own asshole. She hears someone running behind her, panting. She turns to see Dwight hopping up and down, scratching his armpits. He pulls a banana from his pocket, holds it up to his mouth and scratches his head. "Ooo, ooo," he croons, then pants, jutting out his jaw, baring his lower teeth. Alex laughs.

"I made her laugh," he says, holding his arms in the air like a victorious prize-fighter. He hops in circles around her, wielding his banana, screeching and scratching his head. Alex laughs so hard that her eyes water.

Finally he collapses on a lawn, and she flops down beside him. They lie still, staring up at the evening sky. He crosses an ankle over his bent knee. "You know what Nick said after you left?"

"What?"

"He said he felt sorry for you."

"How magnanimous of him."

"There's no winning with guys like that. You shouldn't even try."

"So who should you try with? I mean, are we supposed to accept unethical behaviour? Pretend it's not happening?"

Dwight swats at a fly. "Sure. Self-preservation."

"But that's exactly what they want, the jerks like Nick.

They want us to feel impotent so they can slowly squash our brains."

Dwight nods. "It's a problem."

"So what do we do? Lock ourselves in our houses and tell ourselves the mess outside has nothing to do with us?"

They hear a screen-door open. "What do you think you're doing?" shouts a man in a terry-cloth robe. "You're on my lawn. What do you think this is, public property?"

Dwight and Alex get up quickly. "Sorry about that," Dwight says.

Alex points down the street. "We were just going." The man closes the door and scowls at them through the window. "How were we bothering him by sitting on his lawn?"

"It's his turf," Dwight explains. "He wants to be king of his piece of dirt."

"He's probably never sat on his front lawn in his entire life. He was probably watching TV, letting his brain turn to mush."

Dwight brushes the dirt from his shorts. "Let's go get a popsicle." As they walk down the street, he kicks a small stone in front of him. "Did you know that there's an animal, some little furry animal, that rolls over on its back and exposes its belly to predators? Big predators it knows it can't beat."

"Are you being profound?"

"No, I just think it's interesting that the animal has it all worked out in his head. I mean maybe the big predator just ate and isn't that hungry and wouldn't eat the little guy if he wasn't lying there, belly up."

"So you're saying we shouldn't take it lying down?"

He kicks the stone. "I don't know what I'm saying. I just think it's interesting."

"A minute ago you said there's no winning with guys like Nick, that I shouldn't even try."

"That's what I mean, I don't know what I'm saying." He smiles at her, showing his crooked teeth. "Want to see my gorilla impersonation again?"

•

Alex stares through her mask at the unfamiliar shapes. She'd imagined that reefs would be pink and blue, like the pieces of coral she sees in souvenir stores, but here she sees only khaki and grey. The guide had warned them that, because of the rough water, they would not sight as many fish as they would on a clear day. When she does see a fish, she tends to forget to breathe through her mouth. She inhales the water in her mask and has to lift her head above the surface to cough and sputter it out. She can't believe how beautiful the fish are. Shouldn't they be grey like the coral so that bigger fish can't see and eat them? Why are the bigger fish dull and ugly with whiskers and the smaller fish full of light and colour? Shouldn't it be the other way around? A jellyfish shimmers in front of her. The guide instructed them to stay clear of jellyfish, but if they did get stung not to panic, just to swim back to the boat immediately. Dwight told her that he saw a woman's chest after she'd been stung by a jellyfish. Her skin looked like spaghetti. Alex pumps her legs and arms frantically to push away from the path of the jellyfish and looks around for Dwight, her "buddy". The guide warned them to always keep one eye on their "buddies". Alex lifts her head above water, sees the boat bobbing not far off and gets smacked by a wave. She ducks back below the surface, feeling safe so long as she keeps her head underwater and allows the waves to wash over her, lull her. She needs to pee, considers returning to the boat then realizes that she can pee in the ocean. Her pee will become part of the ocean, will drift to foreign lands. Her bladder resists her, not used to relieving itself in the cold. Finally the pee streams out of her, warming her rubber wetsuit. She notices that her hands are wrinkled from staying in so long. She doesn't care, doesn't want to return to shore, wants to stay here with the fish. Everything works here, she thinks. Everything is in sync. There is no stress. For the first time in months she feels no tension in her neck. She wants to stay here. Maybe she should take up diving. Except she would always be an intruder, an outsider, would never belong. She wonders what the fish think of her, flailing her arms and legs, blowing bubbles, peeing in their ocean. She tries to imagine how she would feel if a fish came out of the water and stared at her in her apartment. She wouldn't like it. No wonder the fish swim away from her.

A large, flying-saucer-shaped dark creature hovers close to the reef not far from her. She's heard about mantas and sting-rays and wonders if this is one of them and if it has the power to kill her. She suspects that it will kill her if she continues to invade its privacy. She feels something touch her heel and panics, kicking out her leg. It's Dwight who points to the creature, shakes his head, then points in the direction of the boat, indicating that they should head back. Reluctantly, she follows him, thinking how peculiar and ineffectual his little legs and body look against the backdrop of green water. She wonders if she can retain this sense of the ocean, this feeling that she is microscopic, just a tiny dot floating on the sea. A bug floating on a pond. She likes this feeling because it frees her of responsibility, allows her to let go because she knows that the bug can do nothing but wait and see if a fish or a bird comes along and eats it.

TWENTY-TWO

Zee wonders why black-widow spiders eat their mates after the sex act. Is it because they're hungry or because they just don't want them around? The spider he's been watching makes a right-hand turn and starts crawling across the carpet towards his face. Zee wonders if it will climb onto his forehead and bite him. He hears knocking on his door. "Zee," Daisy says, "come out, it's an emergency." He drops his feet to the floor and opens the door. Daisy pulls her cardigan tight across her stomach. "Jenny's gone." She hands him a piece of paper. Zee reads:

Dear Mother and Brother,

When shall we three meet again? I don't know. I know only that I love you both. A la prochaine fois.

Daisy points to the last sentence. "What's that mean?"

"Until next time." He hands the note back to her. "What do you want me to do?"

"Find her."

"Mum, I'm sure she's fine. It's not like she's never been away from home before. She's thirty-eight years old."

"What did you say to her?"

"What do you mean what did I say to her?"

"You were mean to her all Christmas."

"I wasn't mean to her."

"Yes, you were." She stares at him. He notices that her eyes are slightly red; he suspects that she's been crying. He looks away and fondles the doorknob.

"I'm worried," Daisy says.

"So call the police."

"I did already, they don't believe it's an emergency."

"They're probably right."

Daisy stamps her foot. "What did I do to bring you up so selfish? What did I do?"

"Settle down, Ma." He puts his hands on her shoulders, but she pushes them away and covers her face with her hands. "What did I do to make you have no feelings?"

"Alright, listen," he says, "I'll make some calls. Do you have her boyfriend's number, Satan or whatever his name is?"

"Damian."

"Do you have his number?"

"I phoned him already. There's no answer. I want you to go and see if she's there. I have the address." She pulls a crumpled piece of paper from her cardigan pocket and hands it to him.

Zee looks at it. "Can't we wait and call again in a couple of hours?"

"No. A man chopped a woman into little bits and stuck her in a fridge."

"What's that got to do with anything?"

"Who knows what could happen."

•

Zee climbs the eight flights of stairs to Damian's loft and knocks on the door repeatedly. Finally the door opens a crack, and a gaunt young man with dyed black hair hanging over his face stares out at him. "What do you want?"

"I'm Jenny's brother, I'm looking for her, have you seen her?"

"You're her brother?"

"Yes."

"Which one?"

"Her older brother."

"The pig?"

"Is she around?"

Damian allows the door to swing open and steps back into the loft. Zee follows him, noticing that the large windows have been covered with black polyethylene and that the only light in the room comes from the television. "She's a basket case, man," Damian says. "You made her into a basket case. I don't want her around."

"Is she around?"

"She went out."

"Is she coming back?"

Damian points abruptly to the TV at a beer commercial featuring a rock band. "I auditioned for that!" he shouts and leaps over to the set, his eyes inches from the screen. "Man, they're not even playing. Bullshit, man! They're a bunch of fucking models."

Zee fidgets by the door, watching the light from the TV bounce off Damian's face. He'd expected someone older, with a face ravaged by Rock and Roll, drugs and alcohol. He'd expected Keith Richards not Donny Osmond off his nut. "Do you expect her back?"

"Who?"

"My sister."

"She's fucked up, man, I don't know what you said to her, but she's fucked." Squatting on a piece of foam rubber, Damian stares at a commercial for Wrestle-Mania. A hulk of a man wraps his arms around the neck of a man with long blond hair and throws him over his shoulder. As the blond man crashes to the mat, Damian slams his fist into the foam rubber. "Aced him, man!"

Zee takes another step into the room. "So she's staying here, then?"

Damian, still focused on the TV, holds up his hand, silencing Zee. "There's something you don't understand about your sister," he says, then abruptly points at a cereal commercial in which a dozen squirrels sit in a group, nibbling nuts. "Most of those are fake," he says. "They're stuffed. The first time I saw that I couldn't figure out how they got the squirrels to sit like that. They're stuffed."

Zee adjusts his winged cap. "Do you know where Jenny went?"

Damian adjusts his body into a lotus position, resting his hands on his knees. "People like me and Jenny are sensitive souls. It's hard for us. This city's cold, man. There's nobody to exchange with, nobody to echo off. You're totally alone." Zee looks down at his sneakers and taps his toe a few times. "I've had it with this plastic shit, man. Nobody plays real anymore, it's all bullshit. I want to make a video that's raw." On TV, a man and woman "make love" against a wall. As the man thrusts into her, the woman moans "Yes, yes" ecstatically. "Bullshit, man!" Damian shouts, pointing at the screen. "No woman ever looks that excited when you're fucking her. Bullshit!" Without taking his eyes off the screen, he feels around for the converter. "I've seen this movie," he grumbles, gripping the converter and flicking through the channels. "She kills him."

Zee clears his throat. "Is Jenny's band playing anywhere?"
Damian nods. "The Jack Hammer."
"The what?"

Damian points to the TV. "Oh, this is cool." On screen a commercial for donuts uses clips from a black and white Clark Gable movie.

"Well, if she does come back," Zee says, "could you tell her I was here and ask her to call home? Her mother's worried about her."

Damian nods dismissively, channel surfing as Zee slips out the door.

•

When he arrives home, Daisy is sitting at the kitchen table playing Solitaire, waiting for him. She looks up at him.

"She's at Damian's."

"Did you talk to her?"

"She was out when I was there."

"You couldn't wait?"

"I left a message for her to call."

Daisy looks back at the cards. "She won't call." She turns over a card. Zee starts down the hall. "She's in trouble, I have a feeling," Daisy says and plods to the middle of the kitchen so she can see him in the hall. "Zee, you have to go see her, you have to find her, bring her home."

"Ma, she left of her own free will. It's none of my business what she does."

"You have to tell her you love her."

"I don't love her."

Daisy stares at him, her eyes widening until he can see the whites around the irises. "How can you say such a thing?"

"It's true."

Daisy folds her hands over her heart, gasps and leans against the sink. The tap drips. Zee walks over, tightens it then turns to look at her. She stares through him. "Look, Mum, I'll see what I can do."

Daisy shakes her head slowly. "I don't know what I did."

"You didn't do anything. Who says brothers and sisters have to love each other?" Daisy keeps shaking her head. Zee looks at the apple-shaped clock then back at Daisy. "Okay maybe I do love her." Daisy doesn't move. "Alright, I'll tell her I love her."

"I don't know what I did," Daisy repeats and sits back down at the table, shoving the cards into a pile, organizing them into a deck. Zee slides his hands into his pockets, taps his sneaker a few times and sighs. "Alright, I'll see if I can find her."

•

Pressing a finger against one ear to block out the music blasting from the corner speaker, Zee sips his beer and studies the graffiti penned into the wooden table. "Pornography is a social mechanism to keep women in line. In history it intensifies when the male status quo is challenged." Beside this, carved in another hand he reads: "You're a disgrace to women." Beside this: "Fuck me, whip me, make me write bad checks." Above this: "Jody loves Rob."

Zee gave the bartender five dollars and asked him to give Jenny his note before the show. In it he told her he loved her but that he's going through a rough period and sometimes says things he doesn't mean. He found it easy to lie in the note. Facing her will be more difficult. He hopes that if she receives the note before the show, by the time her act is over, she'll have softened.

He looks around the room, surprised that it's crowded. At a neighbouring table, an Asian man wearing a black Stetson and a leather motorcycle jacket glances repeatedly at the entrance. A girl in black leggings jerks away from the bar to strut up and down in time with the music. At the table beside Zee, a man in a worn army jacket with lank, greasy hair and twitching eyes, pinches a cigarette between his fingers. He stares at Zee, looks away then back at him. "Do you play music?"

"Ahh, not really," Zee says.

"It's a gift. People that play music have a gift."

Zee nods. "They do."

The man looks around the room then back at Zee. "Do you play?"

"No."

"I wish I could play."

Zee sips his beer. "You probably could if you worked at it."

"I could play if I worked at it?" the man asks. Zee nods, noticing an inch of ash on the end of the man's cigarette. "It's a gift," the man repeats. "Some people have it." Zee nods. The man jerks his face away then back at Zee. "Anybody can play if they work at it, right?"

"That's right," Zee says.

"It's a gift." The ash from the man's cigarette falls to the floor. "Anybody can play if they work at it, right?"

"Right."

"Do you play?"

Realizing that the man is mentally disturbed and that this conversation could continue for some time, Zee excuses himself and heads for the bar, hoping to buy some peanuts. When he sees Alex sitting at a table with a man he has never seen before, he wants to run but can see that Alex has spotted him. "Hi, how are you?" he asks, knowing that she can see through his shit-eating grin into his brain, see his heart beating a thousand times per minute. "What are you doing here?" he asks. Alex doesn't smile, but he notices that the tension has lessened around her eyes.

"What are you doing here?" she asks. "You don't like Jenny's music."

"I've never actually heard it. I thought I'd give it a shot."

"She'll be thrilled. She thinks you hate her."

"So I hear."

"Are you with somebody?" she asks, scouting the crowd for the buxom brunette.

"No," Zee says.

"Oh. Well, would you like to join us? This is Larry."

"Hi, Larry." Larry offers Zee his hand. They shake.

"Larry fixes my car," Alex says.

"Oh, really?"

Larry pulls out a chair for Zee. "How is the car by the way?" he asks as he sits down.

"I think it's having a mid-life crisis. I'm hoping from here on it will age gracefully. Larry's putting in a new clutch." Zee smiles what feels like a half-wit smile at Alex then at Larry who does not smile back but drinks from his beer mug then wipes his moustache with the back of his hand. "How was Christmas?" Alex asks.

"Oh, I got through it."

"How's the New Year look?"

"Alright. You?"

"Alright, I guess."

Zee has a feeling that if he and Larry stood up, Larry would be taller than he is. He has a feeling that Larry is the kind of man who doesn't mess around, who makes decisions, drives fast cars, eats steak and eggs and doesn't worry about cholesterol. "I was just on my way to find some peanuts," Zee says. "Can I interest anyone in peanuts?"

"I'd like some," Alex says.

In the old days, they always ate peanuts in bars.

Alex watches him wending his way through the tables and thinks that he hasn't changed a bit; has the same pigeon-toed walk, the same not-quite-there expression, the same saggy overcoat.

"You okay?" Larry asks. "Is he somebody important?"

"Yeah."

"Do you want me to go?"

"No."

The truth is, she invited Larry to the club because, when she arrived at the service station, he hadn't finished replacing her clutch. When she panicked, afraid she would be late for Jenny's show, he offered to drive her, said he was closing up anyway. En route she invited him to come along, admitting that she wasn't too excited about going to the Jack Hammer by herself. He'd agreed casually. It was not like they were having a date. She wonders whether she should explain all this to Zee or take this opportunity to make him squirm.

"Here we are." Zee returns, tearing open a bag of peanuts and placing it in the middle of the table.

"Thanks," Alex says and takes some.

He can't get over how pretty she looks; she really looks pretty. He'd forgotten how stylish she is, in her own way, with her cropped hair, baggy sweaters and jeans. He is about to tell her how nice she looks when lights flash on the stage, and the band starts up, derailing any attempt at conversation. He notices Larry put his arm over the back of Alex's chair. A possessive gesture, Zee thinks, signaling, "If you mess with the little lady I'll knock your block off."

Zee reaches for some peanuts and looks up at the stage, surprised to see the band wearing nylon stockings on their heads with holes cut out for their eyes and mouths. Stamping her feet, the singer shifts her hips from side to side, belting out the lyrics with force and clarity. If Zee hadn't known it was Jenny,

227

he doesn't think he would have recognized her. She sings:

If I was a cowboy, nobody'd bug me.
Nobody'd say,
Let me stick my prick up your hairy cunt.
If I was a cowboy,
I'd wear alligator boots with spurs
That would rattle like snakes
If I was a cowboy,
Nobody'd snicker "Nice ass"
Because I'd blow their heads off.
If I was a cowboy,
I'd swing my legs over tables.
I'd take a leak when I wanted.
I'd chew tobacco and spit.
If I was a cowboy,
I'd drink Tequila with worms in it.
I'd eat corn bread and beans
And fart when I wanted.
If I was a cowboy,
Nobody'd snicker "Give me some pussy,"
Or "Baby, sit on my face."
If I was a cowboy,
I'd wipe my mouth on my sleeves
And my hands on my jeans,
Sit by the campfire,
Rub my belly and scratch my balls …

Zee notices Alex leaning in to Larry to say something. When
Larry nods, Alex leaves the table and heads for the rear
of the bar. Zee stares back at Jenny, hearing but no longer
absorbing, realizing that this is his chance to catch Alex alone.
He could follow her nonchalantly, hang around the Ladies
room and nab her when she comes out. Maybe that's what she

wants, maybe by leaving the table, she's given him a cue. Larry wouldn't notice. Larry's guzzling beer and staring at the band. Zee sets out to find Alex and discovers her leaning against a cigarette machine near the entrance. He waves. She waves back. "It's loud, isn't it?" he says. She nods. "I wonder if Jenny will lose her hearing," Zee continues. "That happens. It happened to Pete Townshend."

"Do you think she's any good?"

"The lyrics are different."

"I guess it's some kind of an outlet for her."

"Let's hope so."

Alex smiles, acknowledging the joke, and absently pokes at the buttons on the cigarette machine. "So you look alright."

"I am alright. Not great, but alright."

Alex nods. Zee waits for her to say something. Usually she says something. A man with hair shaved around his ears and neck leaving a cap of hair on his crown, wearing a nose-ring in one nostril, approaches the cigarette machine. Alex steps out of the way and notices, as he inserts his coins, a silver skull-shaped ring on his finger. She wonders what it signifies, some Satanic brotherhood? Does he rip out animals' entrails and offer them to the Devil? He pulls the cigarette pack from the machine and unwraps it as he heads back towards the bar.

Zee realizes that he must say something, otherwise it will become obvious that they aren't talking. "Are you okay?" he asks.

"Oh yeah, I was just wondering what his ring was about."

"His ring?"

"He had on a skull ring."

"Maybe he's into Satan," Zee says.

"That's what I thought."

Zee adjusts his winged cap. "I can see why a guy would want to believe in Satan. It's easier than believing in God."

Alex sighs and slumps back against the cigarette machine. Zee wonders what he's said that has pissed her off. She can't be offended. She's as sceptical as he is about the existence of an omnipotent, omnipresent being. He considers asking her what's wrong then stops himself, realizing that he's falling back into old patterns.

"One of the babies died at the Centre," she says. "Well, he didn't die at the Centre, he died in the hospital. Viral meningitis. I'm worried about the mother." Marika has not contacted her since the baby died. Her phone has been disconnected. Alex suspects that she has left town, gone home to a mother who constantly tells her how wonderful other people's daughters are.

"I'm sorry," Zee says.

Alex nods. "Babies aren't supposed to die."

"No." Zee watches her jab again at the buttons on the cigarette machine. She looks tired, lost. "It's interesting," he says. "I haven't heard about anybody dying since I last talked to you. It seems you know a lot of people who are dying or sick or something."

"What's that supposed to mean?"

"Nothing. I just think it's interesting."

She stares at him. "I come into contact with a lot of different people. I'm not sitting around my mother's with my thumb up my ass."

"No, of course, I realize that."

"You think I attract tragedy?"

"Not at all, I was just making an observation."

"People are getting sick and dying all the time. Everything's fucked, and there's nothing we can do about it." She turns away from him and stares at a poster of a naked man bound with rope. "Why doesn't he have any balls?"

Zee steps closer to her and studies the poster. "I think he does, I think they're tucked between his legs."

"I was reading an article," Alex says, "about forms of torture they used in Vietnam, like cutting off a man's balls and stuffing them in his mouth. Why would you do that to a person? Why would you want to? In South Africa, in some prison, the guards buried a man up to his neck and pissed in his mouth when he cried for water. It's stuff like that that just makes me not even want to look at people. I mean that must be inside all of us. That evil." She looks down at the floor and shakes her head. "I don't know, maybe I should move to Alaska or something." For a moment he pictures her in a parka on a dog sled, snapping a whip above a team of huskies. She looks up at a flashing neon Coor's Light sign. "It just seems like a constant battle."

"Yup," Zee says.

"What are we fighting for though? That's what I can't figure out."

"Beats me."

They look at each other like two strangers who have spent a long train ride together exchanging confidences and now, on the platform, are wondering if they should exchange phone numbers or let the trip contain their shared experience, prevent it from leaking into their real lives.

Zee pulls his cap low on his forehead. "Larry seems like a nice enough guy."

Alex claps a hand over her mouth. "Oh, my god. Larry," she says and hurries off. Zee trails after her, wanting to stop her, wanting to ask her something, he doesn't know what. What could he ask her? What could he say?

What would be the point?

•

Jenny bounds into the subway car and throws herself into

a vacant seat, crossing one leg over the other, swinging her cowboy boot. "I'm all revved up. It takes me a while to come down after a show."

Zee sits beside her. "Understandably."

"Thank you for the note. It was really sweet. If you ever want to talk about some of the stuff you're going through, I'm around. It's not like I'm new to heartbreak."

Zee avoids her eyes, afraid she'll see that he doesn't take her seriously. He hums quietly to himself and stares up at a chocolate-bar ad. He could use a chocolate bar right now.

"So did you like the show?" she asks. "Well, I guess it's not a show that a person likes, but I mean did it affect you at all?"

"Oh, sure."

"In what way?"

"Well, I think some of the lyrics are interesting."

She hooks her hair behind her ears. "What do you mean, 'interesting'?"

"You've obviously put some thought into them."

She swings her boot. "What did you expect?"

"I don't know," Zee says. "Most songs are about love gone wrong, aren't they?"

"Or love gone right."

To escape her stare, he leans forward in his seat, his forearms resting on his knees. "Daisy will be glad to see you."

"Maybe I'll surprise her, bring her breakfast in bed."

"That would be nice."

She also leans forward with her forearms on her knees. She looks at him. "So you really liked it, honestly?"

"I did." He sits back.

"I wasn't sure you'd get it," she says, also sitting back. "I mean, I thought you'd think it was feminist or something. I'm not a feminist, I believe in equality."

"Of course."

She adjusts the bandanna around her neck and pulls the collar of her jean jacket up around her jaw. "A lot of men are pigs, though," she adds. Zee nods. "What did you think of Damian?" she asks.

"I didn't really get a chance to talk to him."

"He's a lot younger than me, but he's brilliant. I know outwardly he comes across as a bit of a schmuck, but underneath, he's a genius." She slides down in her seat and stretches her legs into the aisle. "My problem is, I can't figure out if I love him enough to put up with all his shit. I mean he's a pig, there's no two ways about it. He tried to make me eat cat food, can you believe that? He said it was as good as tuna when you added mayonnaise."

"Did he eat it?"

"He never eats. I've never seen him eat."

"He seems to like television," Zee says.

"He's an addict. I don't think he'll ever be able to adjust to real life because he's hooked on TV. Once he screamed at me because I didn't act like some girl on a commercial when he gave me this bottle of puko perfume. Later I saw the commercial for it. The girl's wearing a slinky dress, and this guy comes up behind her and puts some perfume on her neck, and she kind of melts, and he starts to slide the dress off her shoulders. It's really hokey. I wasn't even wearing a dress when he gave it to me." Zee wonders if the man sitting across from them with the bleached-blond brushcut is staring at them through his dark glasses. Or if he's blind. "Who was the guy with Alex?" Jenny asks.

"Her mechanic."

"Her what?"

"He fixes her car." Zee stares up at an ad for A Week in the Sun; a tanned, lean man and woman lie intertwined on a wet and glistening beach.

"Are they like an item?" Jenny asks.

"I don't know, didn't ask."

"You were sitting with them, couldn't you tell?"

"I was watching you."

Jenny makes a "tsk" sound and shakes her head. "Why don't you just admit that she's found someone else and it bugs you?"

"Because I don't know that she's found someone else."

"It seemed pretty obvious to me."

"Then why did you ask me?"

"So you could talk about it. I thought maybe you'd like to talk about it."

"I don't," Zee says. The man with the dark glasses has not moved. Zee pictures himself as seen through the man's lenses; sees himself as a middle-aged, paunchy, long-haired nobody in a saggy overcoat and stupid, purple-winged cap.

"She looked good," Jenny says, "looked relaxed. The guy looked nice, dependable."

"Can we not talk about this?"

"So it does bug you?"

"We're in a public place," Zee mutters. "I would prefer that the whole world doesn't hear about my personal life."

"Nobody's listening. Do you think anybody's listening? You think you're so interesting? Nobody's listening." She waves at the man in the dark glasses, "Are you listening?" The man shakes his head. "See. He's not listening."

Alex didn't mention the cap. Did she think it was stupid? Did she think he looked like a paunchy, middle-aged nobody? Did she think, How could I have stayed with him so long? and What did I see in him? Does she go to the gas station and watch Harry pull cars apart? She's always admired men who work with their hands. Zee pictures Harry's hands on Alex's body, Harry's tongue in Alex's mouth, Harry's penis ... He jerks his head abruptly, trying to shake the thoughts from his mind.

"What's wrong?" Jenny asks.

"Nothing's wrong."

"You look like you just saw a ghost or something."

"Maybe I did."

TWENTY-THREE

While Larry mounts her from behind, doggy-style, Alex decides that she must be wacko. Why else would she let a man penetrate her from every possible angle? She must want to beat up on herself, punish herself. Larry told her that, where sex was concerned, he likes to try everything. This should have given her some indication of what coupling with Larry would be like. They started on the couch in the living-room, slid to the floor, rolled onto the beanbag chair, tried it against the wall, on the the edge of the bed, over the edge of the bed, in the missionary position, with her straddling him and now with him behind. Initially Alex found this exciting, unaccustomed to being madly desired or to the man taking charge. She felt light and small when he carried her into the bedroom with her legs wrapped around his waist. But now her vagina is sore, and her back aches. She would like him to ejaculate, not because she wants his baby but because she wants to go to sleep. When he finally does come, he rolls onto his side, pulls her to him and kisses her neck. "You didn't come," he says.

"That's okay."

"I want to make you come."

"It's alright, really," she insists. "Don't worry about it. I enjoyed it anyway."

But he rolls her onto her back and pushes her legs apart. Initially her cunt resents further disturbance, but as his tongue skillfully caresses and sucks her clitoris then slides down to her vulva then back up again, she begins to writhe and groan. She arches back, crying out during orgasm then pushes him away and rolls onto her side. He curls his body around her. They lie very still for a long time.

"You make a lot of noise," he says.

"What do you mean?"

"When you come."

"Does that bother you?"

"I like it." He presses his face into her neck. His beard tickles her.

"Why are we doing this?" she asks.

"Two lonely people ..."

"Two lonely people what?"

"Two lonely people."

She stares at her clothes on the floor, her laundry basket, her life.

"Don't think about it," he says.

He slides his rough, large mechanic's hand onto her waist and tucks his strong solid legs behind hers. His breath against her neck feels warm. She relaxes slightly, no longer resisting the shape of him.

She wonders if he snores.

JUNE

TWENTY-FOUR

As soon as she steps into the apartment, Abby reaches into her handbag, pulls out the Eskimo sculpture and hands it to Alex. "I thought it was a walrus, but it doesn't have any tusks. It seems big for a seal."

Alex runs her hand over the smooth, cool surface of the soapstone. "Maybe it's a fat seal."

"Lucas told me that walruses kill seals."

"You're kidding."

"He said they hack them to death with their tusks." She feels around in her bag and pulls out a pack of cigarettes. "I'm sorry it took me so long to deliver it, but I've been extremely busy, sorting out Lucas' affairs." She looks around. "Did you paint in here? It seems different."

"Yeah."

"Looks nice."

"Thanks. Can I get you tea or anything?"

"No, thanks. But I wouldn't mind sitting for a minute."

"Please do."

Abby sits on the edge of the couch and pulls a Kleenex out of her bag. "My allergies are driving me crazy. I always pine for summer, then my allergies take over, and I pine for fall." She blows her nose, wipes it, tucks the Kleenex into the side pocket of her bag. "Do you mind if I smoke?"

"I didn't know you smoked."

"I did before Lucas." She shakes a cigarette from the pack. "It feels strange to be here. I really don't know you. All I know is that Lucas liked you a lot."

"I liked him." Alex offers a saucer as an ashtray.

"Thanks." Abby places it on the end table. "I know that some of his friends felt rejected towards the end; felt that we shut them out. Did you feel that?"

"No."

"It just became too difficult for him to be with people. He wanted to socialize but didn't have the stamina. We'd go somewhere, and he'd have to lie down after twenty minutes. Everyone would worry about him. He hated that." She lights her cigarette. "I get the impression that some of his friends think I kept him away from them because I was jealous."

Alex squats on the beanbag chair. "Jealous?"

"Of his affection for them." Abby pulls her hair back from her face. "He weighed a hundred pounds when he died. His friends criticize me because I took him to the hospital for the last three weeks. They think I should have kept him at home. That's what he wanted." She shakes her head. "But they don't know what it was like. I couldn't manage on my own. He couldn't walk, I had to carry him, change his diapers, wash him without hurting him. You have no idea how difficult that is. Every part of his body hurt. It used to drive me crazy that I couldn't know his pain." She inhales on the cigarette. "He hated being a burden, was always telling me not to do chores, housecleaning etcetera. I'd say, 'Then how is it going to get done? Who's going to do it if I don't do it?' Once, when I was doing laundry at three in the morning, the washer broke down. I just lost it, completely, was bawling on the kitchen floor, thinking that at least Lucas was asleep. Then I see him

242

crawling on his hands and knees towards me because he's in too much pain to stand. He held me and told me it was going to be okay. I said, 'It's not okay. How can you say it's going to be okay? The washer's broken, you need clean sheets, and I don't have time to deal with it tomorrow.'" She shakes her head. "There were a few times I was harsh with him. I regret that. It's just it became such an issue every time I went out. I had to go out, to make money. I wasn't working full days, I brought work home, but I still had to go out. He couldn't understand that, how I could leave, why I had to do certain things, like banking and shopping. He'd say, 'Why do you have to do that now?' and I'd say, 'When else am I going to do it?' It's only now that I'm alone, I think I can understand some of what he was feeling." She shrugs helplessly. "I wish I'd spent more time with him. I get fixated on things." She picks up a cushion from the couch and turns it over in her hands. "Right afterwards, I felt that he was still around, in the air, I don't know. I just felt his presence, felt he was trying to help me get through it." She puts the cushion down. "But I don't feel him anymore. It was our anniversary last week, and I stayed in the apartment waiting to feel him. I tried talking to him. Nothing. I've never believed in life after death, but I guess right afterwards I believed in it because I had to; had to believe we'd meet again some time in some other place. One night I was standing on the balcony, looking down at his flip-flops— they'd been there all winter, I still haven't moved them—and I swear to you I felt him come up behind me. It was the strangest thing. It scared me. I went back inside and closed the door." She taps cigarette ash into the saucer. "Now it just seems like he's dead. Really dead. I don't believe we're going to meet again in the afterlife or whatever you want to call it. He's just dead." She leans forward and holds a hand over her eyes. Alex worries that she's crying. "I've got the urn by the bed. I don't know what to do with his ashes. We never discussed it. When I finally decided to open it, I couldn't. Couldn't get it open. I'd wanted it to be this private moment between Lucas and me, but I couldn't get the fucking urn open. I had to get my brother to do it." She tries to laugh then stubs her cigarette out in the saucer. "What I can't understand," she says, "is that people seem to think I should be over my grieving. It's only been six months, but everyone expects me to be bright and cheery and starting a new life. For a while I thought maybe they were right. He's dead, there's nothing I can do about it, I should stop feeling sorry for myself and get on with my life. I decided grieving was something only weak people did, and I'm not a weak person. But now I'm just saying, fuck it. I cry when I want. I don't care what they think." She leans back and rests her head against the couch. "I'm not even angry with them for their lack of understanding. I'm just disappointed. People I thought I could count on have stopped calling me. I depress them, I guess. They don't know how to deal with it. Don't want to, don't have the time. They want to forget about it, pretend it's not going to happen to them. Maybe, because there's so much dying going on these days, people are hardened to it. I don't know." She takes another Kleenex from her bag and blows her nose.

"I think we're just scared," Alex says, "because it's so close. We can't ignore it. Nobody's exempt from it anymore."

"Nobody ever was. Everybody's dying. You're dying from the minute you're born."

"I know, I think it's just that ... we don't want to dwell on it, we're afraid if we dwell on it, it might happen to us."

Abby stuffs the Kleenex in her bag. "It's going to happen to you."

"Of course, but we want to put it off for as long as possible."

"So you think ignoring dying people helps you put it off?"

"Abby, I don't want to argue with you. I don't know what to say. I can't imagine what it would be like to be in your position. My problems pale in comparison to yours. I feel like I have no right to complain about anything. Maybe that's why people stay away from you, we feel guilty because we've suffered less, yet we still complain."

"It's all relative."

"Of course, but I feel stupid complaining about my back when you've just lost your husband."

Abby shrugs. "I still complain about my back." She looks down at her belt buckle and fingers it. "The other thing people are saying is that I'm 'pedestallizing' him, which is pretty hysterical, considering I'm doing anything but. The thing about having a beginning, a middle and an end to a marriage is that you can play it over and over again in your mind, study it, analyze it, figure out where you went wrong. It's a waste of time, but it gives you something to do. My mother says I have a bad case of the 'shoulds'. But there are definitely things I should have done, could have done, that would have made our relationship easier. Who knows, maybe he wouldn't have gotten cancer if I'd laid off him a bit."

"You can't think that," Alex says.

"I'm not saying he was perfect. I just think I could've looked at the whole picture a little more. You get so caught up in your own scheme of things. I don't know. Maybe, if he hadn't died, we'd have gotten divorced. Who knows?"

The front door opens, and Dwight steps in with a quart of milk. "They didn't have one-percent," he says, then he notices Abby. "Oh, hello."

"Hello," she says.

He looks at Alex. "So I bought whole milk, is that okay?"

"Sure."

"The lady at the store says you should be drinking at least

a quart a day." He holds his hand out to Abby. "I'm Dwight."

"I'm Abby." They shake.

"I think I'll make some tea," Dwight says. "Do you want some of that blackberry stuff, Alex?"

"No, thanks."

Dwight goes into the kitchen. Abby picks up her bag and stands. "I should get going. Thank you for listening to me. Lucas told me were a good listener."

"Thanks for bringing the sculpture."

After closing the door behind Abby, Alex flops onto the couch. She feels Dwight watching her from the kitchen. "Do you think maybe you could eat some chicken soup?" he asks. "The lady at the store said you should eat at least broths and soda crackers."

Alex doesn't respond but rolls onto her back and stares at cobwebs forming around the overhead light. She has been nauseated for four weeks now, unable to houseclean, unable to do most things. She'd imagined pregnancy to be reasonably pleasant; expected to feel bloated and heavy but not completely debilitated. She'd assumed that she would feel an inner glow and be suffused with anticipation, excitement. She'd wanted to take the nine months to plan, prepare, make as much money as possible in the muffin trade. But all she feels is sick and tired.

"What about some Jell-O?" Dwight says. "I know, when I'm sick, I like Jell-O, or ice-cream. What about ice-cream, nice vanilla ice-cream? That would be calcium."

"Dwight, can you stop talking about food?"

"You have to eat."

She can't see how the baby can be healthy when she feels so lousy. Already, she tells herself, she's failing it. She forced it into existence, and now she's not keeping her end of the bargain. Every night she dreams about failure: failure to bake enough muffins, failure to deliver them on time, failure to swallow large dun-coloured pills that doctors in white coats assure her are critical to the baby's health. She worries that already a relationship is forming between her and her child; already her child has figured out that it can't count on mum. Mum says one thing then does another. Mum wanted to have me then tried to starve me to death.

Her doctor tells her that because she is under thirty-five there is no need for amniocentesis. But Alex has a feeling, a very strong feeling that there is something wrong with the fetus. She thinks that she and the fetus got off to a bad start. She pictures it twisting and turning in the womb, suffering because of her mistakes, her single-mindedness. From a documentary on Down's syndrome children, she learned that approximately one out of three hundred and sixty-five women over thirty give birth to a Down's syndrome child. She knows she'll be the 'one'. She watched the mothers of the Down's syndrome children insist that they didn't regret having them; that they loved them dearly; that the Down's syndrome children were very loving, joyful, trusting, gifted in their own way. But to Alex, the children just looked slanty-eyed and retarded. She even saw one in the park two days ago, stumbling towards the swings calling "Heewa! heewa!" to his dad. The dad, looking dazed, followed the boy and lifted him onto a swing. The boy sat limp in the swing staring at the ordinary boys playing in the sand around him. The dad, blond and strapping, stood by the swing-set watching the boy impassively. When the boy finally began to kick his legs, the dad stepped behind him and gently pushed him forward, then stepped back waiting for the swing and the boy to return to him. Neither of them seemed to be having a good time.

If hers is a Down's syndrome child, what will she do with it? How will she manage? She'll have to spend her life looking after it. How will she afford it? The Centre is only open three days a week now because of government funding cuts. The muffin business is doing alright but can't continue without her. She counted on having the nine months to pull her life together. She feels time running out, but she can't lift herself off the couch without barfing.

Dwight comes into the living-room, stirring his tea. "That Michael guy phoned again, seemed really upset, said his wife is in the hospital."

"So why is he calling me?"

"Don't snap at me, I'm just relaying the message. He wanted to know who I was, got quite aggressive about it."

"What did you tell him?"

"I said I was a friend." He sips his tea. "I don't think he believed me. I think he thinks I've tied you up and gagged you or something."

"Why won't they just leave me alone?"

"Because they're concerned about you."

"They don't know anything about me." She covers her face with her hands.

"Anyway I was reading this book at the store about pre-natal care. It says if you can't stomach meals you should just eat quick nutritious snacks, like bananas and carrots, fruit, maybe a little cheese."

"Stop talking about food."

"Alex, I'm not going to let you perish here."

"Why not? What am I to you, and what are you to me?"

"We're friends."

She groans and rolls away from him, facing into the couch. "This is not your baby."

"I didn't say it was."

"You think it is."

"I want to help you, that's all. You need help right now."

248

Alex pushes her face into a cushion. She can't believe how stupid she has been; can't believe how she has gambled with her life. Why didn't she think things through? She always thinks things through. She's a rational person. How can this be happening? She'd wanted some peace, thought it would bring her peace. But she feels boxed in, and she can't find a way out. Except abortion, and she can't go through that again. Besides, what would it solve? She'd be right back where she started. She doesn't want that. Doesn't know what she wants. She wants some fabulous, gorgeous man to come and rescue her, love and cherish her, set her up in a pretty brick house with skylights. Last night she dreamt that Robert Redford wanted to marry her. She'd hesitated because they had nothing to talk about, but at the same time she was seriously considering it because she knew he had lots of money and a ranch in the mountains.

She hears Dwight walk over to the window. "So what do you want me to tell this Michael guy?" he asks.

"Tell him I'm sick."

"With what?"

"I don't know, pneumonia, mononucleosis. Tell him it's contagious."

"You're crying again."

"Bug off."

"It said in the book mood swings are normal."

"Bug off!"

TWENTY-FIVE

Zee leans into the weeping fig, checking it for pests, then he sprays it with water. He likes coming to the Morton building because, from the upper floors, he can see the entire west end of the city spread out beneath him, sparkling in the night. He's amazed by how pretty it looks. From up here, you can ignore the garbage and despair in the streets below. A blimp floats by, advertising real estate. It annoys him that corporations can invade the sky. He wonders how much it costs to float a blimp, how many people could they feed and clothe for the cost of floating a blimp? He hears footsteps behind him, Mary's footsteps. "Are you going to wait for me later?" she asks.

"Sure," he says, although he doesn't want to. He has grown weary of Mary, her big watery eyes and her mouth that can't hold a shape.

"Maybe we can have breakfast," she says.

"Sure."

Fortunately, it is not easy for them to sleep together because Zee insists that Daisy would not appreciate him bringing a girl home, and Mary lives with a roommate who plays loud rock music that Zee claims gives him migraines.

"Karen's at her boyfriend's tonight," Mary says, which Zee

knows means that they can go to the apartment at dawn and copulate in privacy. He considers complaining of a migraine anyway, but instead he holds his hose over the fig and listens to the water spattering against the earth.

"I've got eight more washrooms," she says.

"Alright. Well, I'll meet you downstairs."

"Okay."

Becoming involved with Mary is one of the worst things he has ever done. He knew from the start that he would end up hurting her, that all he wanted was to explore her large jiggly breasts and see if his penis still worked inside a woman. He knew that, once having confirmed this, he would drop her. Why couldn't he have chosen someone with more resilience? On Valentine's Day, Mary gave him a silver ID bracelet with her name and 'love' engraved on the back of it. He gave her nothing because it hadn't occurred to him that it was expected. He forces himself to wear the bracelet at work. It disturbs him to think of the sizeable chunk it took out of her meagre paycheck.

Jenny's right. He is a pig.

Only once, so far, has he been impotent with Mary, but he feels that this is a warning and that, in spite of her expert blow-jobs, his interest is waning, and he'd better jump ship soon. But each time she approaches him with her mournful and trusting face, he can only put his arm around her and tell her that everything's going to be alright.

After they'd been sleeping together for six weeks, Mary told him that she had been sexually abused by her father from age three to fifteen. Zee had seen victims of sexual abuse on "Oprah" and had listened to their stories as he might news from Bosnia. It horrified him but didn't touch him because it was over there somewhere. When Mary confided—after weeks of what was, for Zee, sexual vindication—that she'd been abused, he tried to remember how the victims on "Oprah" had wanted their sexual partners to behave. Immediately he'd pulled his hands from her, but she'd held onto them: insisted that it was okay, that it was all in the past. She'd just wanted him to know.

Now when he touches her, he can't help wondering what her father did to her. Did he teach her to give blow-jobs? Zee knows this is exactly the opposite of how he is supposed to react; knows that if he were a mature, well-adjusted man he would continue to make love to Mary as before. But he can't. He tries to convince himself that it's because of who Mary is, not because of what her father did to her.

After the break with Alex, Zee had planned to simplify his life, rid himself of guilt and duties and emotional debt. Now he feels as entangled as ever. It angers him that he could have deluded himself into thinking he could just have sex with someone, as if "just having sex" were possible outside of prostitution. He tries to excuse himself for using Mary by telling himself that she uses him. For what he isn't certain. He can't offer her financial or emotional security. She doesn't seem to want him for his mind, and he can't imagine that she lusts after his body. She seems to take solace from holding his hand or having his arm around her as they walk. Once she told him it had been two years since she'd hugged a man. At first he liked it when she clung to him because it made him feel big and strong. But now he has to fight an urge to shake her off.

•

"Don't you want your bacon?" she asks.

"No, you have it." He picks it up, places it on her plate then wipes his mouth with his napkin as he reaches for his coffee cup. While he sips, he watches her pick up the bacon with her fingers and nibble at it. She reminds him of a bunny with a piece of lettuce. "Any problems tonight?" he asks.

"Somebody flushed a sanitary napkin down eight's toilet."

"Will they ever stop doing that?"

Mary shrugs and wipes her hands with her napkin then tucks it under the plate. Zee can hear two construction workers in the booth behind him comparing a six-cylinder Malibu's mileage to an eight-cylinder Buick's. Mary looks at him. "There's something wrong with one of the palms on fourteen."

"I know," Zee says. "I've made a note."

"It looks like somebody chewed on it."

Zee nods, listening to the construction workers discuss the difference between two- and four-barrel carburetors. Then he smiles his shit-eating grin at Mary. "So what are you up to today?"

"Nothing."

Zee nods and looks down at the dirt under his fingernails.

"I think maybe I should take my canary to the vet," she says.

"Why?"

"He's stopped singing. My neighbour said if I put a mirror in his cage, he would think it was another canary and be happy. But he just stares at it."

"Why does he have to sing?"

"They sing when they're happy." She folds the corner of her paper place-mat. "Maybe I should let him out of the cage. Karen knows some people who let their parakeets fly around their basement."

"I think parakeets are different," Zee advises. "I think they're tamer than canaries. I think you can train them to sit on your shoulder and things."

Mary folds another corner of her place-mat. "I feed him apple. I clean his cage. I do everything I'm supposed to. I don't know why he doesn't like me anymore." Now the construction workers are discussing the pros and cons of fuel injection.

"I don't think it has anything to do with you," Zee says. "He probably just stopped singing because of something in himself. Maybe he's going through a phase. Maybe you should just wait and see what happens."

Mary stares out the window at early morning traffic. "I had a guinea pig that I let out of his cage, and he got chewed by a dog."

"A dog? Really?"

Mary nods glumly. "I shouldn't have let him out. I just thought it would be nice for him to run around in the grass. I didn't think he'd run away. I found him in a ditch."

"How did you know a dog did it?"

"Tooth marks."

"I'm sorry. That's terrible."

She nods. "It's hard to know what to do. You think you're doing what's best, then they run away. I'm scared to let the bird out of the cage."

"I don't think you should. I think you should just wait and see what happens."

She opens her purse on the seat beside her and pulls out some money.

"It's on me," Zee says.

"You don't have to."

"I want to."

She rests her purse on her lap and looks at him. "Are you coming over?"

Zee pretends to be occupied with pulling bills out of his wallet. "Actually I think I'm fighting something, I don't want to give it to you."

"You look alright."

"I do? That's funny because I feel a little feverish."

She reaches across the table and holds her hand, rough

from cleaning fluids, against his forehead. "You don't feel feverish."

"I don't?" She shakes her head. "I guess then maybe I'm just tired," he says. "In any case, I don't want to take any chances."

She stares at him with her most baleful expression and nods. "I guess I'll see you at work then."

"For sure."

TWENTY-SIX

Dwight raps on the bedroom door. "That Michael guy is here to see you. He seems really upset."

Alex lifts her head off the pillow. "Did you let him in?"

"I said I'd ask you first."

She sighs and starts to get up. "Let him in. Oh, and Dwight ...?"

"Yeah?"

"Do you think maybe you could go out for milk or something?"

He pinches his lip between his thumb and index finger, considering. "Okay."

•

Michael avoids her eyes as he sits down on the couch, sets his briefcase beside him, then stares at his hands clasped between his knees. Alex leans against the bookshelves, watching him.

"Laura's in critical condition," he says.

"I'm sorry."

"She was starving herself while I was betraying her, and I didn't even realize it. I mean I could see she was thin, but I didn't think you could die from it."

"She won't. Now that she's in hospital. They'll save her."

He stares down at his polished leather shoes. "I sit by the bed and hold her hand and try to understand it, but I can't. I just can't understand how she could do this to herself, and her children." He shakes his head. "I don't even see her when I look at her now. It's as if … it's as if she's lost her soul. This disease, as they call it, has destroyed her soul."

"I'm really sorry, Michael." And she is. She just doesn't know what he expects her to do about it. Why do people come to her with their problems? As if she doesn't have enough problems.

"I've been trying not to feel guilty about us," he says. "I mean, it wasn't as though she and I were functioning as man and wife. She didn't notice what was going on, she was too busy starving herself. At least that's what I keep telling myself." He looks out the window then back at his shoes. "Do you think I'm right to think that?" Alex shrugs. Michael scratches his nose absently. "I really don't want to believe in God. I mean I … I don't think I could stand it. Believing she's suffering because of my sins." Abruptly, he yanks off his tie and undoes the top button of his shirt. "It's hot in here."

"Yeah. Well, I don't have air-conditioning."

He folds his tie and places it in his briefcase. "Do you regret what we did?"

"I'm not sure."

"I don't understand why you stopped seeing me. Are you really sick?"

"I think I'm just burnt out."

He nods. "You've had a very emotional time." Alex turns on the fan by the window and stands in front of it. Her oversized T-shirt billows around her. Michael clasps his hands between his knees again and looks at the floor. "I don't really know how to say this, but I … I need you at this time. There aren't many people I can talk to." Alex hears the catch in his throat. She worries that he is about to cry, and she will have to console him. "I mean," he says, "I think they see me as the villain. I think they think that somehow I'm responsible. And I suppose, in a way, I am." He unclasps his hands and looks at his palms. "I do regret what we did, there was something forced about it, desperate, I don't know. There was no need for it, really, I don't think. It wasn't healthy for either of us. And I'm afraid it's jeopardized our friendship."

"Do you blame me for it?"

"God, no. Is that what you think?" Alex shrugs. He walks over to her and holds both her hands. The breeze from the fan makes his hair stand up as though he's being electrocuted. "Don't desert me, Alex."

"Don't worry about it, Michael. You know where to find me."

"Thanks." He hugs her then glances at his watch. "I have to pick the kids up from school." He grabs his briefcase. "They still expect Mommy to come home and bring them presents. We always give them presents when we go away. How in God's name am I supposed to explain this to them?" He opens the door then looks back at her. "I'm glad we had this talk."

"Me too," she says automatically, wondering what he thinks "this talk" has accomplished. What did he come here for, absolution?

No Michael, it is not okay to screw around on your wife.

He touches his index finger to the side of his nose and closes the door behind him. She goes to the toilet and throws up then slumps against the wall, cursing herself for meddling with other people's lives. She'd intended to keep it clean, uncomplicated, was determined to bear the responsibility on her own. She told herself that what they didn't know wouldn't hurt them. But the hard fact remains that she stole from them, these men who wanted to believe in her. These men who formed an idea of her that had nothing to do with the real Alex, the sperm thief. She leans over the sink and rinses her mouth then dries it with toilet paper. Is it her fault that they only saw what they wanted to see? Should she beat herself because they never questioned her motives but assumed that she was throwing herself at them because they were irresistible? Larry used to say that good sex was the foundation of a good relationship. Alex asked him how he knew if the sex was good for the woman. He'd said, "You just know."

"But how can you be sure it's good for her?"

"You just know."

"Do we have good sex?"

"It took us awhile to get started, but it worked out alright, don't you think?"

Dwight knocks on the front door of the apartment before entering then pokes his head around the door. "Is he gone?" he asks. Alex nods. Dwight holds out a paper bag. "I bought some ice-cream. Do you think you could eat some ice-cream?"

"I surrender."

"You'll like it. Trust me." He scampers into the kitchen, where she can hear the sounds of drawers and cupboards opening and closing. "So how was the Michael guy?" he asks.

"His wife is anorexic."

"Is he the father?"

"I told you. I don't know."

He comes back with two bowls of ice-cream, hands her one then sits cross-legged on the floor. "I saw this crazy lady on the street. She had a banner across her chest with Miss Sweden written on it."

Alex stares down at her ice-cream, trying to imagine how

it will feel in her stomach. "Maybe she was Miss Sweden once."

"Maybe. She was old with dyed blond hair, kind of a Marilyn Monroe do. And she was wearing this tight, turquoise, sleeveless dress, like they used to wear in the sixties. The heels of her high-heels were so worn down, they looked flat." He holds the spoon in his mouth, pondering. "Imagine that being the highlight of your life? Being Miss Sweden."

"At least it's a highlight. What's the highlight of your life?"

"It hasn't happened yet. I don't think. I hope." He spoons more ice cream into his mouth then grins, showing his crooked teeth. "Unless it slipped past without me noticing."

•

Alex worried that the smell of McDonald's would make her sick, but she didn't want to discourage Marika from seeing her by insisting they meet somewhere else. She'd expected Marika to be sad, subdued in mourning. But Marika chews on her Big Mac and sucks on the straw of her milkshake as though nothing out of the ordinary has happened. Not once does she mention the death of her baby. Instead she describes in detail a system she's worked out for selecting lottery tickets. Not once does she meet Alex's eyes. Her hair has been dyed red, which Alex realizes she must have done herself because the colour is uneven, actually orange in places. Alex knows that if she allows it, Marika will talk about everything except her grief for the next hour. "How was the funeral?" she asks, suddenly.

Caught off guard, Marika meets her eyes for a second then looks away. "Small."

"Did your mother come?"

"Of course not."

"Why 'of course not'?"

"Because she thinks it was my fault."

"Do you think that?"

Marika chews at her chipped nail polish. "They said I could've saved him."

"Who said that?"

Marika swivels in her chair, facing into the restaurant, away from Alex. "I don't know. One of those guys."

"Which guys?"

"A doctor. I don't know. He said if I'd brought him in sooner they could have given him antibiotics."

"That's not true. It was a viral infection. There was nothing anybody could do. Whoever told you that didn't know the details of case." She stares at Marika, willing her to look at her. But Marika won't. "There was nothing you could do, Marika. It wasn't your fault."

"He had red splotches all over his body," Marika says. "He couldn't move."

Alex reaches across the table and grips Marika's wrist. "You're going to have to work at believing that it wasn't your fault."

Marika tries to free her wrist, but Alex holds tight. "Alex, if I'd wanted counselling I would've gone to the Centre."

"It's futile to blame yourself. You'll only hurt yourself."

"Alright, I get the point. Can we talk about something else?"

Alex releases her wrist, drains the last of her orange juice then sits back, crossing her arms over her stomach. "Has Travis been around?"

"He showed up a couple of times."

"And how's that?"

Marika shrugs indifferently. "He wants it to be like it was before."

"Have you told him that's not possible?"

"Why isn't it possible? You get over things. That's what

makes me sick about it. I know I'll get over it. I'll forget my baby. That's what happens. You think you'll die. You say, If this happens, I'll die. It happens, and you don't die. Time goes by, and you get other problems, so you stop thinking about it. It's like your mind does this trick so you can keep living your bullshit life. Otherwise you'd go crazy, right?" She grips her milkshake. Four tables away, two little boys in matching striped T-shirts screech as they throw plastic cups, napkins and styrofoam containers at each other. Marika sucks on her straw. "I wouldn't mind killing myself."

"Why don't you?"

"Because I don't know how. It's not like you can just get up and do it, unless you want to jump off a building, and I don't have the nerve to do that. Jane tried emptying the medicine cabinet and lived through it." One of the little boys hops off his chair and begins to strangle the other little boy, who screams.

"Why wouldn't you mind killing yourself?" Alex asks.

"Because I'm tired of waking up to nothing. It's not like anybody's going to miss me. It's not like I'm going to be president or anything."

"Lots of people aren't going to be president, but they don't kill themselves." The boys' mother returns, slaps both of them on the back of the head and herds them out of the restaurant.

"There's no point in my being around," Marika says, reaching back and combing her hair with her fingers. "I mean what am I supposed to do, slave in some shit job for the rest of my life? Forget it."

"You could go back to school."

"I'm already way behind."

"That's no reason to give up. Lots of people are behind."

Marika stares at her. "Lots of people don't have their babies die." She grabs her cup, squashes it and pushes into the trash can beside her. "I keep thinking, If I kill myself I won't forget him." She picks up the Big Mac container and stuffs it into the trash can. "Already I can't remember stuff about him. Like the noise he made when he was hungry, that little martian scream he used to do. I can't remember it. And his eyes, I can't remember the exact look of his eyes." She resumes combing her fingers through her hair then looks back down at her fingernails. "I remember his body pretty much, how it felt to hold him. I can still feel that. It's like my body can remember the feel of his body. But his face, his exact expressions, I'm starting to forget." She leans forward in her seat, resting her elbows on her knees, shielding her face with her hands, making it impossible for Alex to read her expression. "I wish I had pictures," she says. "I never took pictures. I've always hated those people who show you pictures of their babies all the time. I used to think all babies looked alike."

A red-faced man approaches their table and places a card in front of them. Alex reads it: "Hello ... Please excuse me. I am suffering from deafness and am selling this Information on Deafness to make my living. Please buy one for one dollar. Thank you." Marika shoves the card back at the man, "No," she says and shakes her head. The man turns to Alex. Marika tries to push him away. "Get out of here!"

"Take it easy, Marika," Alex says and hands him some change. He smiles meekly, nods then moves to another table.

"Why did you give him money?" Marika asks. "He's a fake."

"Do you know that for sure?"

"How do you think he paid to get those cards printed up?"

"I don't know."

"God, Alex, you're such a softy." She rolls up the sleeves on her T-shirt.

"So what are you going to do now?" Alex asks.

"I don't know. Go back home so my mother can scream at

me. It keeps her happy, and I don't have to pay rent."

"What about Travis?"

"What about him?"

"Do you miss him?"

Marika chews more nail polish off her thumbnail and spits it out. "It's like I don't want to be with anybody right now, you know? I don't want anybody getting at me. My mother, Travis, my dickhead dad and his stinking wife. They're always getting at me. It's like they don't have anything better to do."

"They're worried about you."

"They don't want a crazy daughter, that's all." Marika pulls a cigarette pack from her purse. "They want a normal daughter they can show off to their dweezle friends."

"Travis doesn't want that."

"Travis wants to rescue me."

"What's wrong with that?" Alex asks.

"Because he thinks he can rescue me by marrying me. He's been watching too much TV." She lights her cigarette and inhales deeply. "He keeps humming the tune from that beer commercial, where the nerdo guy gets the girl just by making eyes at her. This guy is a total nerd, but he gets this gorgeous girl. Like that really happens in real life." Smoke drifts out of her nostrils as she studies the cigarette between her fingers. "At least I can smoke as much as I want now."

•

Alex tosses some bagel into the murky water and watches the four ducks paddle over hurriedly. After they gobble up the bagel, the two colourful male ducks swim away with one of the brown female ducks, leaving the other female behind. They dip their bills into the water and shake their heads. Alex can see their orange feet flapping beneath them. The lone female duck seems unconcerned that she has been deserted. She doesn't even glance in their direction but stares at Alex out of one eye while drifting sedately with the movement of the water. Alex wishes she could signal to the duck that the others have left without her. She wonders how the duck-husband can be so fickle as to run off without his wife. As the gap widens between them, Alex wonders how the wife-duck will be able to catch up with the other ducks, if she'll fly or dive under the water. Suddenly one of the male ducks paddles speedily back towards the wife-duck. Alex waits for them to exchange some form of greeting, but they don't. They just float around each other, looking off. Alex admires the wife-duck for holding her ground.

She read somewhere about a species of brown ducks who are becoming extinct because the females are being wooed away from their mates by the males of another more colourful species. It saddens Alex that ducks, like humans, can be fooled by appearances.

She takes another bite of her bagel. After inhaling the greasy air of McDonald's for two hours, she'd suddenly craved a fresh, clean sesame seed bagel. Now sitting in the sun eating it she feels content. She has no idea why. Nothing has changed. Marika is still suicidal.

Once the bagel has settled in her stomach, undisturbed, she feels certain that the worst of the pregnancy is over.

As the wind caresses the back of her neck, and her toes stretch in her sandals, she notices a clarity to everything around her: the water, the trees, even the buildings looming above them. The people dressed for summer are no longer blurred; they jump out at her, dazzling her with their uniqueness, no longer threatening but making themselves available for her entertainment. Not even the Coke cans and styrofoam containers bobbing on the pond disturb her. Even they have a place in her world. She lies back in the grass and places her hand on her stomach, wondering when it will start to kick.

TWENTY-SEVEN

My bird died," Mary says, jabbing her mop into the bucket.

"I'm sorry." Zee watches her, unsure of her mood.

"I should have taken him to the vet."

Zee doesn't know what she expects him to do. He considers hugging her, but she is gripping the handle of her mop with both hands and staring down at the grey water. "I'm really sorry," he repeats. When she looks at him, he pretends to be reading the ingredients on a bottle of aphid killer.

"I didn't have any place to bury him," she says. "I had to wrap him in Kleenex and put him in the garbage."

"You should have told me. We could have buried him in the park or maybe in a pot here. One of the big pots." Mary sniffs and wipes what Zee suspects are tears from her cheek with the back of her hand. "Have you thrown the garbage out yet?" Zee asks. "Maybe we can retrieve him and give him a proper burial."

Mary stares down at her bucket of dirty water. "You told me I should wait and see."

"Well I ... I thought maybe it was just a phase. I mean I don't see why canaries have to sing all the time. Humans don't talk all the time."

"He must've been really sick, and I didn't notice." Leaning the mop handle against her shoulder, she pulls a crumpled Kleenex from the pocket of her uniform and wipes her eyes. "I should have taken him to the vet."

"Well, you can't say what you should have done, Mary. I mean that doesn't help. It's too late. Anyway, who says the vet could've helped him? Maybe he would've died anyway. Maybe he was old."

"He wasn't old," she says fiercely, stuffing the Kleenex back in her pocket.

Zee holds his hands out at his sides. "Well, what can I say? I'm sorry. I shouldn't have said anything."

"It's not your fault," she mumbles and grips the mop again. He waits for her to move, but she doesn't. Her knuckles turn white. "Do you think," she asks, "if Karen hasn't taken the garbage out, we could bury him?"

"Sure," Zee says, knowing that he will have to reach down into potato peels, coffee grounds and sanitary napkins to fish out the dead bird.

She loosens her grip on the mop and looks up at him hopefully. "Can we do it after work?"

"Sure."

"Can we do it in the park? It'll still be dark. There won't be anybody around."

"Sure."

•

Of course, he intended to end it, knows he must end it. But as Alex says, he's a coward. And he's decided that since it doesn't particularly pain him to be with Mary, he shouldn't cause her undue pain by ending it abruptly. He's hoping that, as they spend less time together, the relationship will gradually, gently expire. He plans to tell her that he's attending a technical school during the day to learn how to fix TVs. Already he has her believing that he has to stay home to look after his invalid mother.

Fortunately, Mary's roommate drinks beer. On the bottom shelf of the fridge is a twelve-pack. Already Zee has drunk three while fumbling through the garbage bags piled behind the building. Mary stands behind him, watching anxiously, her hands curled into fists under her jaw.

"Mary, surely you can recognize your own garbage."

"It's mostly her garbage."

"Don't you have any idea what she eats? What about yoghurt? This bag has a yoghurt container on top."

"She doesn't eat yoghurt."

He holds up a pizza box. "What about pizza?"

Mary shakes her head.

He has drunk four beers by the time he wraps his fingers around the soggy Kleenex containing the stiff bird. He drinks another during the cab ride to the park.

Standing under the dark, damp foliage, he looks around, then at Mary. "Where do you want to bury him?"

"Under a tree."

"There's a lot of trees here, Mary."

Trying to decide, she looks up and around at all the trees then points across the park. "Alright," Zee says and trudges across the grass holding the plastic bag containing the bird in one hand and his beer in the other. Under the tree he holds out his hand as Mary pulls a serving spoon from her purse. When he begins to dig, the handle bends under the pressure. He kneels and digs with his hands. When he has burrowed a hole four inches deep he looks up at her.

"It has to be deeper," she explains, "or a dog will get it and choke on the bones."

He takes another slug of his beer and digs deeper. Suddenly a bright light blinds him. "What do you think you're doing?" a gruff voice says. Zee squints into the glare and sees the outline of a policeman's cap above the flashlight.

"Oh, hello, officer," he says.

"What are you doing?"

"Ahh … burying a bird."

"A what?"

"A bird."

"What do you mean?"

"You know, a bird, that flies?"

"A canary," Mary offers.

The officer rests his hands on his hips; he looks sceptical. Zee takes note of the gun in the open holster on his belt. "Let me see it," the cop says. Mary hands him the plastic bag. He feels around inside it then pulls out the bird. "That's disgusting," he says. "What do you think you're doing burying a dead bird on public property?"

"We don't have a yard," Mary explains.

Zee nods. "Otherwise we would've buried it there."

"You can't just dig holes in public property. What are you, crazy?" The cop aims the beam of his flashlight at the beer bottle. "How many of those have you had?"

"Just a couple," Zee says.

"I don't think so. What do you think you're doing drinking in a public place?"

"Is that illegal?"

"I think you better come with me."

"What do you mean 'come with you'?"

"I mean, come with me."

"Oh no, no. You see, you don't understand." He points to Mary. "This is my friend, and her canary died. She was justifiably upset and wanted to bury it. I," he holds his hand against his chest, "being her friend, felt compelled to help her dispose of the body. I see nothing illegal about burying the bird. We're not disturbing anyone. There is nothing in the Criminal Code stating that burying birds in public places is against the law. I know because I happen to be a lawyer."

"You happen to be loaded is what you happen to be," the cop says. He points his flashlight at Mary, "You, go home."

"Can I have my bird back?"

"I'll take care of this bird," the cop grumbles.

"Oh, come on now," Zee says, "let her have the bird."

"I'd keep quiet if I were you. You're already in enough trouble."

Zee holds up his arms as though the cop were pointing the gun at him. "What have I done?"

"You've destroyed public property, and you're resisting arrest."

Zee places a hand over his chest again. "You're arresting me?"

"You said it."

"I want my bird," Mary says.

The cop takes Zee's arm. "Excuse me," Zee says, trying not to slur his words, "but I am well acquainted with the law and I can assure you that none of my actions substantiate an arrest."

The cop tugs on his arm. "Why don't we let the judge decide?"

"You're crazy." Zee tries to shake his arm free.

"I'm crazy?"

"I want my bird!" Mary shrieks.

The cop stops still and looks at her. "Is she retarded?"

Mary jumps up and down, wailing.

"Give her the bird, and I'll come quietly."

The cop throws the bird at Mary's feet. "I'm warning you,

young lady, if you try to bury that bird, I'll come after you."
Mary, weeping, cradles the bird in her hands. The cop escorts
Zee across the park and shoves him into the patrol car.

•

While he listens to the phone ringing on the other end, Zee
stares at the wide, fat back of a cop sitting at a desk, flipping
through a tabloid. Zee wonders why cops are fat. What is it
about the job that makes them fat? Too much time spent eating fast food in cars? Do cops have to be fat? Are rookie cops
allotted a certain amount of time to fatten up, and if they fail,
are they ostracized from the force?

Zee hears Alex pick up the phone. "Hello ...?"

"Hi. It's me." He pictures her waking up, squinting at the
digital clock on the bedside table.

"What is it?"

"I'm in trouble."

"What kind of trouble?"

"I'm in jail." He listens. "Do you think maybe you can
come and get me out?" The fat cop glances up from his
tabloid, swivels around in his chair and stares at him indifferently. Zee turns his back on him and lowers his voice. "I keep
telling them that I'm a law-abiding citizen, but they don't
seem to believe me. I think, if I can provide proof of a fixed
address, they won't press charges."

"Don't you have I.D. on you?"

"Yeah but it's got your address on it. I explained that I'm
staying at my mother's, but I don't want them calling her
because it will freak her out. I think if you come to collect me
and back my story about being a lawyer and just say that, yes
we've separated, but that I did live there and that you don't
mind taking me home for the night ... I mean, you don't have

272

to, just tell them that and I'll go to Daisy's." He listens.

"Which jail?"

•

Alex starts the Mazda. "Where do you want to go?"

"I sort of feel like a coffee," he says. "Do you think maybe we could go for a coffee?"

"Alright."

They stop at a Donut King and sit across from each other. She waits for him to explain; she's determined not to ask. Once she would have asked. Now she will wait.

"Thanks for coming," he says. "I couldn't think of anybody else I could count on."

"You look terrible."

"Well, it's pretty scary in there. Most of the guys seem used to it. I think some of them like it because they get to spend the night in a dry place. One of them had this huge gargoyle tattooed across his chest and shoulders. He told me he believed in the occult, witches and things. Paganism." He bites into his chocolate-coconut donut and stares out the window at the pink sky spreading above the buildings. "I was burying a canary. That's why I was arrested."

"A canary?"

He nods. "A friend of mine's canary died. She wanted to bury it, so I thought the park would be a good place for it."

"I see." Immediately she senses that he's been intimate with this friend. "Why didn't you ask her to get you out?"

"Well, she was with me when I got arrested."

So they were frolicking in the park at four in the morning. What were they doing the rest of the night?

"She's ... a little unstable," Zee continues. "I don't think she would've made a convincing case."

273

"I see." Good old dependable Alex, she thinks, the door-mat, someone you can count on. "Well I should get going," she says.

"Please don't. I mean, I wish you wouldn't. You haven't even drunk your coffee yet."

"I can't drink coffee. I'm pregnant." She hadn't intended to tell him, but now that he has hurt her, she sees no reason not to strike back.

He feels as though a basketball has hit the side of his head. "When did that happen?"

"It's been happening for a couple of months now."

"Well, that's wonderful, that's … that's what you wanted. Congratulations."

"Thank you. You've got coconut on your chin."

"Oh." He wipes his chin then looks down at what's left of his donut, wishing he could eat it, wishing he could act like she hasn't just destroyed him. "Well, I'm very happy for you."

"Thank you."

He pulls a napkin out of the dispenser. "So it will be a Christmas baby."

"That's right."

"I've always wondered what that would be like, having your birthday so close to Christmas. I wonder if you get shortchanged on presents." He takes a hearty bite of the donut, chews and tries to swallow. But it sticks in his throat, choking him.

"Are you alright?" Alex asks.

He nods, swills coffee, pounds his chest and coughs. "I'm really happy for you."

"You've said that."

"Well, I am."

"Well, I'm glad."

Obviously she is not going to tell him who the father is.

Obviously she is waiting for him to ask, to grovel, to writhe in pain.

"So you're still at Daisy's?" she asks.

"That's right."

"How's that?"

"Okay. I've got a job."

"You're kidding?"

"I look after plants in office buildings. I actually quite like it. I feel like I earn the paycheck."

"Paychecks are nice."

"When you feel you deserve them."

Suddenly a young man in cut-off jeans smashes his head into the counter. The black waitress shakes a finger at him, "Don't you start with that now." The young man freezes.

Zee shoves his cup around on the table. "So you're still living in the apartment?"

"That's where you phoned me."

"Right. So you're not getting married or anything?"

"No."

He flicks bits of coconut off the table, enormously relieved but still suspicious. It must be the mechanic, Harry, with the beard. Alex hates facial hair. How could she let a man with a beard impregnate her? Maybe Harry is living in the apartment, sleeping in his bed, sitting on his beanbag chair. Maybe neither of them believe in marriage and are happy to have a bastard. This isn't fair to the child, Zee believes. Children should have parents, real parents with the same last name.

"The car going okay?" he asks, hoping she'll mention Harry.

"Sure. Why do you ask?"

"Oh, I'm just curious. You seemed to be having so many problems with it."

"It seems to be going okay."

"Good. That's good."

She wishes he would just come out with it, scream, "Who's the father?" But, of course, he won't. He'll meander, determined to appear unconcerned, until he gets lost in his own head, disappears up his own asshole. "I really have to get some sleep," she says. "Do you want me to give you a ride to Daisy's?"

"No. That's okay. You go get some sleep." Who with, he wants to know. Is old Harry keeping the bed warm? Waiting up in his baby-blue Jockeys with a gun in case of trouble? "You disturb the little lady one more time, and you die, pal."

She stands. "Okay, well ... Go home soon, hunh?"

He smiles his shit-eating grin. "Don't worry about me." He pats his stomach. "Look after that little pardner of yours."

"I will."

"Thanks for helping me out," he calls after her, not sure if she's heard him.

Through the window, he watches as she gets into the Mazda. She doesn't look pregnant. Maybe she's lying, testing him. How can he pass the test, he wonders. And what is the test exactly? And does he really want to pass it? The boy at the counter bashes his head again. "I'll call the police," the waitress warns. The boy sits still.

•

On the subway, Zee watches a man slumped on the seat opposite, holding his arms protectively over bundles in plastic bags stuffed into a rusty laundry cart. Zee wonders how the man can think that anyone would want to steal his possessions. He doesn't look insane, just homeless, very sad and very dirty. Zee suspects the man has lice because he keeps reaching under his filthy trenchcoat to scratch. He has no shoes, only plastic slippers and shredded socks. Zee wonders if he should give the man money, or look away, or cry. He used to believe that this could never happen to him.

He has been saving money lately, so that he won't become homeless. Rationally he realizes that a few hundred dollars won't keep him off the streets. But still, he likes to have money in the bank; has discovered that he'd rather save than spend; gets a thrill out of depositing. Alex would be shocked. He plans to pay off and cancel his credit cards. He wants to simplify his life.

Maybe, he tells himself, if the baby looks like Alex, it won't be so bad. Maybe, if Harry doesn't shoot him, he can become Uncle Zee. Or maybe she only used Harry for his sperm and has discarded him, banned him from her life as she has banned Zee. Maybe the baby will be born dead like Mel's friend's baby, and Alex will call him from the hospital, distraught, hysterical, begging him to come and take care of her. She'll look up at him from her hospital bed and greet him with outstretched arms. Tears will stream down her face and she'll say she's made a terrible mistake, that she loves him, will always love him, can no longer live without him.

Maybe not.

TWENTY-EIGHT

Mel pushes the plate of carrot-cake across the table towards Alex. "Have some." Alex shakes her head. Mel pulls the plate back, takes a forkful and puts it in her mouth. "She won't kill herself. People who talk about it don't do it."

"Teenagers are different from ordinary people."

"A woman who works in our office tried to kill herself. She took a bottle of Librium and turned on the gas. Two days later her boyfriend found her. Apparently she was blue." She stirs her cappuccino. "Anyway they rushed her to the hospital, but she didn't die because the Librium slowed her heart rate so she wasn't inhaling deeply enough for the gas to kill her. Meanwhile they discovered she was five months pregnant."

"She didn't know she was pregnant?"

Mel shakes her head. "She thought she was missing her periods because of some thyroid condition. Her quack had her on diuretics because she was retaining liquids and gaining weight." She sips her coffee. "I tell you one thing, if a doctor isn't helping you, switch doctors. This guy must have been out to lunch. Anyway, she was so far along that they took her to the hospital and dripped some kind of saline solution into her arm to induce contractions. It didn't work because she'd been on these diuretics and had hardly any fluid in her uterus. Finally it came out, dead of course. But she'd bled so profusely that she had to stay in the hospital for three weeks getting blood transfusions. She says the hospital staff treated her like shit because, the way they saw it, she'd murdered her baby. Anyway, when it was over, she went home and tried to pull herself together but she still felt lousy. A couple of weeks later she felt contractions again. It turned out she had twins so she had to go through it all over again."

"That is too horrible."

Mel points her fork at her. "You think you've got problems."

"No, I said I'm feeling better about it now. I still feel nauseated some of the time, but it doesn't upset me like it did." She attempts to pour tea into her cup, but the teapot leaks from its lid.

"Why can't they make those pots so they pour properly?" Mel asks. "Someone could make some serious money if they designed a small, stainless-steel teapot that doesn't spill."

Alex lifts the lid as she pours. "How is the woman now?"

"I don't know, she doesn't work for us anymore."

"Why not?"

Mel shrugs and looks down at her plate. "I think the boys lost patience with her. She took a lot of time off and hadn't been with the firm very long. Apparently she wasn't that good to begin with. Norm said if she'd been a good secretary they would have found a way to keep her because he knows how valuable a good secretary is, but he said she was difficult to have around, that she affected other staff, brought them down."

"Do you think that's true?"

"I don't know, when you're working twenty-hour days, you're too exhausted to notice what's going on with the secretaries. God knows I have enough trouble keeping Norm off my own back."

"How's your eye infection?"

"Terrible, I still can't wear contacts. I hate these glasses, they make me look like an owl."

"Get new ones."

"I don't have time." Mel takes her glasses off and gently rubs her eye. "I tell you one thing. Next winter, when I get the flu, I'm taking antibiotics right away, no matter how many white blood cells they annihilate. I can't afford to be sick all winter. This has happened two years in a row."

Alex rests one foot on the edge of her chair, wrapping her arms around her knee. "Don't you think maybe your job has something do with you being sick? I mean there's always something, remember you had that cyst, then the eczema ..."

Mel scrapes icing off her plate with her fork. "Believe me, I would love to quit. The problem is, I have to make a living."

"Maybe there's something else you can do."

"Like win the lottery." She licks her fork. "What's Zee doing, by the way? Did he say?"

"He's watering plants in office buildings."

"You're joking."

Alex shakes her head. "I think it suits him."

"What's he making, five dollars an hour?"

"I didn't ask."

"You didn't ask? How unlike you."

"It's none of my business." Alex stares down at her sandal. "I just think, since you say you give half your money away in taxes anyway, you might as well do something that doesn't make you sick."

"It doesn't make me sick, Alex. I'd get sick anyway. Everybody gets sick."

"Okay." Alex sits back and looks around the cafe. A blond couple near the window are tearing apart croissants for their two-year-old twins. The boy stands on his chair, his little hands gripping its wrought-iron back. He puffs up his pudgy cheeks and stares at Alex. She stares back. He lets the air out of his cheeks, looks away then back again. Noticing him staring, his mother hooks her hand into the back of his pants and forces him to sit down.

"So how's Marty?" Alex asks.

"I prefer to call him Martin. 'Marty' makes me think of a short Jewish man."

The little boy, gnawing on a piece of croissant, turns in his seat to stare at Alex. "He is Jewish isn't he?" she asks.

"Sure, which is fine. He's circumcised, which is more hygienic. I just can't stand the name Marty. Everybody calls him Marty." She pushes her plate away. "Anyway he's fine. He's really nice. I've finally met a nice guy. He keeps discussing marriage in a general way, which means he wants to get married."

"Do you want to?"

"I don't know. I guess I should. I mean I'm not getting any younger. And he's really nice. He calls me 'beauty'." She snorts and brushes crumbs off the table. The mother of the little boy tries to get his attention by waving a bottle of juice in front of his face. "He's a pig, though. His apartment is disgusting. The man doesn't know the meaning of caps—toothpaste caps, mouthwash caps, shaving-foam caps. It's disgusting. I won't go anywhere near his sink."

"He'll probably still be a pig if you marry him."

"That's occurred to me." Mel feels around inside her bag, pulls out a lipstick, runs it over her lips and drops it back in the bag. She sighs. "There must be somebody out there."

•

When Alex sees Larry sitting on the front steps, she considers ducking into the corner-store until she realizes that she's actually glad to see him. She likes him. She just wishes she hadn't had to use and abuse him.

He doesn't notice her approaching; he appears to be studying a crumpled piece of paper. He stuffs the paper back in his jeans pocket, drinks from a can of Coke then massages the back of his neck. A baseball rolls towards him. He picks it up and tosses it back to two boys in new, white, high-topped sneakers. Alex admires his throw; suspects that he used to play ball, used to spit and grind his feet into the dirt. "Do you still play?" she asks. His head jerks up.

"There you are," he says. "I knew you'd show up some time. Who's the guard dog who won't let me in?"

"He's just obeying orders." She sits on the steps beside him.

"Is he your new man?"

"There is no new man."

"What about the old one?"

"No old man either."

He shakes his Coke can to see if there's any left, holds it to his lips, tilts back his head and drains it. He squints into the sun as he squashes the can in one hand. "Are you going to explain any of this to me?"

"I thought I did," Alex says.

He exhales abruptly, shakes his head, rests his forearms on his knees and stares at the boys playing catch.

"I had to try it to find out," Alex says. "I thought I was over him. I really did."

Larry looks down at the can in his hand then back at the boys. One of them misses his catch. He scrambles down the street after the ball. An oncoming car honks at him, the driver yelling out his window. The boy ignores him, scooping up the ball and pitching to his friend.

"Who's looking after your car?" Larry asks.

"Nobody. It's going alright."

"That's good to hear."

She would like to explain that her rejection has nothing to do with him, but she worries that this would only hurt him more. She would like to say, "Let's be friends." But then he would want to see her again and would notice her ballooning belly. She almost longs for the old days when men and women screwed and didn't ask questions, didn't want to know, just wanted to move on to unconquered ground.

"So you're not really sick," Larry says.

"No."

"So why did you lie to me?"

"Because you didn't believe me when I told you the truth." It sickens her that she can lie so easily. She never used to lie. *This child is being born of lies.*

Mrs. Merchant's daughter waddles towards them, weighed down by plastic shopping bags of groceries. Alex shifts closer to Larry to make room for her to climb the steps. She feels heat as her thigh presses against his; she realizes that she misses the feel of him, his solidity. She smiles at Mrs. Merchant's daughter. "How's your mother?" she asks. "I haven't seen her."

Mrs. Merchant's daughter grimaces then turns sideways to step past them. "Not too good. Her friend's daughter got killed. She was driving to pick up her wedding dress, and some teenager hit her head-on."

"I'm sorry."

Mrs. Merchant's daughter nods. "There's always something." She pushes open the front door of the building. "Bye, now," she says then lets the door slam shut behind her. Alex slides away from Larry and leans against the railing.

Larry massages the back of his neck. "Teenagers shouldn't be allowed to drive." A grey cat streaks out from under a parked car and through the open window of a basement apartment across the street. "My kid wants a Trans AM."

"You never mentioned a kid."

"No. Well, most of the time he doesn't feel like mine."

"Why not?"

"He doesn't want anything to do with me. He's a Nazi."

"What do you mean 'a Nazi'?"

Larry shrugs. "He's a Nazi."

A lady-bug lands on Alex's jeans. She places her index finger in front of it and watches it climb onto her hand. "Have you tried talking to him about it?"

"He doesn't give a flying fuck what I think. He carries around an empty briefcase with the antennae from a cellular phone sticking out of it. It doesn't work. He just wants people to think he's a businessman. He's got himself a beeper. It doesn't work, but he thinks it looks good."

"He'll probably do very well."

"Probably." He nods at the lady-bug. "Let's hope that's lucky."

"So he lives with your ex-wife?" Alex asks. Larry nods. The lady-bug opens its wings and takes off. "So you must have married very young, then."

He examines a small scab on the back of his hand. "Mistake of my life."

"Why? At least you have a son."

He looks at her and shakes his head. "You're pretty funny."

"Aren't you glad you have a son?"

"He's just another guy. Started out small, got bigger, turned into an asshole."

"Don't you feel responsible at all?"

Larry shrugs. "What am I supposed to do about it?"

"I don't know. I would have thought you'd want to do something."

"Leave him alone. His mother hassles him enough." They listen as the baseball thuds into the gloves. He rubs a patch of grease from his palm with his thumb. "So I guess that's it, then. Between you and me." Alex looks down at ants swarming over a popsicle stick on the sidewalk. She tries to think of something to say that won't sound so final. Larry stands and tucks his T-shirt into his jeans. "Well, it's been nice knowing you."

"Don't be like that."

"Well, how do you want me to be?" He drops the Coke can to the ground and kicks it into the street. "It seems to me you should think a little more before you start screwing around with people's heads."

"I agree."

He seems about to say something else, but with a wave of his hand he dismisses her instead, as he starts down the street. "Ah fuck, I don't even want to talk to you."

She watches him, thinks sadly what a nice bum he has and wonders who will fix her car now, and what she'll tell the child when it asks who its father is. She has wondered about this before and can only come up with 'Your Daddy died before you were born.' How would he die though? In a plane crash? Maybe he was killed in the war. Which war? But he'd have no medals. A father killed in the war must have medals. What if the kid decides to become a soldier to emulate his dead father? And what about pictures? It will want to see pictures. No, she'll have to tell it the truth, explain that she wanted it so badly she risked her life to get it. Who knows, maybe at this very moment the AIDS virus is multiplying in her bloodstream. Maybe she and the child will live a short life together, watching each other die. She hears the front door open.

"What's up?" Dwight asks. "You coming in? I'm trying to make Baked Alaska. Your mother called. She's coming to visit, says she has business in town."

"She doesn't have business in town."

"She said she did."

"She's lying." Alex drops her head into her hands. "God."

"I couldn't think of a way to stop her," he says. "She wanted to know what I was doing here." Alex expects him to climb down the steps and sit beside her, but he stays in the doorway. "I guess I'll have to move out," he adds. "Let her have the sofa." She knows he's waiting for her to say something like, "it will only be for a few days", but she doesn't because she wants to be left alone now, to be forced to take responsibility for her actions. She's been a chickenshit. "That's okay," he offers. "I should be getting my own digs anyway."

"'Digs'?"

"You going to be okay? You and Junior?"

Alex shrugs. "We're going to have to face each other some time."

TWENTY NINE

Z ee falls asleep mid-afternoon on Daisy's couch while studying the ad for Swedish Girls One-On-One Phone Fantasy. Candy pouts at him from a photograph. "It's dark," the ad reads, "And I'm playing romantic music. Call me and I'll tell you what I'd like to do to you …"

He dreams that Alex is in a car accident and loses both legs. He rushes down the pale-green corridor to see her, trying to think of what to say, how to make it seem alright that she has no legs. But when she greets him outside her room, her prostheses already in place—hard, shiny, flesh-coloured plastic—barely concealed by a mini-skirt, he stands dumb. She does a grotesque little dance, hopping from one foot to the other, demonstrating her mobility. Aghast, he tries to look impressed and suggests they go for a pizza. As they walk down the crowded street, people stare at Alex tottering on her artificial legs. Zee keeps reaching for her elbow, as if to steady her, but never actually touches her. She asks if he thinks her legs look alright. She says she thinks the nylons dull the shine of the plastic and make the legs look more real. He wants to reassure her, but he can't; he feels a swelling in his throat, tries to smile. Her cheerfulness, hopefulness make him weep. He lags behind, turning his face away from her, quickly wiping tears from his cheeks. She needs him now, he thinks, now that she has no legs. He tells himself that he will never leave her and feels almost glad that she has no legs, because no one will want her now. She's his now, forever.

When he wakes up, it takes him a moment to realize that he has been dreaming and that, in fact, Alex doesn't need him at all, not even his sperm. Alex is self-sufficient, needs no one. He remembers a scene from a German movie in which a small boy stands on a pile of rubble, formerly his home, in bombed Berlin. For the first time it hits Zee that really, really, really, it's over.

•

In the park he ponders the dead duck. It has been floating face down on the pond for two days. Zee wants to bury it but fears he'll get arrested and suspects that the cops won't let him off easy this time; they'll think he has a dead-bird fetish. He wonders how the duck died and how the other ducks feel about his corpse floating around the pond. Zee told a cop on a motorbike about the duck, but he just went on writing out a parking ticket and muttered that Zee should phone Parks and Recreation. He did. A Mr. Smiley was supposed to return his call but hasn't. Meanwhile the duck is covered in flies.

A bride and groom bustle down the gravel path towards him surrounded by swarthy, middle-aged men carrying video and still cameras. A young woman in a lilac dress walks alongside the bride holding her train off the ground. Even so, the groom catches his foot in the train and has to kick it free. Zee wonders why anyone would want to wear such a silly dress. They all gather by the pond, the swarthy men hovering around the bride and groom, clicking and rolling their cameras. The woman in the lilac dress fusses over the bride, arranging her veil and train, then hands her a bouquet of flowers and backs out of the shot. The bride and groom smile steadily until, Zee imagines, their cheeks begin to ache. Periodically the groom leans over and kisses the bride. Zee wonders if, when they get the pictures back from the shop, they'll notice the dead duck.

Dave has assured him that he and Glenda are not trying to fix him up. He explained to Zee that they had invited someone besides Maggie, but that person couldn't make it. But he's not trying to fix him up, Dave repeated. Zee had managed to postpone the dinner for several months until, finally, he ran out of credible excuses. Now, feeling the paper bag containing his bottle of wine dampened from his sweaty grip, he considers calling up and saying he's in hospital with a hernia.

The woman named Maggie throws a tanned, slightly thick leg over the arm of the easy chair and stares directly at Zee. "David tells me you're a crusader but couldn't tell me what you're crusading for." When they were introduced, her British accent had surprised Zee. Now it seems to him that she's speaking too loud.

"Nobody knows exactly what Zee's about," Dave says. "That's what's so great about him."

"How interesting," she adds. Her strident tone and walking shorts make Zee think she should be hiking over moors singing about jolly old England. "Zee can't be your real name, surely."

"Theodore."

Glenda places nachos and dip on the coffee table. "So we should call you Teddy," she says, sitting beside him on the love-seat. He realizes that this is the first time he's seen her out of tight-fitting clothes. Even the points of her nipples are hidden behind the stiff cotton of her blouse. Zee wonders if, now that she has Dave in the cave, she no longer exposes her body to strangers; or to Dave. She pats Zee's knee. "So what do you think of my interior decorating?"

Zee noticed the changes to the apartment as soon as he came in but withheld comment since the place now reminds him of department-store furniture displays. He looks around at the apricot walls that match the new sofa set, the dried flowers shooting up from a hand-blown glass vase, the oil painting of a weathered barn in a field of wild flowers. "It's very nice," he says, reaching for his scotch. When he first sat down, Glenda provided him with a coaster, but he keeps forgetting to use it. Instead, he places his glass directly on the antique pine coffee-table, causing a ring which Glenda quickly mops up with a napkin. He decides to keep the glass in his hand.

Maggie reaches for a nacho. "Dave tells me you're a lawyer but that you're taking a sabbatical." Zee nods vaguely, staring at the parquet floor. Dave stands, pulling on his nose.

"Next I want to buy a couple of area rugs," Glenda says. "A hundred-percent wool. I don't want any nylon in here."

"Honey …" Dave asks, "do you think maybe we should take a look at the fish?"

They exchange a look. "Oh, right," she smiles at Zee and Maggie. "I hope you both like sole." Both Zee and Maggie say yes, and Glenda goes into the kitchen, trailed by Dave. Zee stares at a wooden wall-clock while it chimes eight times.

"Are you taking a sabbatical to study …? Or travel …?"

"Actually, I'm just … lying fallow for a bit."

Maggie nods. "Very wise. At a certain point in your life, you just have to step off the treadmill and take a look at yourself." Zee wonders if that's what he's doing. He studies the barn painting. He tries to imagine who did it and how many they made just like it, and if painting the same painting over and over again drove them bonkers.

"I'm in a similar situation myself," Maggie continues. "My life couldn't be more chaotic at the moment." Her reddish hair, tied into a ponytail, swings as she talks. "I could, of course, be in a complete panic about it, but fortunately I'm not that type of person. I rather welcome a change." She holds the bowl of nachos out to him. He takes a handful. "Be warned. The dip is very hot," she says. They both crunch nachos. "Would it be accurate to say that you're experiencing a transition?"

"That would probably be accurate."

She nods, her ponytail bounces. "Many people are in the same situation. Times are changing; people are rethinking their values. I must tell you, I'm sick to death of this preoccupation with money."

She sips her wine. "Unfortunately, you can't escape it. Everything is so expensive. I heard someone on the street the other day say," she imitates a male voice, "'If you've got the money, you spend it. If you don't have the money …' he paused here and his friend chimed in, 'You're in deep trouble'." When Zee doesn't appear amused by her anecdote she laughs self-consciously. He takes another swig of his scotch, wondering why women talk more than men. Why can't they be silent? Then he remembers that Mary is silent, and he never knows what she's thinking. Sometimes he suspects that there is another world inside Mary's head, a separate planet, filled with canaries and animated creatures from Walt Disney pictures.

Maggie brushes nacho crumbs from her fingers then slides her hand nervously over her ponytail. "Dave told me you just ended a relationship?"

"Not 'just'. It's been six months."

"I'm sorry. It's difficult at our age; starting fresh, meeting new people. I must tell you, I've even tried a dating service. Well, not a dating service exactly. It was called Meeting Gourmands. I thought it would be tolerable because you meet in a group and feast on culinary delights. I must tell you, not only was the food disgusting, but there was a grand total of three men at my table. Three men and seven women. Hardly a fair ratio. I demanded a refund. I don't see why I should pay to eat mediocre food with a posse of women."

"Were the men nice?"

"I didn't get a chance to talk to them."

Zee nods and juts out his lower lip, hoping to appear deep in thought. He hasn't drunk for weeks, hasn't felt the need for it, working at night. Now he welcomes the haze settling over him.

"I must tell you …" Maggie goes on, and Zee wonders why she 'must tell' him anything. "I've even tried the personal columns, in a reputable paper, of course. You wouldn't believe the mail I received. There are many lonely people out there." Zee nods and stares at the pink marble ashtray beside his coaster on the coffee table. "I must

291

have met twenty men," Maggie says. "They were pleasant, nothing particularly wrong with any of them, they just weren't for me, I'm afraid."

"What did you say in the ad?"

She tugs on her ponytail. "Oh, I can't remember. Something along the lines of 'attractive professional woman, mid-thirties, looking for a long-term relationship with heterosexual male under forty-five. Enjoys sports, travel, the arts,' something like that."

Zee raises his eyebrows. "Humm."

"I didn't lie about a thing. I was very straightforward."

"That's the way to do it."

"I just thought I'd try it. Couldn't see as I had anything to lose. Occasionally you just have to stick your neck out, don't you think?"

"Absolutely."

After dinner, Dave takes Zee into the den for cognac and shows him his new laptop. "You have to get one," he says. "The software they're coming up with will blow your mind." Zee stares at the screen, the cursor flitting from word to word, number to number and wonders who designs these things, what do they look like? Wizened old men? Sixteen-year-old whiz-kids with greasy hair? Japanese with glasses?

"She talks a lot, I know," Dave says, "but I thought you'd like her. I mean she's intelligent." He shakes his head. "I wasn't trying to set you up."

"I know that." They both sip. "So how's married life?" Zee asks.

"Different. I think I like it. Sometimes I get a little weirded out about it. I mean everything you do has an effect on this person."

"And vice versa."

"That's right." Dave flattens his hand over the rim of his glass. "Sometimes I forget that. I get caught up in my own thing. Like with the computer. She says she's a 'computer widow'." He tries to laugh, switches off the computer, leans back in his chair and rests his feet on the desk. "And sometimes, I don't know, I get scared she's getting bored with me. I mean I think maybe she thought, because I'm a broker, I'd have an exciting life. You know, risky and all that. I don't. I'm a really ordinary guy. Sometimes I think I let her down." He pulls on his nose. "Like she hates my sweat-pants, you know those sweat-pants I wear? As soon as I come home I'm out of my suit and into my sweats. She hates it."

"What does she want you to wear?"

"Designer jeans, I guess, I don't know."

Zee sniffs his cognac. "I don't think you should be worried about boring her. I think you should just do what you gotta do, and if she's bored, then let her go."

"Don't say that."

"Well, what are you going to do, spend the rest of your life worrying about boring this person?"

Dave picks up a pen and doodles on a newspaper. "You can't just 'do what you gotta do'. I mean you're married. There's another person there."

"Okay. So why is that person there?"

Dave pulls on his nose again and stares at the desk. Zee notices the crease deepening between his eyebrows. "Were you ever afraid of boring Alex?" Dave asks.

"No."

"Did she ever bore you?"

"No."

"Like I'm even scared of boring her in bed now."

"Does she say she's bored?"

"She never says anything," Dave says. "It's a feeling I have."

"Does she bore you in bed?"

"No, I'm crazy about her. I want to fuck her all the time."

Zee nods solemnly. "She has perky tits."

"She has great tits."

"Well ..." Zee walks over to the window and pulls back the curtain so he can look at the city lights. "It seems to me that you can't be afraid of boring the person. It seems to me that you should be able to relax with the person."

"If the person is your wife."

"Exactly."

Dave sighs heavily and scratches his head. "I don't know. Maybe it's all in my head. Maybe I'm just scared of losing her."

"How can you relax with her if you're scared of losing her?"

Dave starts doodling again. "So why did you split up with Alex?"

"She wanted a kid."

Dave looks up at him. "You don't want a kid?" Zee shakes his head. "Why not?" Dave asks. "You'd be a great father."

"I'm emotionally retarded myself. What am I supposed to do with a kid?"

"Talk to it. Treat it like a person. It's no big deal. I'd love a kid. You take it to the park and tell it to watch the ball. You see that all the time. Dads in parks pitching to their kids, telling them to watch the ball. It looks like a lot of fun." He folds the newspaper and chucks it in a wastepaper basket. "Glenda wants to wait."

Zee lets the curtain fall back over the window and leans against the sill. "You have to give up a lot of things."

"So what's to give up?" Dave asks. "Like guys say to me, they say they don't want to give up their freedom. Like what are they doing with their freedom? Diddly-squat is what they're doing. It's not like they're travelling around the world, taking time off to soul-search or whatever. They're dicking around at their jobs, eating in restaurants and looking for sex that usually sucks anyway. So what's to give up?"

Zee walks back to the desk, picks up a small digital clock and watches the seconds flash. "So why does Glenda want to wait?"

"I don't know." Dave stands and goes to the window. "I don't know why she put these curtains up. Nobody can see in, we're too high up." He yanks back the curtains and stares out. Zee puts the clock back down. Dave slides his hands into his pockets. "I think she's holding out on me," he says, "because she wants to make sure she hasn't made a mistake by marrying me." He shakes his head and turns to Zee. "It's like all I want now is for her to want to have a baby with me. I feel like if she'd just want that, with me, then I'd relax, you know, I'd believe she was in for the full term. I mean a person who wants to have a kid with you isn't about to skip town tomorrow."

"No."

"I mean, talk about commitment."

"Yeah."

•

Alex opens the door and leans on it as though she can hardly stand. "What are you doing here?"

"I came to pick up my beanbag chair."

"At three in the morning?"

"I've been meaning to do it for awhile."

"Oh, Zee, you are so full of shit. How are you going to carry it?"

"I'll get a cab."

She throws up her hands and backs into the living-room. "Fine. Okay. Take your beanbag chair and go."

"Can I sit for a minute?"

"You're pissed out of your fucking mind. Why can't you face me sober?"

"I'm sorry."

She puts her hands on her hips and stares at him. "Do you want to sleep here or what?"

"I want to talk."

Alex sighs and slumps onto the couch. Zee stumbles over to the beanbag chair and squats into it. She jerks a hand towards it. "I won't be sorry to see that go," she says. "A relic from the seventies."

"I didn't think the seventies were all that bad."

"Oh, please." She sighs again and rolls onto her side. "So what

295

do you want to talk about?"

"Where's Harry, is he asleep?"

"Harry?"

"The man."

"What man?"

"The man who was at the bar."

"What bar?"

"Jenny's bar. Where she played."

"Oh, you mean Larry."

"Is he here?"

"No."

Maybe they broke up, Zee thinks; maybe she got bored with him. "You feeling okay these days?" he asks.

"Pretty sick but okay. I hate getting fat. And I have to pee all the time. And I'm constipated. The womb cramps the colon and the bladder."

"That must be uncomfortable."

"It is." She stares at him.

"Well, you don't look fat."

"Thank you."

The tap drips. The electric clock hums. Zee rests his forehead against his arms on his knees and stares at the fake Persian carpet between his feet. "I really miss you."

"I miss you too," she says.

"I never thanked you for getting me out of jail."

"Yes, you did."

"I mean, you didn't have to do it. I really appreciated it."

"It wasn't a problem."

"Well, I appreciated it. Thanks." He wants to lift his head off his arms and look at her, but it feels too heavy. "I really miss you," he repeats.

"It's too late now, Zee. We blew it. It's different now."

He wishes he could jump up and scream at her, knock her

around a bit, demand to know how she could just go off and make somebody else's baby, but he can't feel his legs. Besides he doesn't want to piss her off. He wants to stay here, in the apartment. He feels how he imagines the dog must feel when he's been allowed back in after being thrown out for peeing on the mat. He realizes that he must behave, not cause a disturbance. Maybe, if he stays the whole night, he'll find out more about Harry. He manages to lift his head. "What are you going to do about your job?"

"I'm not sure," she says. "I'll work something out."

"Does Harry have money?"

"Zee, there is no Harry, so quit with the Harry stuff, alright?"

"No Harry?"

"No Harry."

He stares at her. "So whose is it then?"

She sighs and examines one end of the belt on her bathrobe. "I don't know. There are three possibilities."

Three! This is too much. If he weren't so drunk he would take a stand, point the finger, call her a slut, something. But he feels at one with the beanbag chair, mushy and grainy. She doesn't even know three men. Where would she find three men, three studs, three dumb pricks? How could she do it, use any old sperm? Did she screen these guys, or did she just pick them up off the street? Did she pay them? He can't imagine three different pricks invading her vagina. It's too horrible, as she would say. How could she put herself at risk like that? This doesn't sound like Alex. Not his Alex. Where's his Alex? She's been invaded by the Body Snatchers.

"Alex?" he says. When she doesn't respond he crawls on all fours to look at her because he doesn't have the strength to stand. "Alex ...?" When he sees that she's asleep, he stares at her, reacquainting himself with her features. He'd forgotten about the mole on her temple that she worries will become malignant, spread to her brain and kill her. He leans over and gives her the lightest kiss possible on her cheek. A butterfly kiss. He used to press his eye against her cheek and blink, brushing her skin with his eyelashes. He used to call it a butterfly kiss. He pulls a cushion off the couch, lies down on the floor beside her and slides it under his head. He can even hear her breathing; little furry-animal snores. Then everything goes black.

•

When he wakes up he is still on the floor but wrapped in a blanket. He listens for her, peers around. When he doesn't see or hear her, he drops his throbbing head back into the cushion.

Later he feels someone prodding his shoulder. "Zee, what's going on? What are you doing here?" He forces his eyes open and sees Dear Old Fish Face. She hands him a note. "This is for you, I imagine."

He reads: "My mother is arriving some time this afternoon, can you lock up when you leave and drop the key in the mailbox for her? Thanks."

"What time is it?" Zee asks.

"One-thirty."

"Jesus."

"Did you miss an appointment?"

"No … no." He pushes off the blanket, leans against the couch and rubs his face.

"Are you not feeling well?" Elizabeth asks, still looking down at him.

"I'm a little hungover."

"I see." She fingers the pearls around her neck. "Well, I think I'll make some coffee. Would you like some?"

"Please." The pressure from his brain swelling against his skull is unbearable. "I think I'll have a shower," he says and walks as steadily as possible to the bathroom. Under the shower head, he wonders where Alex went and if she's pissed off at him. He doesn't understand why he has to get drunk before he comes to see her. *Because he's chickenshit.* And now he has to face Elizabeth. He could make a run for it, streak through the living-room and out the door, but then Dear Old Fish Face would tell Alex that he took off without a word, escaped like a criminal. He can just hear her, "He ran from here like a bat out of hell." No, he must face Elizabeth, convince her that he is a man in control of his life, unafraid, taking everything in his stride. He must convince Elizabeth that Alex has made a grave mistake by letting him go.

"Do you take anything in it?" Elizabeth asks while he towels his hair.

"Ah, just milk."

She hands him a cup. "You don't shave either. That seems to be the thing these days. Quite frankly, I find it singularly unattractive."

"Actually, I usually do." He squats on the beanbag chair. "I just didn't want to use one of Alex's razors."

"So you haven't moved back in, then?"

"Oh, no."

"I see." She sips her coffee and glances at her watch. "Do you know when she'll be back?"

"No." He combs his fingers through his hair, flattening it against his head. He'd forgotten how nice Alex's towels smell. He keeps one around his neck.

Elizabeth sits on the edge of the couch. "Did you two have some kind of an encounter last night?"

"Encounter …? Ah … we talked, yes."

"Was it productive?"

"Productive? How do you mean exactly?"

"Well, obviously you two loved each other very much. That's not something you get over in a week. I imagine you've had to talk things through. Are you friends now?"

"Ah, yeah, I guess we are. I try to help out. She's having a difficult time right now."

Elizabeth picks a piece of lint off her skirt. "How so?"

"I understand that the first few months are always difficult."

"The first few months?"

Only now does he realize that Old Fish Face doesn't know about the baby. Alex probably doesn't want her to know. Alex will be even more pissed off with him if Elizabeth finds out. "The first few months after a breakup," he says, "are always tough."

Elizabeth tightens her lips. "I see." She takes off one of her pumps and flexes her toes. It shocks Zee to see how much her feet resemble Alex's. "How are you weathering the ordeal?"

"Weathering?"

"Why do both you and Alex repeat what I say?"

"We do?"

"Oh, for goodness sake." She slides the shoe back on her foot.

"I'm sorry. Ah … weathering. I think I'm not weathering badly."

"I would like to hear your side of the story, if you don't mind telling me. I know that Alex was devastated. You know she came to see us at Christmas?"

"Actually, no. I didn't."

"Well, she did, and she was not happy. Quite frankly, I wondered if the whole thing hadn't been a bit sudden." Zee holds the end of the towel up to his nose and sniffs it. "Who initiated the breakup?" Elizabeth asks.

"I think it was a mutual decision."

"There is no such thing," she says firmly, reminding him of Alex. Both mother and daughter make declarations that instill terror in the recipient.

"Then I guess she did," he concedes, "initiate it."

"I see." She sighs heavily and fingers her pearls. "Well, it's always difficult."

"I don't necessarily see it as definitely over," he says, not daring to look at her but rubbing his face in the towel.

"Really?"

"I mean, people work out their differences."

Elizabeth sips her coffee and stares at a point in mid-air. "Is that what you were discussing last night?"

"In a manner of speaking."

"And what is her feeling on the subject?"

"I think she's afraid of her feelings. I mean, Alex isn't a feeling kind of person. She's more a head person."

Elizabeth crosses her legs and adjusts her skirt over her knees. "It's this negativity I'm concerned about. I don't know where she gets that from. Negative things happen to negative people. It's as simple as that."

"I don't think she's negative exactly, more prudent."

The door opens abruptly, Alex steps in and looks straight at Zee. "You're still here," she says dully. "Hi, Mum." Elizabeth stands, and they hug. "Have you eaten?" Alex asks.

"I thought maybe I could take you out," Elizabeth suggests.

"I bought some things to stir fry."

"Why don't we save them for dinner?"

"Okay."

Elizabeth tenderly brushes hair from Alex's forehead. "Is there anywhere special you'd like to go?"

Zee realizes that he has been dismissed, that he is no longer welcome. "Well, I guess I should get going." He stands.

"Are you taking your chair?" Alex asks.

"Oh, right." He looks at it.

"Do you want me to call a cab?" she asks.

"No, that's alright. I'll flag one down." As he bends down to pick it up he feels nauseated and has to steady himself, leaning a fist into the chair. He takes a big breath then wraps his arms around it, trying to get a firm grip on its bulk.

"Are you sure you'll be alright?" Alex asks.

He straightens, clutching it, wavering slightly. "Oh, yeah."

She holds the door open for him. "What about your back?"

"I'll be fine."

He cannot believe that she doesn't even see him to the front steps, just closes the apartment door behind him.

Holding the beanbag chair against his chest, he can barely see in front of him. He walks for a block before dropping it to the sidewalk and sitting on it. A small black boy skips up to it and kicks it, "Cool, man," he says.

"Don't kick it."

"What's in it?" the boy asks.

"Beans."

"Beans?"

"Yeah."

"Cool."

"Would you like to sit on it?"

"Can I?"

"Go ahead." Zee stands and gestures towards the chair.

The boy plops into it. "Cool," he says, bouncing up and down and patting it with his hands.

"Would you like it?" Zee asks.

"You mean you don't want it?"

"I don't really have space for it."

"Sure man, I'll take it."

Zee can't imagine what this small boy will do with the chair. He reminds Zee of little Miss Muffet sitting on her Tuffet. "You have it, then," Zee says, then slides his hands in his pockets, turns and walks away, determined not to look back.

THIRTY

*I*t is not until dinner that her mother really starts to irritate her. "You're peeing an awful lot, love. Do you think you might have some kind of bladder infection? Lots of people get them, especially women. It's very common. With antibiotics, you're better in no time." Elizabeth pokes at her stir-fried vegetables. "I think I need a little salt on this." Alex takes the shaker from the shelf and sets it on the table. "What do you do when you have a dinner party?" Elizabeth asks. "You can barely fit two people in here."

"Take the table into the living-room and open the flaps."

"You should see Nick's house. The dining-room is the size of your whole apartment. Quite frankly, I think Courtney is lacking in the taste department, but even so, it's very grand, the whole thing. And of course they have a pool."

"Of course."

"Don't be like that. He's worked hard for every penny. I just wish he'd married someone a little older, more mature. I don't trust that girl."

"Do you want more wine?"

"I'm fine, thank you." She nibbles a broccoli spear. "I must say I'm pleased to see that you've put a little weight on. You were looking emaciated. I read somewhere that people who grow up eating meat, then suddenly stop, have degenerating connective tissue."

"I didn't suddenly stop. It just worked out that way."

Elizabeth pats her mouth with her paper napkin. "You're looking very tired. Are you working too hard?"

"No."

"I'm worried about you. You're putting on a brave face, but there something's wrong isn't there? Is it Zee, do you miss him?"

"Of course."

Elizabeth looks down at her plate and spears a slice of red pepper. "It's really none of my business, but he told me he thinks a reconciliation is a possibility."

"He said that?"

Elizabeth nods. "I don't know why I'm telling you, I don't think he's right for you, I really don't. He's a weak cup of tea if ever there was one."

Seeing Zee last night, meek and drunk, reminded Alex, yet again, that he drags her down and makes her feel like a bitch. Lately, she doesn't think of him in this condition, remembers only the easygoing Zee, the one she can talk to, who soothes, cajoles and hugs her. The Zee who can wiggle his ears and roll his eyes simultaneously. The dejected Zee who turns up on her doorstep fades from her memory. She mustn't let this happen, she tells herself. She must see it like it is. She mashes a chunk of tofu with her fork. "I'm better off on my own."

"I'm sure you are, love, but you never know, you might meet someone else. Look at Art and I." Elizabeth sits back from the table, holding her napkin in her lap. "I'd like to see your muffin factory."

"It's not a factory. It's a room with an industrial oven, a freezer and an assistant."

"Are you planning to expand?"

"I already did."

"I see."

Alex excuses herself and goes for another pee, furious with herself for letting Elizabeth get to her. She knows that she can never please her mother, why does she even try? Why did she tell her about the muffins? Why tell her anything about her life? Elizabeth will never be satisfied, will only tighten her mouth and hold her hand under her chin looking worried or sceptical or just plain bored.

Alex sits on the toilet and tries to force a bowel movement. When she has no success she leans her head against the cool of the sink and closes her eyes. She feels as if every one of her bones were filled with lead. More than anything right now, she wants to be alone, wants to crawl into her bed and hide. Mixing muffins today, she nearly fainted from the heat. Marika will have to work overtime to fill the orders. The Mazda is making strange noises again, and she has to spend two more entire days with her mother.

"Are you alright, love?" Elizabeth asks through the door.

"I'll be right out." She pulls up her jeans and splashes water on her face.

Elizabeth has started to do the dishes. "I thought I'd make some coffee."

"Go ahead." Alex sits, leaning an elbow on the table, propping her head on her hand.

Elizabeth studies her. "You really are sick aren't you? Please tell me Alex, I can't bear it when you conceal things from me."

"When have I concealed things from you?"

"What is wrong with you? Why won't you tell me? Please tell me." Elizabeth looks scared now, her mouth hangs slack, the coffee filter shakes in her hand.

"I'm pregnant."

Elizabeth's hand holding the filter drops. She looks towards the window then back at Alex. She turns to the stove and carefully places the filter in the pot. "Does Zee know?"

"It's not Zee's. I don't know whose it is, and I don't care. I'm very tired, and I don't want to talk about it now."

"You're going to have it by yourself?"

"That's right."

Elizabeth turns to her, knotting her fingers together. "Sweetheart," she pleads, "do you have any idea how difficult it is to raise a child? It's full time. When it wants you, you have to be there for it, twenty-four hours a day. That's why men and women share the responsibility, a person can't do it alone. Believe me, I know."

Alex crumples her napkin, stands and pushes it into the garbage can. "I'm really tired," she says. "I'm sorry. I have to go to bed. I'm sorry Mum, really. Maybe there's something on TV you can watch."

•

The first time Alex wakes she stumbles, squinting, to the bathroom, barely noticing Elizabeth vacantly watching Jay Leno parade around in a cowboy costume. "Are you alright, love?" Elizabeth asks.

"Yeah."

Later she dreams that Paul Newman wants to marry her. He places his hands on her stomach and tells her he misses the sound of a baby in the house. He tells her not to worry about money, he'll take care of everything, she can come and live in his house in California and swim in his pool. Not once does he mention Joanne Woodward. He looks very grey and frail and is shorter than Alex. She likes the idea of the house and the pool and not having to worry about money, but she doesn't want to break up his marriage. Also he doesn't really know her. She worries that if they get married, he'll find out how neurotic and bitchy she is and won't want her in his house or his pool. Besides she doesn't want to upset Zee any more than she already has. She knows that if she marries Paul Newman, Zee will know she did it for the money and will never forgive her, will despise her.

•

Sun blasts into the kitchen. Standing by the stove, Elizabeth greets her with her gum-revealing smile. "How about a soft-boiled egg?"

"Oh please, Mum, don't even talk about it."

"I know how you feel, but you have to eat, a little protein at least."

Alex sits, resting both elbows on the table. "Maybe I'll try some cereal."

"Good girl."

Alex points to a cupboard. "There's some Mini Wheats in there."

Elizabeth pours the Mini Wheats into a bowl, adds milk, pulls a spoon from the drawer and sets it and the bowl in front of Alex. "I've been thinking," Elizabeth says, "how would you like to come and stay with us?"

Alex sinks a Mini Wheat with her spoon. "Oh, Mum, I can't do that."

"Why not?"

"I have a business going, a job."

"We can support you. And I can help you when the baby's born."

"I'll think about it."

"You won't. I know you won't. Why are you so stubborn?"

Alex stares down at the cereal then scoops up a Mini Wheat with her spoon. "The woman at the corner store says I'm supposed to drink a quart of milk a day. I hate milk. It gives me pimples."

"Oh, for goodness sake."

•

Elizabeth says nothing as Alex leads her into the dark warehouse and through a warren of potters' and sculptors' studios. Alex pushes open a door at the back of the building and guides her into a small, neat space barely containing a freezer, a refrigerator, an industrial oven and a worktable. Elizabeth stares at Marika dripping with sweat, wiping her hands on her floury apron.

"Mum, this is Marika."

"Hi, Elizabeth," Marika says then pulls open the oven door, blasting heat into the room. Marika nods at the muffins. "These guys are pretty close."

"How can you stand this heat?" Elizabeth asks, fanning herself with her hand.

Marika takes a swig of Coke. "You get used to it."

"Do you want to wait in the car, Mother?" Alex points to the muffins cooling on racks. "I have to pack these up."

"Maybe I will," Elizabeth says.

"Do you think you can find your way?"

"Oh yes," Elizabeth affirms, looking uncertain. After the door closes behind her, Alex picks up the clipboard and starts to fill the orders.

"Is she going to make deliveries with you?" Marika asks, brushing muffin tins with oil.

"I'm afraid so."

"If you dressed like a woman, you'd look exactly like her."

Alex lines a box with waxed paper and begins to fill it with muffins. "How was Travis last night?"

Marika shrugs. "We went to see some dumb karate movie."

Alex places a layer of waxed paper over a layer of muffins. "He's not giving up, though, is he? He keeps trying."

Marika uses an ice-cream scoop to dollop dough into the tins. "He doesn't understand what I'm feeling."

"Nobody can. You can't expect that from him. The important thing is that he doesn't tell you not to feel it. Lots of guys would lose patience, expect you to get over it."

"I'll never get over it."

"I think Travis understands that. He knows your demons and wants to be with you anyway. I give him full marks for that."

"You're supposed to be objective."

"Well, I think it's rare that a person is willing to accept all sides of you."

Marika sprinkles rolled oats over the unbaked muffins. "I don't know, I think he's just a wuss."

"A wuss?"

"A softy."

·

When Alex sees the beanbag chair on the pavement, she gasps. She approaches it cautiously, holding her hand over her chest, then leans over to examine it, to verify that it's Zee's. Someone has slashed it with a knife. Greyish particles leak from the rip. It stinks of urine. Nausea grips her, she turns away quickly and continues home, stunned that he could do such a thing; desert a possession he has sheltered through changing times, despite derisive comments regarding its practicality and design. Many times she pleaded with him to donate the beanbag chair to the Salvation Army, but he always refused. And now he has left it on the pavement to be mutilated.

He has left it on the pavement for her to see.

THIRTY-ONE

Outside the movie theatre, Mary leans on Zee for support while she bends over to adjust the ankle strap of her sandal. "Can we go see an American movie next time?"

"You don't like French movies?"

"I always feel depressed afterwards."

"I found this one uplifting."

Mary straightens up. "You did?"

"Well, sure. I mean, he doesn't get what he thought he wanted, but he found out that he really didn't want it."

Mary examines the sunburn on her right shoulder. "Then he should've been happier at the end."

"I think he was happy. Just a quiet sort of happy." He pulls his cap low over his eyes to block out the sun. "Do you feel like an icecream, or a beer maybe?"

"I'm sunburned."

"Well, next time we'll sit under a tree." They walk past a group of teenaged boys leaning against a store window where wheelchairs and walking aids are displayed. One of them, with a cigarette dangling from his mouth, asks Zee for change. Zee shakes his head. "Fuckin' asshole," the boy calls after him.

"I phoned your house a couple of days ago," Mary says. "You weren't there."

"I thought I asked you not to call my house."

"Because it disturbs your mother."

"That's right."

"I talked to your mother. She said she isn't an invalid."

Zee clears his throat and pretends to be absorbed in a shoe-store window, although he's really watching Mary's reflection. Pressing the side of her index finger against her front teeth, she looks down at the pavement. "So why did you tell me that she was an invalid?"

"She is an invalid. She just doesn't like to think of herself as one." He scrutinizes a loafer, aware that Mary is pondering this information. She takes her hand away from her mouth and stares at the side of his face. "She asked me and you to come over after the movie today."

"What?"

"She wants us to come over. She wants to meet me."

Zee turns to her. "She doesn't even know who you are."

"That's why she wants to meet me."

"What did you tell her?"

"Nothing."

"You must have told her something," Zee says, starting to walk, "otherwise why would she want to meet you?"

Mary trails him. "Because I'm your girlfriend."

"You told her that?"

"Well, it's true, isn't it?"

Zee avoids her eyes and looks at a small group of Pro-Life demonstrators carrying signs displaying a photo of a fetus and the words, "Abortion is the worst form of child abuse." Immediately he thinks of Alex, wonders what her fetus looks like, if she's scared of giving birth; of the pain, the blood, the gore.

"I am, aren't I?" Mary asks. "Your girlfriend?"

"Of course. It's just that I don't want to worry my mother."

"She wasn't worried. She said she was worried before because you weren't seeing anybody."

Is she going to be alone in the delivery room? With no one to wipe her brow and hold her hand and breathe with her?

"She sounds really nice, your mother," Mary says. "She doesn't sound sick at all."

·

When they step through Daisy's front door, Jenny is the first to jump out at him. "Surprise!" she shrieks. Standing in the living-room are Daisy, Durham, Kyle and Damian, who plays Happy Birthday on his electric guitar. They all sing along. Zee turns to Mary who giggles. "You knew about this?" he asks. She kisses him on the lips. "Happy birthday, Theodore."

He'd thought it had slipped by without anyone remembering. The only person he'd wanted to remember was Alex. He'd wanted her to think about him all day, and feel bad. Last year she'd roasted a chicken, and they'd driven into the country for a picnic. They'd sat in the grass, listening to the birds and the wind in the trees until they could no longer ignore the mosquitoes.

"Give us a hug, bro," Jenny says, throwing her arms around him.

"We baked a cake," Daisy announces. "Devil's food, your favourite."

"I'm going to take him upstairs," Jenny says, grabbing his hand and yanking him up the stairs. Outside his bedroom, she stops and looks at him. "You ready?"

"For what?"

She pushes open the door and pulls him inside then quickly closes it and clasps her hands behind her back. "Do you notice anything?" she asks. Zee notices that the air feels cool. He can hear a hum. "It's an air-conditioner," Jenny says, bouncing on the balls of her feet. "We all chipped in because you get so grouchy when you're hot."

"Does it always hum?"

Jenny sighs and plants her hands on her hips. "Zee, just try to be grateful for once, okay?"

He walks over to the air-conditioner and studies its buttons and dials. Jenny follows him and leans against it. "There's instructions in the box."

Zee turns a dial down to low. "Are you and Damian back together again, then?"

"Why?"

"Just curious."

"You think it's destructive for me to be with him?"

"I don't think anything. I was just asking."

Jenny hooks her hair behind her ears. "I really don't think you're in a position to judge my relationship." She walks across the room and spins his globe. Daisy bought it for him when he was nine and wanted to know where Africa was. "I mean who's this Mary person?" Jenny asks.

"She's a friend."

"Mom says she's your girlfriend. I can't believe that after Alex, you'd go for a cow brain."

Zee steadies his globe with his hand. "You've only just met her."

"Obviously Alex threatened you, and now you just want to bury your face in big boobs."

Zee heads for the door. "I'm going downstairs now."

"It's men like you that make women think men are pigs."

Zee's always felt that they should leave pigs out of it. He likes pigs, with their flat, cushiony noses and their squiggly little tails.

In the living-room, Durham performs card tricks for Mary, Kyle and Damian. "That's not your card is it?" he asks sadly. Mary shakes her head. Durham tosses the cards on the table. "It didn't work," he mutters and pulls on an earlobe.

"So try it again," Kyle says.

"Zee, is that you?" Daisy calls. "Come into the kitchen." He walks down the hall and stands in the doorway watching her stick candles into the cake. "I don't have forty-four," she says.

"That's alright. Thanks for the air-conditioner, Ma."

"I hope it will make you less cranky."

"Actually I've been thinking of moving out."

"Where to? Are you going to move in with the girl?"

"No, I thought I'd get a room somewhere."

"You have a room here."

Jenny stomps into the kitchen. "Don't even try to talk to him. He's a pig. He says the air-conditioner hums."

"I was just making an observation."

"Is it supposed to hum?" Daisy strikes a match and lights the candles on the cake.

Jenny sticks her finger into the icing and licks it. "It blows air, of course it's going to hum."

Durham comes into the kitchen. "Do I hear arguing?"

"Zee doesn't like the air-conditioner," Jenny says.

Zee shakes his head. "I didn't say that."

Durham pulls on his earlobe. "You think maybe it puts toxic chemicals into the air?"

Jenny sighs and picks up the cake. "Can we please do the cake thing now?" They follow her in single file back to the living-room where Damian, Mary and Kyle are watching a soap opera. "Damian," Jenny says, "I thought we agreed you weren't going to watch TV."

Damian holds up his hand, silencing her. "I just want to see if they hump."

Jenny sets the cake on the coffee-table then stomps over to the TV and switches it off. Damian gives her the finger; she ignores him. "Sit down Zee," she says, "and make a wish." He sits on the couch, trying to think of a wish, but his mind goes blank. When he was small, he used to wish to be a famous singer or a millionaire. "Hurry up, Zee," Daisy says. "The candles are melting." He closes his eyes, pretending to make a wish, then blows the candles out. They all applaud.

What does it mean when you can't even think of a wish?

"Kyle says he'll cut your hair for free," Durham says.

Kyle nods slowly, like Frankenstein. "You should make use of that natural wave."

After the cake, Zee agrees to have his hair cut because it excuses him from making conversation. Sitting on a stool in the kitchen, he enjoys the sound of the scissors snipping around his ears and the sight of his hair dropping in clumps to the floor. He asks Kyle to cut it an inch long all over his head. He wants to shed his old hair, imagines that hair soaks up your past and that, to be free of it, you must cut it all off.

Durham sits watching in his hound-like pose, with his chin resting on his hands folded on the table. "Your ears are almost as big as mine," he observes.

"I had a client," Kyle says, "who wanted me to shave his head. I was against it, but he insisted."

"Why?" Durham asks.

"He said he saw no point in having hair. He said the only reason to have hair was so women could run their fingers through it, and since he'd given up on women, he didn't need it. He says all he does is go to work then go home and watch his VCR."

"Why did he give up on women?" Zee asks.

"Oh the usual reasons: they're too aggressive, desperate; they don't like sex; they want babies; they hate men. He said he loved this one woman, but she loved somebody else. Some other woman loved him, but he didn't love her. He said he always falls in love with women who love somebody else, so what's the point?"

"Especially when you have a VCR," Zee says.

After the haircut, while Damian and Mary try to outguess the contestants on a game show and Kyle, Daisy, Jenny and Durham play Hearts, Zee escapes to the back porch. He remembers batting a ball back here, tossing it up in the air and swinging at it because he had no dad to pitch for him. It was on these very steps that he dreamed about wearing a mohair suit and singing on the Ed Sullivan show; or at least being a folk-singer, standing under a spotlight and strumming a guitar.

Forty-four years old.

He should know more by now, he thinks, should be in charge of his life, should be able to steel himself against ignorance, cruelty and just plain evil. Things shouldn't get to him like they did when he was twenty-one.

Daisy pushes open the screen door. "You're not happy, I have a feeling."

"I'm fine."

She huffs and puffs, arranging herself on the step beside him. "Nobody likes getting older," she says, then glances around the foot of the steps. "I'm scared those wood ants are coming back. They'll eat the whole house." She pulls up grass poking through cracks in the concrete.

"Ma, you must have had ideas about what your life would be like."

"When?"

"Whenever. All through your life. Didn't you think things would turn out a certain way, and they didn't? I mean you didn't expect Dad to take off."

"No."

"So how did you live with that?"

"You get used to it."

He doesn't want to get used to it; doesn't want to go numb and no longer feel anything.

"You try to be decent," Daisy adds.

"What do you mean?"

"I can't be decent to everybody, but I try to be decent to people close to me. Otherwise they'll go away, and I'll have nobody. You,

you aren't decent to people close to you. You push them away. When I'm dead, you won't have anybody."

"Maybe that won't be so bad."

"You wait and see."

He runs his hands over his cropped head. "What do you mean by 'decent' exactly?"

"You don't hurt people for no reason."

"I'm not hurting anybody."

"Who's this Mary girl?"

"I met her at work, she's a friend."

Daisy pulls her cardigan closed over her stomach. "You wait and see. You'll end up with nobody."

●

He decides to tell Mary in the utility van while he's driving her to work. This way he won't have to face her, won't be tempted to hug her and tell her everything's going to be alright. "Mary, I've been thinking that maybe we should stop going out."

"How do you mean?"

"I mean that we should stop seeing each other." A car in front of him suddenly stops. Zee jams on the brakes. They both lurch forward in their seats.

"Why?" Mary asks, steadying herself on the dash.

"Because I can't give you what you need."

Mary presses the side of her index finger against her front teeth. "You said you couldn't give your old girlfriend what she needed."

"That's right."

"So how do you know what we need?"

"I'm not making you happy." He glances at her. She looks away, out the window, and drops her hand into her lap.

"I don't mind if you see other people," she says.

"It's not that."

"What is it, then?"

"It's just a feeling I have."

Mary looks at him. "So don't make it sound like you're doing it because of me. You always make it sound like you're doing things for other people, but you're really just doing things for yourself. You act like you're really nice, but you're not. You think you're better than other people. You think it's everybody else's fault, but it's your fault." He stops at a green light, waiting to make a left-hand turn. Never before has Mary said so many words in a row. He stares at the light, stunned, until finally it changes to yellow. "I'd like to get out now," Mary declares.

"Let me drive you to work at least," he says, but she's already opened the door. He slams on the brakes again. They both lurch forward. She doesn't look at him as she climbs down, but her skirt gets caught in the door as she slams it. When she opens it to free the skirt, he can see that she's crying. "Mary …" he says but she slams the door. A Mack truck bears down on him, honking. He drives on, catching a glimpse of her in his rearview as she examines the damage done to her skirt.

You think it's everybody else's fault, but it's your fault.

All this time he has told himself that he can just walk away from the dung heap, that he doesn't harbour resentment or anger or blame. But he knows he's kidding himself. On the bad days, the hopeless days, he still blames 'them' for his failure, still dreams of blowing up government buildings, still scans the paper for scandalous news of his former colleagues. When he finds a story that applauds one of their endeavours, envy singes the walls of his stomach. He realizes that his freedom has no meaning as long he allows resentment to ferment inside him. So how to purge himself of this bile? How to barf it up, shit it out? To be free of them, he must convince himself that the choice was his, that he has no one to blame but himself. But so far he can't and he's scared, really scared he won't be able to. He'll grow old and stooped with this boil festering inside him. And pretty soon his life will be over.

Early for work, he squats on one of the concrete parking dividers outside the Morton building. At his feet an ant tries to climb over a crack in the asphalt while clutching in its jaw a white particle twice its size. Zee bends down to take a closer look at it, trying to determine what the particle is made of. It seems to be styrofoam. What is the ant going to do with a chunk of styrofoam? Does he think it's food? Is he planning to live off it all winter? The ant continually changes his strategy on the crack; backs off then starts again from a different angle. His perseverance awes Zee. He remembers the story about the ant and the grasshopper. When Daisy told it to him he always hoped that the ant would change his mind and invite the grasshopper inside to warm up a bit. The ant didn't have to share all his food, but if the grasshopper was repentant, couldn't the ant give him a crumb or two? Daisy shook her head resolutely and insisted that the grasshopper had to go back out into the cold and pay for playing his fiddle all summer.

Finally the ant approaches the crack backwards, dragging the styrofoam behind him. He mounts the crack without difficulty and in that brief instant, Zee feels his chest expand with hope.

THIRTY-TWO

*E*lizabeth starts to cry in the airport bar. At first Alex wonders if she's had an allergic reaction to the tomato juice or maybe to the peanuts. She watches Elizabeth take the napkin from under her glass and blow her nose several times. "Are you okay, Mum?"

"I just wish we could be close again." Alex considers asking her mother when she thinks they were close, but decides not to because she doesn't want to hurt her. Instead she eats some peanuts.

"You shut me out," Elizabeth says. Alex, hoping to avoid confrontation, looks over at a Sikh family several tables away. They are all eating and speaking at once. "I don't know what I've done to deserve this," Elizabeth says.

"You haven't done anything," Alex says, wondering how to explain that, after years of building self-doubt in your child, you can't expect it to suddenly drop all the baggage and love you unconditionally. You can't expect it to suddenly trust you with its fears and concerns after years of being told that its fears and concerns pale in comparison to yours; or to the one-legged man's. What have you got to worry about? Look at the one-legged man. What have you got to worry about? I had to raise two children on my own. You know what your problem is? You've had it too easy. You're too judgemental. You take things too seriously. You wish you were your brother.

Now Alex tries to pretend that everything's fine so Elizabeth won't tell her what her problem is.

Alex eats another peanut. "Do you remember the one-legged man?"

"Oh yes. What a sorry sight he was. I wonder what's become of him."

"He's probably dead. He was old." In winter he camped over a subway grid, warmed by the rush of air that rose from the tunnel when trains passed. Sometimes when they saw him asleep on the bench in the bus-stop shelter, his pants would be wet around the crotch. Alex always wondered how he could pee in his sleep. She always woke up when she had to pee.

Although Elizabeth often referred to the one-legged man, she never seemed to see him. She'd stride past him, looking straight ahead, commanding Alex not to stare.

"Remember when you had the abortion," Elizabeth says. "You phoned and asked me to go with you? Remember that?"

"Of course."

"I was so happy that you needed me. You cried in my arms, remember that?" Alex nods. Elizabeth looks down at the napkin in her hand and shakes her head. "It was one of the few times in my life I've felt successful at mothering."

"You're a great mother," Alex says, glancing at her watch, hoping that the imminent departure time will end this heart-to-heart discussion.

Elizabeth folds her hands on the table and stares at her. "Why won't you let me help you this time?"

"Because I'm alright on my own this time, really."

"I don't believe that. My goodness, why can't you be vulnerable for once?"

"Because, when I'm vulnerable, you tell me I'm feeling sorry for myself."

"That's when you're moping."

"Well, that's when I'm vulnerable," Alex says. "When I mope. I was vulnerable at Christmas."

Elizabeth dabs around her eyes with her napkin. "Christmas was difficult for everyone."

"Right. So I had no right to feel sorry for myself."

"I didn't say that."

"Whenever I tell you what's wrong," Alex says, "you tell me I'm making a fuss over nothing, that I'll get over it. I know I'll get over it, Mother. It's just that, at the time, I feel like crawling into a hole and dying."

Elizabeth stirs her drink with a swizzle stick. "You make your own life. If you want something badly enough you can make it happen."

"Right. So why waste time talking about it?" Alex watches the Sikh father laying out snapshots on the table. His chubby little boy holds up a photo and laughs, covering his mouth with his hand, then points at his chubby little sister who buries her face in her mother's soft shoulder. The mother snatches the photo from the boy and scolds him, but as soon as she looks away, he sticks his tongue out at the little girl.

Elizabeth sips her Bloody Mary. "I just think you're too sensitive. You take things too much to heart."

"There you go criticizing me again. Mum, this is who I am, right here." Alex raps her chest with her knuckles. "I don't want to be rich or famous. I don't have what it takes. I want to live a quiet little life, pay my bills and look after my child. Nick is the go-getter. Fix your attention on Nick. He loves it."

"You've always been jealous of him. I think it's hindered you."

"I envy him for not giving a shit about anyone but himself. I wish to God I didn't give a shit about a lot of things, but unfortunately I've been stuck with a conscience."

"You use that conscience thing as an excuse."

"An excuse for what …? For failure? Thanks Mum. Once again

you've filled me with self-confidence and a zest for life."

"You can't blame me for what's happened to you."

"I don't regard what's happened to me as all that bad. I'm doing what I want to do, and yes, you're absolutely right, you make your own life. So let me make mine. In my own way, on my own." Alex picks up her bag. "We should get going."

"Why are you so hostile?"

"I'm sorry. I just wish we could stop having this conversation. I wish we could just … go bowling or something."

Elizabeth grabs Alex's wrist and stares at her. "I love you. You and Nick are more important to me than my life."

"I love you too, Mum."

"I only want what's best for you."

"I know that. Have you got your ticket?"

At the gate, they hug each other tightly while the baggage inspectors discuss the renovated cafeteria. Suddenly Alex doesn't want to let go and senses that Elizabeth doesn't want to either, as if they both realize that physical contact is the only way they can circumvent the history between them. If only they could hug by phone.

"Please call me if you need anything," Elizabeth whispers.

"I will." Clinging to her mother in the stark departure zone, Alex feels weak, lost, desperate, convinced she can't manage on her own, can't manage without her mother. But she tells herself this feeling will pass. Once the plane has lifted off the runway and she is safely in her car, she'll feel like a grown-up again. "You'd better go, Mum."

"Yes."

Alex breaks the embrace, picks up Elizabeth's hand-luggage and places it on the conveyor belt. Elizabeth shows her ticket to a security guard and passes through the gate. On the other side, she picks up her bag, blows a kiss to Alex, then steps onto the escalator. As she sinks out of sight, she waves like the Queen. Panic jolts through

Alex, heat floods her face. She feels like she did when Elizabeth dropped her off at summer camp. Always, she had to fight the urge to run after her mother's station wagon. Always, she feared that she would never see her again, that Elizabeth would die from a fatal illness or a car crash. Always, she regretted that she'd argued with her mother about what clothes to pack, how much spending money to take, how often to call home. Always she felt that she hadn't loved her mother enough, cursed herself for not realizing how much she loved her mother—needed her mother—until she was driving away.

At the Center, certain young mothers have admitted to Alex that they lock their children into a room because they can't cope with their constant demands. Alex sees the same mothers slap their children's heads, call them moron and fuckface. Yet the children love them, cry out to them, wrap their arms around their legs and bury their faces into their thighs.

"Are you boarding, Ma'am?" one of the security guards asks.

"Oh, no, no, I'm just leaving." She turns abruptly and sets off in search of a Ladies room.

She notices the bleeding when she's sitting on the toilet. She tells herself not to panic. The doctor said that spotting is not unusual, that it is not necessarily a cause for alarm. Even so, staring at the dots of blood on her underpants, she begins to sweat. Outside the cubicle a mother reprimands her little girl for touching a garbage pail. "What did I tell you about public trash cans …? They're germy. Tess, make up your mind. Do you need to go or not …?" The little girl whimpers. "Okay," the mother says and guides the child into the cubicle next to Alex. "Let's put paper on the seat," the mother says. "Remember we always put paper on the seat because it's germy." Alex wipes sweat from her forehead then presses toilet paper against her vagina to see if she's still bleeding. Nothing. She'll be fine, she tells herself. She must remain calm. This happens all the time. "Don't touch the toilet," the mother says, then flushes. Alex can see the little girl's tiny pink sneakers and the mother's canvas slip-ons as the mother pulls up the little girl's shorts.

There is an accident on the highway. Alex's Mazda sits sandwiched between a Jaguar and a BMW, each driven by groomed men wearing sunglasses and talking on cellular phones. She envies their air-conditioning, wonders how she must look to them; harried, poor, over-heated in her hatchback. Do they detect her distress? Would they notice if she collapsed over the wheel? Would either of them leave the safety of their sealed vehicles to give her mouth-to-mouth resuscitation? Or would they honk, call her a stupid bitch and shove the noses of their cars into a neighbouring lane to pull around her?

Two hours later she arrives home feeling nauseated and regretting having eaten the peanuts. She calls Marika, asks her to work overtime, then phones Emergency. After holding for fifteen minutes, she speaks to an intern who advises her, if she is miscarrying, to "collect the remnants" in a plastic bag so they can do an analysis afterwards. Alex, revolted by this prospect, fails to ask what kind of analysis but then decides that, if she is miscarrying, which she isn't, the "remnants" will help the doctors to determine why. After two hours of lying on the bed, trying to read a *House and Garden* magazine that Elizabeth left behind, Alex realizes that she has started to bleed again. She presses a towel between her legs and curls into a ball, hoping to fall asleep, hoping to wake up and find everything as it was. Only now does she realize how lucky she was, truly lucky, to be pregnant. She wants to stay pregnant. She will stay pregnant.

This is not a miscarriage.

At eleven-thirty the contractions and the vomiting begin. She sits on the toilet expelling stool then what appears to be water. It's as though her body is rebelling, forcing her to relinquish foreign substances. She can't stop peeing, getting up from the bed to run to the toilet and back again. She lies on the bathroom floor, hoping to stall the process by keeping still. Initially the contractions occur once an hour but by four in the morning they rip her apart every twenty minutes or less. She gets back into bed, trying to find a comfortable position. She lies on her side, her back, then kneels on the bed with her head between her elbows. She bites the pillow case, fighting the pain, the feeling that a knife is slashing inside her. She is not miscarrying, she tells herself. When the chunks of flesh begin to slip from her—unrecognizable flesh, the consistency of liver but pink—she sits on the toilet, holding her hand between her legs and dutifully "collects the remnants" in her palm then drops them into a plastic bag. She tells herself that, if she were miscarrying, the flesh would look like a fetus. It would look like a baby. This is not a baby, this is just flesh.

The chunks become bigger then stop and only water seeps from her. She washes the blood from her hands and looks in the mirror at her face, drained of blood. Only in the past few months has she noticed the lines around her mouth. Then again she feels liquid gushing through her and sits back on the toilet, dropping her head in her hands, staring at the plastic shopping bag at her feet. The entire world is sleeping through her pain. Zee is sleeping through her pain. Never in her life has she felt so alone. So unwanted. So deserted.

By six-thirty she has vomited eleven times, but the contractions have abated. She twist-ties the plastic bag closed, showers and dresses, determined to make her muffin deliveries. She phones her doctor at nine. He tells her to go to Emergency in case they have to do a D&C. When she hands the nurse her bag of remnants the nurse says, "What did you do that for?"

"An intern told me to."

"Why?"

"He said you would do an analysis." The nurse holds the bag at a distance, staring at it with distaste, then walks down the corridor. Alex calls after her, "What are you going to do with it?"

"Don't worry about it, we'll take care of it."

A doctor wearing bifocals performs an ultra sound to make sure that she has lost the fetus. "We have to freeze you now," he says. "We have to do a D&C, to clean you up a bit."

"Are you sure I've lost it?"

He peers at her over his glasses. "Yes."

It is only then that Alex starts to cry. There on the examining table with her legs spread and strangers gawking at her vagina. "It's okay, dear," a middle-aged nurse with a bulbous red growth over one eye says.

"It's not okay," Alex gasps. "How can you say it's okay? It's not okay." She wants to pull her feet out of the stirrups, kick their faces in and run. She wants to tell them to fuck off, that they don't know what they're talking about. But she can't, knows she can't, knows she's lost.

The doctor pats her knee. "Try not to upset yourself now, you've been very brave." He brandishes a needle then aims it at her abdomen. "What about the bag I gave the nurse?" Alex asks.

"What bag?" he asks.

"I gave a bag to the nurse containing my remnants."

At a loss for words, the doctor pulls off his glasses and exchanges a look with the nurse. "Oh … well …"

"Forget it," Alex says as she drops her head back on the table and closes her eyes, surrendering, not wanting to watch as they suck out what's left of her baby. After the sting of the needle, she feels only a dull scraping; similar to the sensation she felt in her frozen mouth when a surgeon dug out her wisdom teeth. She tunes out the doctor's and nurse's murmurs, thinks only that at some point this will be over, and she will have to continue living. She will have to get into her car and drive, will have to go home and eat, and sleep and shit and piss. She will have to make muffins and convince teenagers that they can control their lives. She will have to get over it. She doesn't want to get over it. She's tired of getting over things.

"Alright, dear?" the nurse asks.

Alex turns her face to the wall. Tears slide down her temple into her ear, tickling her.

THIRTY-THREE

Zee likes his room. The sign outside the house says "Clean rooms for rent", and his is clean. And Zee has been keeping it that way, has bought a dust pan and broom and has been sweeping up. Next pay-cheque, he plans to buy a sponge mop and some Mop & Glo for the linoleum floor.

He asked Mrs. Zuppetti if he could take the bed that came with the room down to the basement and replace it with a futon. She agreed if he would mow the tiny patch of grass in front of the house once every two weeks, otherwise he'd have to pay extra for storage.

When he's not working or sitting in the park, he sits in his room on his futon. Today he's been thinking about the dream he had last night. For some reason he had a duck that he took wherever he went, cradling it close to his body to protect it. He took it on a plane, passing it by the stewardess unnoticed. At one point he was riding a chairlift up a mountain, still holding the duck, wondering why it didn't try to fly away. He can't figure out what the duck symbolizes: his heart, his soul, his integrity, his feelings for Alex, Alex's heart or soul or integrity? He can't figure it out.

A few days ago he bought a book on how to meditate and tried Breath Counting. He had liked the idea of simply counting and breathing. But in practice he found it frustrating. He prefers to let his mind wander, even if it takes him to thoughts he'd rather not to dwell on, like what a bastard he is and why Alex doesn't love him anymore.

A mouse shares the room with him. Initially it scurried back and forth across the floor, but during the past week, it has slowed down considerably. He thinks the mouse is sick so he has made a bed for it out of a shoe-box lid and a face cloth. He offers the mouse bits of cracker and cheese, but it won't eat. Zee has a feeling that the mouse is going to die. When he comes home in the mornings, he checks to see if it's still breathing. He's not sure how he'll feel if the mouse dies. He tries not to think about it, tells himself it's only a mouse.

In the room next to him lives Pete, a Phys. Ed. major, who has been trying to coax Zee into accompanying him to the gym. Pete wants him to work on his abdominals. In Zee's room, he demonstrated the correct way to do sit-ups. Zee watched, fascinated, and actually lay on the floor and tried it. But he couldn't stand the pain. "You got a long way to go, pal," Pete said, patting Zee's belly. Zee likes Pete, enjoys his energetic conversation, the way it follows no apparent logic but shifts abruptly from topic to topic.

He invited Daisy over for pizza. She climbed the stairs clutching the banister, walked into the room and turned a slow circle, shaking her head, then asked why he hadn't installed the air-conditioner. He claimed that he would, although he hasn't because he can't stand the hum or breathing treated air. The air-conditioner sits in its box by the futon, functioning as a bedside table.

He has asked Daisy not to tell Jenny where he lives, has decided that he will no longer put himself in the line of fire; has decided that the good thing about getting older is that you know what to avoid.

Stacked in one corner of the room are newspapers that he plans to dump into a recycling bin. He no longer reads the headlined news about corrupt politicians and oil spills. Instead, he studies the small stories. Today, he read about a man who wants to freeze his head before a brain tumour destroys his brain. He believes that, if his head is quick-frozen while he is still alive—a process known as cryogenic suspension—scientists some time in the future will discover a cure for his tumour and be able to attach his head to a healthy body. Whose body? Zee wonders. It fascinates him that this man considers his head worth saving. He tries to imagine what it would be like to know that tomorrow you are going to have your head quick-frozen and severed from your body, and that if you ever wake up, it will belong to someone else. You won't recognize the body. It will feel like you're touching someone else's body, wiping someone else's bum, shaking pee off someone else's penis. The new body will have a past all its own: scars you don't recognize, injuries you didn't get. What if you don't like the body, don't like the hair growing out of the navel or the bandy legs? Has the man thought about that? What if he feels trapped inside someone else's body?

Zee, himself, sometimes feels that his head isn't connected to his body. About a year ago, Alex told him to go and see a doctor about it. He did, and the doctor said it was possible that Zee suffered from low-grade ear infections.

He followed the story about the woman who died from liposuction. She was only thirty-three. How large were her thighs, he wonders, that she felt compelled to have the fat sucked out of them.

But the story that fascinated him the most concerned the maniac who shot ten women at a post office, then shot himself in the head. From his suicide note, which read, "Feminists have destroyed my life", the press surmised that, because he had been denied a position by the post-office supervisor, a woman, he hated women for succeeding where he had failed. Zee is less curious about the maniac's motives than he is about the men who stood by or ran when the shooting began. The maniac began the massacre in one department, separating the men from the women before firing, then walked up two flights of stairs to another department. What were the men doing? Couldn't they have tried to stop him? Zee wonders what he would have done, wonders if he would have had the guts to oppose a maniac with a gun. Probably not.

He would like to pretend that this senseless killing has nothing to do with him, that it was the work of a maniac, but he can't help feeling partially responsible, can't help feeling that there is a maniac lurking inside himself. There have been times when he has hated women. When they haven't laughed at his jokes, haven't noticed him, have treated him like an over-sexed, self-absorbed jerk with an inflated ego. Often he has felt that he has had to prove to women that he's "sensitive", that he's aware of their struggle against male domination. To avoid confrontation, he has pretended to concur with their sweeping generalizations and condemnations of male behaviour. Why doesn't he stand up for the male gender? Why does he cower when the women with hairy armpits and legs make assumptions about him that are just not true? Of course many men are over-sexed, self-absorbed jerks with inflated egos. And not all feminists have hairy armpits and legs, so why does he think that? That's the hatred he's concerned about, the resentment, the maniacal tendencies. At the office, he hired a woman who later insisted that the things he asked her to do did not fit her job description. He dreaded asking her to do things and began to do the work himself because he couldn't face her. Eventually she formed a Women's Group that met once a month to discuss office policy "relating to women's concerns"; beef sessions, Zee called them when he met his male colleagues at the urinal. Why didn't he just approach her, man to woman, and ask, why aren't we men invited? If you have a problem, shouldn't we all talk about it? Instead, he cowered in his office and tried to ignore them.

That woman is now doing his job, probably more efficiently than he did.

And so the resentment builds. He wishes Alex were around so he could discuss it, defuse it. Alex loses patience with people in general, male and female. She doesn't discriminate. Does he resent Alex? For doing what he can't seem to do: make life-changing decisions and facing the consequences? Alex gets things done. Alex isn't afraid.

Does he hate her for this? Is that why he ran away? Because he's afraid he won't be able to keep pace with her, that he will disappoint her? Did he back out rather than chance losing face?

He hears Pete knocking on the door. He knows it's Pete because he knocks four times in quick succession then twice slowly. "Come on in." Pete pushes open the door. "Hey, pal, how ya' doin'?"

"Okay."

"I hope you like bagels and stuff." He sets a brown paper bag on the floor, then sits in front of it, cross-legged in his bicycle shorts. "I work at this bakery on Saturdays, right? The pay's not great, but I get all this free food." He reaches into the bag. "You like back bacon? I didn't know if maybe you were a vegetarian."

Zee squats on the futon. "I love back bacon."

"Far out. Well, you'll love these, then." He hands Zee a kaiser. "Back-bacon sandwich. They're the best."

Zee takes a bite and nods, chewing. "Good."

"Can I ask you somethin'?"

"Sure."

"Okay. I don't know if maybe it's just me, but I haven't noticed you buying groceries or nothin'."

"No, well, I eat out a lot."

"I seen you in King Donut."

"Donut King. Yeah, I like donuts."

Pete shakes his head. "They're bad for you, man. The worst. You keep eating donuts, and you'll die at fifty. No joke. I seen it happen. People eat fats, and one day, pow," he thumps his chest, "it's over."

Zee holds out the sandwich. "This is fat, isn't it?"

"Yeah, well, this is different. It's protein, right? You have to take a little fat with your protein. Like if it's meat."

"I see."

"But you can get your protein from other stuff, right? Like legumes and shit. They're low-cholesterol. They give you gas, though. I eat beans, and I fart for days. You want a cornichon?" He

332

hands Zee a pickle.

"Thanks."

Pete takes a healthy bite of his sandwich and looks around the room. "I've just been wondering if you're okay. I mean what do you do in here all day, read? I don't see no books or nothin'. Well, newspapers."

"I sleep a lot."

"Cause you work at night, right?" Zee nods. "Man, I'd hate that. Going to work when everybody else is going to sleep."

"It's kind of nice," Zee says. "Nobody's around."

Pete nods, considering. "That's a point." He bites a pickle and stares at the mouse in the box. "The mouse any better?" Zee shakes his head. "You know what," Pete says, "maybe Mrs. Zuppetti's been putting poison out. That's real vicious stuff. It's like acid, right? Burns up their stomachs." Pete finishes his pickle and wipes his hands on his shorts. "You want to hear something gross? No maybe you better finish eating."

"What's gross?"

"Okay well you know what I heard?" Zee shakes his head. "This guy at the gym told me that certain people put mice up their anuses." Zee blinks, trying to assimilate this information. "They stick them in a condom," Pete explains, "and shove it up." He pulls off one of his Nikes and shakes out a pebble.

"Do the mice die?"

"This guy told me that's why they do it, right? So the mice squirm while they're asphyxiating. It turns them on or somethin', I don't know."

Zee wonders if this is true. And if it is, how anyone could do such a thing to a mouse. And if it isn't, why is Pete telling him this? Maybe Pete has a maniac lurking inside him.

Pete crawls on his hands and knees to the window and looks out. "You're lucky you got a front room." He leans his forearms on the window sill. "There's a fight goin' on down there. Holy shit, it looks like he's about to hit her. Man, is he fat, he must have some kind of disease or somethin'. Boy, is he steamed. She's going back inside. Man, I didn't know anybody lived in that place. It's got boards over the windows."

"Maybe they can't afford glass."

"That's a point." Pete crawls back and finishes his sandwich. "You know what a guy at work told me?"

"What?"

"He said 'Yes dear' has the same number of letters in it as 'Fuck off'." Zee furrows his brow, trying to understand what this means. Pete shakes a finger at him. "So next time somebody says 'Yes dear' to you, think about it." He raises his eyebrows, emphasizing his point, then reaches into the brown bag. "You want another one?"

"Not right now, thanks."

"How 'bout I leave you some so you can nosh later?"

"Thanks."

Pete lies back on the floor, supporting his head with his hands. "I don't know if maybe it's just me," he says, "but I get the feeling you're doing some kind of hermit thing."

"Hermit thing?"

"You were married before, right?"

"Not really. I mean I was living with someone."

"For how long?"

"Five years."

Pete makes a sound as though he has just burnt his finger. "That's rough, man. I broke up with my fiance sixty-seven days ago, and I'm still feeling it."

"It takes awhile, I think."

"You're right there." He sits up, grabs the bag, pulls out two brownies and hands one to Zee. "I don't regret it or nothin'. It had to happen, I know that."

"How do you know?"

"Oh we were just … we were just … I don't know. We didn't

talk hardly at all, right? We'd sit across the table from each other, jesus it was weird. It was like we were just killing time before we watched TV and went to bed. I'm not gonna marry somebody because the sex is good. I mean, there's got to be more to it than that, right?"

"Oh, sure," Zee agrees, staring at the mouse in the box.

"You want to know the worst?"

"What?"

"She started masturbating her dog. No joke. She called it King Kong. It was attacking everybody, so the vet told her it was hyper-active and that she had to masturbate it to release tension or some-thin'. I don't know. I figured he had to be a pervert."

"Masturbating does release tension."

"Sure, but to a dog? Forget it."

"It does sound a bit unorthodox."

Pete sweeps up crumbs and drops them into a napkin. "So, does your ex live in town?"

"In this very neighbourhood."

"Rag on."

Zee knows from experience that when Pete says "Rag on" he means "You're kidding". "She does," Zee affirms. "A couple of streets over."

"You ever see her?"

"No."

"You want to?"

"I'm not sure. For all I know, she might have moved."

Pete folds the napkin carefully so as not to drop any of the crumbs. "We'll feed these to the mouse when he wakes up." He lies on the floor again. "So, if you took a room in this neighbourhood, you must want to see her."

"I like this neighbourhood."

"Yeah, well ... I wouldn't want to live anywhere near my fiance, that's for sure."

335

"Why not?"

"She hates me now."

"Why?"

"She had all these plans," Pete explains. "We were gonna buy a house some day, right? Have kids and all that? I let her down."

"Maybe she set herself up for disappointment by making all those plans."

"I don't know. You gotta make plans, I guess. Some anyway. I don't know. I'm just too young for all that stuff. Maybe later. Like I don't want to be old with no kids or nothin'."

"Why not?"

Pete shrugs. "I'd get lonely."

"That's kind of a selfish reason for having kids, don't you think?"

"I don't know. It's natural, right? I mean what else are you going to do?"

"I don't know."

"I think you'd get pretty bored. With yourself, I mean." Pete crawls over to the mouse in the box and stares at it, then lowers his face to the floor so he can look at it from the side. "I think he's dead."

"Really?"

Pete gently places his index finger on the mouse. "No heart beat."

"What a bummer."

"Hey at least he's not suffocating up somebody's asshole."

"That's true," Zee says.

"It's all in how you look at it."

THIRTY-FOUR

Alex lies in the tub watching her toes turn to prunes. She never used to take long baths, used to be a shower person. Now she kills time by sitting in the bath, watching TV and trying to sleep. Marika has taken charge of muffin production and delivery, which leaves Alex only the paperwork. Alex has stopped driving because she no longer reacts quickly enough to avoid collisions; she drives carelessly, daring any "stupid shit" to ram into her. Sometimes, depending on the driver's gender, she yells "dickhead" or "stupid cow" out her window. Although tempted by the idea of sudden death in a car crash, she's worried that she might live through it, without legs or arms or eyes. And she doesn't want to kill anyone else.

Her doctor, whom she's always trusted because of his resemblance to Papa Hemingway and because he was quick enough to discover pre-cancerous cells on her cervix and freeze them off, told her to expect depression, that the body takes time to adjust to the loss of a fetus. "A huge change occurs," he explained in his Hungarian accent while she sat staring at the cactus on his desk. "The hormones that have been pumping away for months, preparing for birth, don't quit immediately. The blood has thickened and doesn't thin out the moment you miscarry. You must give yourself time," he'd tapped his temple and his stomach, "Emotionally and physically. Don't be in a hurry. Try again in three months." She'd gripped the potted cactus and turned it slowly clockwise then counter-clockwise. "You have nothing to do with it," he'd said, studying her and tugging on his white beard. "It was most likely a chromosome misalignment. Most likely the baby wasn't healthy anyway." Abruptly, he sneezed repeatedly. Yanking tissues from a box, he wiped his nose and peered at her. "After three months, you become pregnant again, and you forget all about it."

His explanation had no effect on her. She felt like the fish in the tank in his waiting-room, staring out at the people tapping their fingers against the glass. The fish must know the people can't reach them, must wonder why they persist in tapping their fingers against the glass. What do they expect from them? What do they want from them?

She wishes she believed in God so that she could blame someone else. *How could you do this to me? What have I done to deserve this?*

She feels as though her centre has been cut from her. She no longer has the energy to stand straight but leans on walls, doorknobs, chairs.

She won't try to get pregnant again. She no longer has the will. For anything. When she remembers who she was, she can't believe she had the energy, the obsession to create her own little world. Now she doesn't give a flying fuck, as Larry would say.

When Michael phoned to tell her his wife had died, she started to laugh and had to clamp her hand over the mouthpiece so he wouldn't hear her. He was moved, thinking she was choking back tears. He told her that he was seeing a therapist and that she'd advised him not to see Alex for the time being.

Big fucking deal.

After she put the phone down, she tried to figure out why she'd laughed when it sickened her that this stupid woman had starved herself to death, leaving behind two children. It had been an ugly, alien laugh, swelling in her gut and forcing itself out her throat. She

338

would have preferred to cry.

Marika tells her that she'll get over it, a person can get over any-thing. Alex doesn't doubt this: if the person wants to get over it. If the person cares.

She has contemplated suicide but can't figure out how to go about it. Papa Hemingway wouldn't prescribe Valium for her, insist-ing it wasn't necessary. When Alex asked if there were any other drugs she could take, he must have understood her intentions because he suggested she might benefit from counselling.

Sometimes when she thinks of Zee she laughs that same ugly, alien laugh. Zee, the king of potted plants, shuffling around high-rises with his watering can, contemplating the meaning of life, screwing anyone who'll have him. Zee, the king of "waiting and see-ing with his thumb up his ass".

Well, he's won.

If he knew her pain, would he smirk, inwardly? Outwardly she knows he would appear sad and say he was sorry.

At other times, some stupid thing will make her think of him, some stupid thing like a duck or a guitar or a place they used to sit, and she'll start to cry, in public. She realizes that she's out of control and that people passing will think she's desperate, but she doesn't care. She cries until her eyes burn.

When she can't sleep, she slides over to his side of the bed, rolls onto her stomach and flattens herself against the mattress.

Not even Mel can stand being with her anymore. She says Alex is not even trying to "break through this thing".

"What thing?"

"Lots of women have miscarriages," Mel insists. "Especially the first time around. Get pregnant again, if you want."

I don't want! That's the fucking problem, I don't want!

She's been swearing much more than she used to. Mostly at TV commercials. She hates daytime television but watches it anyway, because she doesn't want to think. She shouts at the actors and actresses in the soap operas, calling them "dickheads" and "stupid cows".

At the bathroom window, she hears dogs growl and bark at each other. She bangs against the pane, trying to scare them off. Startled, they glance up at her briefly then start barking again. "Fucking dickheads."

•

Alex sits on the couch examining her thick toenails. How disgusting that toenails thicken as you get older. She used to look at her mother's thick, yellow claws and think that hers would never look like that.

On "Oprah", pale, doughy housewives are being given the opportunity to gawk at, and even touch, male soap-opera stars. Each hair-sprayed, tanned, tailored male star sits regally on stage with an arm around a woman selected from the audience. Each responds to the woman's inane questions with answers deliberately weighted with sexual innuendo. The women on stage blush and swoon while the females in the audience squeal with envy. It astonishes Alex that these vacuous men can illicit such orgasmic cries. She realizes that, for the women on stage, a dream has come true. One of them seems almost catatonic with ecstasy. It amazes Alex that the women don't even notice the stars' discomfort. Clearly, it seems to her, the male stars would prefer to have their arms around beautiful soap-opera starlets. One of the women proudly boasts of watching four soap operas a day. Does she do anything with the rest of her life, Alex wonders, or does she stay inside her soap-opera dream while serving Hamburger Helper to her indifferent husband and squabbling kids? Alex wishes that she had a dream she could switch on for four hours a day. It seems to her that she doesn't have one dream left in her head. Not even the handsome man rescuing her from all this, installing her in the nice brick house with the hardwood floors and the skylights.

Someone knocks on the door. "Alex, it's me, Dwight."

Alex sighs and brushes her toenail clippings onto the floor.

"Alex! Come on, let me in. I know you're in there."

She opens the door and stares at him.

"Hi." He tries to smile cheerily. "I brought you a kite. I don't know if it will fly or not but it's really pretty, Japanese." He hands her a paper kite.

"Thank you," she says, staring at it. "Nice colours. It's a beetle or something."

"Yup, a flying beetle." He hooks his thumbs in his suspenders. "I'd love a coffee."

"Sure."

He follows her to the kitchen and leans against the door-jamb. "So I talked to my Dad. He says Elizabeth has settled down. He thinks she's secretly relieved you're not going to be a single mother."

Alex opens the fridge. "I don't have any milk."

"Black's fine."

The dogs outside start barking again. Alex slams two cups onto the counter. "What's the fucking problem with those dogs?"

Dwight looks out the window. "I think one of them's tied up."

"I hate this neighbourhood. It's filled with stupid people with stupid dogs." Dwight watches her apprehensively, pinching his lip between his thumb and index finger.

In the living-room, Dwight nods at the TV. "Do you mind if I turn it off?"

"Go ahead."

He switches it off just as one of the doughy women runs her fingers through the hair of one of the male stars, gasping as though she has just climaxed.

"After coffee," he says, "we should go to the park and try out the kite. Have you ever flown a kite?"

Alex stares at the blank TV screen and shakes her head.

341

"Oh, well, you'll love it. You feel like you're up in the air with it, riding the wind. Today's a good day for it. Nice and gusty."

"Dwight, I don't want to fly a kite."

"I'll fly it then, you can watch."

Again she has that fish-in-the-tank feeling. *Why won't he stop tapping on the glass?*

He curls his fingers around his cup and looks down at it. "I just think you have to start going out, Al. I mean, it isn't healthy to stay in all the time. You lose your sense of place in the world."

"Your sense of place?"

"You know what I mean."

"No, I don't. I never had a sense of place. The world doesn't give a fuck about me, and I don't give a fuck about it."

Dwight taps his fingers against the side of his cup. "I just think you have to try to let it go."

"Dwight, you're a really nice person, and I don't want to be mean to you, so don't tell me to let it go when you don't even know what 'it' is."

"All I know is you're bitter and bitterness eats up your insides."

Alex rubs her palms against her eyes; she suppresses a scream.

"That's what's happened to Elizabeth," Dwight continues. "She's consumed with bitterness, thinks nobody's had it tougher than she did. She shuts my dad out, patronizes him because she thinks he hasn't suffered like she's suffered."

Alex stands, goes over to the window and stares out at a boy on a skateboard trying to flip it onto the sidewalk. "I don't think I'm suffering more or less than anybody else. I don't even know what I'm feeling, if I'm feeling, and when people like you come in and tell me how I'm feeling or should be feeling, I get very angry."

"I'm sorry."

"That's okay. I appreciate your concern."

Dwight watches her for a moment then takes his coffee cup into the kitchen and rinses it. He steps back into the living-room and watches her staring out the window. He grips his suspenders and hunches his shoulders then lets them drop. "So I guess I should get going."

She faces him. "Thanks for the kite."

"You're welcome. If you change your mind ... I mean if you want ..." He rams his hands into his pockets. "Anyway, you've got my number."

"I do. I'll call you."

After he's gone, she takes one of the Kit Kat bars from a kitchen shelf, unwraps and eats it. The dogs bark. She smashes her hand into the window, cracking it. "Fuck," she says, "Fuck, fuck, fuck."

Then she takes out the masking tape and seals the crack.

THIRTY-FIVE

t first when he sees her, tossing the kite into the air and running zigzag across the grassy slope, he thinks it must be someone else. Someone who looks like Alex; same short hair, same baggy jeans. It couldn't be Alex because she must look pregnant by now and wouldn't be running around. But after sitting and watching her try again and again to launch the kite into the sky, he realizes that it is Alex. He freezes, not wanting to draw attention to himself, his heart thunders in his chest. He's not sure if he wants her to see him, not sure if he wants to break the silence between them. Won't that just make it harder? Isn't he okay now? Now that he has his room and his plants and his peace of mind? She'll shatter him with one blow, one battleship-grey-eyed stare. But still he doesn't move, decides to wait and see if she's with anyone. If she's with someone, he'll turn and go. If she isn't, maybe he'll stroll down the slope and pretend to bump into her. But what if her face tightens into one of those don't-talk-to-me-asshole expressions? He doesn't think he could stand it. Maybe he should just leave now; go have a donut, a double chocolate.

"Hey, dude, how's it goin'?" A small boy straddling a bicycle points a plastic pistol at Zee.

"Hello," Zee says. The boy clicks his pistol at him twice then pedals off. Zee looks back at Alex who throws up her hands, giving up on the kite, letting it crash to the ground. She slumps down onto the grass, resting her elbows on her knees. For a moment she looks in Zee's direction. He stops breathing, considers waving, but she looks away.

What if she saw him and looked away because she doesn't want to see him?

She stares across the green towards the trees for a long time and Zee feels certain that she's looking for someone. Then, abruptly, she lies back in the grass, folding her hands behind her head.

She definitely doesn't look pregnant. Maybe she's one of those women who carry the baby around their middle instead of up front. He's heard that women carry babies differently and that some women don't look pregnant until the seventh month.

His legs feel numb from sitting so still. He uncrosses them and stands, then moves stealthily towards a tree and leans against it. Maybe he should follow her at a distance, hiding in doorways and behind trees like private detectives do in movies.

Then he tells himself he should just face her. What is he afraid of, rejection? He's already been rejected. He has nothing to lose. The worst she can say is go away. And he will. At least then he'll know about the baby thing. He doesn't want to go away without knowing about the baby thing.

She has her eyes closed when he sits down beside her. Suddenly, she springs up, fists clenched. He holds up his hands. "It's only me."

"My god," she says. "What are you doing here?"

"You thought I was an attacker?"

"Well, what was I supposed to think?"

"No, you're absolutely right. Daisy told me about a woman who was chopped into little bits and stuck in a fridge."

"There's all kinds of stories like that."

Zee nods. "A woman was raped in a hotel recently. The guy got into her room by pretending to be hotel staff then gagged her with her own clothes."

"I heard about that."

"Horrible."

"Yeah." A big plastic ball bounces towards them. Zee catches it and tosses it to a dad in a baseball cap who tosses it to his kid in a baseball cap. "So how are you?" Zee asks.

"Alright."

"How's the pregnancy going?"

"Do I look pregnant to you?"

"Not really, but then I don't know about these things."

"I miscarried."

Zee studies her face for some sign of how this has affected her, but she only stares towards the trees, expressionless. He pulls a blade of grass from the ground and chews on the stem. "I'm sorry to hear that."

And she looks at him, to see if he is, really. But he has his face turned away from her. "My doctor says there was probably a chromosome misalignment."

Zee nods, not exactly sure what this means but not wanting to ask for fear of upsetting her.

So there is no baby.

He waits to feel something; relief, sorrow. But all he can think about is what she must be feeling.

"How are you?" she asks. "Still watering plants?"

"Yeah. It's okay; it's decent." He realizes that it would be ridiculous to ask if she's alright. She can't be alright. What is a miscarriage like? How does it feel? How long does it take? He pictures her cringing on the bed, bleeding, crying out in pain. Where was he? What was he doing? How could he not have known? He feels as though his rib cage is shrinking, squeezing the breath out of him. "How's the muffin business?" he manages to ask.

"Okay. I have a partner now."

"Who?"

"One of the girls from the Centre."

346

"Great." Not far from them, a dog on a leash squats down to crap while its owner stares at it. Zee clears his throat. "You still at the Centre?"

"I took a leave of absence. I haven't been too well." The dog owner covers his hand with a plastic bag and picks up the dog's stool. A child in coveralls approaches the dog. A woman in stretch pants grabs his wrist. "Don't go touching strange dogs," she warns. "You want him to go bitin' off your hand?" The child withdraws his hand quickly and curls it under his chin.

"What's been wrong with you?" Zee asks.

"I miscarried."

"Well, I know, but other than that."

"Other than that I just feel like I'm rotten, the whole fucking planet is rotten, and I might as well be dead."

Zee nods, wishing he could think of something helpful to say. Now that she doesn't seem unhappy to see him, he doesn't want to annoy her by saying the wrong thing, like "the world isn't all that bad, really. You just have to avoid the things that bug you; focus on other things, good things, like ducks." He saw some ducks sleeping the other night, their heads twisted around, their bills buried in their feathers. It looked very contorted, but it must be comfortable for them. If they saw humans curled up in a fetal position, they'd probably think it looked pretty contorted.

"You know how you used to talk about being brain-dead?" Alex asks. "Well, that's how I feel. Like there's no fucking point." She grips her hair in her hands then releases it slowly through her fingers. "Before, when I used to feel shitty, I knew it would pass. I knew if I just kept going, I'd start to feel better, you know, if I stayed occupied. Like in some stupid Chekhov play. You know how they're always talking about how they'll feel better if they work? Now keeping occupied just seems like a joke. I mean, why bother?"

Zee stretches out his legs and crosses his ankles. "I've actually been kind of enjoying being occupied. I kind of like having a simple task and doing it well."

"Has it ever occurred to you," Alex says, "that slimeballs work in those buildings? Slimeballs employ you. I mean you go around talking like you've opted out of the system and are getting back to the earth, but the fact is, you're still working for slimeballs."

"It depends on how you look at it," Zee says. "I never see the slimeballs. Their offices are quite pleasant when they're not in them."

Alex rubs her palms against her eyes. "Well, I just think you're fooling yourself."

"I'm trying to look at things a little differently, instead of bashing my head against the wall. You taught me that."

"Oh, please."

"It's true, when things don't work out the way you want them to, you come at them from another angle. Like the baby thing."

"The baby thing was obsessive."

"But it was important to you, so you did it. A lot of people wouldn't have had the guts."

"Well, I'll never do it again, that's for sure." She watches a boy and girl, lying on the grass, start to roll sideways down the hill, yelping excitedly.

"Is that your kite?" Zee asks.

"It's a stupid kite. It won't fly."

"I think it needs a tail."

"Where do you get a tail?"

"You make it, out of string and paper." Zee gets up and retrieves the kite. Alex watches him, surprised at how familiar his movements still are to her, how natural it feels to be with him. "Organic" is the word used these days; it feels organic to be with him. She pictures the spotty, wilted vegetables in the health-food store. Then she realizes that this is the first time she has said what's on her mind and not been accused of moping, or of not trying to break out of this thing or of not letting it go. She feels a little better for saying it, as though a plug has been pulled, creating an air passage. As Zee clambers back up the slope towards her, she tries taking deep breaths. For so long now, she has felt that if she exhaled completely, she would snap in half.

He holds up the kite. "It's pretty, a beetle or something. I think it will fly with a tail. It's pretty sturdy, considering it's made of paper."

"And bamboo. I think it's bamboo."

"Or wood maybe." He sits, placing the kite between them. The two children, squealing with delight, scramble back up the hill and start to roll down again.

"You cut off all your hair," Alex says.

"Yeah." He slides his hand over his head. "You like it? It's grown in a bit. At first I looked like a boot-camper. Durham calls me seal-head."

"I like it. It's greyer though."

"Yeah. Well, I turned forty-four."

"I know. I was going to call you, but then I thought, why? I'll only depress him. Nobody can stand being around me anymore."

"Not even Dear Old Fish Face?"

She smiles. "Not even."

He lies back in the grass, crosses an ankle over his bent knee and stares up at the sky. "Somebody's got a kite going up there."

Alex looks up. "It's got a tail."

"See how it balances it?"

A ten-year-old boy wearing jeans ripped at the knees and carrying a clipboard walks up to Zee. "Do you want to sponsor my swim team?" the boy asks, lisping slightly.

Zee sits up. "Why should I?"

The boy, surprised by the question, looks down at his high-topped, lime-green sneakers. "Because ... we need money. For the team."

"But why should I give you money?"

"Well ... because I want to be in the Olympics some day."

"Do you think you'll win?"

"I don't know." The boy, still looking at his feet, nervously taps the clipboard against his thigh.

"Okay. Well, here," Zee takes some change from his pocket and hands it to the boy. "Thanks," the boy says and notes the amount on the clipboard. He moves off, approaching the dad in the baseball cap playing ball with his kid. "He's working the whole crowd," Zee says.

"An entrepreneur."

"Kids are interesting, aren't they? They don't mind not having answers for everything. In five years, he'll know how to bullshit." He lies back on the grass. An airplane streaks white above him. An ice-cream van, at the foot of the hill, signals its arrival with a tune. Children swarm around it. "Remember," Zee asks, "how you used to have baby dreams?" He rolls onto his side to face her. "Remember the one you kept having where you forgot to feed it?"

"And it died."

He rests his temple against his palm. "Right, well a couple of nights ago I had a dream where there was this baby crying on a raft. It was in a baby carriage."

"Where was it, the raft?"

"I'm not sure, a reservoir or something. Anyway I swam over and picked it up, and it stopped crying." He chews on another piece of grass. "It felt nice, you know, wriggling against me."

She wonders what he expects her to say to this. "What happened?"

"Nothing. I just stood there, trying to keep my balance on the raft. I didn't know what to do. I mean there I was with this baby in the middle of this water." He sits up and wraps his arms around his knees. "But I felt really good about stopping it from crying. I mean it must have felt secure with me holding it."

"Little did it know."

She suspects that he expects her to ask what he thinks the dream means. *Does it mean you've changed your mind and suddenly want to be a father?* But she doesn't ask, doesn't want to play games, doesn't see the point.

"I wondered what the dream meant," he says.

"I always wonder what dreams mean."

"Yeah." He would like her to say that it must mean he would be a wonderful father, that maybe it's time for him to start thinking seriously about the baby thing, now that he's being responsible and doesn't hate himself.

"Your shoelace is undone," she remarks, and he realizes that he can't expect her to understand, right away. Can't expect her to believe in him, right away. Maybe later. He looks at his sneaker and ties his laces. "Do you feel like maybe getting something to eat?" he asks, without looking at her because he doesn't want her to see his face if she says no.

"Umm ..." she says, "I don't know, do you?"

"I'm hungry. Maybe we can find a falafel or something."

"Actually what I feel like is a burger."

"You don't eat burgers."

"I've been doing a lot of things I don't do." She picks up the kite. "I think it's the hormones."

"You shouldn't eat too many burgers. A friend of mine tells me that if you eat too much fat," he thumps his chest. "Pow. It's over."

She stands, brushing the seat of her pants. "Yeah. Well, it's not like I'm eating lots of burgers. I think it's just a phase I'm going through."

"It'll pass."

"That's right."

As they walk across the grass, he reaches over and smooths down a tuft of hair still poking up from her head.